JAMES W. HUSTON

BALANCE

OF POWER

A NOVEL

AVON

U.S. $6.99
CAN. $8.99

EAN

ISBN 0-380-73159-2

9 780380 731596

5 0 6 9 9

BALANCE OF POWER

The admiral was dumbstruck. His heart raced as he considered what the President was doing. "Mr. President, do you realize what this will say to the rest of the world? That we have a rogue battle group, that we have to send our own military force to stop it. It looks like a civil war, with part of the military fighting for Congress, and part for the President."

The President looked around the room. No one dared to speak, or even move.

"Isn't that exactly what we have?"

"James W. Huston's military thriller hits the ground running . . . Huston handles both battle scenes and courtroom confrontations with skill. The pace is fast and the suspense is gripping as his story careens toward a guns-blazing, here-come-the-Marines climax . . . Indeed, if you like Tom Clancy, Huston is a good step up."
Washington Post Book World

"A heart-stopping story of military action combined with Washington politics and law."
Library Journal

"A great summer read . . . fast-paced . . . engaging and clever . . . James W. Huston may be stepping into territory dominated by Tom Clancy, but Huston more than stands his ground."
CNN online

JAMES W. HUSTON

BALANCE
of POWER

AVON BOOKS  NEW YORK

AVON BOOKS, INC.
1350 Avenue of the Americas
New York, New York 10019

Published in hardcover by William Morrow and Company, Inc.; for information address Permissions Department, William Morrow and Company, Inc., 1350 Avenue of the Americas, New York, New York 10019.

First Avon Books Printing: April 1998

AVON TRADEMARK REG. U.S. PAT. OFF. AND IN OTHER COUNTRIES, MARCA
REGISTRADA, HECHO EN U.S.A.

Printed in the U.S.A.

WCD   10   9   8   7   6   5   4   3   2   1

For Dianna

United States Constitution. Article I, Section 8: The Congress shall have Power . . . To declare War, grant Letters of Marque and Reprisal, and make Rules concerning Captures on Land and Water.

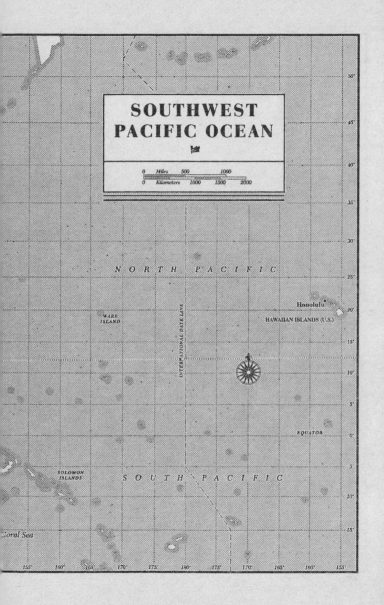

SOUTHWEST
PACIFIC OCEAN

| 0 | Miles | 500 | 1000 | |
| 0 | Kilometers | 1000 | 1500 | 2000 |

NORTH PACIFIC

Honolulu

HAWAIIAN ISLANDS (U.S.)

WAKE ISLAND

INTERNATIONAL DATE LINE

EQUATOR

SOLOMON ISLANDS

SOUTH PACIFIC

Coral Sea

155° 160° 165° 170° 175° 180° 175° 170° 165° 160° 155°

50° 45° 40° 35° 30° 25° 20° 15° 10° 5° 0° 5° 10° 15°

BALANCE OF POWER

1

THE FASTEST SHIP IN THE WORLD COASTED SILENTLY to the Jakarta pier just before dawn. Its six jet engines idled for the first time since leaving San Diego ten days ago. Captain Clay Bonham leaned on the rail of the flying bridge and shook his head in disgust as he watched the dockworkers eight stories below struggle to tie the ship to the pier. The cargo ship had set a new world record for crossing the Pacific and there wasn't anyone there to greet them. Lindbergh's welcome to Paris it wasn't. Preoccupied with his place in history, he didn't notice the dark 0blue bus as it turned onto the pier two hundred yards away. He walked back onto the enclosed bridge of the *Pacific Flyer* as the Indonesian harbor pilot climbed over the portside rail down to the tug. "Nice job, Bacon," Bonham said to the helmsman grudgingly. "Maybe I'll let you go back with us."

"Ford people are here early," said John Franklin, the chief engineer, as he squinted at the bus, just now able to make out FORD on its side. His thick glasses made his eyes look unusually large, as if he were always surprised.

"I guess they need a bus full of mechanics to get their new cars running." Bonham smiled sarcastically. "Did you *see* those cars when they were brought aboard? Look like they were designed by a committee." He sipped his coffee slowly. "Probably were. 'The car for the world— the new international sedan.' Stirring. What's it called?"

1

he asked, looking at Franklin. "The . . ." He groped for the name.

"Ascenda."

"Right. What the hell kind of name is that?" Bonham looked at the bus as it neared the ship. "Better get down there and give 'em a hand," he said. He forgot the bus and watched the beautiful city lights extinguish themselves at the start of sunrise.

Dawn in Jakarta. Ships, boats, people, and heat everywhere. Mind-stifling heat, but not on the *Flyer*—Captain Bonham always kept the ship's temperature at seventy-two degrees. Bonham glanced over at Franklin to see if he was moving. He tolerated Franklin because he was a good engineer, but deep inside he thought Franklin was a misfit. Probably president of the short-wave club in high school.

"Who's supposed to be here?" Franklin asked.

"Chairman of the Board of Ford," Bonham replied. "But not for a couple of hours. And the Secretary of Commerce and a bunch of"—the word stuck in his throat—"politicians . . . at ten or so. New car to a new dealership, big ceremony, cutting of some ribbon or other—the usual waste of time and taxpayers' money." He watched the crane move slowly toward the ship with the gangplank. The Ford bus stopped next to the *Pacific Flyer*. "Get *down* there and help those Ford guys."

Franklin nodded and walked off the bridge. He slid down the ladders at a quick, experienced pace and crossed outboard to the main deck access hatch where the gangplank was being attached.

"Everything okay?" Franklin asked Phillips, a brawny sailor in his thirties who had sailed with Bonham and Franklin on several trips.

Phillips stood smoking a cigarette, watching the crane lift the long metal gangplank. "No problem. The guy on the crane seems to be drunk, but he's coming close."

Franklin watched the swaying gangplank. Two men stood on the pier waiting. The Ford bus was twenty feet away. Finally the gangplank touched the ship. Phillips grabbed it, secured it to the *Flyer,* and walked to the middle of it to unhook the four crane cables. He released the shackles and the gangplank was in place. The two men on the pier yelled to Phillips, who waved them aboard. Franklin stood at the top of the gangplank and waited. The men stepped off and extended their hands to him. He shook their hands and nodded. "Morning. You speak English?"

"Yes, a little," said one of them. "Are you an officer?"

"I'm the chief engineer," Franklin replied.

"You have your papers?" the official asked.

"Sure. Come to my office," Franklin said, walking ahead of them down the passageway. He stopped and turned. "Hey, Phillips."

"Yeah?" Phillips said, interrupting his conversation with another sailor.

"Would you give those Ford guys a hand?"

Phillips frowned in confusion, looked over at the pier, and saw men in blue coveralls getting out of the Ford bus; he turned to Franklin, rolled his eyes, and nodded. Thirty Ford mechanics picked up their blue satchels and walked quickly onto the ship. Phillips stepped aside and let them onto the deck. The space was only large enough for about twenty; the others stood restlessly on the creaking gangplank. Their satchels look heavy, Phillips thought. Probably tools. He chuckled at the idea of these Indonesian mechanics bringing new starters for all the brand-new American cars they assumed weren't going to start. The leader of the workers approached him. "Morning," Phillips said, extending his hand.

"Good morning," the man said in English, not taking Phillips's hand.

Phillips looked into his dark brown eyes. There was no joy at being a Ford mechanic in them. "You boys here to get the cars ready?"

"Where is captain?" the man asked. He had a perfect

complexion and dark eyes. His eyebrows were thin lines. He was much shorter than Phillips, who was six feet tall and weighed two hundred fifty pounds. The small man weighed half as much.

I could crush him like a bug, Phillips said to himself as he unconsciously sucked in his belly. "What do you need to see the captain for?" Phillips asked, annoyed. "Can I see your papers?"

"Where is captain?" the man said in a quiet voice, standing steadily, unintimidated by Phillips.

"I suppose he's on the bridge. But before we do anything, I need to see your papers."

The man put his satchel down and squatted next to it. He opened the zipper halfway and quickly pulled out a Chinese Type 64 machine pistol with a long silencer. He came up suddenly and placed the barrel under Phillips's chin. "Where is captain?"

"What the hell . . . ?" Phillips's mouth suddenly went dry.

"Shut up," the man said quietly.

Phillips nodded.

"Take us to captain," the man insisted. "Now." He eased the pressure of the barrel on Phillips's chin. Phillips swallowed hard. His heart raced. He tried to think of some way to deflect them, to get them into a compartment he could lock, but his mind wouldn't work fast enough.

"Now," the man said again.

Phillips walked forward down the passageway Franklin had used. He stopped at the foot of a series of ladders that led to the bridge. As he missed the first step, his boot smacked the tiled deck with a loud noise. The leader moved up behind him and put a hand on his shoulder. He leaned forward. "More noise, I shoot." He put the pistol in Phillips's back. "Understand?"

Phillips nodded. He climbed the ladder carefully. As his head reached the next deck, another sailor was waiting to go down the ladder. "Get out of here!" Phillips said in a terrified whisper with a wild look in his eyes.

"Why the hell should I?" asked Bart Jenkins in his usual cavalier tone as he stood waiting for Phillips.

"Now!" Phillips whispered, wanting to scream at him.

The leader noticed Phillips had slowed. "What doing?" he said, pushing up through the hatch with surprising force. Phillips rolled off the top of the ladder onto the deck. The leader stuck his head up through the hatch and saw Jenkins, who froze as the man raised his gun and shot.

Jenkins's knees gave out and he fell as two bullets screamed by just above his head. His adrenaline took over. He scrambled on his hands and knees through a hatch and around a corner.

The leader pushed his way past Phillips and stood. Two other men in Ford coveralls climbed up next to him and looked around hurriedly with their AK-47 assault rifles ready. They pointed anxiously in the direction Jenkins had gone. The leader shook his head, clearly not concerned.

Phillips stood.

The leader looked at him closely. "Who that?" he asked.

"Bart Jenkins."

"What does he do?"

Phillips almost answered automatically, almost told him Jenkins was the radio operator. "Engineer," he lied.

He looked at Phillips for several seconds before speaking again. "To the bridge," he said.

Phillips made his way up the next ladder, and the one after that, followed by a long trail of men in Ford coveralls. As they moved snakelike through the ship, the *Pacific Flyer*'s crewmen assumed they were the Ford mechanics they had been expecting.

They stopped behind the bridge, and Phillips pointed to the door. "That's the bridge."

The leader looked around and put down his bag. The next five did likewise and removed their AK-47s. They spoke rapidly in what Phillips guessed was an Asian language, walked quickly through the door onto the bridge,

and covered every entrance. Bonham leaped to his feet
from his captain's chair, confused. Tommy Bacon stared
openmouthed. The leader crossed to Bonham and lowered
his gun. "You captain?"

"Yes, I am. Who the hell are you?" he replied, trying
to control his anger.

"Shut up." He pointed to the other men in coveralls
with a wave of his handgun. "They do what I say. Understand?"

Bonham stared into his eyes, trying to read his intentions. "What do you want?"

"Ship."

Bonham tried to hide his surprise. He lowered his
voice. "You can't have it," he said, his blue eyes burning.

"Already have," the man replied gruffly.

"The *hell* you do. You can do anything you want to
me. The rest of the crew won't do what you want."

"Yes, they will," said the leader. "You have weapons
aboard?"

"No," Bonham said.

"Yes, you do. Small-arms locker on second deck," the
leader said, shaking his head. "You think we not find out
before, Captain Bonham?"

"How do you know my name?" Bonham asked,
stunned.

"You lied," he said to Bonham sternly. He motioned
to one of the men, who pulled Phillips to the center of
the bridge. "Need punishment." The second Ford man
took Phillips's hand and held it on the brass railing around
the helm. He smashed his rifle on Phillips's left forefinger.
Everyone on the bridge could hear the bone snap. Phillips
fell to his knees in pain.

"You son of a bitch!" Bonham yelled at the man with
the rifle as he held Phillips's shoulder.

Phillips's face turned bright red as sweat beaded on his
forehead. He held his left hand with his right, fighting the
pain, trying not to scream.

"Small warning," the leader said. "Next time more

serious. Understand?'' He looked up at Bonham.

The captain stared at him without speaking.

''You have weapons?''

''Just in the small-arms locker,'' Bonham said through gritted teeth. He watched Phillips trying to get up. He looked like he was going to cry, or throw up. Bonham looked at the leader again. ''Who are you?''

''No security for morning ceremony?''

''They're supposed to meet us here. What's your name?''

The leader showed a hint of a smile. ''George Washington. I fight for freedom for my country. Just like him. What time?''

''What time what?''

''Security come.''

''Eight.''

''Washington'' looked at his watch. ''Where is radio room?''

Bonham didn't respond.

Washington pointed his gun at Phillips and spoke to one of his men, who pulled Phillips up, grabbed his right hand, put it on the railing, and smashed his right forefinger with his rifle. Phillips cried out and his knees again buckled.

''Where is radio room?'' he asked again, more insistently.

''Behind the bridge,'' Bonham said. Washington signaled to two men at the back of the bridge.

''Correct. Now get under way,'' he said.

''What?'' Bonham said, not believing what he had heard.

''Give command. Get under way.''

''Why?''

''I say so. Five minutes.'' He looked around the bridge to make sure nothing was happening without his direction.

''It'll take longer than that to get the boilers up.''

''No boilers!'' Washington said, raising his voice. ''Jet engines. Start them. Give commands!''

Bonham turned to his control board and picked up a phone. "Cast off from the pier!" he yelled into the receiver. "No, I'm not kidding. Cast off! . . . You don't need to know why. Just do it!" he said, slamming the phone down. Bonham started to walk across the bridge.

"Where are you going?" Washington asked.

"To the wing of the bridge. I have to see when they've cast off."

Washington nodded and followed him.

Bonham went outside, not believing what he was doing. His mind raced for some way out. He saw the lines being taken off the bollards by confused dockworkers. Bonham looked for the crane to remove the gangplank, but didn't see it. He walked back inside the bridge and crossed over to Phillips, who was bent over the radar repeater. "You okay?" he asked, bending over to talk into his ear. Phillips didn't respond.

"Give the command—get under way," Washington said.

"I can't," Bonham said. "We have to wait for the crane to come back to lift off the gangplank."

Washington crossed to him and spoke directly into his face. "No. Don't care about gangplank. Give command."

Bonham crossed to the engine-order telegraph. He rang it, set it at all reverse one third, and spoke into the microphone next to it. "All reverse one third," he said.

"Are you serious?" came the reply from the engine room. "We were just shutting her down."

"I know. All reverse one third!" Bonham looked around, his eyes full of hatred and confusion. He watched the RPM of the shafts climb. The helm wasn't manned. He didn't care. Let her run aground.

"Who steers?" Washington asked.

"What?"

"Who steers the ship?"

"It depends."

Washington looked at Bacon. "You steer?" he asked.

Bacon nodded as blood drained from his face. Washington pointed to the helm. "Steer."

He reluctantly took the helm.

"Left rudder," the leader said to him.

Bacon looked at Bonham, who nodded slightly. He turned to ten degrees left rudder. The ship began backing slowly away from the pier.

Washington moved outside to the bridge wing and looked over the side. The dockworkers looked up at him, then spoke to each other animatedly as they watched the gangplank slide along the pier still attached to the ship. It skidded sideways for thirty feet, then hit a bollard. The gangplank ripped away from the ship and fell into the water next to the pier as the *Pacific Flyer* pulled away from Indonesia.

Washington went back onto the bridge, "Rudder middle," he said.

Bacon looked at Bonham, scared, confused, trying to breathe with his mouth closed.

"Amidships," Bonham said.

Bacon centered the rudder as the ship backed into the harbor until it was clear of the pier and other boats.

"Left rudder, all the way," the leader ordered. "Full speed, Captain."

Bacon spun the small brass wheel to the left.

"All ahead full," Bonham said resignedly.

"Tell crew to come to front of ship. Down there, where we can see them," he said pointing to the deck on the bow. He saw the hesitation on Bonham's face. "Now!"

The captain grabbed the PA microphone, "All hands to the bow. All hands to the bow."

"How many men are on the ship?"

"Twenty-five."

"Shipping records say twenty-six," the leader said disapprovingly.

"Twenty-six includes me," Bonham said.

The door to the bridge burst open and the two terrorists who had left earlier came in dragging Bart Jenkins. They held a gun to the side of his head and spoke quickly to their leader.

Washington turned to Bonham, "Get men to bow. Now!"

The crew had begun to assemble on the bow in confusion.

The phone from the engine room rang. Bonham answered it. "Yes, I mean all hands. Leave the engines unmanned for now. I want everyone on the bow."

Washington stood in front of Bonham and looked at him with his cold brown eyes. "Crewman transmitted on radio. Mistake." He looked at the bow, counted twenty-four. He looked back at Bonham. "There should be twenty-two on bow. Four here." He frowned. "Why?"

"I have no idea," the captain answered, intentionally not saying that two Indonesian port officials were on board. Bonham was grasping for anything that would confuse or slow the terrorists.

Washington spoke to his men rapidly. Four of the terrorists stayed on the bridge. The remainder followed him and the captain as they made their way down to the bow. Bart Jenkins and Phillips were behind the captain with their two personal escorts. The crew was startled as they watched their captain walk toward them surrounded by men in Ford coveralls with guns.

Washington and the others stopped in front of them. Half the terrorists walked behind the group.

"Do not speak," the leader said in his steady, authoritative, and slightly high-pitched voice. "Do not move. My ship now. We go out to sea. Do what I say." He spoke to the terrorists behind the crew, who began searching the crew members one by one. The sun was up behind Washington and bright enough that the crewmen couldn't see his face well. "One man made bad decision," he said, looking at Bart Jenkins. "Transmitted on radio."

Washington looked to his left at the two men guarding Jenkins. He looked at the *Pacific Flyer* crewmen standing terrified in front of him, and pointed to Franklin. The two terrorists holding Jenkins released him and grabbed Franklin by the arms. Franklin's eyes grew larger behind his thick glasses. Washington looked at the rest of the crew, then at Franklin, and motioned for him to come forward, away from the rest of the crew. Washington looked Franklin in the eyes. "Anything to say?" he asked.

"About what?" he asked desperately, suddenly and acutely aware of the ocean rushing by him, the wind on his back. "I didn't do anything. What do you want?" Franklin looked directly at Washington, then at Bonham.

"Get on knees," Washington ordered.

Franklin looked at him, disbelieving, not moving.

Washington pointed the long silencer of his automatic pistol at Franklin's forehead.

Franklin went down slowly to his knees. The hard steel of the deck made him wince.

Washington looked sideways at Bart Jenkins and asked him, "You send radio we taking over the ship?" he asked.

Bart Jenkins began to sweat; he saw the terror on Franklin's face. He didn't know whether to lie or confess. "If I did something," he said haltingly, his voice shaking, "you should deal with me . . ."

"No!" Washington shouted. "I punish him *instead* of you!" His face changed into a ball of anger. "You talk on radio?" he yelled.

Jenkins tried to swallow as he struggled to anticipate what would happen next and which was the right answer to avert a disaster. He watched Washington carefully while looking around for some way to escape. Over the side was the only thing even remotely possible, but that would only leave him in the middle of the ocean, miles from any shore, facing an almost certain death. Perhaps he was too worried. He stole a glance at Bonham, who gave a barely perceptible nod. Jenkins looked at Washington and nodded slowly.

Washington pushed the silencer hard against the side of Franklin's head, pressing the skin against his skull, and pulled the trigger.

2

"HEAR THE NEWS?" JIM DILLON ASKED AS HE RUSHED into the office of the Speaker of the House.

John Stanbridge turned slowly away from his evening view of the lighted Washington Monument to frown at his staff member. "I *hate* it when people quiz me. *What* news?"

"Hijacking," Dillon said, walking around Stanbridge's desk and turning on the small television the Speaker kept there for just such emergencies. "It's on CNN."

The news anchor was talking: ". . . it appears a large U.S.-flagged container ship . . ."

"It's not a container ship," Dillon interrupted.

". . . was attacked and taken over in Jakarta, Indonesia, early this morning Indonesia time. Just a few minutes ago we learned that the *Pacific Flyer* out of San Diego was transporting new cars to Indonesia for the grand opening of a Ford dealership. The Chairman of the Board of Ford and the Secretary of Commerce were both expected to attend the ceremony in Jakarta. But as the ship pulled into Jakarta it was hijacked by a large unidentified terrorist force. Our information comes from the Department of Defense. The U.S. Navy, which has a Battle Group operating nearby, intercepted a mayday call from the *Flyer* that it had been taken over. According to those sources, the radioman making the call sounded distressed. He has not been heard from since his first transmission. The President has called a news conference to begin in thirty minutes. The *Pacific Flyer* is the first of a brand-new class of ships built in San Diego. They are the fastest cargo ships in the world, called FastShips, and operate on the principle of a jet ski . . ."

The narration went on as Stanbridge yelled, "Robin!"

Stanbridge's secretary ran around the corner. "Yes, sir," she said.

"Get the President on the line. Now!" He stopped, seeing her confusion. "Tell him I want to speak with him before he goes on the air. Go!" he said, motioning with his hand. He turned back to Dillon. "I don't trust him. He'll say the wrong thing, give these terrorists the wrong signal. I know he doesn't care what I think, but he *has* to when we face things like this . . . he's never even been in the military." He shook his head in disgust. "Commander in Chief," he mumbled. "Only in America."

The phone rang. It was the Senate Majority Leader. Senator Pete Peterson was a fellow Republican and one of Stanbridge's closest friends.

"Yeah, I heard," Stanbridge said. "I have no idea what he has in mind. He doesn't consult. . . . I know. . . ." He nodded.

Dillon strained to hear the small television.

"I *know*. . . ." Stanbridge continued. "I've got a call in to him right now. If you'd get off the damned phone maybe I could talk to him. . . . No, I don't need you in on the conversation . . . it won't matter. Thanks, Pete, I'll call you right back," he said, hanging up.

"President on line one, Mr. Speaker," Robin announced from her desk.

"Good evening, Mr. President." Stanbridge looked out his window toward the White House even though he couldn't see it. "I wondered if you know anything more than is on the news. If you do, I want to come over and hear it for myself. . . . Oh . . . Nothing at all?" he asked, looking at Dillon, who was listening carefully. "What do you plan . . . ? I suppose you're right . . . okay. I agree. Fine. Thanks for calling.''

Stanbridge hung up and told Dillon, "He's not going to say anything. He'll condemn it, say how outraged he is, how cowardly they are, that we're not going to negotiate with terrorists . . . the usual.''

Dillon frowned, "What do you want him to say?''

Stanbridge looked out the window again. "Robin! Get the staff in here as soon as possible. I want everyone in on this,'' he said, then turned his thoughts back to Dillon. "I'm not sure what he should say. I just know he can't carry this sort of thing off. He has no ability to express *outrage*. He . . . I don't know, he doesn't seem to have any fire in his belly. It's hard to describe. He doesn't have any, any . . . *sand*.'' Stanbridge stopped as he shook his head. "We need to keep all our options open at this point. We don't know what's happened, or what we need to do.''

In the year Dillon had been working for the Speaker there had been no international crises, none of the gut-wrenching "what do we do?'' sessions that he had hoped for. They spent most of their time doing what Congress had been doing for years—arguing endlessly over how much to decrease next year's increase in the budget, and where the money was going to come from. He had begun to realize it was unlikely he was going to change the world in this job, or any other in Washington, for that matter. But he was trying to resist the irresistible conversion from idealism to ambition. The Speaker's inability to distinguish between the two made it more difficult.

Dillon's excitement rose as the staff filed in. He tried hard not to look like the typical staffer with a blue suit and perfect haircut. His hair hung over his forehead, slightly uncombed, giving him that all-American-yet-mischievous image he liked. At six feet one, he was athletic, but more explosive than graceful. His smile could light up a room, but he didn't always smile when expected to. It made people look at him more than they otherwise might, almost for approval.

The staff gathered on the couches and chairs, and many stood. Everyone was talking about the hijacking. Twenty bright young people, all trying in their own way to save the world. There was an equal number of men and women. A few were over forty—the professional staffers, the ones who had found their niche in politics without ever running for office. They wanted to be on the general's staff, but never the general. They loved the derivative power they got from working for the Speaker of the House, the second most powerful elected figure in the world. Stanbridge was just a congressman, reelected from his home district every two years like all the others, but his position as Speaker told of longevity, durability, and ultimately of leadership. His staff shared his power without paying the dues, the decades of banquets and handshaking and smiling at people they didn't care about.

But they also knew John Stanbridge. They knew he was nothing particularly special. He was bright and capable, but all those in the room, including Dillon, believed themselves to be smarter than the Speaker and secretly thought more highly of their own abilities than they did of his. They also knew Stanbridge was irrepressibly ambitious. He wanted one more thing in life—to be President. His ambition gave him a sharp edge that cut in unexpected ways.

Stanbridge stood to address them. "Listen up," he said, waiting for a lull in the chatter. "This one could get hairy."

Stanbridge was in his late fifties. He was of average height with dark brown hair that was stiff and unruly. He wore it parted on the side, but the only time his hair looked neat was in the morning when it was still wet. He tucked his shirt in more tightly with the military tuck he used out of habit. He had served in the Navy in Vietnam in riverine patrol boats—one of the few places Navy officers actually got shot at. He looked reasonably trim, but his body was softening.

"We don't know who these terrorists are or what they have in mind. What we do know is that they've taken one of our ships and are out at sea with it, just north of Jakarta." The staff was hanging on every word. He loved it. "The President is holding a press conference in half an hour," he said, looking at his watch, "actually, twenty minutes. I want to be ready to help, if I can. You all know it's the President's job to act—we just help. Right?" He smiled. They smiled back.

"Rhonda," he said, turning toward a staffer in the back, a woman with a Ph.D. in American history from Stanford. "Do the history on all the hostage and terrorist crises we've had in the last twenty years. I want to know what the situation was, and what we did." She nodded in response, having already started a file on just that topic. She adjusted her squarish wire rims and mentally patted herself on the back for her foresight. He always wanted the same thing—the history of what the United States had done in similar situations, and the history of the people on the other side. He thought policy consistency should be a guiding factor and might help predict the outcome. But he didn't believe in slavish duplication.

"Chuck," he said to his staffer who had been an Air Force officer. "Get with the Pentagon. I want to know every military asset in the area. I want to know what our capabilities are."

"Yes, sir," Chuck replied.

"The rest of you, pay attention to what you hear, and if you think there's something I need to know, or an angle I haven't considered yet, let me know. This isn't a contest to see who can look the best." He sighed. "Questions?" There weren't any. "Get started. Be back here for the press conference." He yelled past them, "Robin—get the chairmen of the National Security and Intelligence Committees too. I want them in on this. And International Relations." He looked back at Dillon. "I want you to be the point man for this entire thing." He studied Dillon's face, wondering if he was doing the right thing. "You up to it?"

Dillon looked back at him hard, annoyed that his stomach had jumped. "Yes."

🙚

President Edward Manchester stepped to the podium and waited for the din to die down. He looked over the sea of anxious White House reporters. He had done this many times in his two years as President, but this was the first time he had responded to an act of terrorism. Like many others, he thought international terrorism had seen its day. For the most part he had been right. Except for the ongoing attempts by some factions of Palestinians to undo the peace treaty between the PLO and Israel, there hadn't been a major terrorist attack in over two years, and nothing that involved the United States until now.

His face showed the right combination of anger and sympathy. He had a very expressive face. He was tall, with big clear eyes that showed an uncommon gentleness.

He looked at the cameras and the reporters. "Good evening," he began firmly with a grim look on his face. "We have received word that the *Pacific Flyer,* the first of an exciting new American ship design called a FastShip, carrying the newest model Ford, the Ascenda, has been taken by terrorists while in port in Jakarta. Rather than recite the details, which you already know as well as I do, let me say this." He furrowed his brow, looking severe and angry. "We will not tolerate acts of terrorism." His eyes glowed. "The Americans must be freed immediately and the property taken returned. We don't know the current status of the ship. We haven't heard from it since the original call for help. We will do what we can to assess the situation, then take appropriate steps. That's all I have at the moment. Now, if there are any questions . . ."

Several of the reporters jumped up and began calling out.

President Manchester called on them one at a time. "Bill," he said pointing to an older reporter in the front row.

"Sir, do you think anyone has been killed or wounded?"

"We have no way of knowing. Those on the pier at the time said they saw no signs of violence. Apparently the terrorists—dressed as Ford employees, I might add—took the crew completely by surprise." He looked around the room. "Sally," he said pointing.

"Mr. President, do you think it was too much to ask Ford to open a dealership in Jakarta, which is somewhat unstable since the death of Suharto and the imposition of martial law? Has your 'diplomacy through commerce' policy brought this about?"

President Manchester looked at her intently. "I promised in my campaign that we would continue to be the leader of the world, but would change the emphasis from military leadership to commercial leadership, that we would be the business leader of the world. We already are actually, having had the largest economy in the world for a long time now. But I wanted a new emphasis, a new image, if you will. I wanted to touch other countries through commerce. I promised that we would trade, not dominate; that we would give fair value, and expect to receive it. It would benefit everyone." He shifted his weight and gripped the podium. "Until now it has been working admirably. Combined with our new laws designed to encourage U.S.-built ships delivering goods to and from the U.S., things have gone smoothly. But as we are reminded again, there is always someone there to tear down what we try to build up." He stopped and shook his head slowly, as if he had planned such a dramatic pause for emphasis. "We can't let them defeat us in our attempt to lift the economies of the world." He paused. "Maybe I'm pushing too far too fast. But I think the faster we get the countries of the world trading with each other, the better off we'll all be. I don't think this changes that goal, even though it is clearly a direct challenge to my diplomacy-through-commerce approach.''

''Have you ruled out a military response?''

Manchester shook his head. ''We haven't ruled out anything. Over there. Elizabeth,'' he said, pointing to Elizabeth Duke, a reporter for the *Chicago Tribune*. The shutters on the still cameras clicked as she looked at her pad to find her question. ''Sir, are there military forces in place that could launch an attack on the terrorists?''

''I'm not going to comment on that, Elizabeth,'' he said, looking away from her.

''May I follow up?'' she pleaded.

''Go ahead,'' he said reluctantly.

''Is this the kind of thing the military could respond to? Do we even have the capability, whether or not they are in the area?''

''I'm still not going to comment on that. David,'' he said, pointing to the White House correspondent for CBS.

''Sir, have you been in consultation with Congress on this?''

Manchester nodded. ''I have spoken with the Speaker of the House. We are of one mind on what to do at this point.''

The Chief of Staff gave the secret ''cut'' signal, and the President stepped back from the podium. ''That's all for now. I'll tell you more when I know it.'' He turned around and walked out of the room, with the reporters yelling after him.

Manchester and his Chief of Staff, Arlan Van den Bosch, walked into the Oval Office, where other members of the presidential staff had watched the press conference on television. The President sat down heavily in his chair and looked at his staff. He turned to Van den Bosch. ''Well, what did you think?''

''That was truly excellent, sir. Not too much information to pass at this point, so there wasn't much that could have gone wrong.''

"Thank you for your vote of confidence," Manchester said, removing his coat.

"I didn't mean it like that, sir. Everything was fine. Now we have to decide what to do."

"What new information do we have?"

"Nothing sir. We've moved the *Constitution* battle group toward the *Pacific Flyer* and they're going to start looking for it."

"That's all we can do right now," Manchester said with resignation, then looked at Van den Bosch. "Didn't our intelligence folks have any idea this was coming?"

Van den Bosch shook his head and glanced at Cary Warner, the Director of Central Intelligence. "Cary?" he said, giving him a chance to speak.

Warner shook his head slowly and uncrossed his thin long legs. "No, sir, not a thing. These guys are very close-mouthed and very organized. We would have heard something if it was one of the usual organizations."

Manchester looked at him, unsatisfied. His intense gaze made others uncomfortable. He liked it that way. "And why do you think the Speaker felt he had to call? What could he possibly add to what we might do?"

His Chief of Staff shook his head. "Easy. Anytime he thinks you might stumble, he wants to be there to push—" Van den Bosch was interrupted by the entrance of Richard Benison, Counsel to the President, accompanied by Molly Vaughan, deputy White House counsel. Even though they knew her, they were happy to have the excuse to look at her.

Benison held out his hands apologetically, "Forgive me, Mr. President, for being late."

Manchester waved his hand at him, "Welcome, Richard, not a problem."

"The Chief of Staff said you wanted someone from my office involved in this from the earliest stages. I thought Molly would be just the right person, Mr. President. She has the most experience in international law."

The President nodded at her and smiled warmly.

She looked him directly in the eye and returned his smile. She was five feet seven and thin, her figure both subtle and alluring. Her dark auburn hair was parted on the side, tucked behind her ears, and hung to her shoulders. She wore an elegant, fitted navy blue gabardine suit and a cream colored silk blouse.

"Thank you for coming. This may be overkill, because we're going to have a lot of lawyers looking at this situation, both at the State Department and at the Pentagon. But I told Richard I wanted somebody on my staff, in the office of the Counsel to the President, looking out for the interests of the presidency."

"Of course," Molly replied. It was the fundamental purpose of the job in the office of Counsel to the President. That he felt like he needed to mention it, she found slightly amusing.

"I want you to evaluate all the implications. Rules of Engagement, International Law. . . ." He hesitated, unsure of what the other implications might be. "Anything else that occurs to you. Just look out for my interests. Will you do that?"

Molly nodded. "It would be a pleasure, Mr. President."

The President smiled again and let his eyes linger on her. He then turned to the rest of the staff. "Stay close by. As soon as we have any more information, I'll want to know what our options are. Arlan, get Admiral Hart over here. I want the Joint Chiefs involved in this from the earliest minute in case we have to do a hostage rescue or something else."

"Yes, sir."

3

COMMANDER MIKE CASKEY FOUGHT BACK A YAWN AS he sat down in the ready room chair to brief. They had been at sea for thirty straight days on the USS *Constitution* (CVN-77), the latest and last Nimitz-class nuclear-powered aircraft carrier. He was ready to go home. It had been five months since they left San Diego.

Caskey had been on numerous cruises since he first started flying in the Navy. He had been to sea for a month on many occasions before this, but he'd never gotten used to it. It was always a challenge. He stretched his legs out in front of his chair. He was just under six feet two and in superb physical condition, which he maintained mostly by doing chin-ups on the steel beam that ran through his stateroom. He kept his blond hair so short that it barely held a part. When at sea he would occasionally get a flattop from one of the ship's barbers, but not this time.

"Morning, Skipper," muttered Lieutenant (junior grade) Bill Schmidt, called Messer by his squadron mates. A recent Naval Academy graduate, Messer was crewed with Caskey as a RIO, Radar Intercept Officer. Their squadron, VF-143, considered itself the best fighter squadron in the Navy. They were called the Pukin' Dogs because of their symbol—a Griffin—half eagle, half lion—in a bent-over position to accentuate the wings. When first painted on a VF-143 plane decades ago, it had looked like a dog throwing up. The squadron *loved* that image. They called themselves the Pukin' Dogs until the early nineties, when someone from the Navy brass thought the image of a puking dog wasn't quite proper and forced the squadron to change it. The new name, the Dogs, had been used until Caskey took over. One of his first acts was to change the name back to the Pukin' Dogs. Nobody had forced him to change it back, yet.

"You ready to fly, Messer?" Caskey asked. The battle group was in the area to take part in a naval exercise.

"Sure." Messer smiled casually. "A low level over Bali? *Hurt* me. I can't believe they pay us for this." Messer's smile was infectious. He was regarded throughout the squadron as an extremely competent RIO for a first-tour officer. Even though he was a junior grade lieutenant, he was at least as skilled as the lieutenants in the squadron. He also was easygoing and funny. As much as the other officers in the squadron liked Messer, Messer worshiped Caskey. For him, the opportunity to fly with the squadron commanding officer was an honor. It was also a tremendous responsibility, and a chance to screw up right in front of the guy who would write his fitness report. Messer wore his curly blond hair as long as he could under Navy regulations, in contrast to virtually all the other officers. It was the only thing that ever got him in trouble with Caskey.

"Check the route?"

"Of course I checked the route," he said, looking up at Caskey, miffed he would doubt him.

"What jet we got?"

Messer glanced at the schedule board. "Haven't assigned us one yet."

The second crew on the low level sat down next to them for the brief—Lieutenant Commander Larry Landretti, the pilot, and Lieutenant Bill Warber, the RIO. Landretti and Warber made quite a sight. They were, respectively, the smallest and largest officers in the squadron. Landretti was five feet six and bald; Warber was almost six three and constantly fighting his weight at two hundred forty pounds. Warber was called Beef for obvious reasons.

They settled in for the usual brief: the weather, where not to fly, what not to do, what *really* not to do, and miscellaneous other information.

Suddenly the 1MC, the ship's loudspeaker, came alive. "All Squadron COs to CVIC. All squadron COs to CVIC."

Caskey raised his eyebrows and looked at the others with some surprise. They looked back with equal curiosity. He stood up and shrugged, pulling down the sleeves of his olive flight suit with the blue Pukin' Dog patch on the shoulder. "I've got no idea," he said. "But I'm about to find out." He walked down the starboard passageway to CVIC, the carrier intelligence center. He was the last one there.

Captain Zeke Bradford, commander of Air Wing Seven, strode into the room. He was a handsome black man with a deep and authoritative voice. Loved by the entire air wing, officers and enlisted men alike, he had the reputation of being a great pilot and a gentleman, but one who didn't suffer fools gladly. He had flown A-6s in the old days, then F/A-18s.

"You're not going to believe this," Bradford said. "You're just not going to believe it." He shook his head. "You heard about that Ford deal where they were going to open a dealership in Jakarta? Joint venture, co-ownership with Indonesians or something? 'Diplomacy through commerce,' and all that?" He held up a piece of paper. "I just got a copy of this mayday transmitted in the clear from the *Pacific Flyer....*" He looked at their blank stares. "That's the name of the ship carrying all those Fords to Jakarta—a U.S.-flagged vessel. Someone hijacked the ship."

The COs looked at each other, puzzled.

"How'd they do that?" Caskey asked.

"Walked aboard," Captain Bradford answered.

"What do you mean 'walked aboard'?"

"Get this," he said, reading from the message in his hand. " 'Mayday! Mayday! This is the *Pacific Flyer* in Jakarta. As soon as we pulled in, a bunch of men in blue Ford coveralls came aboard. They have bags with them, and guns. They are taking over the ship. We are being hijacked. I don't know what their intentions are . . . hold on for a second' "—Bradford looked up at them, then continued reading—" 'I can hear us getting under way. We are backing away from the pier. There are at least twenty of them, maybe thirty. I have no idea what is happening, but we need help fas—' " Bradford stopped reading. "And then he was cut off."

Caskey shook his head. "Who are the guys in the coveralls?"

"We don't know."

"What's the plan?"

Bradford shook his head. "Don't have one. We're waiting for instructions from the National Command Authority, but you can bet we'll be doing something soon. In the meanwhile, we're already headed west at flank speed."

The COs looked at each other. Caskey was the first to speak. "Not really much the air wing can do. We can't exactly attack them. Sounds like a job for the SEALs."

Bradford nodded. "My feelings exactly. But I thought we should do a fly-by first, to let them know we're in the area. Let them know anything they do from now on will get them in deep kimchi."

"Won't that tell them there's a battle group around, that we may try something?" said Dave "Drunk" Driver, CO of VFA-136, one of the two F/A-18C squadrons.

Bradford shrugged. "Maybe. But I'd rather let them know we're here, and that we're going to spank 'em if they do anything stupid."

The COs nodded.

"Who can get to them first?"

Caskey raised his hand. "The F-18s can get there at the same time the F-14s can, Captain, but we can also get *back.*'' Caskey smiled, poking at the weak point of the F/A-18C: its constant need for more fuel.

"With the proper tanking assets . . ." said Drunk Driver defensively.

Bradford interposed. "No, this is a job for the F-14. I want a TARPS bird to go so we can get some pictures," he said, thinking of the Tactical Air Reconnaissance Pod System that the F-14 could carry to act as a reconnaissance plane. "But they may have shoulder-fired SAMs; we don't need to lose an airplane. I want you to do a supersonic fly-by too. Let them know we mean business."

Caskey shook his head. "Can't do both. You want TARPS or supersonic?"

"Can you take a hand-held camera with you?"

"Sure. Messer's great at that. We win 'photo of the week' all the time."

"Okay. No TARPS."

"Roger supersonic," Caskey said. "Are we waiting for approval before we go?"

"Absolutely," said Bradford. "Right now the rest of the flight schedule is canceled. The *Constitution* is heading west at flank speed with the rest of the battle group that can keep up. We'll launch as soon as we're close enough and when we have approval. In the meantime, the SEALs on the *Wasp* are getting ready, and the Marines are on alert as well. We're not sure how this is going to go, so stay loose." He looked at Caskey. "MC, I want you to fly this mission yourself. I don't want anyone to screw it up."

"Roger that," Caskey replied, feeling a rush of adrenaline. "When do you want us to go?"

"I'm not sure." He turned to the PLAT. The Pilot Landing Assistance Television in every ready room and in CVIC had a continuous readout of the ship's latitude and longitude. He memorized the numbers and crossed to a wall chart. The ship was north of Bali, heading west at thirty-plus knots. "I'd say we'll launch in about two hours. But before that, I want every up S-3 we've got out there looking for this ship.'' The S-3B, a Viking of VS-31, a hefty two-engine antisubmarine airplane, was well established as the best airplane on the carrier for surface surveillance because of its excellent radar and its ability to stay airborne for a long time. ''We have no idea where she went after leaving Jakarta.''

Caskey looked at the chart and nodded. ''I'll be ready.'' He looked at his air wing commander. ''Flight of two?''

''Yes. One for cover in case anything happens we're not expecting. I want the E-2 airborne too, to keep radar coverage of the entire area, as well as a section of F/A-18s in case somebody else shows up we're not expecting. Could be a surface ship or two involved in this. We've been trying to reach the ship ever since we got the distress call, but there's no response. We don't know if they don't want to talk or if the radio was destroyed.''

''What kind of radars they got?'' Caskey asked. ''Any air-search?''

''We don't think so. We're checking on that right now with the ship's owners. It's a really fancy new ship. The owners are *pissed*. But we think they had only surface-search radars—some air capability—but mostly for surface ships and navigation.''

''So they probably won't see us coming.''

Bradford shook his head. ''*Probably* not,'' he said a hint of caution in his voice.

''Admiral aware of all this?'' Caskey asked.

Bradford frowned. ''No, MC. I thought I'd just run this show on my own. Cancel the flight schedule, order the ship west, fly sorties.''

''Sorry,'' Caskey said, feeling stupid. Caskey knew the admiral well. Admiral Ray Billings. ''Steam.'' His former commanding officer when they were on the *Nimitz* in the Jolly Rogers.

''I've got to see the admiral right now, in fact. Any more stupid questions?'' Bradford asked. He scanned them once, then turned and walked out of CVIC.

''I wonder what they want,'' said Wayne Berry, the

Commanding Officer of VF-11, the other F-14 squadron.

"Notoriety. Always the same thing. Publicize some cause that's important to them," said Drunk. He looked up as if a new thought was struggling to get out. "Who decided it was okay to be a terrorist anyway? That it was like being a soldier?"

"Nobody's ever said that," said Caskey.

"But *look* at us," Drunk said. "Nobody's outraged, nobody's flaming mad, nobody's running up the bullshit flag." He looked around, then went on, not caring whether he had any support. "It's like we've *accepted* terrorism as part of the scenery. We're not upset by it anymore."

"I don't think that's fair," Caskey said, squinting. "It's just that we've seen it for so long we're accustomed to it."

"That's exactly my point. We shouldn't *ever* get accustomed to it," Drunk said as he stood up and walked out of CVIC.

⚑

Two of the men in Ford coveralls took Franklin's arms and dragged him across the deck. The blood ran down his face and neck, soaking his shirt. Bonham tried to control his anger, both at the terrorists and at himself. He was responsible. He had failed to take adequate security measures. He had failed to take *any* security measures and hadn't done anything to stop the attack. If anyone deserved to die it was him, not Franklin.

Washington looked at the rest of the crew and pointed to Jenkins. "He unwise to use radio," he said with cold look in his eyes. "Understand?" he asked. The crew watched sickly as the two terrorists pulled Franklin up over the railing. His body tumbled over the side of the ship and plunged into the ocean below.

"All go back to places," Washington ordered. He spoke to his men, then again to the crew. "One man will go with each of you. If you stupid, they shoot you. Go,'' he said with authority. ''No talking. Go.''

The crew dispersed, slowly, afraid to make a mistake. No one wanted to test the rule against talking. They walked off to their stations, each followed closely by a terrorist with a gun and a blue bag.

🏴

The two F-14B tomcats streaked westward. The S-3s had been scouring the area for over an hour, but couldn't pick the *Pacific Flyer* out of the dozens of surface ships. Messer had plotted its last-known position, charted a circle that described the maximum distance the ship could have traveled since the transmission, and started at the outer limits of that circle. The S-3 had reported the southeastern quadrant clear.

''See anything, Messer?'' Caskey asked over the ICS, the internal communication system.

''There are ships all over the place. I don't know how we're supposed to pick out one.''

''Supposed to be a big ship, or sort of big anyway,'' Caskey reminded him.

''Well, they all look pretty much the same on the radar,'' Messer replied.

''Choose one, and let's go look,'' Caskey said, scanning the horizon.

''Roger that. Come left to 280. There's one about . . . twenty miles off.''

Caskey brought the nose around five degrees in a gentle turn. They stayed at five thousand feet: high enough for a good radar horizon and low enough to quickly descend and check out any ship they found. ''Range?''

''Seventeen.''

Caskey squinted as he looked toward the ship, but saw only the blue unbroken ocean. No ships. The radar screen made the Java sea look crowded. To his eyes it looked empty. They flew toward the contact at five hundred knots, carefully watching their fuel and distance from the carrier.

"Ten miles," Messer said.

"Tally," Caskey said, seeing a large whitish ship on the horizon. He couldn't tell what it was, other than a cargo ship, and big. He lowered the nose of the F-14 and pointed at the ship.

"Five miles," Messer called.

"I'll take him down the starboard side," Caskey said. "He's heading south—not a good sign," he added.

"I don't think they'd be heading back to port," Messer said.

They leveled off at five hundred feet and five hundred knots and flew down the port side of the ship, keeping it on their right. They could see quickly it was the wrong ship. It had a white superstructure, like the *Pacific Flyer,* but it wasn't the right shape at all. They couldn't make out the name as they passed by, but they could clearly make out the Red Star on the stack, from the famous Russian Red Star line, formerly one of the largest cargo lines in the world—state owned, of course. Crewmen standing on the decks looked up at them as they flew by. Caskey could see the white faces turned upward. They waved and the crew waved back.

Caskey pulled back on the stick gradually until the Tomcat was pointing straight up. As soon as they reached four thousand feet he rolled the plane over on its back heading south again, then rolled wings level at five thousand feet. "Next," Caskey said.

"Thirty right, fifteen miles," Messer replied immediately.

"Tally," Caskey said coolly. "It's bigger than the last ship. Can't tell if it's the one," he said as he lowered the nose.

They approached the second ship from the bow. It was headed directly toward them, but not fast; the bow wave was small.

Caskey breathed in sharply. "I think this is it, Messer.

Set up the camera. I'm coming left, then right. I'll take it down the starboard side.''

"Okay," Messer said as he checked the settings on his camera.

"Here we go." Caskey banked hard left as the Tomcat continued its descent, then hard right. They flew by the ship a quarter mile away at five hundred feet and five hundred knots. No one was on deck. With a telephoto lens on his hand-held 35mm camera Messer took as many pictures of the ship as he could while looking for evidence of a missile launcher. They passed the ship and banked hard right. The G forces pushed them down into their seats. Caskey saw the ship's name in large white letters against the red hull: *Pacific Flyer.* Caskey pulled up sharply to get away from the ship without passing down the other side. He went into afterburner to keep the Tomcat climbing at a forty-five-degree angle and increase the distance from the ship.

As they reached ten thousand feet Caskey rolled the plane over on its back and pulled hard. The G forces built up again as the nose passed through the horizon and he pointed the Tomcat directly at the ocean. Caskey looked straight up and back through the canopy to the ocean and picked out the ship, stark in its white and red against the blue sea. Caskey kept his eye fixed on the ship and held the stick back; he held 7 Gs as the nose came up toward the other horizon, completing a split S. As the nose approached the ship he relaxed the back pressure on the stick and pushed the throttles into full afterburner. "Speed," Caskey said.

"Passing six hundred knots, sixty-five hundred feet," Messer said.

The G forces left the airplane as Caskey bunted the nose down to keep the Tomcat pointed at the target. They came out of their seats as the plane went to zero G— weightless. The engines chewed up the jet fuel and threw blue flame out the back of the plane as they pushed the Tomcat forward with more pounds of thrust than the plane had in weight. They could accelerate going straight up. But at zero Gs and pointed down, they could *really* accelerate.

"Super," Messer said matter-of-factly as they passed through the sound barrier.

"Rog," Caskey replied. He kept the nose of the plane on the ship as they lost altitude.

"Passing one thousand," Messer said.

"Rog," he said, holding the throttles in max afterburner.

"Mach 1.2."

"Stand by to mark their position."

"Ready," Messer replied as he leaned forward to see the ship a half mile ahead. They were approaching the ship from the stern at 1.2 times the speed of sound. They would be there in three seconds.

The ship flashed by on the left. "Mark," Caskey said curtly, and Messer immediately pressed the waypoint button on their computer navigation system. Caskey pulled back and the Tomcat's wings bent under the G forces. The moist air condensed behind them and left a vapor trail in front of their sound.

"Break left!" Messer yelled. Over his shoulder he could see a missile tearing straight toward the Tomcat.

Caskey immediately put the F-14 on its side and banked toward the ship in a 7 G turn. The wings were already fully aft since they were still supersonic.

"Come out of burner!" Messer said as Caskey retarded the throttles, already thinking the same thing.

Caskey and Messer were thrown forward into their shoulder harnesses as the airplane slowed without afterburners as if hitting a wall of air.

"Where'd it come from?" Caskey asked through clenched teeth as he fought the G forces and tried to keep the color in his vision.

"Open hatch just aft of the bridge," Messer said, watching the small missile. "It's not gonna make it. It's out of gas,'' he added as the missile petered out and headed toward the ocean.

Caskey reversed course, headed away from the ship, and descended to just above the water to ensure he was out of the envelope of whatever other surprise might be aboard the *Pacific Flyer*. "That was unpleasant," he said checking his fuel and the clock.

"One day, we may have to show them what a *real* missile looks like," Messer said, annoyed at his moist armpits and dry mouth.

📧

From the bridge of the *Pacific Flyer,* the man who called himself Washington watched the F-14 disappear over the horizon. "He not attack us," he said, quickly recovering his composure after two bridge windows imploded from the sonic boom.

"He'll be back," Bonham replied hopefully.

Washington shook his head and frowned, suddenly very angry. "Never. They don't want you hurt." He looked up through the broken windows, trying to catch a glimpse of the Tomcat.

"They're probably waiting for you to contact them," Bonham said. "You should use the radio."

Washington shifted his gun to his other hand. "Destroyed."

Captain Bonham looked at him, worried. "Why?"

"Won't need."

"How are you going to talk to them?"

"Nothing to say."

"No demands?"

"No, not yet."

Bonham felt a chill go down his back. "What is it you want?"

"You see. Soon enough."

"No, tell me now!" Bonham spoke louder than he meant to. "Tell me what you want! Maybe I can help," he said, choking on the idea of helping Washington do anything.

Washington stood directly in front of Bonham as he quickly scanned the horizon for other ships. "This is just beginning, Captain. Soon, fourth largest country in the world will get respect it deserves."

"What are you talking about? Are you Japanese?"

Washington turned his back on Bonham as he walked to the other side of the bridge. "You Americans are so stupid. So *arrogant*," he said with venom. "You learn the hard way."

4

LIEUTENANT JODY ARMSTRONG STARED IN DISBELIEF at Bud Cooper, captain of the *Wasp*. "In broad daylight?"

Cooper nodded as he leaned back on his heels, trying to seem authoritative. But he did not have the confidence in his orders he would like. "We don't know what they're doing. We can't wait until dark."

The *Wasp* was the center of the other half of the *Nimitz* Battle Group, the amphibious half. The Amphibious Ready Group, the ARG. The half that carried the Marines, the helicopters, the SEALs, and the people who wore green and went ashore with guns. The *Wasp* was the newest amphibious assault helicopter ship in the Navy. Its design was unique. Not only could it operate Marine Corps AV-8B Harrier jets, the CH-53 and CH-46 helicopters, but the aft end of the ship contained a well deck in which hovercraft or landing assault craft could be launched and recovered. When the time came, the back of the ship was flooded and the assault craft went ashore carrying the Marines, trucks, and occasionally tanks. Armstrong's SEAL platoon operated off the *Wasp* in support of the ARG.

"We?" Armstrong frowned. He wore his distinctive SEAL insignia on the left breast of his camouflage uniform, the insignia affectionately called the "Budweiser" because of its resemblance to the symbol on a Budweiser can. His uniform was perfect, and his tan highlighted his

35

rugged appearance. He had been interrupted in an inspection of his men, something that occurred only once during each tour at sea, and always with only twenty-four hours' notice. He was not in a good mood.

As the Officer in Charge, the OIC, of the SEAL platoon on the *Wasp*, he expected hard problems. But nothing like this. They usually had days to plan an operation. Now they were expected to leave in half an hour.

"We just got a good position on the ship," Captain Cooper continued. "An F-14 found it. Here's the lat/long." He crossed to a chart of the western Java Sea on the bulkhead tack board. He pointed to a spot sixty miles north of Jakarta. "They're still heading north, but seem to have slowed."

"Where are we?"

"Right here." The captain pointed. "Just north of Bawean."

"That's three hundred miles," Armstrong said, rubbing his do-it-yourself buzz cut.

"Right."

Armstrong studied the chart and thought. He looked at the overhead and thought some more. Finally, he turned to the ship's intelligence officer, Lieutenant Commander Tyler Lawson, a black officer and graduate of The Citadel. "What do we know about numbers?"

Lawson was widely respected by the SEALs. He was a former SEAL who still wore his "Bud" on his chest. After breaking his back on a parachute jump three years before, he was no longer fit enough to be a SEAL. He applied for a change of designator to intelligence and now worked as an intelligence officer, specializing in amphibious warfare, special operations, low-intensity conflict—the use of SEALs. The SEALs trusted him, which was more than could be said for other intel officers who had no warfare specialty and treated intelligence like academic work.

"All we know," Lawson began slowly, "is that there are at least twenty, maybe thirty terrorists." He looked up at Armstrong. "Maybe more. Everything's based on one call from a radio operator. We got a photo from the F-14 that the *Constitution* scanned and sent to us over the satellite, but you can see only a few men on the bridge." He tacked the photo onto the wall next to the chart. He put his hands on his hips and looked at the chart, then the ship. He stared at the *Pacific Flyer*'s position, where the captain had stuck a pin. "Where the hell are they going?" he asked no one in particular, noting the position and direction of travel. "Why out there in the blue water instead of near the coast?" He shook his head as he pondered his own question. "They'd have a lot more leverage and a lot more options if they'd anchored in Jakarta harbor. . . . I don't get it. Unless they're rendezvousing with some other ship. But who? Some combat ship from some navy? Whose? We know where every combatant is in the Pacific, and there isn't *one* that can even be a factor—at least not before we get there."

Armstrong stared at the chart. "If we have to go now, there's only one way we could do it." He looked at the captain. "Are the 53s up?"

The captain nodded.

"We'll have to take the whole det. I can't take one squad onto a ship with twenty or thirty terrorists and . . ." He looked at Lawson. "How many ship's company on the *Pacific Flyer*?"

"Twenty-six."

"Thirty terrorists and twenty-six hostages?" Armstrong shook his head. "Shit! Who wants us to go so soon? We aren't even giving 'em a chance to play their hand." He paused. "This should be a job for USSO-COM," he said, frowning and fighting against the urge to say something he would regret. He knew the Special Operations Command was not only the right command to run such an operation, it would be salivating to get the chance. "This is their op!"

Lawson hesitated. "I think Washington has some info we don't have."

"Like what?"

"I'm not sure. I'm trying to read between the lines in the messages I've read. Maybe they've intercepted something. Something that makes them either think, or know, that these boys aren't going to be around for very long. Like maybe this isn't the usual hostage deal. Maybe the terrorists have something else in mind."

"Like *what*?"

"I don't know. All I know is we've got to go, and they say so."

"*Who* says so?"

"National Command Authority."

"Roger that," Armstrong said, immediately recognizing the brick wall that had just been erected in front of him. "And what *exactly* are our orders?"

"Hostage rescue. No casualties."

"Jump in the ocean, but don't get wet." He thought some more. His arms flexed involuntarily against his taut sleeves as he considered the details of the mission forming in his head. "We'll have to go right at them. I sure can't promise no casualties. That's up to them." He looked at Lawson and Cooper. "Agree?"

They nodded.

"They didn't ask us to *guarantee* no casualties, did they?"

"No, they just said no casualties," Cooper echoed, getting uncomfortable.

"Well shit, sir, excuse my French. What the hell does that mean? Are we supposed to go unarmed?"

"I don't think so. I expect it means to minimize casualties. I'm sure they expect you to be able to defend yourselves. . . ."

Armstrong stood up straight and shook his head. "It doesn't *work* like that. We're not going there to chat— we're going there to get the Americans off the ship. If they won't let them go, we whack them. Simple as that. Is that what I am authorized to do or not?"

"I don't know really," Cooper said softly, frustrated. "I can't give you any guidance. . . ."

"Maybe we should ask for clarification—"

Cooper interrupted. "No time." He looked at his watch. "You've got to get going now."

"This is a shit sandwich."

"Do the best you can."

Armstrong stared at him coolly. He wasn't angry at Captain Cooper; he was angry about the orders he had received. "I'll bet Lieutenant Commander Becker would push back at these orders." Becker was the Naval Special Warfare Task Unit commander in charge not only of the SEAL platoon, but also the RHIB Det (Rigid Hull, Inflatable Boat Detachment) and the MCT, the Mobile Communication Team. But Becker had flown ahead to Thailand for the upcoming Cobra Gold exercise.

"Maybe. But he's not here. This one's on your shoulders."

⚑

Washington clicked on the microphone on the bridge of the *Pacific Flyer*. He listened for the sound. He blew into it until he heard his breath on the ship's loudspeakers. He began to speak in his native language in a way that made it clear he was giving orders to his men. He spoke for thirty seconds and set the microphone down. He turned to the captain. "Come here."

Bonham looked at him but stayed where he was.

"Here, Captain," he said with more intensity.

"Why?" Bonham asked. "What's going to happen? Are you afraid the U.S. Navy is going to come get you? They will, you know. Look what happened on the *Achille Lauro*."

Washington dismissed Bonham's words with a wave of his hand. "Come here. *Now*."

Bonham crossed over to Washington and stood directly in front of him. "What?" he said.

"Put out hands." Washington bent down and pulled a pair of handcuffs out of his bag.

"What are you, some kind of coward?" Bonham said gruffly. "Afraid I'm going to attack you or something?"

"Shut up."

"You shot one of my men like a dog. You're a spineless *murderer*," Bonham said, his eyes blazing.

"You not speak!" Washington screamed as he roughly tightened the handcuffs around Bonham's hands behind his back.

"Why are you doing this?" Bonham asked.

"No talk," he said, inches from Bonham's face as he brought his gun up.

"Go ahead and shoot me," Bonham taunted.

Washington took a roll of heavy tape out of his bag and tore off a piece six inches long. He taped Bonham's mouth and looked at him from two inches away.

Bonham stared at him with contempt.

Washington spoke to his men on the bridge, who pulled handcuffs from their bags and handcuffed Bacon to the ship's wheel. He spoke again to one of them, who opened his bag on the deck of the bridge and pulled out a heavy round device.

Bonham had never seen anything like it.

The man carried it outside to the port bridge wing and left it there in the open.

Washington and the others then reached down and unzipped their bags all the way. They pulled out more of the heavy metal devices. They were gray, circular, eighteen inches or so in diameter and five inches thick. They looked like UFOs. Washington reached under his and threw a switch. He carefully placed it on the deck near Bonham. It touched the deck with extra force—more than just gravity.

Beads of sweat rolled down Bonham's face as he watched the other terrorists remove identical devices from their bags.

Washington glanced at his watch to note the time and began moving faster.

☙

Armstrong checked his op-gear and ordered his chief to inspect that of the other platoon members. They were as trained and ready as anyone could be, but this mission was screwed up from the start. Not enough time, too rough a plan, too much light, too many targets. This could be a disaster, he thought. I could be famous like the SEALs who died in Operation Just Cause in Panama by getting shot up while being forced to push a bad situation. But this was what they had been told to do, so it was what they would do.

"All set, sir," said QMC Lee, his chief petty officer.

"Thanks," Armstrong said.

The SEALs and two Explosive Ordnance Disposal techs, wearing their EOD badges, sat quietly on the webbed seats of the Sikorsky CH-53E, a three-engine behemoth of a helicopter. The remainder of the platoon was in the other CH-53E flying equally fast and parallel to Armstrong's, five hundred feet to the side. The CH-53E could carry more cargo farther than any other helicopter in the Navy or Marine inventory and could refuel in flight. It streaked over the dark blue ocean, less than one hundred feet off the water. Armstrong could smell the JP5 jet fuel from the engines in the humid air pouring into the helicopter through the open hatch.

The pilots spotted a large ship and leaned forward to see if it was the *Pacific Flyer*. They thought they had a decent fix on the location of the *Flyer* from the GPS mark relayed from the F-14, but couldn't know for sure. They couldn't approach the ship close enough to check its identity without being seen, but they had no other way of confirming its identity. The helicopters slowed and descended lower as they approached. Armstrong watched out the side window as the ocean grew closer; it looked as if the helicopter was going to smack into the water any second. He couldn't judge how high they were. The only reference point was the horizon and he had learned a long time ago that the ocean can look the same from five thousand feet as it does from one hundred.

The helicopter crew chief gave him a two-minute warning. Armstrong ordered his men up, "Check gear!" he shouted.

The dark helicopters hovered ten feet above the ocean as they drew closer to the target.

"Two minutes!" the crew chief shouted as he lowered the ramp at the back of the helicopter and waited until it stopped. He then looked at Lieutenant Armstrong, who nodded.

The Marine captains who had been trained to fly the Sea Stallion in special operations accelerated their helicopters to the maximum speed at sea level of one hundred sixty knots. The helicopters beat their way through the moist air, each with its seven massive blades bending under the weight.

The pilots strained to see the ship ahead. The pilot in Armstrong's helicopter could just make out the superstructure of the ship ahead of them. Fortunately, the *Flyer* had a very distinctive look that made the close-up identification easy. "That's her!" he exclaimed as he tried to determine the heading. He wanted to approach from the stern, but they were coming in on the *Flyer's* bow.

The pilot climbed to avoid striking the water with his rotors as he banked left to slow his approach. He circled around low on the horizon to head toward the stern of the ship. They were still three miles away and would be seen only by a diligent lookout who knew what he was looking for. The pilot noticed the ship didn't seem to be moving. Strange. The fastest merchant ship in the world dead in the water. He looked around the horizon for other ships or airplanes. Nothing. He continued in toward the *Flyer* and gave the signal to the crew chief for the SEALs to get ready. The crew chief shouted, "One minute!"

Armstrong gave hand signals to his men as they stood

and lined up in order. The four lead SEALs attached the ninety-foot specially braided ropes to the bulkhead hard-points above the ramp of the helicopter. They had been carefully coiled so that the first men out had only to kick them and the ropes would easily uncoil to the deck of the ship.

The pilot hugged the surface and held his speed, flying as low and fast as safety would allow. At one quarter mile he pulled the nose of the helicopter up quickly, using the rotors as a large brake. The helicopter slowed as quickly as it could be slowed as it approached the stern of the ship. The Super Stallion looked like an enormous bug about to crush something smaller as it approached the fan-tail. Two SEAL snipers hung out of the open door and trained their M14s on the ship, looking for anything moving.

Armstrong reached for something to hold as the Super Stallion came to a deafening, frightening stop two hundred yards aft and left of the *Flyer*'s fantail. The snipers scanned the ship quickly but carefully through their scopes. While continuing to look, one of the snipers gave a thumbs-up to the crew chief, who relayed immediately to the pilot, who transmitted via the radio to the other helicopter that it was clear.

The second Super Stallion charged in, covered by the hovering sniper helicopter, and did a quickstop directly over the fantail of the *Flyer*. The SEALs kicked the braided ropes onto the deck and fastroped down instantly. When the first half of the SEAL platoon was on the deck, the first helicopter jerked up and pulled away.

Armstrong's helo rushed in and stopped over the fan-tail. The SEALs already on deck were covering every possible approach point with their automatic weapons.

Lieutenant Armstrong was the first to leap out of the helicopter and slide down the fastrope to the deck. He landed on his feet and ran away from the rope. He stopped next to the port bulkhead that formed the side of the enormous open area along the entire ship to the bridge. He unholstered his automatic pistol and provided security as the others slid out of the back of the 53 down the fastrope to the deck in less than ten seconds. When the last one was out, the crew chief threw out two large bags, which thudded heavily onto the deck. The helicopter pulled up, banked hard left, and dashed to a quarter mile away, where it hovered with the two SEAL snipers hanging out, their weapons still pointed at the ship. The air was suddenly still. The SEALs crouched around the perimeter of the flat deck and listened.

They spread out, encircling the area with their backs toward each other, looking for any signs of life or danger. They looked quickly over the side of the ship for boats escaping but saw none. Each SEAL wore a small voice-activated Motorola throat mike. Their black helmets had headphones built in. Everyone kept their voices down and mouths shut unless they had something important to say. Armstrong called for a radio check. They answered in order by their pre-briefed number, by seniority, from one to fourteen plus the two Explosive Ordnance Disposal techs, fifteen and sixteen. The entire check took less than ten seconds.

Armstrong looked at each of his men and waited for an all-clear signal. He ran up to Lee, on the port side toward the bridge. "What've we got?" he asked, as he knelt next to him.

"We got nothing. There's no sounds, no movement, no engine noise, nothing. If I was guessing, I'd say this baby's abandoned."

Armstrong shook his head. "You don't go to all that trouble just to abandon a ship like this. I think they're waiting for us." He checked his H&K SOF offensive handgun, a .45-caliber weapon designed specifically for Special Forces. It had a mean-looking silencer and a compact laser-aiming module in front of the trigger guard. He had hollow-point bullets for maximizing stopping power and minimizing the risk of hitting a hostage behind a terrorist. "Plan Alpha, Lee. Command and control stay on the fantail, everybody else to the bridge. Right now. Let's go!''

"Aye, sir," Lee said, acknowledging his complete understanding and looking to see that all the others had heard Lieutenant Armstrong. They gave him thumbs-up. He had been working with Armstrong for three years and knew him to be a natural leader and someone with incredible instincts. He always seemed to know when to charge and when to sit and wait in the mud for two days. Lee checked the safety on his silenced H&K SD3 9mm submachine gun and pointed to the two petty officers who had been preassigned to wait on the fantail. They nodded their understanding and picked their positions for best vision of their area. The other fourteen lined up on the port and starboard sides, their weapons ready, thumbs on safeties. Armstrong waited for three seconds, then motioned for the point man to lead the team. They began a quick run toward the bow of the ship. Everyone stayed in a line and maintained their fields of fire.

The point man crouched to keep from presenting too large a target. He had been trained to always assume someone can see you and wants to shoot you; move like there are crosshairs on you all the time. Every time. He stopped in front of a large hatch that appeared to lead to the bridge. It was closed tight, but not locked. He breathed quickly and steadily as he considered his options. If the door was booby-trapped, they'd be cooked. He signaled those with him to spread out along the steel bulkhead in front of and behind the hatch, as he felt the handle. He felt no vibration, no unusual resistance, and no springs. He moved the handle up slowly, feeling every slight movement for something unusual. The handle swung smoothly to the top and the hatch popped open as if pushed. He stepped back and waited. The hatch swung freely but no one came out. He stuck his head around and back, then around again. He could feel the cold air rushing out of the air-conditioned spaces. He quickly assessed the scene. "All secure. Two dead unknowns. No weapons."

Armstrong listened. When he heard "all clear" from the bridge he approached the steel door that led to the radio room and turned the handle gently. He felt resistance; then he felt the handle give way. He jumped back waiting for an explosion. Nothing happened and the door closed again. He tried the door again and the handle turned easily. He spoke softly into his microphone. "I'm going in. Lee, come in right behind me. I'm going right; you clear behind me. Roach, Davidson," he said glancing at them, "come in straight behind us. Three, right; four, left. Ready?" They nodded. They'd practiced this maneuver a hundred times. Armstrong tried to ignore the pulsating heartbeat in his hands and his neck. He threw the door open and ran into the radio room, scanning its length in less than a second. He went down on one knee and held his handgun in front of him. He looked around the room, puzzled. No one was there. "Stay here!" He turned. "Coming out!" he yelled as he rushed to the bridge. There was a body handcuffed to the wheel of the ship and another slumped next to him, handcuffed to a navigation table. Both had been shot in the head. He lowered his handgun as the rest of the SEALs entered the bridge and saw what he saw.

"Where are the hijackers?" Armstrong asked loudly of no one in particular as he looked out the bridge windows at every part of the ship that was visible.

Armstrong pointed to a suspicious-looking device on the deck. "What the hell is that?" he asked Prager, the EOD tech who had augmented the platoon, who slung his weapon and knelt down to examine the device. Prager was a twin pin—a SEAL and an EOD tech. He set his laptop computer next to the device and began scanning through his data for something similar. The screen filled with images of bombs, triggers, and wiring diagrams as Prager scrolled down and selected images deftly.

Prager looked up with a puzzled look on his face. "Never seen anything like it. Might be able to disarm it." He turned back to the device and said, "No obvious timer, no obvious access door, no way to tell what's inside." He felt it gingerly. "Arming switch is on the bottom. Final activation magnetic. If it's C4, one of these would blow the whole bridge off the ship."

Lieutenant Armstrong nodded grimly as he considered the options, growing impatient as he checked his watch. "Can you disarm it or not?"

"I'm not supposed to do this under field conditions. But it's your call, Lieutenant."

"Do it," Armstrong ordered. "Everyone clear the area."

"I'll need to drill a small hole and use a probe." Prager shrugged. "It's the arming mechanism that matters. There just aren't that many to choose from." He looked at Armstrong, then at some of the modern arming devices listed on his CD-ROM. "Let me give it a try."

"Nothing stupid," Armstrong said. "No heroics . . ."

"No heroes here," Prager said enthusiastically as he took out a small electric drill the size of a dentist's instrument. Prager knew using the drill was the quickest way to disarm the bomb if all went well. If he miscalculated, it was also the fastest way to detonate it.

Armstrong went outside and told Lee, "We've got to check the rest of the ship. How many crew were we looking for?"

"Twenty-six," Lee replied. "And maybe two Indonesians."

"Get on the PA," Armstrong said. "Announce that the U.S. Navy is here, and we're going to be abandoning ship. Tell them we're coming to find them, and if they can help us by yelling or any the hell other way, start now." He looked around for BM2 Roach. "Start lowering the lifeboats. We're going to need them all." Armstrong turned to another SEAL. "Contact Golf November and tell them we're aboard the ship and it's booby-trapped. Tell them we're going to check the rest of the ship for the crew, and then we'll abandon ship. We'll be off in"—he checked his watch quickly, suddenly feeling the time pressure of the explosives on the bridge—"ten minutes."

"Aye, aye, sir," he said.

"And give them a posit from your GPS," Armstrong added, referring to their handheld Global Positioning System receiver that gave them an exact readout of their latitude and longitude.

"Yes, sir," the SEAL replied.

Armstrong addressed the other SEALs. "We'll go find the rest of the crew. Be careful. There may be more surprises. There may still be some sleepers aboard—looking to do the suicide thing. Give 'em the opportunity if they're looking for it. Otherwise, we're gonna get off this ship before this little present they left us"—he glanced to the deck—"goes bang." He looked at his watch. "We have no idea how long we have. Could be seconds, or hours. We're going to be on this ship exactly ten more minutes. After that, I want everybody over the side. And I mean over the side. Don't walk aft and do it the easy way; jump off and swim away if you're not off by then." To Lee, "Get the motors going on the boats. We'll need to get a hundred yards away as soon as we're in them. I don't want 'em pulled down if this thing starts to blow." He ordered another SEAL to override the fire doors within the ship to avoid being trapped. He paused to think. No one spoke. "Let's go," he said quietly and headed toward the door.

The radioman ran to Armstrong's side. "Sir, it's the 53," he said. "They've spotted three fast movers. Three cigarette boats heading west, about ten miles from here. They're asking if they should go check them out."

Armstrong shook his head quickly. "No, they'll need to maintain their thirty-second orbit to come get us. Tell them to relay the position to the E-2."

The radioman nodded and relayed the OIC's message.

Armstrong led his men down the ladders into the interior of the ship. No sounds at all. No one calling or yelling. He ran down the passageway checking each hatch. He found another body handcuffed to a pipe fitting, slumped over a table, one bullet hole in the side of the head, with an identical bomb on the deck at his feet. Armstrong's face turned red with rage. He checked the body to see if it was booby-trapped. It wasn't.

They ran on, down the ladders and decks, dreading each turn. They finally turned another corner on a dead run. It was the same thing. Crewman, shot once in the head, handcuffed to the bulkhead, a bomb at his feet.

They ran faster and faster, one location to another, as Armstrong tried to find every crewman, without having to backtrack. Another one. Dead.

"Let's get outta here!" Armstrong yelled, suddenly fearing the corpses had been placed just to get them into the bowels of the ship in time for the bombs to explode. "Everyone to the fantail."

Armstrong turned and headed that way. As he did, his feet were jarred off the deck for an instant by a huge explosion. It started with a deep boom and then a pounding crack as the sound wave made its way directly into his face in one tenth of a second.

Armstrong spoke into his throat mike. "Talk to me, Lee, what the hell was that?"

Lee's voice came through strained and full of static. "Prager, sir! He must have dicked it up!"

"Shit!" Armstrong yelled as he ran back the way he had come, the other two SEALs following, having heard the same conversation.

"Did he try and clip a wire?" he asked, looking around for other mines as he ran.

"Don't know, sir!"

A thought suddenly hit Armstrong. "How do we know he dicked it up? How do we know that wasn't just the first one to go off on a timer?"

"I guess we don't, sir!" Lee said, realizing the implications.

"Everybody out! Everybody out!" Armstrong shouted into his throat mike. "Muster on the fantail! Roach, get on the radio to the 53. Emergency extraction! Emergency extraction!''

Armstrong continued to run with his offensive handgun in his hand, but it was utterly useless. Armstrong's mind raced. ''Davidson! Get to the fantail. Set up the SPIE rig. Roach, tell the 53 we're going to extract on the SPIE rig.

''Listen up!'' Armstrong said with forced coolness as he climbed a ladder toward the open deck. ''I want everyone hooked onto the SPIE rig in thirty seconds. Drop whatever you're doing and head to the fantail now!''

All the SEALs immediately ran toward the fantail.

The two CH-53s raced from the horizon toward the ship. The fourteen SEALs and the remaining EOD tech gathered on the fantail and looked around, each unconsciously counting the number of SEALs missing as the seconds passed.

Armstrong was the last to arrive. He watched the CH-53E Super Stallion tear toward them, less than half a mile away. All the other SEALs were hooked up to the SPIE rigs. ''Prager buy it?'' he asked no one in particular.

''Yes, sir.'' Lee unhooked himself from the SPIE rig and ran back to Armstrong. ''Take a look at this,'' he said, handing Armstrong something. Armstrong looked around, assessed the situation and checked for the helicopter, then took what Lee was offering. It was a Polaroid photograph.

''What's this?'' Armstrong asked.

''Looks like a picture taken on the bridge. I picked it up off the binnacle before the bridge blew. I think they wanted us to find it.''

Armstrong studied the picture of a crewman with the silencer of an automatic weapon pressed against his ear. Electronically superimposed on the photograph was the date and time of one hour ago.

Armstrong handed it back frowning, ''What kind of weapon is that?''

''Can't tell for sure, but it looks like it might be a

Chinese Type 64. I'm prepared to bet that's the captain. I think they took him with them.''

Armstrong looked at him and narrowed his eyes. Lee returned to his position and attached his chest ring to the eye hook on the SPIE. As Armstrong hooked on, he and the rest of the SEALs were nearly knocked off their feet as another mine went off three decks below them, disabling the engines, gearing, and steerage.

''Stand fast!'' Armstrong said, reassuring them as they watched the helicopter pull up over the fantail and hover directly overhead. The helicopter crew chief kicked out a length of rope, which touched the deck near the front of the SPIE rig. Chief Lee reached down and connected the rig and gave the helicopter crew chief a thumbs-up as another explosion went off in the bow. Every one of them heard it and the helicopter pilot saw it. The crew immediately began pulling up. Half the SEAL platoon was lifted quickly off the deck of the *Pacific Flyer*. The second CH-53E raced in behind the first. Its crew chief threw the line out and Davidson hooked up the second SPIE rig. The Super Stallion jerked the eight remaining SEALs off the deck and pulled away from the ship. The SEALs hung from the Special Insertion and Extraction Rig underneath the helicopters like a clump of grapes, as the helicopter banked away and flew toward the horizon.

Armstrong thought about Prager and allowed the rage in his belly to climb to his head. Whoever hijacked the cargo ship and slaughtered the crew had set a trap to kill anyone who came to the ship's rescue. The *Pacific Flyer* receded as they gained altitude and pulled away. Almost instantaneously, explosion after explosion rocked the *Flyer*.

5

IT WAS DILLON'S TURN TO HOST MOLLY AND BOBBY at his place to watch the basketball game. They had considered canceling after the hijacking was announced. But a couple of hours after the President's news conference they thought they would sneak out for the last half of the game.

Dillon helped Molly take off her coat in the entryway to his apartment. He loved the opportunity to study her from behind, to stare without being noticed. He caught the scent of her perfume and thought it might be a good sign, since she rarely wore a scent. He also knew that he would have to maintain the appearance of perpetual nonchalance.

They went way back—Dillon, Molly, and Bobby Nichols, who came in a few minutes after Molly. They had gone to law school together at the University of Virginia and had been in the same study group, commonly known as Dillon's Study Group.

He and Bobby had been close friends, sharing dreams and fears. They had played basketball and taken classes together during the last two years of law school. There wasn't any ambiguity or conflict about their friendship. When Dillon moved to Washington, reuniting three fourths of their study group—the fourth, Erin, had gone to New York—he had reestablished his friendship with Bobby. He frequently walked across the street from the

Capitol building to the Supreme Court where Bobby was the Chief Justice's clerk. Bobby and Dillon would play basketball in the Supreme Court gym.

But with Molly it had been different. They had been rivals: intellectual, political, and academic. Even though they were very close and had feelings for each other that were often confusing, those feelings had for the most part gone unexpressed. They had dated a few times, and Dillon had found her not only stunningly beautiful but also challenging. She was everything he had ever wanted in a woman. But for a reason he couldn't identify he wouldn't let her get close to him. After three years of ambiguity and unexpressed feelings, they had graduated and gone their separate ways, each knowing that they could become more than friends if they made the effort, but neither wanting to be first. That was four years ago. Now they were back in Washington on opposite sides of everything.

"Y'all mind if we turn on the damned game?" Bobby asked as he took off his jacket and threw it in the corner. "Got any food?" He turned on the television and changed the channel. The noise from the fans filled the room. "I'm starved," he said as he sat down on the couch beside Molly and Dillon. "Got any brew?"

Dillon looked at him, "Why, I'm fine. Thank you. Nice of you to ask. Yeah, I've got brew. Get it yourself."

Bobby smiled enthusiastically and got up. As he walked into the kitchen, he yelled over his shoulder, "Hey, what about Indonesia? What is *that*?"

"I've got a bad feeling about that," Dillon replied as he reached out to turn down the television. "It doesn't look like the usual terrorist game at all."

"People are pretty uptight at the White House," Molly added. "I just can't imagine what they hope to accomplish by taking an American ship."

"Notoriety, I guess. I just hope they're able to get the Americans off the ship without anybody getting hurt. What do you think will come of it?"

"I don't know," Molly said. "I'm not even sure what happened."

"How are things at the White House?" Bobby asked Molly as he returned and sat in the overstuffed chair next to the couch, placing three beers in front of them. Although the Chief Justice of the United States, for whom Bobby worked, had been appointed by President Manchester and was therefore automatically expected to be liberal, Bobby wasn't.

People's politics were important but not critical to Molly. She was more interested in their integrity and honesty. "Fine. How are things at the *Big* Court?"

"Fine."

"Okay. We got that out of the way," she said.

They watched the second half of the game between the University of Virginia and North Carolina and tried not to think about the hijacking that dominated the thoughts of each of them, particularly how each might be involved.

Dillon went into the kitchen to get some snacks.

"You dating anyone?" Molly asked Bobby.

"Not a soul. You'd think that in Washington, D.C., capital of the country and the world headquarters for professional black women, I could find *one,* but no. Not me. Must be my looks."

"Right."

"What else could it be?" he asked.

"Molly? Could you give me a hand?" Dillon called out.

She stood up and headed for the door. "What?"

"Could you carry that tray, please?" he said handing her one full of dip and cut vegetables as he carried another with chips and pretzels.

The familiar voice of Johnny Hines, the ACC basketball announcer, filled the room. The crowd in Charlottesville was yelling so loudly the announcer was pressing his headphones against his head to hear himself. Molly placed the tray with vegetables and guacamole next to the chips.

Dillon carefully removed the sagging cellophane from the bowl.

"What's with the soggy cellophane?" Bobby asked.

"Keeps the air out," Dillon replied. "Air turns guacamole brown."

"What are you, the guacamole expert?" Bobby asked.

"Sure. We had avocado trees in our backyard the whole time I was growing up."

"Where'd you find avocados in February in D.C.?" Molly asked.

"You can find *anything* in D.C. if you're willing to pay enough for it." Dillon heaped guacamole onto a large potato chip. His eyes fixed on the television as the Virginia point guard hit a three-point shot from the corner. The crowd screamed its approval.

The phone rang and Dillon reached for it without looking away from the television screen. He punched the button on the portable phone and grunted with his mouth full, "Umhm."

He suddenly stood up and grabbed his beer, taking a deep gulp to wash down his food. After a pause, he blurted, "Yes, sir. Sorry, I had my mouth full. . . . No, sir, just watching the basketball game." He covered the phone with his hand and mouthed to the others: "*The Speaker!*"

Molly and Bobby looked at each other and raised their eyebrows.

"Yes, sir. Any military nearby? . . . What did . . ." He listened. His face became more and more serious, then angry. "Damn. Yes, sir . . . I don't know, sir. Whatever you say. Want me to call . . . okay. I'll see you then." He looked at the phone, then pressed the button to hang up. He walked over and turned off the television. The eerie silence accented the grim look on Dillon's face.

"What?" Molly said.

He spoke reluctantly, "You know that ship that was hijacked?"

They nodded.

"Well the Navy had an entire battle group nearby, including an Amphibious group with SEALs, Marines, the whole thing. The SEALs went to take the ship back, and they found it booby-trapped with dozens of mines or bombs. Every member of the crew was executed. Murdered. Shot in the head.''

"Holy *shit*," Bobby said.

"The SEALs tried to disarm the mines. One of the SEALs was killed. He got blown up. The rest of them got off the ship. The mines exploded and the ship sank.''

Molly sat back stunned. "What are we going to do about it?''

Dillon breathed deeply, "Don't know. Up to the President. I'm sure we'll have to do something. Probably something pretty drastic. Especially with that much force already in the area.''

"Who *did* this?" Bobby asked.

Dillon shook his head. "I don't know. I don't know if we can't tell, or I just don't have all the info. One other thing," he said remembering. "They took the captain hostage." He sighed and put his hands on his hips. "You guys can stay here if you want, but I'm going to the Hill. Speaker wants the whole staff there to explore the options.''

Molly stood up. "I'm sure there'll be some midnight oil at the White House. I'd better go, too. I left the President some material on international law before coming over here, but that may not be enough now.'' She stood up and started toward the hallway, then stopped. An angry frown clouded her face, "Why do people do these kinds of things? It never accomplishes *anything*.''

"Sure it does," Dillon answered bitterly. "Terrorism pays *big* dividends. Look at the PLO. They blew up people all over the world, killed innocent children, and now they have their own country, right where they wanted it.'' He paused. "They do it because it *works*. They do it because too often people like us don't ever *do* anything about it.''

"But it's so cowardly," she said, her eyes burning. She

hesitated. "And we do too usually do something about it."

"We don't even know it's terrorists, really," Bobby said.

Dillon looked at him with surprise. "What do you think, some country is declaring war on the United States by attacking a defenseless cargo ship?"

"I don't know. I'm just saying, don't assume you know what's happening until you know."

"Fair enough," Dillon said. "I've got to go."

Bobby reached for the remote control as Molly and Dillon were leaving. "I doubt this will involve the Supreme Court so I'm going to watch the game. I'll lock the door behind me when I leave."

Dillon didn't reply as he walked out the door with Molly right behind him.

↤

"What do we know, Admiral Hart?" President Manchester asked, looking carefully at Hart and the others gathered in the Situation Room on the ground floor of the White House. They sat around a table, like any ordinary conference table, but the walls were covered with screens, charts, and electronic information. The closest wall was at least ten feet from the table. The large map of the Pacific nearly reached the floor, allowing everyone to see clearly.

The admiral walked to the map of the Southwest Pacific and Southeast Indian Ocean areas and looked at them for a moment, gathering his thoughts. He was a man in his fifties, of average height with graying brown hair. Known for his intensity and his brilliance, he had come up through NROTC and Penn State University, had had a stellar career in Naval Aviation, including command of a carrier and a carrier battle group, then CINCPAC—Commander in Chief of all Pacific forces. Now he was the Chairman of the Joint Chiefs of Staff. "We know there were twenty to thirty terrorists aboard the *Pacific*

Flyer, that they took over the ship posing as Ford employees when the ship docked in Jakarta, that they were well organized, knew the ship, and took it to sea.''

He turned back to look at President Manchester and the rest, who included the Vice President, the Chief of Staff, the National Security Adviser, the Secretary of Defense, the Director of Central Intelligence, and the Secretary of State. They all listened carefully. ''They took the ship out to sea, then set sophisticated mines all over the ship, inside and out, mines like we'd never seen before, and murdered the entire crew, except the captain. They then abandoned the ship, were picked up by cigarette boats, and made their escape, leaving mines which later killed one of our Navy SEALs,'' he said grimly.

''What's a cigarette boat?'' the President asked.

''It's basically a very fast, offshore race boat. They're capable of seventy knots or so in the open ocean. They're used a lot by smugglers because there isn't much that can keep up with them, other than an airplane. They were first used to smuggle cigarettes.''

''Where'd they go?''

''We don't know, Mr. President,'' the admiral said, casting a glance at Cary Warner, the Director of Central Intelligence. ''A helicopter spotted them, but the E-2 never saw them after that.''

''We didn't have any birds in place to do any imagery during this event,'' Warner said, picking up on the cue. ''It isn't exactly one of our hot spots. . . .''

Manchester stood up and looked at his group of advisers. ''How could this have happened? We didn't have any idea this was coming?''

Warner shook his head, moving the unlit pipe he kept in his mouth. ''No, sir. I'm afraid they caught us with our pants down.''

''We don't know who. Anyone care to speculate why?''

Nathaniel Corder, the professorial Secretary of State, spoke up. ''I see this as a direct challenge to your new foreign policy, sir." Corder had taught International Affairs at Yale, and then served as ambassador to Spain. He still wasn't completely comfortable as Secretary of State, a position he had held only for six months. His forehead reddened when he spoke.

Manchester interrupted him by saying to the chief of staff, "Arlan, would you get Ms. Vaughan here? I want her in on every meeting. Somebody needs to watch my backside."

"We're all watching out for your interests, Mr. President," Van den Bosch replied.

"Well then, one more won't hurt, will it?" Manchester said. "You were saying, Nathaniel?" he asked, watching Corder's glowing forehead.

"Your peace and diplomacy through commerce program's goals are to have the military play less of a role in the world and increase our maritime presence in the world. To rejuvenate our shipping industry, you proposed a law that requires fifty percent of the goods carried into U.S. ports to be on U.S.-flagged vessels by the year 2010. And half of those had to be built in the U.S."

"So?" Manchester said, growing impatient.

"Sir, I think it was the right strategy. But someone else out there may fear that the U.S. is going to expand its influence in the world through shipping and exporting U.S. goods. An American Empire, built on our new ability to facilitate trade. Like England's of the nineteenth century, but with no colonies, no compulsion, no force. Simply put, sir, they don't want you to succeed."

"But who?" said Van den Bosch impatiently.

"Let me finish," Corder said. "Which ship was it that was sunk?" he asked rhetorically. "The *Pacific Flyer*. The very first of the newest design of ships, built by NASSCO in San Diego, and a U.S.-flagged vessel carrying U.S. goods to a foreign port. A symbol if there ever was one. And not just any U.S. goods. The newest Ford, the Ascenda, designed to take on the global market. And not just any shipment of Fords. The first shipment to a brand-new Ford dealership in Jakarta. This one was being followed in the press. A new era in American business. A new way of doing business.''

"But who?" Van den Bosch asked again.

Corder shrugged. "I don't know. I'm just trying to identify a possible motive. That may help us discover the who.''

"My guess, if I may, sir," said Warner. "This wasn't done by someone who wants to remain anonymous. We're going to hear from these people again." His dry deep voice showed no emotion whatsoever.

Manchester nodded and looked at Admiral Hart. "Admiral, what are our options?"

Hart looked at the President, then back at the chart. He studied the hundreds of islands of Indonesia, the immense area of ocean and finally said, "Frankly, to wait. We don't know who did this, or why, or where they have gone. We'll certainly be looking for the cigarette boats—we have every airplane with infrared and ISAR radar airborne right now looking for them, but it's going to be very difficult. Inverted Synthetic Aperture Radar allows for good definition, so you can tell one ship from another with it; but there's an awful lot of ocean there, and more islands than you can count." He breathed in noisily through his nose. "And unless they decide to tell us who they are, it may be virtually impossible to respond."

"We got anybody on the ground in Jakarta that can tell us anything?"

Molly opened the door quietly and sat down without speaking. They glanced at her, then back at Warner.

Warner responded, "We have very limited resources on the ground in Indonesia. We had no warning of trouble brewing in the region. I'm not optimistic they'll be able to find out much after the fact, but they have already been instructed to try, sir."

Manchester clenched his fists. "We are going to look like fools. We have the largest military in the world, an entire battle group in the area, and the best intelligence in the world. We are the only superpower left, and some terrorists can sink one of our ships, kill a score of Americans—and we can't do anything about it?''

"That's about how I see it," chimed in Dick Roland, the short and intense Secretary of Defense, then hurriedly tried to recover. "But it's only because we have limited information. We'll know more by tomorrow. We are working closely with the State Department and the CIA to identify all known terrorists and guerrilla organizations operating in the Southern Pacific. I expect we will hear from the terrorists themselves within the first twenty-four hours. They'll want to tell the world who they are and why they have done this.''

"So that's it? We sit and wait until tomorrow morning?''

"*We* sit, Mr. President," said Admiral Hart. "But our aircraft keep searching, the battle group steams to the exact location where this happened and inspects every wave, and we find the people who did this," he added.

"I want to be kept fully informed," the President said. "I'm going to have a press conference at seven A.M. to catch the morning news shows, and I'm going to announce that the American crew has been killed and the ship sunk. I don't want anyone leaking that until I've had a chance to announce it. But before then, I want to know who did this. Understood?''

They all nodded and rose to leave. "Stay here, Ms. Vaughan," said the President. Molly looked embarrassed. She had no idea why the President had called her, nor why he'd singled her out after the meeting. She felt awkward and out of place. She waited for the President to speak again.

"Thank you for staying, Ms. Vaughan," he said when they were alone.

"Certainly, Mr. President," she replied stiffly. "What is it I can do for you?''

"So that's all we know," the Speaker said to his entire staff in the large conference room next to his office. "It's gotten ugly. We've been ordered not to talk to the press about it until the President's news conference at seven in the morning. Everybody clear on that? If anyone talks, it will make me look bad, and it will make you unemployed. Clear?" They all nodded. "It's already late," he said, glancing at his watch. "If you need to, go home and get some sleep. But be here early."

Frank Grazio, a young assistant, nudged Dillon as everyone rose to leave. Grazio asked, "What do you think?"

"About what?"

"About the hijacking," Grazio said. "What do you think is going to happen?"

"How would I know?" Dillon said, annoyed.

Grazio stopped, "Did I say something stupid?"

"No. I just don't know what to say. We don't know who did it, so it's hard to know what the right response is."

"No, the proper response is easy. We go and kick their *asses*," Grazio said in his Long Island accent. "The question is whose ass to kick."

Dillon walked into the hall and headed toward his office.

"Where you going?" Grazio said.

"To my office," he replied. "I'm going to find out everything I can about Indonesia. I don't really know much more about it than what I saw in a weird Mel Gibson movie ten years ago. *A Year of . . .* something or other."

"Well," Grazio said, slowing down, "I think I'll call a friend of mine over at the Pentagon and see what Indonesia has in its military."

Dillon looked at him. "Get with Chuck. He's probably already doing that. I doubt Indonesia itself is the one we're dealing with, but it won't hurt to know what they've got."

Grazio nodded and left.

Dillon went into his office, sat down, and began to organize his thoughts. He had done research before, but never for anything *this* important. And never out of anger.

6

"I DON'T THINK YOU CAN HELP." CAPTAIN ZEKE
Bradford appreciated the enthusiasm of his two best
fighter squadron commanders. They were always out
front, ready to do whatever needed to be done. But this
time it might just muck things up. "Those cigarette boats
eluded the S-3, but we're sending out attack planes to find
them."

"We can help," Caskey said. "We can check out ships
on our radar, with our IR or our TVSU—we might be
able to ID 'em."

Bradford regarded them with skepticism. "They're
probably all fiberglass and going like hell. Besides, the
bastards launched a missile at you when you flew over
the cargo ship and they probably still have shoulder-fired
missiles—it could be a real problem." Bradford shook his
head. "I don't think so."

"Come on, Captain. We'll be flying anyway. May as
well let us try," Caskey said. "If we don't find anything,
no harm done."

Bradford frowned, "Unless one of your junior officers
with his fangs out flies into the water . . ."

"Won't happen," Caskey said, trying to answer every
objection. "I'll make sure the crews are second cruise or
above only."

Bradford's resistance weakened. "What do you think,
Drunk?" he said to Commander Dave Driver.

64

Drunk nodded almost imperceptibly. "We can definitely help. I'm just wondering whether we should assign quadrants or radials so we're not all out there running into each other."

Bradford nodded. "I already did, but we can make them smaller areas though, if there are more of us airborne."

Drunk looked at the air wing commander. "What are we supposed to do if we find 'em? We supposed to shoot 'em?" he asked, almost rhetorically. He pulled up the sleeves of his flight suit. "What looks like a sixty-knot cigarette boat to one pilot may be a thirty-knot ski boat to someone else."

"That's the big problem. The plan isn't to shoot 'em, it's to find 'em. Then we can watch where they go and do what we need to later."

"You think they're going to let us follow them?" Drunk said. "If they've got any sense at all, they're going to be in those boats only about a *minute*—just long enough to get over the horizon. They'll transfer to another ship as soon as they can—some ship that looks like your generic cargo ship found by the thousands all over these oceans. This is only about the busiest ocean in the world."

Caskey nodded. "I agree, CAG," he said, calling the air wing commander by his generic initials. The title Commander of the Air Group was used widely in the Navy even though air groups haven't existed since the fifties. "But we've got to look. One thing's for sure—if we don't look, we'll never find them."

"You have an amazing grasp of the obvious," Bradford said as he unconsciously straightened up, pulling his shoulders back. "Let's get everybody airborne as soon as possible."

"Roger that," said Caskey enthusiastically. "I'm gonna go rewrite the flight schedule. We gonna go with a flex deck or cyclic ops?"

"I'd like to do a flex deck, but with two cycles of planes up at once. We can burn more gas to find them

and not worry about recovery times. We'll keep everybody out there for four or five hours. After that, we'll go
to cyclic if we haven't found them. And if we haven't
found them by sunset, we're cooked. We'll have to report
our failure to Washington and wait for further instructions, which will probably be to come home and turn in
our commissions.''

Caskey and Drunk left quickly to order their squadrons
into the air.

Caskey walked into his squadron's ready room. ''Messer, Mario, and Beef, we're first up. Ops O,'' he said,
looking at his operations officer, ''find three aircrew to be
ready for the next go, which will be in a few hours. We'll
do flex deck for four hours to look for the three cigarette
boats, then cyclic after that if we haven't found them.''
He looked at Lieutenant Barry Thacker, the SDO, the
squadron duty officer. ''You got a good ship's posit on
the chart?''

''No, sir.'' The lieutenant jumped up. ''I haven't updated it in a couple of hours.''

Caskey stared at him. ''Why not?''

''I just haven't sir, sorry.''

''Sorry doesn't cut it, Barry. Make it happen.''

''Yes, sir.'' Thacker copied down latitude and longitude and crossed to the chart on the sliding cork board in
the front of the ready room. ''We're right here, sir,'' he
said, sticking a pin in the ocean north of the island of
Java.

''How far are we from where the *Pacific Flyer* went
down?'' Caskey asked.

Thacker measured the distance on the chart with his
pen. ''About two hundred miles,'' he answered confidently.

''No sweat,'' MC said. He looked at his watch and
turned to Messer. ''CVIC brief in five minutes. They'll
tell us which radials we'll be searching. We'll go to the
last known location of the *Flyer,* turn outbound, and start
looking. We'll look for anything fast, and after that, we'll

look for anything at all. But we'll have to be careful of flying into controlled airspace. Little islands that are part of Indonesia are all over the place. Last thing we need is for them to get mad at us for flying into their country with armed airplanes without permission. Capiche?''

They all understood perfectly. They also understood it was an exercise in futility.

≈

''I've got lots of ships and boats, MC,'' Messer said, leaning toward his radar repeater as the F-14B turned southeast at five thousand feet. They could see other *Constitution* airplanes turning outbound on other radials at different altitudes, probably saying the same things either to themselves or the other aircrew.

''Anything fast moving?''

''Can't tell.''

''Well, let's just start looking.''

''Roger that. First contact—is five degrees left, ten miles.''

Caskey banked the Tomcat gently to the left and headed for the first ship on the radar. The first of hundreds. They approached it carefully, mindful of CAG's warning that the terrorists might have shoulder-fired missiles aboard and their own, more vivid memories of flying past the *Flyer*. They flew down the side at one thousand feet and looked carefully at the ship. It was clearly not a cigarette boat. Not even close. A hundred times too big. Just another tramp steamer.

The next ship was less remarkable, and the next less remarkable still. Their enthusiasm softened gradually, imperceptibly, as they went from one target to another, all equally unlikely to hold any key to the cigarette boats.

They flew outbound again and again, then turned around and headed back and looked at every ship or boat in their sector. It was always the same story. Too big, too slow, too something. Not even a good candidate as a mother ship—although Caskey had no idea how they might know if the cigarette boats had been hoisted aboard one of these ships.

"Well, Messer, this has been a flail," MC said as he turned back toward the ship for the last time. The sun set behind him toward Malaysia and Singapore. He raised his dark-colored visor to get a better picture of the darkening sea ahead of them.

"Flail ain't even the word," Messer said, frustrated. "Never had much chance of finding these guys anyway. Too small."

"Too small, and we got too late a start."

🢒

It was another beautiful day on the equator, just as hot as the one before, just as hazy from the humidity and oppressive heat, and just as comfortable in the air-conditioned cabins and staterooms of the world's largest warship. Comfortable in temperature but not temperament. Billings stewed as he thought of the men that had done this and tried to imagine why. It would be some "cause," no doubt, some supposed reason to commit murder.

The air wing had continued the search for the three elusive cigarette boats all through the night. As dawn approached, Admiral Ray Billings realized his one mission for the last twenty-four hours had been a failure. It hadn't been a particularly tough mission: Find the three cigarette boats that carried off the men that murdered the Americans. Didn't have to do anything else, just find them. Total, complete failure.

Billings summoned his staff, the air wing commander, and all the squadron commanders to his wardroom. The group gathered around the table and took the offered coffee.

"That it?" he began with no introduction, no preliminary statements. "We done looking?"

Captain Bradford spoke in his deep voice. "We're not done, sir, we'll continue to look. But the circle of how far these guys could have gotten in"—he looked at his watch—"twenty-three hours, is a big one. They could have had a mother ship that craned them aboard, they could have been refueled, they could have scuttled the boats and climbed aboard a steamer, they could be tucked in some cove or cave somewhere waiting for time to pass. It's hard to know."

"Wrong answer," Billings said, leaning back in his chair. "What am I going to tell the Secretary of Defense and the Joint Chiefs? That we failed? That the most dangerous battle group since World War II, maybe ever, can't find three shitty little motorboats?" His eyebrows angled angrily down toward his nose.

"Sir," said Drunk, "it's a needle in a haystack, and it's *their* haystack. They could be anywhere."

Admiral Billings shook his head and looked into the eyes of each officer present, one at a time, slowly. "Anyone got any more ideas? I think I've heard enough for this morning on how hard this is. What I want to hear is how to find them."

The skipper of VAW-121, the E-2C squadron, spoke. "I think we should keep our surface search radars active in the area all day. Carpet coverage. They've got to know we're looking for them, but they probably don't appreciate how well we can pick them out if they go too fast. They will be more inclined to rely on their speed than on hiding. And if they're hiding, we wait for them to make a move."

"You all concur?"

Bradford nodded, and put up one finger. "I'm changing the entire day's schedule into surface search, so every airplane will still be devoting its entire flight to looking for these boats. That's all we can do, unless you want to go full out, get every airplane airborne we can, and keep them airborne as long as we can." He hesitated. "But that will exhaust the air wing and the planes in a day and we'll have to cut back."

Billings shook his head. "No, no point in getting someone killed.'' He thought to himself. ''Anything else?''

Captain Black, his chief of staff, spoke. ''Admiral, even though we don't know where these guys have gone, I think we should prepare contingency plans, so when we're asked to do something about this, which seems likely, we're as ready as we can be.''

Admiral Billings glanced at him and nodded quickly. ''I agree. Prepare a message to the Amphib group, give them an update. I want the Marines ready to go ashore on any beach within five hundred miles of here. Make it seven hundred. And from looking at the chart, that's a lot of beaches. Tell them to find out what beach studies they have, and start working on the rest. I don't care if there are ten thousand of them; start at number one and keep going until I say to stop.''

He looked around for his intelligence officer, Commander Beth Louwsma. ''I want every chart of this area pulled out and pored over by every intel officer on board, down to the lowest ensign. I want the charts all over the walls in CVIC, and I want all the aircrew studying those charts like their lives depend on it. I want everyone to look for where you'd hide if you were in a small fast boat and an American battle group was looking for you. We have to know this area like the back of our hand, and I mean *every* island.''

Admiral Billings stood up, his juices flowing. ''Beth, I want you to get messages off to whomever you need to— I'll sign them—asking for imagery of every suspicious inlet, bay, cove, and port within seven hundred miles of here. We'll send the Tomcats with TARPS pods into some of those places, but we may need permission from Indonesia to go in.''

''Yes, sir,'' Louwsma said, writing.

Admiral Billings looked at his operations officer. ''Get messages off to get us carte blanche from Indonesia to overfly some of their territory to find these murderers.''

His operations officer nodded knowingly.

''Everybody listen up,'' he said and paused until all

eyes were on him. "We don't know if we'll be going after them in an hour or three days. We have to be ready for anything. Get the ordnance ready. I want everything available, from Tomahawks to cluster bombs. Keep the laser-guided bombs ready—we may have to drop them into a cave. Alert the SEALs too—it may be their show."

"Yes, sir," the operations officer said, as he wrote furiously in a small green notebook.

"Anything else?" The Admiral looked around the table. "Okay. Let's go. I'll let you know if I hear anything else. Dismissed." The officers hurried out of the cabin.

The *Constitution* forced its way through the ocean, pushing mountains of water aside as it dashed westward toward the point on the surface of the ocean above the mangled hulk of the *Pacific Flyer* and the bodies of twenty-six Americans and two Indonesians. Billings was acutely aware of each one of lives that had been lost. He could picture their families, their houses or apartments, their normal lives.

He looked at his watch and called for his communications officer to draft the message he had been dreading, the message to Washington telling them he had failed to find the men who murdered the American merchant sailors and a SEAL.

7

THE PRESIDENT STEPPED ONTO THE PLATFORM WITH Secretary of Defense Dick Roland and the Chairman of the Joint Chiefs at his side. Just like the night before. He looked at the same tired faces of reporters who were constantly eager to undo him and make him look foolish. He sighed deeply.

Roland, who had been chosen to run this particular press conference, took a paper out of his coat pocket and began. Unconsciously, he stood on his toes to look taller and more imposing. "We have received word from the U.S. task force on the scene that the *Pacific Flyer*, which was hijacked yesterday, was taken out to sea. Once in open ocean, the terrorists who had taken the ship murdered the crew and set explosives in the ship."

The President looked up when the press corps let out their audible gasps.

Roland continued, "By the time Navy personnel located and boarded the ship all the crew had been killed, except the captain, and the terrorists had escaped. The captain has been taken hostage. The explosives found aboard were evaluated and it was determined that it would be too dangerous to try to disarm them. Our men abandoned the ship, but the explosives went off as they were evacuating. One Navy sailor was killed. Shortly after the rescue team was safely evacuated the ship exploded again and sank. Twenty-five members of the crew were murdered, all Americans, as well as two Indonesian port inspectors, and the ship and all its cargo were lost." He looked up at the press. "That's all I have. Are there any questions?"

"Mr. Secretary," a woman from *The Washington Post* asked quickly, "did they get the bodies of the Americans off the ship?"

"No," Roland replied. "They were chained to hard points on the ship. They couldn't cut them loose."

"They went to the bottom with the ship?" The press corps was astonished and energized. This was turning into a huge story, if a horrible one. They shifted in their seats and sat up straight.

"Yes."

"Mr. Secretary," yelled a popular New York columnist. "You said the captain was taken. Where is he now, and has he been harmed?"

"We have no idea, other than he wasn't on the ship."

"How do you know that the Navy personnel didn't just miss him, not find him on the ship?"

Roland hesitated. "Because the terrorists left behind a photograph of the captain with a gun to his head. We've identified him from the picture. You'll each get a news summary at the end of this conference. It contains the names and backgrounds of the captain and all the deceased."

"Did the terrorists leave anything else to indicate who they were or what they wanted?"

"No. Nothing at all."

"Have they made demands of any kind? Do we know who did this?"

"As you were told last night, there were twenty to thirty men dressed in Ford coveralls who walked aboard the ship when it docked. That's all we know about them."

"Mr. Secretary," said a woman in the back.

"Yes?"

"What are you planning on doing about this?"

"Very simply, we're trying to find out who did this

and why. We're using every resource available to find whoever is responsible. When we do, we will respond appropriately. We aren't ruling out anything.''

''Will you take military action?''

''I said we aren't ruling out anything. That's all for now. I will give you more information when we have it.'' Roland stepped back. He, President Manchester, and Admiral Hart headed down the hall to the Oval Office, leaving the hubbub of unanswered questions behind them.

President Manchester sat down heavily in his chair. Molly was there with the other advisers and Cabinet members sitting on the couch or standing around the desk. The President rubbed his forehead and sat forward.

''The great United States can't find three motorboats. That's how it will play around the world.''

The Secretary of Defense shrugged his shoulders. He had never been one to care too much about world opinion. His approach was to get the job done, and world opinion be damned.

''Find them,'' the President said standing up, indicating clearly that the discussion was over. The others stood to go, but thought much more needed to be said. What approach? What to do?

''If I may, sir,'' offered Nathaniel Corder, the Secretary of State. ''What about Admiral Billing's request to contact Indonesia and get permission to overfly their air space?''

''Of course. Why do they even have to ask us about that? Isn't that automatic?'' His tone exposed his frustration. ''Please expedite that request.'' The President looked around the room. ''Anything else we absolutely have to deal with? I didn't get much sleep last night. I'm tired.''

They considered several things, then remained silent.

''Fine. I'll call you if I need you. Let me know if you hear anything or have any brilliant ideas. Oh, Ms. Vaughan,'' he said as they were leaving.

''Yes, sir?'' she replied, not sure whether to stay or go.

"How's that one-page memo on the War Powers coming?"

"Fine. I should have something very soon." She smiled hesitantly. "It's not hard getting the information; what's hard is reducing it to one page. Any limitations on font size?" she asked mischievously.

Manchester smiled. "Have to be able to read it with my glasses off. Fourteen point."

Molly held the door, about to close it behind her. "I'll try to get it to you this afternoon."

Manchester nodded. His mind was already on something else.

>=<

"What'd you think of the press conference?" Grazio asked as he sat in Jim Dillon's office. They were going over the agenda for the day.

Dillon noticed the playful look in his eyes. "I thought it was weak. The President should have run it himself instead of dishing it to the Secretary. Made him look like he wasn't sure what was going on."

"They did answer the most important questions."

"But they didn't say anything. 'We haven't ruled anything out.' I guess there isn't much more to say, but I'd like to hear that we will pursue these people to the *ends* of the earth. That we'll do whatever it takes, no matter who it turns out to be. Why do we have to wait and see who it is to be able to say what we're going to do about it?" Dillon stood up, almost involuntarily, "It's like the police saying we know there's been a murder, and as soon as we find out who did it we will decide whether to make an arrest. What difference does it make *who* it is? Why do you have to know about all the angles when U.S. citizens have been murdered and valuable property ruined?"

Grazio nodded and smiled. "Exactly," he said, pointing at Dillon. "*That's* what sets you apart as a nonpolitician. To a politician everything is relative, everything has to be examined from all possible angles before any commitment can be given. In my opinion, a *gifted* politician also knows when not to waffle. But that instinct is found only among the truly developed political animal. I'm afraid our President, of the other party, I might add, fails on that test.''

"Oh, and *you* happen to have a perfect feel for the use of that instinctive response, instead of a careful political response.''

"I was just evaluating the President's performance. I didn't know we cared about mine,'' he said wryly. "So what'd you find out about Indonesia?'' he continued, carefully changing the subject.

"Quite a bit, actually,'' Dillon said. "I admit to being basically ignorant about it before today. I knew where it was, but I sure didn't know it was the fourth-largest country in the world—in population.''

"Seriously?'' Grazio said.

"Yep. Over a hundred ninety million people. Bigger than Russia. Bigger than Japan.''

"You sure don't hear much about it.''

"Not much anymore. During the seventies and eighties they had a lot of trouble with the Communists, the military taking over the government, Sukarno and all that. Some have said up to a million were executed in the seventies when the Communists made a big run at taking over the country.'' He leaned forward and put a piece of paper in front of Grazio. "I copied a page from the atlas. I've circled Indonesia.''

"It's really spread out,'' Grazio said as he examined it. "How many islands?''

Dillon looked at his copy. "Hundreds. Maybe thousands if you consider five square miles an island. There are bays and coves all over the place. There are all kinds of different languages and cultures. Any group could have done this to get back at Indonesia.''

Grazio nodded, thinking. "What's their dominant religion?''

Dillon looked at him intensely. "Guess.''

Grazio frowned, "Buddhism?"

"Nope."

"Taoism?"

"Nope."

Grazio was stumped. "Hindu?"

"Nope." Dillon leaned forward. "Guess which country is the largest Muslim country in the world?"

"I don't know. What does that have to—"

"Indonesia."

Grazio's face showed his puzzlement. "Are you kidding me?"

"Eighty-five percent of the country is Muslim."

"I wonder if that has anything to do with what happened—the country being *Muslim*."

"Beats me. . . . What'd you find out from your pal at the Pentagon?"

Grazio shrugged absently. "Nothing. He said he doesn't have anything you can't find out on CNN."

"Sounds like we're all up to speed. Look, I'll call you if anything else comes up. I've got to do some other stuff."

Grazio stood up. "I can take a hint," he said as he walked out of the office and closed the door loudly behind him, as he always did.

Dillon turned toward his desk. It was stacked high with books and magazines on Indonesia. He threw open a *National Geographic* and began reading about indigenous groups and religious traditions. There were also the usual pictures of naked breasts. He turned the page and frowned at a picture. It was an exotic picture of people on Irian Jaya, a province in eastern Indonesia, one half of the island of New Guinea. He leaned down and looked more closely, his face inches from the page.

The photo showed the men of the island wearing long gourds on their penises. The gourds were held up by cord tied around their waists to look like they had a permanent erection. Dillon laughed. He shook his head as he stared at the picture, imagining the status of the guy in the tribe with the biggest gourd. He wondered what would happen if some young buck found a gourd bigger than the head chief's. Would he have to surrender the gourd? He looked more carefully at one man in the picture. His gourd looked different. He bent down and squinted at the photo.

"No . . . it can't be," he said. The man had a pink plastic doll leg over his penis instead of a gourd. The leg protruded from his abdomen, with a small little foot pointed up at the sky. He looked very proud.

Dillon wondered how in the hell some native got a pink plastic doll leg, and what compelled him to put it . . . there. He wondered if Molly would be impressed if he met her for a movie with a pink plastic doll leg protruding from his fly. . . .

There was a knock on the door, and Grazio stepped in. "Thought I might find you here."

"Good guess. My office and you just left," Dillon said. "Check this out," he said to Grazio, showing him the *National Geographic* article, and pointing to the guy with the doll leg.

"What the hell is *that*?" Grazio said, staring at the picture, his mouth open.

"Doll leg."

"On his crank?" Grazio said, a startled laugh forcing itself from him.

"Sure," Dillon said. "Where else would you put a doll leg?"

"That what Muslims wear under all those big robes and everything? Doll legs? Gourds?"

"You're pathetic," Dillon said. "I think you'd better stop thinking the only Muslims in the world are Arabs."

Grazio ignored him. "Listen, I just got another call from my guy at the Pentagon."

"Good," Dillon said, turning in his chair toward Grazio. "So. What'd you find out?"

"Indonesia has more than I thought," he said. "Did you know they have F-16s and F-5s?"

"Yeah. It was a big deal in Congress when they agreed

to sell them F-16s; then later, they bought MiG-29s."

"They've also got a military of two hundred thousand men."

Dillon whistled. "I had no idea. They any good?"

"Initially trained and supplied by the Dutch when Indonesia was the Dutch East Indies. Since independence in 1948, they've been on their own; they haven't fought anybody but themselves. So it's hard to say how good they are."

"Anybody else in the area that could challenge them? Anybody they're scared of?"

"Japanese. Have been since World War Two. Maybe India and Australia? China, I suppose, except the fifty-trillion-man Chinese Army can't walk there. Indonesia is all islands, it's basically secure unless some real heavy with a navy—like us—decides to pop 'em."

Jim Dillon sat back and put his hands behind his head. "I just don't get it. What does anybody gain from killing those crewmen and sinking the ship?" His chair creaked from the weight on the spring.

"Seems to me they're trying to make some kind of statement. But to who?"

"Whom."

"Whatever," Grazio said. "I doubt this was some Toyota dealer deciding to murder the comp before they could open. I see this as a punch in the mouth to the U.S."— he paused for emphasis—"and in particular to the President. Everybody thinks it's to tell him his diplomacy through commerce is a pile of shit. But who would hate commerce that much? I mean Indonesia nearly *begged* us to let them be first in this deal. It was *their* idea to start with, they wanted Ford to open a dealership in partnership with them."

"I don't know," Dillon said, tired of covering the same ground. "Keep me posted."

"Will do. Next, I'm off to the Library of Congress to do a chart of the political history of Indonesia. Speaker says."

"Sounds like fun," Dillon replied.

8

CASKEY LOOKED AT HIS WATCH AND THE FLIGHT schedule. Ten minutes until his next brief. Not even enough time to look at the message board. He put his head back against his leather ready-room chair and closed his eyes. As soon as he did, he knew he shouldn't have. He could feel sleep crawling over him, sapping his strength. He fought it, and reveled in it at the same time. He wanted to sleep, to surrender to it, to let himself go. But he told himself it wasn't the *time* to sleep. For the commanding officer to be seen sleeping in the ready room was completely unacceptable.

The sound of the television in the front of the ready room coming to life made Caskey open his eyes. He saw the familiar face of the air wing intelligence officer, Lieutenant Commander Carroll Cousins, or Pinkie as he had called him since Pinkie was an ensign in VF-84 and Caskey was a lieutenant. He looked at his watch. Eight minutes too early for the brief. Something was up.

"Good morning," Pinkie said. "No, I haven't lost my watch, and yes, I do know it's not time for the brief, but we've just received a message that CNN is going to carry a live report from Jakarta in one minute that will shed light on the events of the last twenty-four hours. We're getting a good satellite feed, so we shouldn't have any problem picking up . . ."

"Wart!" Caskey shouted to the duty officer. "Get on

80

the horn and make sure everybody catches this report.''

"Aye, aye, sir,'' Wart said, turning toward the phone.

"Here we go,'' Pinkie said, as the television was switched to CNN for ship-wide distribution.

The anchorwoman came on the screen and had the serious look that meant she had hard news, not to be confused with the clever knowing look which meant she had filler. "Good evening,'' she said. It was evening in Washington, but morning in the Java Sea. "CNN has obtained an exclusive first communication from the group which claims to have sunk the *Pacific Flyer*. Early this morning Jakarta time a man on a motorbike dropped off a videotape at our local CNN office in Jakarta and sped away. The videotape had a note on the top in English that said: 'From the FII—those who took the *Pacific Flyer*.' There was no other writing with it and no way to trace its origin. The CNN engineers in Jakarta played the videotape and believe it is authentic and is indeed from the men who attacked the American ship yesterday. We are now going to show you the videotape in its entirety. This is a CNN exclusive.'' She turned her head sideways to look at a monitor.

The image changed, and the focus became clear on a white male in his fifties. He was in a dingy room with his hands placed awkwardly flat on the wooden desk in front of him. He sat stiffly. He stared directly into the camera as he had obviously been instructed to do. His eyes appeared slightly swollen and his hair was unkempt. A voice came from offscreen. It spoke in English with a heavy accent as the speaker obviously read from something he had prepared.

"You Americans continue to believe that as long as you spread your Western poison around the world, the world will improve. You are wrong. The world is tired of your oppression and your self-serving attitude that whatever you want is what is best for the world, especially if it means you make money.

"No longer will the people of the world bow down to

American Imperialism. I am a freedom fighter, like George Washington. I represent the future of Indonesia and the world. We are the Front for an Islamic Indonesia. Through us this country will find its true greatness, by the Koran and obedience to its precepts in this Muslim country. Through us Indonesia will throw off military dictatorship, American support of the dictator, and America itself.

"We took over *Pacific Flyer* as a lesson to you Americans. You do not control us, nor can you buy us with your Commerce through Democracy. We want none of your commerce or your democracy.

"With America come corruption, prostitution, pornography, blasphemy, murder, and enslavement."

Those watching thought he had finished, but then he started again. "We will not stand for any of it. First, we demand that America promise not to engage in any further commercial relationships in Indonesia for ten years. Second, the U.S. Navy must stay out of the oceans of this area for twenty years. Third, you must take your missionaries home and not try to convert our people. We are a Muslim country and always will be. If these promises are not made, nothing you do will guarantee the safety of Americans here, or elsewhere in the world."

Caskey was transfixed by the broadcast, especially the terrorist's unemotional delivery.

"In case you think we are bluffing, as you can see, we have the captain of the *Pacific Flyer*." A left hand showed in the bottom right-hand corner of the screen and a right hand flashed in the middle of the screen as it slapped Captain Bonham in the back of the head. He jerked forward involuntarily and began to raise his hands. The phantom right hand slapped Bonham again in the back of the head. "I can do whatever I want with your captain. If you do not comply with our demands, he will be executed, just like the others."

Caskey felt his stomach tighten as he tried to control his rage. The nerve. To murder innocent men, and then go on world television and challenge the United States and the *Navy*. Unbelievable.

"If you are listening, President Manchester, you will do as we ask. You Americans are big ones for rights. Rights for yourselves. We ask simply for what you take for granted, the right to be left alone."

The television screen went blank as the tape ended.

💐

President Manchester turned to the Director of the CIA and said in a controlled tone, "You ever heard of these guys before?"

Cary Warner stared at the anchorwoman who was summarizing what they had just heard.

"No, sir, I've never heard of them. Doesn't mean nobody in my shop has. I'll get with them right away and find out. I recommend, sir, if you'll permit me, to contact my counterpart in Indonesia who will, I think, be as concerned about this as we are."

"Why do you say that?" Van den Bosch asked.

"That little speech was meant for Indonesia as much as it was for us. Sinking that ship was perhaps more embarrassing for them because the attack was launched from their territory. This group is implying they are taking over Indonesia, not America. They just want us to keep our noses and our business out."

"What a bunch of crap," the Chief of Staff said. "They're just thugs, trying to get famous. What are we going to do, Mr. President?"

"I don't know," Manchester said, thinking, rubbing his face. "We still don't really know much more than we did. We know it was a small group, not a foreign government or a previously known organization. Terrorists, trying to make a point." He walked around to the back of the desk in the Oval Office and looked out the window. "I need to talk to the President of Indonesia and see what they plan to do about this."

"Should we have the Navy take any steps?" the Chief

of Staff inquired, trying to hint at what he thought the right answer should be.

"Like what?" the President inquired, annoyed.

"They should continue to try to find these guys, and if they find them, they should be prepared to attack."

"Sometimes, Arlan, I think you've seen too many movies. We're just going to sit tight, let the information develop, and take appropriate steps as we can."

"Shouldn't we at least tell them to keep looking?"

"Of course they'll keep looking! We need to find them regardless of what we finally do."

The Chief of Staff nodded, relief showing on his face, a fact that annoyed the President.

"Well," said Cary Warner, "I need to talk to some people. I need to find out more information," he said as he rose.

"Cary," the President said, stopping him.

"Yes, sir?"

"I'd like a brief by your best person on Indonesia as soon as possible."

"Yes, sir. I'll send someone in, but since Suharto died, there hasn't been much trouble. They do have martial law, but it's not all that different than it was under Suharto really," he said. He turned toward the door, then turned back, "But I don't know that we have the whole story either."

President Manchester looked at Warner with his lips tightened into a thin line. He had something in mind, but he wasn't sharing it with anyone—not the National Security Council and not his Chief of Staff.

🙰

"The phones have been ringing off the hook, Mr. Speaker," Dillon said to the Speaker's back as he hurried through the outside office. Stanbridge took off his suit coat and threw it onto a peg behind the door.

"This is unbelievable. I don't remember the last time anyone challenged the United States so directly. Things happen, sure, we end up in conflicts here and there, but I don't remember anyone *ever* thumbing their noses at us like this.'' He turned to Dillon. ''What kind of calls are we getting?''

''The outside calls are from voters who think we should act immediately. A few even said we should resort to nuclear weapons.''

Stanbridge stifled a laugh.

''One guy thought we should invade Indonesia. They think the whole country is behind it and is paying some terrorists to get them out of a deal they have with us when they didn't have the nerve to do it on their own.''

''Anything else?''

''That's about it.''

''I was over talking to Pete Peterson. We've decided to go see the President. We need to get our heads together. Make sure we're on the same page. I don't want to undercut him, but I want to make sure he starts taking some action now. Starts sending some strong signals.''

The Speaker turned to Dillon and said, ''You know what's really bugging me?''

Dillon shook his head.

''I don't trust the President's instincts. I mean, think about it. He was an antiwar protester in the sixties. While I was over in Vietnam getting my *ass* shot at, he was back in Washington demonstrating against the war. He's never been in a situation where he's had to act with the military, and he's never proven he's capable of doing it.''

Dillon wasn't sure whether the Speaker wanted a response or not. He hesitated to say anything but finally spoke. ''I don't know that there'd be any direct relationship between his antiwar efforts in Vietnam and this.''

The Speaker nodded. ''I know. I just don't trust him.''

Dillon looked at a pad he had taken notes on earlier. ''Yes, sir. Anything in particular you want me to do now?''

''Yeah, I want to be the expert on Indonesia. I need a

program to keep the players straight. Get me up to speed before I sit down with the President.''

"Yes, sir.''

The Speaker began examining papers in the middle of his desk. Dillon walked out and headed down the hall and up one floor to his office. He surveyed the myriad of periodicals, computer printouts of research, photographs, and books, and looked at the phone. Someone else was probably doing the same research he was. He picked up the phone and dialed a number from memory. It rang twice on the second floor of the West Wing of the White House.

"Yes?'' Molly said.

"It's Jim,'' he said.

"Hey,'' she said. "Can you believe those guys? Where do they get their nerve?''

"I have no idea. But I've got a feeling they won't be quite as confident when this is over.''

"I'll bet you're right,'' she said. "What's up?''

"You got any idea who FII is? Are you working on this?''

"We're waiting to hear.'' She hesitated. "I'm working with the President, but I'm not sure what that means yet. You call just to ask me that?''

"I figured we could share info about this.''

"It doesn't work that way, Jim. You know that. People in this town will always look for a political advantage out of any event, even if it's a mass disaster. You *know* that.''

"Look, why don't you come over for dinner tonight?'' he asked. "We could debate this then.''

"I guess I've got to eat. I've got a feeling it's going to be a late night in Washington for a lot of people, but I'm not sure . . .''

"What?''

"Never mind. See you about seven-thirty.''

"How about seven o'clock?''

"Okay, I'll be there,'' she said and hung up.

꧁

"This is some mighty special Hamburger Helper, Jim," Molly said sarcastically as she wrinkled her nose.

"Next time *you* cook," he said, eating heartily.

"I will," she said pushing her half-eaten food away. She put her plate on the counter and began making coffee. "What do you think is going through their minds?" she asked, letting the question she was pondering find a voice. "Murder American sailors just so they can have their fifteen minutes of fame?"

"Seems to be the way things are done these days. A few freaks with bombs or guns, that's it. No more big wars, no more mass destruction, just the world slowly bleeding to death." He stood and leaned on the counter, placing his plate in the sink. "What do you think we should do about it?"

She looked over her shoulder, "In general?"

"In general."

She thought for a moment, then pulled her hair away from her face. "I don't really know. Being tough didn't seem to help Israel. Not only did terrorism not stop, now the PLO has its own country right in their backyard. It's as if it doesn't matter what you do."

"You think Israel would have had fewer terrorist attacks if they'd been *easier* on the terrorists?" he asked, amazed.

"We'll never know, will we?" She poured the water into the coffeepot and turned around. "I guess I think we should try a peaceful approach more often than we do."

"Even with the FII, whoever the hell they are?"

She shrugged. "I guess I'm not sure."

He shook his head slowly. "What's to be sure about? If we find them, can you think of any reason we shouldn't attack them?"

"I can think of a lot of reasons not to. We need some more information first."

"What's the President going to do about it?" Dillon

asked quickly. He saw the look on her face. He had crossed the invisible line. She was unhappy with his question.

"You know I can't discuss his plans. I can't believe you even asked."

"Why can't you discuss it?" Dillon asked, handing her the sunflower cup he had bought for her to use at his apartment. She loved sunflowers. "I just want to know."

"It's *inappropriate*. You know that," she replied coolly.

"I just want to know the answer." He leaned on the counter next to her. "It's the President's deal, and you work for him. He is the Commander in Chief, right? If someone is going to act, it has to be him."

She nodded. "But that's no news. That's the way it's always been."

"So what's he going to do?"

She didn't answer. "Sorry," she said.

"Okay, then tell me what *you* think he ought to do."

"I just told you I don't *know*."

"Why are you so touchy?" Dillon seemed puzzled. "What is this? Why is this making you annoyed?"

Molly looked at the ceiling and closed her eyes. She finally lowered her head. "If I were going to be completely honest, I guess I'd have to say that it bothers me personally that you seem all gung-ho to go attack these Indonesians—"

"Well, why shouldn't I? And what does that have to do with—"

"Let me finish," she said. "Whenever I get close to you, something gets in the way." She hesitated, not sure if she should speak her mind. "Our differences seem to go beyond politics. I'm not as anxious for blood as you are. The country needs to *think* about things, not act before we understand the issues. And even then, we have to be willing to *not* act, if that's what's called for."

"Why would that be called for?" Dillon asked, perplexed. "Tell me what you think those circumstances could even possibly be." He smiled, as if amazed. "Look. *Whatever* comes of this, we can't let it get in the way. We were just starting to be comfortable around each other. It's funny that you mentioned us getting together. I've been thinking the same thing." He took a step closer to her and looked into her eyes as he put his hands into his pockets. "Don't let this get in the way."

She looked back at him. "It already has."

9

PRESIDENT MANCHESTER RECEIVED HIS USUAL MORN-
ing briefs, read his usual morning papers—actually ex-
cerpts from countless newspapers around the country—
and thought about what to do. Everyone in the world was
waiting to hear what he was going to do about the attack
on a U.S.-flagged ship in international waters. Would he
strike back like a child on a playground? Try the diplomatic approach that mature politicians were supposed to
prefer and always seemed to choose because at least it
bought them time? Respond like the Israelis, or at least
the way the Israelis used to—never negotiate with terrorists? What was there to negotiate anyway?

He knew he would be second-guessed. He was always
second-guessed by those who disagreed. Even when they
agreed in their hearts, if there was any possible advantage
to be had by questioning his decisions, they would do it.
It was part of the job.

The door opened slowly. "Your secretary told me to
come on in," said Molly. She was wearing a black suit
and high heels.

Manchester rose and said, "Yes, come in. Sit down."

"Certainly, Mr. President."

"Good morning," he said, returning to his seat behind
his desk. "Thanks for coming in so early. I have breakfast
meetings, but I wanted your opinion on how my backside
was doing so far before I talked to the rest of the staff."

"So far, I don't see any problem at all, Mr. President. There's a lot of pressure for you to respond, but that kind of goes without saying."

"You mean militarily."

"Well, that's what everyone seems to want you to do."

"What do you think?"

"That's certainly an option. There are other options, of course."

"Like what?"

"Well, I'm sure you've thought of trying to negotiate, trying to work through Indonesia itself, trying to back off militarily as a gesture of good will . . ."

"Yes, I have thought of all of those. I just wanted to hear from you since you're always in on these meetings and don't have the same inclination to tell me what I want to hear."

"Well, I may very well have that inclination; you just may not know about it," she said, smiling.

He smiled back. "I guess that's right." He sat up. "You know, since I first heard of this attack, I have basically known what I had to do." He looked at her directly. "I've also had the sense that this is going to be the turning point of my presidency."

Molly didn't know what to say.

"Let me ask you a question, Ms. Vaughan."

"Yes, sir."

"Which is more courageous—to lash out in anger or hold back in mercy?"

Molly raised her eyebrows. "Well, I guess it would depend on the circumstances. If you mean *these* circumstances, I think a case could be made for either course."

Manchester nodded.

He had sensed the rest of his staff backing away from him, including his close advisers. The attitude was difficult to pinpoint, but it was there. Backing off so they could watch him make his decision from a distance and, if the plan failed, claim they hadn't really encouraged *that* decision, or if it was successful, claim they were part of the inner circle of trusted advisers who had come to a consensus. That was routine, that was politics.

He hated politics. He hated hating politics. He had gone into politics out of principle, to do something right, to make the country—and ultimately the world—a better place. But like every president before him, he found himself having to bargain with truly difficult people, always being challenged to compromise his principles.

But this was the time to make a decision, unequivocally, because it was *right,* to stand for something, no matter what the polls said, or his advisers, or his adversaries. He got up, walked over to a window, and looked out across the South Lawn, which was winter brown. He was angry at himself for the thoughts that had been coursing through his head. He had been feeling pressure from Congress, from the press, from the private shipping company whose ship had been lost, from the Indonesian ambassador, from his staff, from his wife, from everybody.

Everybody had an opinion in a crisis. And this was the first real crisis his administration had faced, the first time the world hung on every word, wondering what he would do. It was time to lead. He went back to his desk and spoke into his intercom, "Would you get Arlan on the phone, please?"

"Yes, Mr. President" came the immediate reply. "Should I tell him what this is about?"

"Tell him I've decided what we're going to do," he said, looking at the surprise on Molly's face.

Dillon dropped *The Washington Post* and *The Washington Times* on his desk and hung his coat on the hook on the back of his office door. The door came back toward him. Grazio walked in.

"Speaker wants to see you."

Dillon looked at him and breathed deeply. "I haven't had breakfast. I haven't even had a cup of *coffee.*" He followed Grazio out the door. "What's up?"

"Don't know. But he's got that energized look in his eyes."

Dillon walked down the hallway, hurried down the stairs, and into the Speaker's outer office. "Hey, Robin. He in?"

She nodded.

Dillon didn't even break stride as he walked into the Speaker's office. "Morning, sir," he said.

Stanbridge sat up straighter and looked up at Dillon. "You looked at the War Powers Act recently?"

Dillon tried to evaluate the importance of the question as he answered it. "Not in a couple of months," he said, stretching the currency of his knowledge. "As I recall— president can't send troops into hostilities without notifying Congress and getting permission for an engagement longer than thirty days . . . something like that. Reports required . . ."

The Speaker nodded. "Thanks to Nixon and Vietnam," he said, then shook his head as he stood. "Funny history behind that. Congress got the U.S. into Vietnam with the Gulf of Tonkin Resolution. Congress funds the war for a dozen years, then blames the president when he goes into Laos, like *that's* different somehow. Then, when it doesn't work out, they yell at him for even thinking of sending troops without their permission. Unbelievable. What exactly did they think they were funding? Target practice? Pure hypocrisy." He ran his hand through his bristly brown hair. "Anyway, it's in place and it keeps a president from committing a bunch of troops without Congress's permission."

Dillon nodded. "Yes, sir. You want me to do some quick analysis of how it plays into the current deal in Indonesia?"

The Speaker nodded as he crossed to his favorite window. "I've heard the President's going to make an announcement soon. My guess is he's going to make some big move to shore up his image as a military lightweight, which of course he is."

"Yes, sir."

The Speaker paused and looked at Dillon, as if wondering something for the first time, "You ever serve in the military?"

"No, sir."

"How come?"

"No reason really. Just didn't. By the time I was in college you didn't even have to register for the draft. Just never entered my mind as something to do."

"You should have. Builds character," the Speaker said. "Anyway, let me know what you come up with about the War Powers before lunch. I don't want to get caught off guard. I need to have the basics at the tips of my fingers."

"Yes, sir. I'll get right on it. You want a memo or something?"

"One page. Bullet points. What he can and can't do."

"I'll take care of it. Mind if I get some help?"

"Whatever it takes—don't work on anything else right now." He looked up at Dillon. "We know any more about the jerks who did this?"

"Just what's on CNN."

Stanbridge nodded.

The sun had already set on the sweltering Java Sea. Swells were calm and the water was smooth with a slight chop. The engines on the three cigarette boats throbbed as they reduced their throttles entering the beautiful lagoon. Captain Clay Bonham stood behind the small man driving the boat with his hands tied behind him. Another man held a large knife at his back.

Bonham tried to memorize the entire scene in case he could ever break free of his captors and try to describe this island to the Navy. He strained to read the latitude and longitude from the GPS satellite navigation unit on the dash. He knew the chances of getting free were zero. He knew the chances of living through this were about the same. No blindfold. They didn't care what he saw because he wasn't going to be telling anyone about it. He winced as he remembered his crewmen. Even though the F-14 had spotted the *Pacific Flyer*, the Navy had not been able to reach the ship before Washington and his terrorists executed his crew and kidnapped him. There was no hope anyone was going to get him out alive. Bonham gritted his teeth.

The three boats coasted to a pier that had obviously been recently constructed. It was solid and well built. One of the men jumped off the bow of the lead boat in which Bonham and George Washington were riding and secured the bow line to a post. As soon as the aft line was secured, the men scrambled onto the pier and into the jungle surroundings. The man with the knife pulled up on Bonham's arm, causing pain to shoot through his shoulders. Bonham refused to cry out. He stepped onto the side of the boat and onto the pier and marched forward as directed by the man with the knife. There were several tents and lean-tos in what was obviously a temporary setting.

I'll bet they have dozens of these, Bonham thought. Good pier, temporary settings, fast speedboats, and a mother ship to carry them around. He shook his head. The Navy would never find them.

Admiral Billings growled to himself as he stared at the chart. The thought of an entire battle group looking for three speedboats in the immense Java Sea was ridiculous. If there was one thing he hated, it was looking ridiculous. Only seventeen thousand islands in Indonesia. And he was supposed to find three little boats, no matter what. Even though it was considered critical to the security interests of the United States, for some reason they couldn't redirect the necessary satellites to the area to help in the search. Satellites would be able to image and identify the boats if they were in port. But other commitments were more critical—even though no one would tell him what those commitments were.

He looked around the table at his staff, who were all staring at him, trying to read his mind. They knew better than to speak first. He pointed to the chart. "You see how many islands there are? By now, those boats could be on any of them, or none of them. Agree?" he said looking at his intelligence officer, who nodded her head. "I'm up for any ideas you have. We're steaming around here looking stupid, wasting nuclear fuel, jet fuel, and sleep."

"I think we need to start flying recce hops over the beaches of some of the closer less-inhabited islands, Admiral," the CAG said. "We'll never find them in the open ocean. They can't be that stupid."

"What else?" Billings asked, peeved.

The chief of staff looked around, then spoke. "I think we need to be coordinating with Indonesia to get permission to overfly their territory. We've got to lean on them."

The admiral sat back and waved his hand. "You've read the messages on that. We asked Indonesia, and they said no. Don't ask me why, but they did. Probably don't want to look impotent, letting a bunch of Americans run around showing the only way they can catch them is if the U.S. Navy does it for them. I know how those things go. They want us involved but don't want to acknowledge that."

"Well, we've got to lean on them to let us get involved, or nothing will ever happen."

"Can't. Anything else?" No one spoke.

"Until something changes, I want all flights to do surface surveillance and recce, and *find* those three boats. If they can peek into harbors and islands with radars or TV units, then *do* it. But stay in international waters." He looked at his operations officer. "SEALs and Marines ready to go if we find them and get the go-ahead from the President?"

"They're ready, Admiral," the chief of staff replied, jumping in.

The admiral nodded. "I want hourly reports on where our aircraft have gone and whether we've seen anything suspicious. I want every flight charted in SUPPLOT.'' Beth nodded. ''Until we find them, we'll just have to sit tight.''

''Any traces on those strange explosives the SEALs found aboard the *Pacific Flyer*?''

''No, sir. Apparently neither the military nor the intelligence community has seen anything like them before, and no one else has either. All the descriptions in our messages came up with blanks. No one has seen anything anywhere like it.''

The admiral sat back and put his hands behind his head. ''Maybe these guys are more sophisticated than we're giving them credit for.''

Commander Beth Louwsma spoke first. ''Probably just bought them from China or Iran or somewhere. Hard to say where they got them. We can be certain, though, they didn't create 'em. Those devices showed some sophisticated manufacturing. Not something a terrorist group is going to be able to pull off by themselves.''

''Still. Don't underestimate them. If they have access to those, they may have more surprises up their sleeves. We need to be very cautious.''

''Yes, sir. Concur . . .''

The door to the admiral's cabin opened quickly and a first class petty officer came in. ''Excuse me, sir,'' he said to the admiral, looking every bit as awkward as he felt in his dirty denim uniform. ''This just came in and the Ship's Intel thought Commander Louwsma should see it right away.''

The admiral waved him in, and the petty officer crossed to Beth Louwsma and handed her a file. All eyes were on her as she opened the file and examined the contents. She frowned as she stared at the picture in front of her. It wasn't a photograph, but it was clearly from a satellite. A radar satellite, but the United States didn't have any radar satellites anywhere in the area. She motioned for the petty officer to approach and lean down. She whispered in his ear, and the petty officer pointed to a legend on the back of the photo. The petty officer backed away, and Louwsma looked at the admiral.

"Well?" the admiral asked, annoyed at the intrusion.

"I think we've got them, Admiral," Beth said, unable to hide the excitement in her voice. Her chest rose and fell much more rapidly as she tried to catch her breath.

"What? How?" The admiral leaned forward enthusiastically.

Beth swallowed. "Radar satellite. Even though the boats are fiberglass, most of what is in them isn't. They still show a distinctive shape. We had a file copy of the same Italian cigarette boat in the Mediterranean. One of the 53 pilots gave us a lead—said he thought it was an Italian boat."

"So, what do you have?"

"We have a radar satellite image taken"—she looked at the top of the photo—"two hours ago that appears to have caught three cigarette boats under some very nice camouflage in an inlet of an island."

The admiral smiled with satisfaction. "So you got them to redirect the satellites after all. Well done."

Louwsma looked chagrined. "Not exactly, Admiral. This isn't our radar image."

"Whose is it?"

"Russian," she replied.

The admiral tried to disguise his disgust. "How'd we get it?"

"They called us and asked us if we wanted it."

"Why in the hell would they do that?"

She shrugged. "Don't know. Could be the Islamic thing. They've always seen the Islamic fundamentalists as a threat. Many of them think that's what caused the breakup of the Soviet Union, with Kazakhstan, Uzbekistan, Turkmenistan, Tajikist—"

"Could it be bogus?" he interrupted.

"Could be. The specialists will check it. I'm pretty sure it's legit though."

"So where are they?"

Beth Louwsma leaned over the chart, studied it for a minute, looked again at the latitude and longitude on the radar image of the three faint speedboats. She put her finger on a small island southeast of Sumatra, two hundred miles southwest of the battle group. "Here."

As Dillon walked back into his office, the phone rang. He shut the door loudly behind him and reached for the receiver. "Hello?"

"Hi," Molly said. "How's it going?"

"Okay," Dillon said, sounding concerned.

"What?" she asked, perceiving his tone.

"A lot going on. This thing has people pretty wound up."

"I'll say," she replied. "Listen, I know you planned on working tonight, but is there anyway we could get together? I was kind of tired the other night, I was short with you."

"I don't know," he said. "I'm pretty low on Hamburger Helper. I've got some canned tuna—if you bring a fork . . ."

"My turn," she said. "Something healthy."

"Sounds tasteless."

"It won't be. Spaghetti."

"Now that *is* healthy." He looked at the increasing pile of paper on his desk and tried to estimate the work ahead of him.

"You've got to eat, as you always say," she prompted him.

"I really can't. I'd love to, but I just can't. I really appreciate the offer though."

"That's fine," she said, withdrawing before she was perceived as being vulnerable. "I'll talk to you later—"

"Hey, before you go, we just got word the President was going to make an announcement soon. Any truth to that?"

"Not that I know of, but I wouldn't necessarily know."

"I hear ya. What's he got you working on?"

"Oh, just some research."

"What about?"

"You can't ask me that."

"Aw, come on."

"Just War Powers stuff, you know, the usual crisis process."

"Same here, just different perspective. We should compare notes."

"Probably not."

"Yeah, you're right," he said, his mind already elsewhere. "Probably not."

"See ya," she said.

"Yeah, bye," he closed as he began reading a law review article on the War Powers Resolution.

⊯

Commander Mike Caskey looked down at his nav display and saw that they were ten miles from the waypoint where they would begin their TARPS run to photograph the bay where the Russian satellite had spotted the three cigarette boats. Messer, in the back seat, was already slaving the television sight unit, the TVSU, to get a videotape of the area to complement the still photos that would be taken automatically by the TARPS pod they were carrying on the belly of the plane. He increased his speed to three hundred fifty knots and checked his fuel. "See anything yet?"

"Nope. Just foliage. Come starboard ten degrees, prepare for run."

Caskey eased the stick slightly right and descended. The cobalt-blue ocean rushed by. The spot they approached, a small jungle island between Java and Sumatra, was thought to be uninhabited. At least that's what Pinkie, the intelligence officer, had said. But he had said it with such a complete lack of conviction that Caskey knew he had no idea. "Think they've got any SAMs?"

"Where they gonna get SAMs without us hearing about it?" Messer said. "No chance."

Caskey sucked pure oxygen in deeply from his mask and sighed.

"Here comes the waypoint," Messer said. He reached down beside his left knee and turned on the cameras.

10

LIEUTENANT COMMANDER PINKIE COUSINS, THE AIR wing intelligence officer, leaned over the table and examined the photograph from Caskey's airplane. The quality was stunning, especially for an airplane that wasn't designed for reconnaissance using a pod attached to the bottom of the plane. He examined the picture more carefully. The sideways angle of the camera lent itself to revealing things that an overhead photograph, like a satellite, would never see. Like this. Clear as a bell, three cigarette boats at anchor underneath a beautiful camouflage cover in a small inlet on the island of . . . of what? He looked at the chart next to him to find the island. It wasn't even named. Too small.

It may not be named, he thought, but it sure isn't going anywhere. He picked up the phone to the admiral's intelligence officer. He dialed the number he knew by heart. "Hey, Commander," he said, wondering for the hundredth time how a Navy officer could be so gorgeous. He had lusted after Beth Louwsma ever since he was an ensign, when she had been one of the instructors in his intelligence course. But *every* single male intelligence officer had lusted after her to no avail.

"Morning, Pinkie. What you got?"

"Found 'em. I'm sure. TARPS photo confirms that Russian radar satellite. Unless somebody had a sale on white cigarette boats at about five hundred thou each, unless there's a butt-load of these boats running around in the Java Sea hanging out under camouflage netting for fun, then we've found our boys.'' He shifted his feet and looked at the photograph again.

Beth responded without hesitating. ''Let's brief the admiral right away. Bring the photo.''

''You got it,'' he said as he grabbed the photo and slipped it into a file. He walked down to SUPPLOT and fingered the rocker keys on the wall. He moved the spring-loaded keys with the lightning speed that comes from daily repetition of the code and the lock buzzed open. He pushed the steel door and stepped into the dimly lit room. It was small, with charts on the walls and electronic gear humming all around. Less than a minute later, the admiral entered.

Pinkie had been fond of Admiral Billings ever since he had known him as the commanding officer of Fighter Squadron Eighty-four on the *Nimitz*. Pinkie had been a wide-eyed ensign on his first tour an intelligence officer assigned to the Jolly Rogers.

''What you got, Pinkie?'' the admiral asked, skipping the preliminaries as he always did and glancing at Beth Louwsma, whom he trusted completely, not only to provide him with good intelligence but also as a sounding board.

''Recce photos from the F-14 TARPS mission that MC flew.'' He handed a copy of the photo to the admiral, who looked at it carefully. ''Look closely in the shadow toward the left of the middle,'' he said, pointing. ''There are three cigarette boats parked there—''

''Moored,'' the admiral corrected.

''Moored there,'' Pinkie said, ''under camouflage netting. These photos are being shown to the Marine captain who was flying the CH-53 with the SEALs who saw three similar boats heading away from the *Flyer*. I have no doubt he'll confirm these as the ones.''

Billings frowned and looked at the two intelligence officers. "Does the location match up with that Russian radar satellite?"

"Yes, sir. Small island," he said, crossing to the chart of the Java Sea. "Right"—he leaned forward and touched the chart—"here. Just southeast of Sumatra and west of Java."

"What's on the island?"

"I don't know, sir. It's not even named on the chart. Indonesia has a pile of islands, most of which aren't even inhabited—although you'd think with two hundred million people they'd take advantage of every island." Pinkie smiled as he glanced at Billings. Billings stared at the photo carefully, unsmiling. "In any case," Pinkie continued, "I'm trying to find out what I can about the island, but right now all I know is the general terrain—jungle. We're just south of the equator here, and the heat just hovers over these islands, crushing them into submission."

"Very poetic," the admiral quipped. "Any idea how many people are there?"

"No, sir. The jungle cover is too dense to get any good reconnaissance. We really have no way of knowing."

The admiral looked at him and frowned. "What do you mean, 'no way of knowing'?"

"We can't get good imagery of the island, only the water around it, and the radar info is useless, basically."

The admiral sat back in his leather chair and looked at Pinkie and at Beth, who was standing to his left. "Seems to me we need to put someone on the ground there."

Pinkie looked at Beth, then at the admiral, and nodded.

"What?" the Speaker exclaimed as he jumped up from his chair. "What's he going to say?" He listened to the President's Chief of Staff on the other end of the phone explain that the President would address the nation tonight. "That's not good enough. I want to know what he's—I understand that. I am the Speaker of the House," he said slowly. "Fine, just remind him of the War Powers Resolution. If he doesn't think we'll—I don't care!" he said, raising his voice and putting his free left hand on his hip. He stared at Dillon and Grazio as he spoke. His eyes were covered by his frowning eyebrows. "That's a crock. Just tell him what I said. Fine."

He turned to Dillon as he hung up. "I tell you what; if he sends troops over there without consulting us, I'll raise the roof. I'll call him on it—he better not think I won't." He looked at the rest of the staff that had gathered in his office for the brief on the War Powers Resolution Dillon had just finished. "He's going on the air tonight at nine to announce what his decision is."

"Good thing we've already looked at the War Powers. Should we fax him an outline?" Dillon asked smugly.

The Speaker shook his head, lost in thought. "There's something strange about this." He pondered silently. He began to pace near the window. "Gut feeling. He's going to do something different."

"Like what?" Dillon said.

"I don't know. But he hasn't consulted with Congress." He rubbed his chin and looked out the window. "It doesn't feel like he's using this to challenge the War Powers Resolution. Maybe he isn't going to send them at all." He turned. "But if he isn't going to send them, what's he up to?"

They looked at one another, then at the Speaker. No one spoke.

The Speaker went on, "I don't know either. Be back here at eight-thirty. If anything occurs to you before then, come see me. Otherwise"—he held his hands up—"we'll learn about it together."

☙

At exactly 9:02 P.M. the news anchor stopped rambling and looked seriously at the camera. "Ladies and gentlemen, the President of the United States."

Manchester was seated in the usual talking-president

position at his desk in the Oval Office, in the usual presidential blue suit, with the usual unremarkable presidential tie. His hair was perfectly groomed. He looked into the camera and paused—longer than the usual presidential pause—for effect. He had a flair for the dramatic, a sense of timing that most other presidents before him had lacked. He used a TelePrompTer, but spoke from an outline instead of a prepared speech. It gave his staff heart palpitations every time he did it because they were afraid he would say something that hadn't been cleansed by the infinity of staff filters. The public loved it for the same reason.

President Manchester glanced down at his notes, then back at the camera. "Good evening." He never started with the usual presidential "My fellow Americans" because he thought it was trite and he couldn't get Lyndon Johnson out of his mind whenever he said it.

"As you all well know, two days ago terrorists from Indonesia attacked a U.S. merchant ship called the *Pacific Flyer* and took it out to sea where they killed twenty-five crewmen and a Navy sailor, sank the ship and its cargo, and took the captain hostage. This act was clearly intended as an attack on the United States itself and intended to harm not only our citizens but our reputation and our influence in the commercial world and especially the emerging economies of the Pacific. It was a cowardly act and conducted against defenseless and unsuspecting civilians. I cannot express how strongly I condemn this barbarism, nor will I give respect or credence to the terrorists by repeating their demands issued since the murders.

"As President it is my responsibility to deal with events of national importance, wherever they occur." He looked down at his notes and breathed a little more deeply than some would have liked. "It is difficult to find the proper balance all the time, especially when things are examined under the bright light of hindsight. But because decisions are difficult doesn't mean you don't make them. You have to make them. *I* have to make them.

"Tonight, America takes a different course than we have in the past. Tonight, we take the high ground against terrorists, against people everywhere who believe that by being evil they can make us evil, that enough wrongs deafen our ability to hear truth and know what is right. No more. Terrorism has been around for a long time, but is the particular curse of my generation. Since I was a young man, terrorists have been attacking and killing innocent people in order to make a political point. Their attacks so anger people that countries strike back. More killing. A cycle of violence that the society claims is started by the terrorist, and that the terrorists claim is caused by the oppression or political situation in which they find themselves. Then the terrorists conduct more attacks, and the retribution continues. Once the cycle of violence begins, all seem powerless to stop it.

"No longer will America take a leg for an eye, or even an eye for an eye. No longer will our conduct, our response, be determined by someone else. We are not going to participate in the cycle of violence."

Manchester casually looked at his outline and then back up. "As you know, the U.S. Navy has been diligently looking for the terrorists and any base from which they may have operated. The latest information leads us to believe we know where they are. We have indications they are still on Indonesian soil. We will relay their location to Indonesian authorities who can bring them to justice through their judicial system. We will cooperate. We will help with reconnaissance, surveillance, or whatever other means are necessary to assist Indonesia in its quest for justice on its own soil. But we will not not lash back at the terrorists like an angry child.

"I know some of you will be disappointed by this decision. I know many of you were hoping we would bloody their noses. I have those same feelings of anger, of fury at the cheapness with which they view human life. But striking back simply endorses their low value of life. In this country we *treasure* life. Every life. If a life is taken, revenge is not the response. Justice is. Justice based on cool evaluation, not instantaneous rage.

"We need to apply the same coolness to international events, to bring to the problem the same detached objectivity, in spite of the emotions raging inside urging us to strike. Civilization requires that of us, if we ever hope to progress. Because ultimately, progress is measured to some extent by our ability to rise above our instincts, our emotions, and our selfish desires, and to put justice, truth, and goodness in their place. Now is the time to begin to do that, and that is the message this decision will send to the world—that America is different. We base our decisions on justice, on ideals, not on emotions."

Manchester blinked and pursed his lips. He stared at the camera with his huge, soft, but piercing blue eyes. "Thank you for your attention. If you have time, think of the families of the murdered sailors. Pray for their loved ones and work with me to make this country greater than it already is. Good night." The picture faded.

The news anchor sat in his studio stunned, momentarily at a loss for words.

The Speaker was not. "Robin, get my car," he said softly but with double the usual intensity. "I'm going to the White House *right now*. He's finally flipped. That was the biggest load of bullshit I've ever heard." He looked at his staff. "You guys look like you've been watching a silent movie and they got the reels mixed up. Did that make any sense to anyone here?"

No one spoke. Rhonda, the historian with the squarish wire rims, finally answered. "It wasn't exactly incoherent. It was actually a good speech if you agree . . ." She saw the Speaker's furious countenance and changed direction.

Grazio interjected, trying to rescue her, "I know what he was trying to say—it's just incredible to me that he said it. Talk about encouraging terrorism. Smoke a bunch of Americans and we'll let Indonesia put you on trial?

They must be curled up in balls laughing right now, wherever they are. . . .''

"We know exactly where they are," the Speaker said. "They found them about three hours ago."

"Are you kidding?" Dillon asked, concerned.

"You think Manchester would make a speech like that and not be aware of the latest intelligence? Now not only does *he* know it, but the *whole world* knows it, because he just told them we know where they are! He just sabotaged our effort to catch them." He walked to the door of the office and jerked his suit coat off the hangar. He added his heavy blue-wool overcoat and strode quickly to the doorway. He stopped and turned around. The six staff members in his office watched him, curious. They had never seen him so focused. "I want a solution to this. I want a way around this. Find it," he said as he walked out.

Dillon rubbed his eyes and ran his hands through his hair, which flopped back down to its usual carefully unkempt look. None of the other staff members spoke.

Grazio finally spoke. "I've never seen the Speaker so pissed."

"I think the President has lost it," Rhonda said.

Dillon stood up and looked at them. "It's not the Speaker, and it's not the President, it's the *system*. One person decides whether we do anything about it or whether we don't. If we have a president who doesn't *feel* like taking action, then we're the laughingstock of the entire world. If he feels like taking action, then Congress attacks him for taking action, and we're still the laughingstock of the world." He challenged his fellow staffers. "Aren't you sick of everyone passing the buck in Washington? Are we ever going to do anything that matters?" He waited for a response from someone, but most avoided his gaze. "If I *can't* make this thing come out right, I'll quit. Whatever it takes to get those murderers, I'm going to find a way." Dillon grabbed his coat off of the back of his chair and put it on roughly. His tie was askew and he didn't seem to care. He headed quickly toward the door.

"Like what?" Rhonda asked, stopping him.

"I have no idea, but you'd better start looking too. If we don't find something creative, they're going to get away with it. You can count on that. If we're waiting for Indonesia to fix this for us, then we deserve whatever we get." Dillon turned and walked out of the room, slamming the door behind him.

♛

"I'm here to see the President," Stanbridge explained to the Chief of Staff.

"I'm sure he can meet with you tomorrow, Mr. Speaker. This is unscheduled."

"It sure is unscheduled. My reaction to that stupid speech was unscheduled. His disclosure of secret information was also unscheduled, at least I hope it was." He looked at Van den Bosch coldly. "If I'd known what he was going to say, I would have scheduled my reaction so it fit into the President's calendar. But as it is," he said, shrugging, "I'll have to see him now. You should be starting to get all the irate calls, and I want to see him *now*. Just him. Not you, not six other sycophants. Just him and me."

"I resent your insin—"

"Shut up. I don't give a shit what you resent. Are you going to get him, or am I going to?"

"I'll tell him you're here."

"If he doesn't already know I'm here, somebody isn't doing his job. *Get him.*"

Van den Bosch realized he had failed to deflect the Speaker.

Stanbridge paced in the foyer with his coat on for fifteen minutes, his anger building like superheated steam. The Chief of Staff returned. "He will see you in the Oval Office."

"Ah, formal tonight, are we?" he said, glancing at his

watch. He walked directly to the office and opened the door. Manchester was sitting at the desk reading, his glasses low on his nose. He looked up and saw Stanbridge. "Welcome, John. What an unexpected surprise."

"Cut the crap, Mr. President," Stanbridge said, crossing to stand in front of the desk. "I want you to tell me to my face what you were thinking about in making that speech. You may have derailed U.S. foreign policy for the indefinite future, and I for one want an explanation unfiltered by your staff, or CNN, or anyone else."

Manchester looked at his Chief of Staff. "Thanks, Arlan. See you in the morning."

"Good night, sir," said Van den Bosch, backing out with his eyebrows raised, one last chance for the President to enlist his services. The President shook his head subtly. The door closed behind Stanbridge.

President Manchester spoke first. "Why do you say that?"

The Speaker breathed deeply and sat on the couch. "You've given terrorists a license to kill Americans abroad, and the worst that can happen to them is they'll be pursued by the police of some Third World country."

"Indonesia is not a Third World country."

"Of course it is. Who are you kidding?"

"They have a very vibrant economy, one of the Asian Tigers."

"Spare me the marketing brochure. If you think the Indonesian police have any hope of catching these murderers and bringing them to justice, you're sorely mistaken."

Manchester smiled without humor. "I think it is very likely. We'll be giving them intelligence support—in fact, we already know where the terrorists are."

"I know. I got the brief. Some island. Thanks to your little speech, the terrorists know we know where they are too."

Manchester frowned, but wasn't surprised. He went on,

"Yes, some island. On Indonesian soil, subject to Indonesian law."

"Right." Stanbridge stood up and walked around the room, the tail of his coat flapping behind him, sweat forming on his forehead. "Why didn't you send in the Marines who are right there? We know where they are—why not go in and *get* them?"

Manchester stood up, energized. "And do what? Kill them? Murder *them*? We'd make martyrs of them and thousands would be lining up to take their places. It just continues the cycle of violence."

Stanbridge had never liked Manchester. He was too clever by half, too willing to find a complex solution when a simple one would do, just to make a point. "Where'd you get this cycle of violence . . . stuff?"

"Seems to be an accurate reflection of what it is," Manchester said, feeling suddenly warm and rolling up the sleeves of his flannel shirt.

"That it?" Stanbridge asked, incredulous. "That the only reason?"

"Pretty much."

"No political considerations?"

Manchester shook his head. "No. All those considerations seemed to point in the opposite direction. I know everyone will disagree, probably even the public. But I need to do what is *right*."

Since when? Stanbridge thought. He couldn't stand it. "How is it *right* to let people murder Americans?"

"We're not letting them murder Americans. Indonesia will handle it through their system."

Stanbridge shook his head vigorously, "You can't dodge this. As far as the world is concerned, we are letting them murder Americans. No other conclusion to draw."

"I'm tired of this. Did you have anything else to say?"

"Mr. President, you're basically just afraid, aren't you?"

Manchester closed his eyes and held them closed. "Mr.

Speaker, I'm trying to control my temper. I really don't need to sit here and be insulted by you."

"Well, you need to be insulted by somebody, Mr. President. You need to appreciate the seriousness of this situation. You seem to be taking this very lightly. I think it's because basically you're a coward."

"I really doubt that our definitions of courage are the same, Mr. Speaker. Yours seem to reside in your knee-jerk conservative response to everything. Frankly, I'm tired of it. This country needs a new response, and that's what I'm giving them."

"You're not giving them anything," the Speaker said. "What you're doing is worrying about yourself, trying to become some kind of historical figure."

"Are you done?"

"I want to ask you a question," Stanbridge said, crossing to stand directly in front of the desk.

"What?"

Stanbridge leaned forward, put his hands on the desk, and spoke softly. "Will you give me a straight answer?"

"What's the question?"

"Will you give me a straight answer or not?"

Manchester pursed his lips. "Say what you have to say."

Stanbridge narrowed his eyes and pointed to Manchester's chest, "In your heart, way down there where the rest of us can't see"—he paused and looked into Manchester's eyes—"are you a pacifist?"

"What kind of a question is that?" Manchester said suddenly, loudly.

"A direct one. Straight. What's the answer?"

"I'm not going to subject myself to cross-examination by you at eleven P.M. I have other things to do. If you want to discuss this further, I am willing," Manchester said, color coming to his cheeks. "But if you only want to grandstand, or insult me, I've got better things to do."

"What's the answer?" Stanbridge said quietly, pressing.

"Is that it? You came over here for *that*?"

"No. I came over to find out why the President of the United States, whose sworn duty, whose obligation, it is to defend the citizens of this country, has chosen not to do that. I want to know why you as Commander in Chief aren't lining up the forces necessary to go after the murderers who attacked a U.S.-flagged vessel, killed its crew and sank—"

"I know what happened. You don't have to—"

"Do you really? Do you know they shot each one of them in the head like a dog? Do you know they booby-trapped the ship and set the mines so our SEALs had just time enough to get aboard, and almost killed them too? You realize they have flipped you off and you're just walking away?"

"I don't believe in returning killing for killing. It doesn't accomplish anything."

"War doesn't accomplish anything? World War Two didn't accomplish anything?"

"That's a different thing entire—"

"Are you saying killing someone who is the enemy of your country never accomplishes anything?"

"No, that's not what I said. I said this wouldn't accomplish anything."

Stanbridge stared at him. He stood near the couch and adjusted his coat. "I'm wasting my time. Is that it? You've made up your mind?"

Manchester sighed heavily. "That's all I have to say to you. Now if you'll excuse me—"

"This isn't over, Mr. President. I'm going to take this to the people." Stanbridge looked around the office, as if measuring the walls for his paintings. "This is the biggest mistake of your presidency. It may be fatal."

"Foreign affairs and the military are areas exclusive to the president and his administration. What are you going to do? Operate the War Powers Resolution backward? Say that if Congress decides to send troops, the president has to?" He grinned slightly. "Sorry, but it doesn't work that way. Why, I'll bet you had your staff all cranked up to accuse me of not complying with the War Powers if I sent troops without consulting you. Am I right?''

''We certainly were going to make sure you complied with the Resolution by consulting us, but we certainly also expected and hoped you were going to respond to this direct attack on this country.''

''Sorry to disappoint you, Mr. Speaker.''

Stanbridge walked to the door of the Oval Office and stood there with his back to the President. His hand rested on the door handle for ten seconds. He didn't say anything or look around at all. He pulled the door open quickly and walked out.

◣

The press and Washington insiders knew that the Speaker's limo had gone to the White House immediately after the speech. Everyone knew that Stanbridge had stayed an hour, then gone back to the Capitol, not home. There was speculation that something was up: Conflict, Power Struggle, Political Combat. It was the kind of situation that made reporters at *The Washington Post* dream of glory. The press could sense it. They reported it as they gathered information, first of disagreement between the Speaker and the President, then of a looming crisis. They all wanted to talk to Congressman Stanbridge from California. But he wasn't talking.

11

"ROBIN!" STANBRIDGE CALLED AS HE STRODE through the outer doorway to his office. "Who's here so far?"

"I think Mr. Dillon and Mr. Grazio are here, as well as a few others," she said.

"Get 'em all here."

"Sir." She hesitated. "It's almost midnight. Most of the staff has gone home."

He stopped in front of her desk and looked at her for the first time in a week. "Why haven't you?"

"Because you asked me not to," she replied.

Stanbridge hung up his coat and said to the wall, "I did?"

"Yes, sir."

"Sorry about that, but some things can't be helped." He looked at his watch, thought for a minute, then turned to her again. "All of 'em, Robin. I want everyone here in thirty minutes. If they're home asleep, wake their asses up. Order pizza—enough for everyone." He looked at his office without seeing it and spoke to Robin behind him without turning his head. "This one's got hair all over it," he said as he closed his door.

Most did arrive within half an hour, none happy to be there. They milled around, looking for coffee that no one had made, angry at whoever hadn't made it. Rhonda had assumed they would be up all night. She had gotten

116

dressed in a dark suit. Her soaking-wet hair clung to her back, leaving a large dark spot on the back of her suit coat. Others had assumed it would be a short meeting and had gotten dressed quickly in jeans and sweatshirts. They slumped in their chairs in the seventh-grade posture that went with casual dress outside of business hours. The conversations were mostly muffled complaints about being called in. There wasn't any news of a big development in the crisis, nothing that couldn't have waited until morning.

Stanbridge stood beside his desk and looked them over. "Sorry I had to ask you to come back in. I know what a pain that is. But I wanted to tell you about my conversation with the President."

They looked at each other. Great, they thought. Another chance to hear from the Speaker how witty and clever he is, how he can defeat anyone in an argument.

"We all heard the President say he wasn't going to do anything about the attack on the *Pacific Flyer*. Frankly, he caught me by surprise. I assumed we were going to have to make sure he complied with the War Powers Act. I didn't think there would be any problem with that—we would have supported him—but I was going to make sure he complied. . . ." The staff members looked at each other discreetly. Yeah, right.

"But now, everything is different. He isn't going to come to the defense of Americans who were attacked. It's . . . I don't know"—he rubbed his eyes—"unusual, it's . . . spooky."

He looked at them. "I think the President is a pacifist. Not just a dove, politically, but a genuine pacifist." He waited for his comment to sink in. The staffers looked at each other, then skeptically at him.

"I asked him straight out if he was, and he wouldn't give me an answer."

"Excuse me, sir," Rhonda said, "but what difference does that make?"

"What difference does it make?" Stanbridge looked at her as if she had a growth on her forehead. "Rhonda, you ever hear that saying that there's no such thing as a stupid question?''

''Yes, sir.''

''That is one of the stupidest questions I've ever heard. You don't think it would matter if the President was a pacifist? The Commander in Chief of the largest armed forces in the world, unwilling *ever* to use them, to order them to do what they're trained to do? You don't see a problem there?''

Rhonda nodded slowly, yearning for his attention to be directed somewhere else.

''Well, I wanted you to be here,'' he said in a low voice, ''because I need ideas on what we can do about this. The President refuses to act. So is that it? End of story? Are all American ships now subject to attack and murder and sinking? Is that the message we're going to send? We need an alternative. *Fast*. I don't want this thing to get stale—''

Dillon stood up suddenly and walked toward the Speaker. Dillon's approach was so unexpected and inappropriate that the Speaker stopped talking and stared.

''I think I have the answer, Mr. Speaker,'' Dillon said quietly.

''What?''

''The alternative. What we can do.''

''What are you talking about?''

''When you went over to see the President, I started looking, like you asked me to. Since the President is always the one who acts, we all assume he's the only one who *can* act. But if he isn't going to do anything about it, the question is, can anyone else do anything about it?'' Dillon put his hands in his pockets and turned to face the rest of the staff, who were looking at one another in amazement at Dillon's nerve.

''Well,'' the Speaker said, folding his arms defensively. ''Then by all means, share this insight with us.''

''Since the President won't act, then we should act without him.''

The Speaker studied his face for humor, but saw none. "What are you talking about? Get to the *point*."

Dillon nodded understandingly. "Why not issue a Letter of Marque and Reprisal?"

The Speaker frowned. The rest of the staff looked puzzled.

Dillon continued, "Article one, Section eight of the Constitution, Mr. Speaker. It's in the exclusive powers of Congress. The power to declare war, and grant Letters of Marque and Reprisal . . . It's the power to issue a letter, a commission—to an armed merchant ship to attack an enemy's ships. It's legalized piracy." His blue eyes burned. "It's nothing less than the power of Congress to conduct private limited war."

The Speaker stared at Dillon uncomprehendingly, then with stunned appreciation. Stanbridge began in a low intense tone, "Did you do any research to find out if it's still possible?"

Dillon nodded slowly. "I didn't finish, but nothing so far that says you couldn't do it."

The Speaker put his hand on the top of his head, as if to hold it on. He paused, then spoke quickly. "I want you to do the best research job you can on this clause. Every case that's cited it, every article that's mentioned it, every history book that's mentioned it, the Constitutional Convention's discussion of it, *everything*. Rhonda," he said, looking at her, "I want all the history you can find about Letters of Marque and Reprisal." He was energized. He began pacing. "You need to become *the* expert in twelve hours. Split up the research—get everybody here working on it. Within twelve hours, I want to know everything there is to know about it." He paused and looked at their faces. Some were eager and understood the implications; others were still stupid from sleep. "If things are as I suspect, I'm going to keep the House in session all night tomorrow night." He looked at his watch. "Actually, tonight." It was 1:00 A.M. "Let's get going."

The staff started to stand. Grazio was frowning. "If I

might ask the second stupid question of the night, Mr. Speaker, where the hell are we going to find an armed merchant ship to attack these terrorists?''

The Speaker nodded, his countenance clouding slightly. ''That's one of the things we'll need to solve. But I'll tell you what, Mr. Grazio, if Dillon is right, and it's still in effect—dormant but in effect—then it's our *ticket.*'' He breathed deeply and looked at Grazio intensely. ''And the President can't stop us.'' He looked back at Dillon. ''Did you think of exactly who will receive the commission?''

''Yes, I did. I thought about that a lot.'' Dillon scratched his head. ''At first I thought maybe a CIA armed merchant ship or something like that. But then, it hit me.'' Dillon was suddenly transported back to the constitutional law seminar he had loved so much at UVA. He sat directly across from Molly and not only enjoyed her presence but disagreed with her on almost every point. She was always calling for a living Constitution, a document that changes with the times to accommodate a modern world. He found himself fighting for the traditional understanding of the Constitution and the way it was interpreted by those who wrote it. He feared that once the words in a document came to mean whatever the Supreme Court said they meant, then they could mean anything. He was about to turn the tables. ''I realized there aren't any armed merchant ships today like during the War of 1812. So the Constitution therefore must change to accommodate modern times, a living document. The only armed ships that exist anymore are Navy ships.''

The Speaker's eyes grew suddenly large; the rest of the staffers began to murmur as the implications became obvious.

Dillon continued, ''We'll issue it to the USS *Constitution* Battle Group in the Java Sea. If the President won't use them, *we* will.''

The room was full of electricity. The implications were enormous and satisfying. Stanbridge was speechless for the first time in their memories.

Rhonda spoke first. "Has such a commission ever been issued to a Navy ship before?"

"Not that I'm aware of," Dillon said.

"There's always a first time," Stanbridge said excitedly.

☙

Dillon stared at his computer screen as the legal research graphics loaded. Before baring his idea to the Speaker and the others on the staff, he had been able to do some basic research. He had felt strongly about the power to grant Letters of Marque and Reprisal because it was in the Constitution. Nothing trumps the Constitution. Not a treaty, not a law, not a state, not custom—nothing does. Only a constitutional amendment can officially change the Constitution. Sometimes interpretation can gut a concept, but that was certainly not the case here. The number of times the Supreme Court had even dealt with it was minuscule. Still, he wanted to be *sure*.

Dillon was confident that he had uncovered a strong durable weapon that Congress could use as it saw fit, both in ways in which it had been used in the past, and in newer, more creative ways, as a result of the rubber sides the Supreme Court had given to the Constitution, claiming it was a living document.

But there might be something out there that could preclude using the power as he had envisioned. If there was, he had to find it.

His fingers flew across the keyboard, accessing the cases, law review articles, and anything else that cited this provision in the Constitution. He hit more and more wrong keys as he pushed himself. Sweat was beading on his forehead in a way unusual for him. He was perceived as cool, cocky. But he felt a nervousness that ran to his core as he glanced at the clock. This night could mark one of the most dramatic changes in this century's U.S. foreign policy. If he was right. Being wrong would not be simply a question of preparing a memorandum that proved to be embarrassing. This was the kind of thing that could end careers. Not only his, but the Speaker's, and that of anybody else who signed on.

☙

Pinkie sat down in the dirty-shirt wardroom, the forward wardroom on the 03 level of the USS *Constitution* where the air wing ate, and took the food off his tray. He unzipped the leather flight jacket festooned with patches of the squadrons he had been in and ships he had been on as an intelligence officer. Still, he had never actually flown in a Navy plane other than the COD, the Carrier Onboard Delivery plane, the ugly bugsmasher that carried parts and people back and forth from shore. He had shown the requisite amount of ingenuity, though, by getting hold of a leather flight jacket he wasn't entitled to.

Lunch was the usual fare. Lasagna, corn, bread, milk; starch, carbohydrates, and fat. If they had sailed from a port less than ten days ago, there might have been some semblance of a salad or fresh vegetable or fruit, but not here. They were a month out of port with no likelihood of a port call anytime soon. At least not until the latest crisis was over, the latest call for the Great American Aircraft Carrier to steam around angrily and convert jet fuel into noise.

As the air wing intelligence officer, he knew what many on the ship didn't. They had located the terrorists on an island and were about to send SEALs ashore to determine their strength and composition. The sticky part was that they were going ashore on an island that was Indonesian territory, and they had received specific instructions from Indonesia not to overfly their land. He chuckled to himself as he cut into his lasagna. They didn't say don't *walk* over their country, they just said don't *fly* over it.

Since the first contact, the admiral had changed his plan. He realized he needed hard information, and the only way to get it was to do overhead reconnaissance. But even that wasn't good enough. They needed to put some eyeballs on the problem, as the admiral said. The admiral had asked for permission from Washington, and much to his surprise, it had been granted.

Pinkie had been as confused as everyone else on the admiral's staff and others in the know when they had heard the President's speech on CNN. Probably for public consumption, like Eisenhower after Francis Gary Powers was shot down in his U-2, spying on the Soviet Union. Deny it. The USS *Constitution* hadn't been ordered out of the area. The admiral was going to be ready, even if it meant fudging the rules a little.

Caskey and Messer strolled over carrying their trays and sat down across from Pinkie.

"They got you on that special TARPS mission?" Pinkie asked.

"Yeah. I was going to do another challenging air intercept hop this afternoon, but some things take priority." He looked at Pinkie. "What'd you think of the President's speech?"

"I don't know," Pinkie said, his freckles suddenly becoming more pronounced. "If he meant it, he's more naive than I thought. If he didn't mean it, and we're about to go whack them, that'd be cool 'cause we'll surprise them, but everyone will accuse him of being a plain old liar, which is uncool."

"Exactly what I thought. I don't get it. Let them attack a U.S.-flagged vessel, murder the crew, scuttle the ship, kill a shipmate, and let Indonesia take *criminal* action against them? I'll bet the Indonesians can't even get them off that island. They have a military, but not much of one." He tried to take a bite of food before finishing his thought, and spoke with a full cheek. "I'll bet they're still there a year from now if the President's serious."

Pinkie leaned forward to MC. "We're sending SEALs ashore tonight."

Caskey stopped eating and looked around. No one else was listening. "Are you kidding me? On whose authority?"

"Admiral's."

"Did he hear the President's speech?"

"Yep. Whole staff did."

"And he's still sending the SEALs ashore? Didn't they cancel the authorization to do that?"

"Nope. At least not yet. And they sure haven't given him orders to withdraw from the area. The admiral figures the speech is for public consumption only, and we're going to spank 'em."

"What if he's wrong?"

"I guess we'll find out. If the SEALs get caught ashore, it could be ugly," Pinkie said, drinking the last of his coffee. "But if they don't get caught, we may go finish the job tomorrow."

🖙

Dillon rubbed his tired eyes and looked at the pile of printed cases, law review articles, and books on his desk. He was nearly done with his research on the Letters of Marque and Reprisal. The adrenaline came again every time he thought about it. Every time he imagined himself telling the Speaker it was still intact, that he was clear to go ahead with it, clear to stand the entire country, or the world, on its head. This wasn't politics, it was *action*. He had never felt so galvanized in his life.

Congress could issue Letters of Marque and Reprisal, and no one could say they couldn't. Unused for almost two centuries, but still there, enshrined in the Constitution, protected from attack by the difficult requirements of amending it. Congress could start its own little private war, and *no one* could stop it.

Dillon looked at himself in the reflection of the photo on his desk. It was a picture of his study group from law school, the best friends he had ever had. It had all four of them with their arms around each other at their graduation on the Lawn of the University of Virginia. Dillon, Molly, Bobby, and Erin. Happiest day of his life. The world was theirs to conquer. They had all graded onto the

Law Review, giving them the ticket to the most prestigious law jobs in the country. Any firm, any clerkship with any judge, any public interest job defending whales, trees, or criminals, any private firm. Whatever they wanted.

Dillon thought of himself as being on top of the tallest hill. Capitol Hill, working for the Speaker of the House. He had just discovered a power in the Constitution that could change the entire way the government operated, that could give Congress a power it didn't realize it had anymore. It was intoxicating and he loved it, but he had a gnawing feeling he was missing something.

12

ROBIN HATED THIS PART—WHEN HER BOSS DID SOME-
thing controversial and it caused ten to twenty times the
usual interest from the press. He had a press secretary and
a private public relations consultant—not many people
knew that—but she had to take the calls. And every newspaper reporter and television reporter had this number.
There was no hope of answering all the calls. None. She
had learned to deal with these crises, but she had never
seen anything like *this*. Never. Her boss hadn't been the
Speaker that long, but this was ridiculous. She had
stopped hanging up the phone. She just depressed the button and answered it again. There was always someone on
it. And they all wanted to talk to the Speaker, to ask him
why he was keeping the House in session on Friday night,
knowing they would have to work all night. The press
had gotten wind of it before most of the members of the
House. And the Speaker wasn't taking any calls. Not until
his staff meeting was done; they were preparing for the
press conference that was scheduled for . . . she looked at
her clock . . . one hour from now. Ten-thirty East Coast
time, just in time for the morning news shows on the West
Coast to pick it up live as their lead-in.

Inside his office, Congressman Stanbridge from the
Forty-ninth District in San Diego was in a beatified state.
The tension in the office was audible, a humming of hu-
man energy: excitement and fear, jubilation and an in-

stinctive desire to run for cover—or to change one's name.

"Robin!" he yelled through the closed door.

She put a call down on hold without even determining who was on the line, and rushed into his office. "Yes, sir."

"I want you to change the location of the press conference. I want it to be in the Rotunda, right under the Dome. In the center of congressional history," he said, smiling at how appropriate that would be.

"You've never had one there, sir," she said, puzzled.

"I know that, Robin. I know that."

"But the press has never set up there."

"I guess the ones who can will be the ones who get this story."

"Should I tell them anything else?" she asked, hoping for some other morsel to offer the inquisitive press other than that the Speaker would be holding a press conference at 10:30 about a "major development."

"Nope. Keep them guessing. Has Pete Peterson called yet?" he asked, hoping the Senate Majority Leader was still on his side. Peterson hadn't been very receptive to the idea initially, but said he would consider it. Stanbridge was counting on him to get the Democrats to agree to a debating schedule that would let them consider it tonight. Peterson said they knew their best chance to defeat it was tonight, when it was new and uncomfortable to everyone.

Stanbridge looked at those staff members gathered again, every one of whom had been up all night and showed it.

Dillon stood next to him, assuming a position of leadership without being asked. The Speaker did not object. "Anybody else have anything before I ask Mr. Dillon to give us the results of his research?"

No one spoke. "Okay, Jim?" the Speaker said.

Dillon looked at the staff and tried to force his heart back down his throat. He answered slowly. "There isn't anything out there in American law, or constitutional law, or cases, and not much in law reviews, that says we can't do this. It's really never been argued, because nobody has ever thought of it.''

The Speaker hesitated and looked at the ceiling. He glanced at his watch, measuring the time between now and his press conference, when he would announce this to the entire world. He could not afford to be wrong. ''Do you realize the implications?''

''Yes.''

''It could be the end of me politically.'' He turned his head quickly to Dillon. ''You understand that?''

''Yes, I do.''

''We can't be wrong.'' He looked as serious as Dillon had ever seen him. ''You willing to take that risk?''

''Mr. Speaker, the attack on the *Pacific Flyer* has already meant the death of twenty-six Americans. They're not just politically dead, they're *really* dead. I want to do whatever we can to get these guys. If that means taking a position that is marginal in someone's eyes, then fine. But I don't think it's marginal.''

''So, the bottom line, Mr. Dillon, is that there is nothing that says we can't do this?''

Dillon shook his head slowly. ''Nothing.''

Stanbridge lowered his voice. ''Not only could this mean a new era for Congress, it could mean the end of this President.''

☙

Stanbridge walked into the Rotunda, the large circular room underneath the dome of the Capitol building. The center of power in Washington, or at least the center of the power not resident in the White House. The cameras whirred and clicked as Stanbridge walked to the small, hurriedly constructed wooden platform in front of a huge painting of General George Washington resigning his commission to Congress as Commander in Chief of the Army. The reporters hurled questions at him, annoyed at not having been able to find out what this was all about.

He paused behind the mountain of microphones and phalanx of reporters without saying anything, a grave but
confident look on his face. Standing slightly above them
on the platform made him look taller, and he kept the
microphones low, near the middle of his chest instead of
in front of his mouth so that he towered above them in
any picture. He waited until the hum died down. CNN
and all the major broadcast networks were carrying the
press conference live. He stepped to the microphone and
raised his hand.

"Good morning. Before I open for questions, I thought
I would tell you what this is all about. Otherwise you
wouldn't know what questions to ask." There was a political chuckle, meaning no one thought it was truly funny.

"As you have all heard, the President has decided not
to pursue the terrorists who killed innocent Americans
aboard an American-flagged vessel carrying American
goods to a country that is our trading partner." He stared
coldly into the cameras. "I am not going to let it rest
there. My staff and I have been up all night since then,
evaluating our options. I will be calling on the House, and
I have word from my counterpart in the Senate that he
will do likewise, to *intervene*." He paused, looking at
them. "To do what the President is afraid to do." He
waited until the murmur died down. "I will be asking the
House and the Senate to authorize direct action through
the issuance of a Letter of Reprisal. As I'm sure you
know, the Constitution of the United States authorizes just
such a Letter to be issued by Congress in Article one,
Section eight. I'm also sure, though, that you're not inti-
mately familiar with it, because it hasn't been used since
the War of 1812. Until now . . ."

He tried to go on but the clamor of shocked reporters
was too much. He waited and watched the tumult. Finally
he continued. "If the . . . if the President won't do what
he is required to do, to protect citizens and the property
of citizens, then we will." He held up his hand as the
reporters fought to get their questions out. "In due time,"

he said calmly. "In due time. Frankly, we were hoping it wouldn't come to this. We expected the President to take the appropriate steps, especially in light of the presence of the U.S. battle group already there. But we were wrong. Therefore, Congress will be in session until this is done. The Rules Committee is meeting right now in special session to consider a rule to allow this to be heard and passed tonight. I expect we'll be here all night, but we're prepared to do that. I'm sure my fellow members of Congress will have questions, but we've done the research necessary to answer those questions quickly. Now, if there are any . . ."

The reporters cut him off before he finished his sentence. "Is this legal?" asked the correspondent from *Newsweek*.

"Absolutely," responded the Speaker in the first of many answers. He knew there would be intense interest but had underestimated the firestorm his announcement would generate. Reporters were on cellular phones, the cameras were rolling, and the networks showed no intention of cutting away to their regular programming.

The questions came at him like baseballs from a runaway pitching machine, and equally hard. The frustration the reporters felt at not being able to prepare questions on the topic, and their ignorance of the subject matter, flustered them. One finally asked about the Constitution, and why, if the action was legal, no one had taken it recently. Stanbridge told him exactly what he thought, that no one had done it because no one had thought of it.

☙

Word spread quickly through the House and Senate and the rest of Washington. In the offices of the Counsel to the President, Molly Vaughan stared at the television in disbelief. The Speaker was out of his mind. Usurpation. Betrayal. A politician run amok. Her anger rose as she thought of Jim Dillon working away on something he wouldn't talk about. She felt sick.

Dillon watched the small television he kept on the top of his desk. The newspeople had been caught off guard. That was rare. They usually had some idea of what was coming. Not this time. Even if they had heard rumors, they wouldn't have had any idea what it was about. Nobody did. When Dillon had raised the idea with others on the staff, he hadn't found one person who even knew what a Letter of Marque and Reprisal was, let alone that it was a still existing constitutional power of Congress. Dillon was so nervous his hands were shaking. The Speaker had accepted his research. He had notified Congress that they were going to be in session all night if necessary to debate and vote on issuing a Letter to strike against the terrorists. Stanbridge made it sound as routine as he could, but everyone involved—and most who weren't—saw the implications of Congress being able to conduct a private war without the President, and in fact in direct conflict with the President. Most doubted that the Constitution said it was possible, but no one knew enough to say it didn't.

Even the constitutional law professors whom the reporters always called, who were always happily on standby to contribute their remarks in low, controlled, knowing tones, were baffled. Most had never given ten minutes' thought to the clause they were being asked about. Some tried to bluff, but most said frankly that they were surprised, didn't know the history of the clause, and would have to "look into it" before commenting further. Dillon turned off the television and put it away.

He waited with sweaty palms for the phone call. For someone to call and tell him about some case or treaty or whatever it was that he had missed that proved him wrong, dead wrong. But no calls came.

He glanced up at the clock. 11:00 A.M. He drew a deep breath and read the copy of the Letter of Marque and Reprisal from 1812 that he had found in the Library of Congress and put it next to his notepad. He began copying the language and unconsciously updating it. "To all those who shall see these presents, Greetings. BE IT KNOWN, That in pursuance of an Act of Congress, passed on the . . ." Stanbridge had asked him to have a draft ready for the afternoon to be distributed to the other members.

Suddenly Dillon's heart froze. He stared at the bottom of the 1812 Letter of Marque and Reprisal. How could he not have noticed it before? How could he have done all that research and never wondered how the Letter actually worked? He stared at the bottom of the Letter. It was signed by James Madison. Dillon breathed deeply as he tried to think his way around it. Manchester would *never* sign it. That was the whole point. He sat back and looked at the ceiling and closed his eyes. Did the President have to sign it, or was that just window dressing? His heart pounded. He could feel his pulse in his fingertips. He imagined the next press conference that the Speaker would have to give: "Just kidding about that Letter thing. Turns out the President would have to sign it, and we know he isn't inclined to do that, so we'll be meeting later in the week to discuss options of monitoring the Indonesian criminal investigation. . . ." Dillon filled his lungs with as much oxygen as he could hold so he wouldn't pass out.

❧

"I didn't think you'd come," he said as Molly stepped into the apartment.

"Why wouldn't I?" she asked warmly.

"Because of the Speaker's press conference, and the debate," he said as he leaned over to kiss her on the cheek.

He could feel her coolness. "They're just going to make fools of themselves," she said, shrugging off her coat and throwing it into a chair.

He held his tongue and studied her. Why now? Why did this thing have to happen now, just when she had started warming to him and looking at him differently?

"Was it your idea?" Her tone was direct and clinical.

"Think we should talk about it? I mean with you at the White—"

"Maybe I can talk some sense into your head so you can stop this lunacy before you commit professional suicide." Her cheeks were red.

He changed the subject. "I thought I'd fix one of our old student dinners, carbonara. That be okay?"

"Don't try and avoid the subject," she replied quickly. "Come on, Jim. You start a constitutional crisis and you're worried about carbonara? What have you been doing all day? I was researching this stupid Letter of Marque and Reprisal, and whether you can still use it."

"Look," he said, "I've got to be back on the Hill in an hour or so. Let's just eat. Okay?"

She relaxed slightly. "I've got to get back too. To undo whatever you're going to do next."

She watched him without a word as he finished preparing dinner. He set two places at the small kitchen table. In his hurry, he spilled water on the table when filling her glass. Finally, he pointed to the chair, and they sat down together.

They started eating without a word.

"You can't do it, you know," she said, halfway through the silent meal.

He rolled the spaghetti noodles onto his fork with a large spoon, catching some of the chopped bacon inside. His stomach jumped. Oh, no. He tried to look unconcerned. "Why not?"

"Because we don't do it anymore."

"Doesn't mean we can't."

"But there's a *reason* we don't," she said somewhat smugly.

Dillon felt his stomach tighten more, "Like what?"

"That was a power that used to exist. It doesn't anymore. It is a *former* power."

"Why do you say that?"

"Jim, it's well known." She looked around the room. "Do you have a law dictionary?"

"Not here."

"Look up *Letters of Marque*. It says it is 'A power *formerly* granted.' We agreed not to do it anymore. We formally agreed. In a *treaty*. The Declaration of Paris."

He put his fork down. "Did you research it?"

"A little. The Declaration was signed in 1856. All the major powers agreed not to use it anymore. We can't do it, Jim." She drank from her coffee cup and watched him. He didn't show any emotion. She was disappointed. It was why she had come—to tell him and watch his face. She had hoped to handle it better, but had finally just blurted out the facts. She had been torn between keeping him from driving off the political cliff and showing him up because she loved to compete with him. He was clearly caught off guard, but she had expected more of a response.

"Is that it?" he said finally.

"Is that what?"

"Is that the only reason we can't do it?"

"No, there are others, but that's good enough. We promised the whole world we wouldn't. It would look pretty foolish to do it anyway, wouldn't it?"

Dillon got up and opened the refrigerator. He took out the milk and poured a glass. He held it out to her and raised his eyebrows. She wrinkled her nose. He put the milk carton back. He sat down and drank deeply from the cold milk. He exhaled, and gazed intently into her eyes. "We didn't sign the Declaration of Paris."

"What do you mean, we didn't sign it?"

"We didn't sign it. I don't know how else to say it."

"But the law dictionary says . . ."

"They're wrong. I saw that too. About had a heart attack, because it was after I'd done most of my research. It sure seems to say we gave that power away. But I went and found the actual treaty—the Declaration of Paris— and we didn't sign it, because of this and a few other things. The kicker is, though," he said, moving closer to her, perhaps to convince her, "that when the Civil War broke out, the Europeans suddenly thought they should agree to the restrictions we wanted on Letters. We said okay, but wanted to exclude the Civil War. They wouldn't do it," he said, throwing up his arms in apparent disgust over the diplomatic discussions of a century ago, "so the thing was never signed by the United States."

"How can that be?" she asked, truly puzzled, confused.

"Simple. We never agreed. Even if we had, I'm not sure it would have mattered. You know con law. Treaties can't trump the Constitution. We can't sign a treaty with France agreeing to disregard the First Amendment. . . ."

She leaned forward against the table and lowered her voice, as if talking to someone who was truly ignorant. "You mean you really think Congress can do this?"

He nodded and finished his noodles.

She took advantage of the silence to make her point stronger. "But even if we haven't agreed in a treaty, it's ancient history. Those kinds of ships don't even exist anymore."

"We're going to do it differently."

"How?"

He glanced up and considered whether to tell her. "The Letter is going to the USS *Constitution* Battle Group, not a private ship."

She sat back with her mouth open slightly and tried to absorb what he had said. It was impossible. It was one thing to imply that Congress could commission an armed merchant vessel and conduct some mischief, but to send a Letter to a U.S. Navy aircraft carrier? "That's *impossible*."

"Not impossible."

"How can you do that? There isn't one thing in the Constitution that even *implies* Congress has that power." She stood and paced around the table, breathing harder than she would have liked as the implications of a Navy battle group under the control of Congress alone sank in. "It would be *unconstitutional*."

"Says who?" Dillon replied, his voice raised slightly.

"Whoever looks at it will come to that conclusion. They *have* to."

"No, they don't. There's precedent for using the Letter of Marque or Reprisal with government forces."

"Where?"

"In due time. You'll see it in due time."

She sat down again, agitated. "You think this is a game? You come up with some clever idea to jerk the President around to get him to do what you want?"

"No. It's no game," he said. "The President chose what he wanted to do, or *not* do, and now he has to live with the consequences. This isn't some ploy to get the President to act, it's Congress acting legally when the President won't."

"But nobody can read that into the Constitution! It's not there," she said, her voice rising involuntarily.

"Yes, it is. Plus," he added with an edge to his tone, "you've always liked the liberal scholars and judges, the ones who find new rights in the Constitution all the time. Right?"

"What are you talking about?" she said, anger growing.

"You *love* constitutional law when it's going your way, when Earl Warren and William O. Douglas are discovering new rights that aren't even remotely in the document, all in the name of privacy and individual rights. Well, it's your bed. Now you're gonna have to sleep in it. They always said it's a 'living document.' It has to change to accommodate more modern times. Right? Fine. So be it. Since it's a living document, these are the times to which it must adapt and this is what it means. We don't have armed merchant vessels anymore. Assigning a Letter of Reprisal to an unarmed merchant ship would be futile. Obviously, the only ship that could receive such a letter today is an armed ship, and the only armed ships are Navy ships." He finished his sentence more loudly than he meant to.

She looked at him as if she were seeing a complete stranger. "I never figured you for someone who was *dishonest*. I never thought I'd see the day when you, of all people, would be saying things so blatantly wrong that you couldn't look at yourself in the mirror." Her words were filled with disappointment. She breathed in quickly. "President of the Christian Law Students Association, encourager of honesty, ethics, character—the one who always used to say: 'Do whatever is *right,* and let the chips fall where they may—you have to live with yourself.' "

She smiled. "It's one of the reasons I liked you then. I thought you were a person of incredible integrity. I didn't always agree with you, but you were always trying to find the truth, to make things better. You made life exciting. For a while recently, I thought you still might." She shook her head sadly. "I guess not anymore. You're the one who was always calling the Supreme Court dishonest for coming up with interpretations that you said were ridiculous. Driven by policy, you said. That was you, wasn't it? That was . . ."

"What are you getting at, Molly? You used to go to those meetings. You believed the same things. You still do, I'll bet. You said you didn't want to work for a big law firm because you were *sure* they'd make you compromise your principles or your"—he groped for the right word—"righteousness." He paused. "You end up working for the President, the king of all compromise, a man with *no* principles—"

"How can you say that? How is it 'no principles' to choose not to enter the cycle of violence—"

"*Spare* me the cycle of violence. The only reason he doesn't want to do anything is because he is beholden to the Chinese Indonesian investors who bought a bank in his hometown in Connecticut. . . ." He watched her face. "Didn't know that, did you?" he asked pointedly.

"No," she said defensively.

"How can you argue how right he is and not even appreciate he may have been bought?"

"The Speaker wants to run off half-cocked because the precious shipyard that built the ship is in San Diego, and the owner of the shipping line is a contributor to his—"

"What a crock!" Dillon exclaimed. "He wanted to stop, to offer peace, but he couldn't. The President has an obligation to protect the citizens and property of the United States. He is the Commander in Chief, and has a duty—"

"That's right! *He* is the Commander in Chief, *not* the Speaker, *not* the Senate, not the whole Congress put together. They don't have the power. If they try to exercise it, it is usurpation! It's like a . . . a . . . coup!"

Dillon found himself breathing as hard as he did when he ran in the morning. His heart was beating furiously. He realized they had been shouting. He watched Molly. He leaned back in his chair, looked at the cold food, and closed his eyes. He wondered what to say next. "Look, Molly, this thing is legit. We're not making this up. We believe—"

"It is *not* legit. It is a political move, and a violation of the Constitution. If the Speaker goes through with it, there will be consequences."

"Like what?" he asked, sitting forward quickly. "What is the President going to do?"

"You'll find out soon enough." She stood and looked around for her coat.

"Is that it? Is that how we're going to leave it?" he said, following her to the front door.

She turned to look at him as she pulled on her coat. "I just hope the Speaker comes to his senses before he does this. If he doesn't, it will be the largest constitutional crisis this country has ever seen." She lowered her voice and leaned toward Dillon. "I promise."

Dillon looked at her without speaking. He read the hardness in her face. He stared at her beautiful eyes, like a third grader in a stare-down contest, and blinked as she turned and walked out the door and down the stairs. He went slowly back to the kitchen and began putting the dishes on the counter. He picked up her coffee cup with the sunflower on it and tossed it into the trash under the sink.

13

THE MOON WAS BRIGHT, DIRECTLY OVER THE TWO dark boats as they raced north toward the island. The two coxswains from the Special Boat Det were highly trained in high-speed ocean transits. They worked their throttles carefully and expertly to avoid being launched off the top of a wave or stuffing their boats in the trough of the next swell as they tore through the dark ocean at thirty-five knots, well short of the maximum speed of their new NSW 30' Rigid Hull, Inflatable Boats. RHIBs were very fast SEAL insertion craft with fiberglass bottoms and inflatable sides, equipped with the newest electronics and weapons.

The lead coxswain watched his GPS position on the monitor in the dash of the RHIB as they approached the dropoff waypoint. He turned and looked over his shoulder at Lieutenant Jody Armstrong. "Six minutes," he said loudly, so as to be heard over the pounding sound of the ocean on the rigid fiberglass hull. Armstrong did not reply but passed the word and continued to scan the horizon for any signs of boats. He was particularly wary of a cigarette boat charging up unannounced.

As they approached the waypoint, the coxswain reduced his throttle and gradually slowed the RHIB to idle. Armstrong and the other three SEALs in the two swim pairs moved quickly to the F-470 Zodiac atop the engine cover, forward of the console.

The moonlight made it easy to see the SEALs silhou-etted in the other RHIB doing the same.

"Let's go," Armstrong said as they pushed the Zodiac into the water and climbed aboard. The SEAL coxswain scrambled to the fifty-five-horsepower motor and started it up immediately. The four SEALs settled into the Zodiac as the coxswain turned it away from the RHIB and toward the island. He checked his portable GPS receiver for a heading to the dropoff point two thousand yards from the beach where the SEALs would go ashore.

They wore dark jungle camouflage uniforms and jungle boots with swim fins over them and had blackened faces and dark Nomex hoods over their heads. Under their uni-forms, each wore a diveskin, a thin stretchy fabric that gave them some protection from cold, but helped primar-ily in protecting them from jellyfish, parasites, sea snakes, and sand fleas. Their dive masks were down around their necks as they awaited the signal to ease into the ocean.

As the Zodiac crossed over the satellite-designated waypoint, Armstrong gave the signal. Four SEALs rolled silently out of the boats. They pulled their masks onto their faces, ensured their weapons were safely attached, and began the two-thousand-yard swim to the shore. They kick-stroked and glided, so that nothing broke the surface except part of their heads and shoulders. The water was warm, even in the dark night hours. The surf was small and no cause for concern as they approached the shore-line.

Lieutenant Jody Armstrong felt the sand underneath his hands, which trailed slowly underneath him in the black ocean. He drifted slowly to shore, driven by the waves. He hovered there, just below the surface of the Pacific, waiting, listening, suspended in two feet of water, just off the beach. He slowly lifted his head sideways. He could see the dark island silhouetted by the moon. No lights showed from the island. Armstrong looked for the other black heads penetrating the surface of the lagoon. His swim buddy, QMC Lee, looked at him and gave him a thumbs-up.

Lee reached down to the pocket on his right thigh and pulled out a waterproof bag, opened it, and took out a monocular goggle. He slowly pulled off his mask and slipped on the battery-powered night-vision goggle. As he switched it on, his left eye immediately perceived the world in shades of green. He scanned the beach and the jungle, right and then left, for any signs of life. He looked over at Armstrong, who waited for the signal. Armstrong's eyes looked eerie to Lee because his pupils were completely dilated in the darkness.

Armstrong pulled out his own night-vision goggle and strapped it on after removing his mask. The other two did likewise. They lay in the water for three full minutes, only their heads exposed, looking for anything unusual, including dogs or birds that could warn of their approach. They removed their fins while the others provided security. When he felt secure, Armstrong began his slow crawl up the beach. The others rose to a crouch and followed him into the jungle.

Armstrong scanned the jungle and listened to the foreign sounds. His primary concern was of a sentry with a thermal imaging device. They stood and walked, their fins hanging from their left forearms, just behind their weapons. They made sure their dripping-wet MP-5 submachine guns were covering the entire beach.

They looked left and right as they walked carefully over the beach into the dense jungle. Armstrong had picked this lagoon as an easy place to go ashore where they were unlikely to be discovered. It was three miles from the small bay where the cigarette boats were docked. Between them was dense jungle. It was unlikely the terrorists had guards this far away from their base—if they had a base.

Armstrong thought of the limited information they had about the island and who might be on it. They could be walking into an anthill. It was impossible to tell what was on the island under cover of the jungle canopy.

Armstrong pulled his infrared signal laser out of his shoulder pocket and pointed it out to sea. He turned it on and signaled to the four SEALs in the other Zodiac. A few minutes later the boat scraped against the sand and the rest of the squad jumped out and pulled the boat into the tree cover.

Armstrong turned on his small red light to look at his chart and examined it for sixty seconds under his poncho with the point man, while the others provided security. Satisfied his chart coordinates matched his GPS position, he motioned to move out into the jungle. The point man walked carefully as he led the group inland for ten minutes, and turned east, parallel to the shore. Their footing was slippery and wet from the saturated ground and rotting vegetation. The air was pungent and moldy. The night sounds were less noticed than their own breathing.

Each of the SEALs kept his automatic weapon at the ready as they watched for any movement or sign of life. Although there was real danger, Armstrong and the others felt at home. Each jungle was different, but they had been trained well by the Negritos of the Philippines. They knew most of the ways you could die in a jungle. This time shouldn't be much different.

*

Admiral Billings aimed his knife at the top of the soft-boiled egg perched in front of him. Just as he prepared to strike off the top he stopped, as did the conversation of the three other usual invitees to breakfast at 0600 in his private wardroom. CNN was about to repeat its headline broadcast of the amazing story out of Washington that had been dominating the news, the Letter-of-Marque-and-Reprisal. The announcers said those words as if they were all connected together.

These newscasters had been around for a while. They had heard every word out of Washington for so long they could almost write most stories before they happened. But this one they had never heard of. Nobody had. The phones were ringing off the hooks of the few naval historians in the country who could speak intelligently on the subject. Even the constitutional law scholars still seemed confused, put off by the entire subject. They wanted to talk about Substantive Due Process, or the First Amendment, the things they had spent their whole lives trying to understand. They simply weren't prepared to discuss a topic from left field, especially without knowing the political implications.

Unlike most of the people trying to speak intelligently about the issue, Admiral Billings was a student of naval history. He thought that to be an effective naval officer, one needed to know what had come before, how battles had been lost and won, and what lessons the modern Navy could learn from the old Navy. He liked to think he had learned the lessons of Admiral Nelson, John Paul Jones, and David Farragut well enough to become an admiral.

His chief of staff ate breakfast in three minutes as he always did, eating only dry toast and drinking his morning tea. The operations officer reviewed the message board and ignored the television, having heard the same lead story every thirty minutes for the last two hours. But Beth, the admiral's intelligence officer, watched the television screen as she picked up a piece of bacon and chewed it thoughtfully.

They listened as the newscaster said what they knew, that the Speaker was holding the House in session and the Majority Leader in the Senate was doing the same thing, until they issued a Letter of Marque and Reprisal to strike back at the terrorists in the Java Sea.

When she moved on to another "expert," the admiral interrupted. "What do you make of this?"

All three looked at him and saw that he was talking to Beth.

"Never heard anything like it, sir. I don't know where they get the authority. I just . . ."

"Right out of the Constitution," said the admiral, "according to the Speaker. He was on earlier. He read the section; I don't remember what it is, but it's right there.''

Beth shook her head. ''I've just never heard of anything like it. It just doesn't feel right . . .''

''Why not?'' the admiral asked, digging for the last of the soft egg, trying not to break the shell. ''If it's in the Constitution, how can there be anything wrong with it? What I don't get is what ship they have in mind. A Letter of Marque used to go to armed merchant ships in the old days—ships that could attack with some force. Merchant ships today probably have a couple of rifles and shotguns aboard, but nothing significant. What's Congress going to do, send a couple of able-bodied seamen from a container ship after a bunch of terr—''

The Admiral stopped as a radioman came in and handed a message to the chief of staff. He read the message and turned to the admiral, his face quite serious. ''It's the report from the SEALs ashore, sir. They're in voice communication and reporting their findings.''

''Well, what did they find?''

''Nothing.''

The admiral's eyes narrowed automatically, as if keeping out smoke, as his mind began to work on the problem. ''What else did they say?''

''The bad guys had definitely been there. They found the camouflage netting in the bay where it was imaged. Only there isn't anything underneath.'' He paused as he read the message again. ''The cigarette boats are gone. Not a trace. There are signs of life around—rotten food, cartons, ammo—but no people. They say it looks like they left in the middle of the night. The SEALs are RTB.'' Returning to Base.

The admiral sat back and looked at the others at the table. ''Well,'' he said softly. ''Looks like they're not as dumb as we had hoped.'' He pressed his lips together in a tight line of frustration. He looked up. ''Any word from the *Los Angeles*?''

''No, sir,'' Beth answered. She looked at her wristwatch. "They're on an eight-hour reporting schedule. Next report is in two hours, at 0800."

The admiral nodded. "I sure hope they didn't screw this up. If we lose these clowns, we'll never be able to go home." He picked up his coffee cup and began reading the morning sports page of the ship's paper, the *Daily Constitution*. The others, knowing the unspoken signal, excused themselves and went to work.

The admiral stepped onto the admiral's bridge and his aide called the rest of the bridge to attention as he always did and the admiral uttered "as you were" and they all went about their business. He sat in the leather captain's chair welded to the deck by a sturdy pedestal; the elevation and angle allowed him to see out the windows both toward the bow of the ship and down to the flight deck. He took the cup of coffee his aide offered him with the message board as he did every morning. It was his favorite mug, a white porcelain cup that had a Jolly Rogers flag with a skull and crossbones and VF-84 underneath—his last fighter squadron. The squadron that he had commanded. There was something special about being the commanding officer of a fighter squadron. He would never forget it—the camaraderie, the sense of belonging, the mission. Even when there wasn't a particular mission, there was *the* mission: defending democracy and freedom from tyranny and oppression.

The bridge was cold even though outside it was already in the high eighties. Billings pulled his blue ball cap down closer to his eyebrows and looked at the lightening sky over the dark sea. The turbulent sea was a dark, purplish blue that looked as if it were covered with oil and was fighting to break through. The clouds were gathering their energy to fight the brutal sun, hoping to make it through the day as adult clouds. The sun was just about to the horizon, about to transfer the light from Washington,

D.C., exactly on the opposite side of the world, exactly twelve hours away.

The F/A-18s started their engines on the flight deck below. The first launch was scheduled for 0700. Another routine day on the USS *Constitution*. The biggest, fastest, strongest, most powerful warship ever built.

Lieutenant Rick Reynolds, the admiral's aide, put down a telephone receiver attached to the bulkhead and crossed to the admiral. "Sir, that was the chief of staff. He asked if the admiral had his television on."

Billings looked at him without saying anything.

"He believes if the admiral would turn on CNN, he would find something very interesting being discussed."

The admiral waited for Reynolds to do something. "Well turn it on, Drano."

"Aye, aye, sir," Reynolds said as he reached to the overhead and turned the button on the small receiver.

Beth came through the door. Billings glanced at her and then back at the television. CNN came on in a clear picture that they could pick off the satellite anywhere in the world. He studied the picture. It wasn't the usual House of Representatives scene of someone making a passionate speech before an almost-empty floor. This scene was full of energy, full of people with red cheeks and messy hair.

Beth stood next to Billings. "What's up, Admiral?"

"Don't know. Chief of staff just called, said I should turn it on. So I did."

"I thought you'd want to see this right way, Admiral," she said, handing him a Navy message.

The admiral read it quickly, watching the television out of the corner of his eye. He read it again, and handed it back to Beth with a pleased look on his face. "Do we know where that is?"

"Yes, sir. I'll get the chart." She saw it on the starboard side of the bridge and walked back opening a large chart that she had folded like a road map from a gas station.

She laid the map out on a table near the admiral's chair

and smoothed the folds. She leaned over the table and looked for the latitude and longitude listed in the message. The admiral leaned over her shoulder as she worked.

"Zero degrees, thirty minutes north, and"—she grunted as she pressed against the table—"one hundred four degrees . . ." She drew two faint arced lines with the compass that intersected on a small island.

"Bunaya?" the admiral asked. "What the hell is there?"

"Nothing, sir," Beth said. "Uninhabited. One of the many uninhabited islands of Indonesia. They have seventeen thousand, but only six thousand or so have people on them. They've even tried forced resettlement on some of them, to relieve pressure on Java."

The admiral picked up the message lying on the chart. "Good call to have the submarine park offshore."

"I think this is it," Lieutenant Reynolds said as he stood watching the television. "Here we go."

Billings and Beth looked up at the television. Reynolds turned it up so it could be heard easily. A reporter was following the Speaker of the House down the hallway, one of about twenty or thirty reporters trying to get his attention. He was waving them off without turning around. He walked quickly to the door to his office, only to find more reporters stationed there to block his retreat.

"Give us something," one woman finally yelled in a piercingly high voice.

Speaker Stanbridge turned and raised his hands in surrender. "All right. I'll answer questions for"—he looked at his watch—"ten minutes. We're taking a fifteen-minute break. I've got to do a few other things. But if I do . . ." He stopped and looked up, then shouted, "But if I *do*," then waited for a semblance of quiet, "you have to leave me alone until we adjourn. Agreed?" They all nodded, not meaning it for a second. "Okay. What?" he said.

The closest one spoke first, a television reporter. "Is it true that if you can get it through Congress, you intend to issue this Letter of Marque or Reprisal to the USS

Constitution Battle Group already on the scene?''

"That's right. That's exactly what I plan to do."

"Do you think you have enough votes to do it?"

"Yep. They're ready to go, to authorize our Navy to defend American interests, since the President isn't willing to do it."

"Isn't this a usurpation of the President's power?"

The Speaker shook his head and smiled. "Nope. Right in the Constitution. 'Congress has the right to Declare War, and grant Letters of Marque and Reprisal.' The power to fight a limited private war, if you will, is Congress's power as well. You might say the presidents through the ages have been usurping *Congress's* authority, like in Panama, in Granada, or with the Contras against the Sandinistas. The whole War Powers Resolution was intended to rein in the president from unauthorized acts of war or hostility. Those powers rest with Congress. We should either declare war, issue a Letter of Marque and Reprisal, or stay out. The President isn't authorized to go to war without Congress, nor should he fight a limited war or action. It's our power, and we are about to exercise it. Now if you will excuse me . . .''

"What is the President going to do about it?"

"I don't know, " he said. "Ask him."

"What did he say when you met with him last—"

"That was a private conversation." He stopped, looked around, and decided to finish his thought. "But I can tell you that the Letter didn't come up at all."

"You never mentioned it to the President? He's never told you what he thinks about it?"

"Exactly," he said finally, looking at his watch. "He's probably hearing about it for the first time right about now." He quickly went through the door to his office and disappeared as it closed behind him. The reporters turned to face their cameras and began to report on what everyone watching had just seen live.

The admiral turned down the volume and looked at Beth. "Now that's amazing. That is a twist." He seemed almost amused. "If he's trying to rattle the President's cage, this ought to do it."

The first F/A-18 was hurled down the flight deck by cat 2, the catapult on the port side of the bow, and made a clearing turn away from the ship before resuming the ship's heading and leveling off at five hundred feet. The admiral watched his bridge clock click over to 0701.

"Rick," the Admiral said. "Get a staff meeting together at 0800. We need to talk about this Letter of Marque. Ask the ship's captain and the CAG to be there too."

"Aye, aye, sir," said Reynolds, reaching for the phone.

"And make sure Lieutenant Commander Falls is available."

Reynolds picked up the phone to track down the staff officers.

Admiral Ray Billings took a deep breath. He could feel things closing in on him, as he usually did when he had to make a big decision, the big decisions that separate admirals from lieutenants. "Good thing we had our submarine station itself offshore from those cigarette boats," he finally said, returning to the tactical problem at hand.

"Yes, sir. That was good thinking."

"It was obvious. Those boats were intact for only one reason—to use again. If they weren't going to use them, they could have scuttled them, or loaded them aboard a mother ship, like they have now." He looked up. "What is the name of that tub we saw crane them aboard?"

Beth looked at his memo. "The *Sumatran Star*. Indonesian registry."

"And where did they go?"

"Bunaya."

"Right. Bunaya." He drank from his coffee, then realized how cool it had become and put the cup down on the table. He watched the airplanes shoot off the deck, one after the other, thirty seconds apart. The sun was above the horizon now, scorching everything in its path.

The admiral walked to the chart and stared at it.

"What's our current position?" he asked no one in particular.

His aide looked at the PLAT television in the corner of the bridge, which carried a constant readout of the ship's latitude and longitude. "Four degrees ten minutes south, one zero eight degrees thirty-four minutes east," he called out loudly.

The admiral stood over the chart motionless. He picked up the handset of a heavy red phone on the bulkhead as an F-14 went to full power on catapult 1 beneath him. He looked out the bridge windows as the captain picked up the other receiver. "Morning, Captain," he said cordially. "Please set a course for Bunaya."

14

"BOBBY, HOW YOU DOING?" DILLON ASKED, HOLDING the phone on his shoulder as he typed on his computer.

"Dillon?" Bobby replied from his desk deep in the U.S. Supreme Court building.

"Yep."

"That place must be about to explode. You can't turn on the news without seeing your boss, or the debate, or somebody standing somewhere in the Capitol building talking about it. It's unbelievable."

"The reporters are even starting to recognize *me*. That's a first. They used to look right through me. They're trying to talk to anybody they figure knows something."

"So what's up?"

"Wanted to see if you're going to Molly's tonight."

Bobby paused. "What for?" he asked finally.

"For the game, stupid. Don't you have your schedule? Games on red days are at my place, blue for hers, and green for yours. This is a blue day. Clemson. Only a few more regular season games."

"You talk to her about this?"

"Well, no. Why?"

Bobby hesitated. "I don't think she's very happy about you right now. This whole Letter thing. She thinks it's all your doing."

"It is. Mine and the guys who wrote the Constitution."

"I think it's personal, really," Bobby speculated. "It's

a matter of integrity. She sees politics in you, not integrity. She says you've become political."

"What a crock," he said, sitting forward suddenly. "Where does she get off saying that?"

"The Letter."

"I looked into it because I didn't know what it was. Then after I'd looked into it more, it just . . . well, it got momentum of its own."

"Well, she thinks it's your idea."

"Brother." Dillon sounded exasperated. "Well, I'm not backing off. So you going to her place or not?"

Bobby sighed. "Can you get away?"

"Sure." Dillon shrugged as well as he could with the phone cradled on his shoulder. "I've done what I need to do. I need to get out of here for a couple of hours. I'll be here all night again anyway."

"What time is the game?"

"Seven-thirty. I'm going to take the Metro, so I should be there about ten after."

"All right," Bobby finally agreed. "I'll see you there."

They stood on Molly's doorstep, waiting for some sign of life. The windows were dark and her car wasn't there.

Bobby looked at Dillon. "You call before we came all the way out here?"

"I didn't figure she'd stand us up. I can only stay for a quarter anyway. I need to be on the Hill." He looked at his digital watch in the dark.

Bobby shuffled from one foot to the other, trying to stay warm. "I think the Supreme Court is the only branch of government not burning midnight oil. Kind of fun for a change."

"Not yet, anyway," Dillon said.

"What's that supposed to mean?"

"I don't know. I've just got a feeling about this one."

Bobby knocked loudly and looked at the windows for any light. "She's not here," he said after giving Molly enough time to react to the knock. "Would you stipulate to that, Counsel?"

"So stipulated."

"What the hell you doin' dragging me out here when you didn't even call?" He was becoming more aggravated the more he thought about it.

Dillon looked around, then interrupted, "I say we go to the Bear and the Rugged Staff."

"The pub? What for?"

"They show every UVA game. There'll be a bunch of alums there. It'll be great. What do you say?"

"You sure you're not supposed to be somewhere? Researching some obscure question of admiralty law for your boss's next move?"

"You coming or not?"

"Yeah, sure. Why not?" Bobby said as they walked off the porch.

The pub was dark and warm. In the main room a fire burned brightly in a fireplace large enough to walk into. The crowd was more interested in the game being shown on a television hanging from the ceiling in the corner farthest from the door. Dillon chose a table close to the fire, but with a clear view of the television. "How's this?" he said as they sat down with their backs to the fire.

Bobby shrugged.

"How're David Ross and the Supremes?" Dillon asked, making the same joke that had been made a thousand times since David Ross was sworn in as the Chief Justice of the United States two years ago.

"How long do I have to hear that?"

"Probably until they break up for their own recording contracts," Dillon said smiling. "What're you working on?"

"Couple of *real* exciting cases. *In personam* jurisdiction for a foreign corporation through its wholly owned sub, and whether Indians can have gambling on their reservations when the state doesn't want them to."

"Enjoying it?" Dillon asked, getting the attention of the waitress.

"It's pretty heady, writing opinions that become the supreme law of the land, signed by a judge. Sometimes the justices change a lot from the draft opinions we write; sometimes they don't change a word. Kind of scary."

"Two Bass ales," Dillon said, ordering for both of them.

"It's like I've always said," Bobby continued, "the United States is run by people under thirty. We're the ones who do all the work. It's the old guys who take all the credit."

Dillon smiled. "We're living proof," he said, sitting back. "You tell the Chief Justice of the United States what to do, I tell the Speaker of the House, and Molly tells the President. The three most powerful men in the world." He paused, then looked at Bobby. "It really is kind of scary, isn't it?"

The waitress placed a glass of dark beer in front of each of them. Dillon paid her with a single bill and motioned her to keep the change. Behind her the referee threw up the ball in the center of the floor for Virginia and Clemson. Dillon looked hard to see which team was wearing the orange away jerseys since they both wore orange.

"So, you think Molly's really mad?" Dillon asked.

"I'd say that's fair. I think you set her off. She's probably figuring some way to outdo you right now. I'll bet that's why she wasn't home. It's like in law school when you got the best grades of any of us the first semester. Remember?"

Dillon nodded and winced.

"She looked at you with this stare and said, 'That's the last time that will happen,' and tried to bury you every semester after that. Friendly competition, she said." Bobby laughed. "She's driven, man. Don't forget it."

Dillon changed the subject. "So what do you think would happen if this Letter thing came before the Supremes?" he asked nonchalantly as he took his first drink.

Bobby, who had been watching the game, looked quickly at Dillon, his usual easygoing face clouded over. "Why're you asking me that?"

"Just interested."

"Don't—" Bobby said, shifting his weight in his chair.

Dillon spoke without looking at him. "Why not? There's no case in front of you, or even on the way. I just wondered if you'd thought about it."

Bobby sat silent, suddenly cool. He kept his eyes focused on the television as he answered Dillon in a soft, direct voice. "I don't think that's it at all. I think you want to know what I think and what I'll say in the bench memo, if there ever is one." He looked at Dillon, remembering. "You said you had a *feeling* about this one. You didn't really expect Molly to be there, did you."

"Of course I did," Dillon said defensively. "You think I'd go all the way out to her house knowing she wasn't going to be there?"

Bobby's eyes burned holes in the side of Dillon's head. Dillon finally turned and looked at him. Bobby didn't speak.

Dillon felt uneasy. "What?" he protested.

"You know what. This whole thing was a scam. You called me but not Molly. Why? You meet me there and we're by ourselves, so you recommend this nice warm place with English beer and try to find out what the Supreme Court is going to do with what may be the most important case in fifty years—"

"There isn't any case! I told you that! How can you accuse me of setting you up?" Dillon sat up, shaking his head. "This thing is making people go crazy. You know me. You know if I were trying to influence you I'd argue the case outright; I wouldn't come to a bar and try to pump you for information. Geez, Bobby."

Bobby softened, thinking perhaps he had been too quick to judge. "Sorry. I think this whole thing has people edgy. It's not like the usual political debates. This is the kind that could change the government." He looked around. "Or the world."

Dillon nodded. "I'm just trying to do my job. I've researched it till I'm blue in the face. But there isn't much authority at all. I just thought, if you've looked at it, and know of some silver bullet that says we're dead wrong and way off base, it'd be nice to know now. To prevent whatever's going to follow"—he looked at his watch again—"if Congress adopts it tonight. So, do you know of any reason why we're dead wrong? That this isn't even arguable?"

Bobby swirled the beer around in the tall glass and stared at the distant television without seeing anything. He drank a last sip and put the glass down. He finally looked at his old friend Jim Dillon, the head of his study group in law school, the one who was in some way responsible for his grading onto the Virginia Law Review. That had given him access to any law job he wanted and put him where he was right now. He studied Dillon, feeling the palpable strain on their friendship, hoping there wouldn't be more. He looked him in the eyes and shook his head slowly, as if in disappointment. Without saying anything else, Bobby stood up, tossed a bill on the table, and walked toward the door of the Bear and the Rugged Staff.

Bobby stopped as the image on the television changed from the basketball game to a news bulletin. The anchor looked extremely serious. He couldn't hear what was being said, nor could anyone else at the bar. Somebody closer to the television yelled, "Turn it up!"

Bobby walked back toward the table where Dillon was still sitting. They watched as the image changed to a rough videotape clearly taken outdoors in a jungle setting. The camera zoomed in on Captain Clay Bonham, who was suspended from a bamboo pole that had been passed between his arms and his back so that his elbows were pointed to the sky and his head was toward the camera. The pain was clear on his face, which was swollen from being beaten and covered with nick marks and bruises. His feet dangled six inches off the ground. A voice came on the tape. "You Americans don't learn. You think we stupid. You try to come ashore and get us on an island. You flew airplane over island. The Navy has not gone away from the Java Sea. You have not complied with our demands."

Bonham began to moan.

"The U.S. Navy must leave. Now!" A man moved onto the screen in front of Bonham and struck him in the head with a bamboo stick. The image went black.

Bobby turned to Dillon, "Did you see what those mother . . ."

"Can you believe that?" Dillon said, standing up.

"I'm outta here," Bobby said. "I'll catch you later."

Dillon watched as he walked out of the pub. He shifted his attention to the basketball game, but after a few minutes, he realized he didn't even know who was ahead. It didn't matter.

15

ADMIRAL BILLINGS HADN'T LEFT THE BRIDGE ALL DAY. The airplanes had come and gone, doing their usual missions—fighter intercepts, ocean surveillance, electronic warfare, bombing practice, strafing practice—all the missions intended to maximize the ability of the carrier battle group to attack and kill anything within reach. Anything.

In the past few years though, Billings, like most admirals, felt like a chainsaw at a woodcarving contest. Very effective, but maybe not the right tool. Not that there wasn't a role for the carrier battle group anymore; there was—perhaps more than ever. But the politicians didn't seem to know what it was.

Bunaya would be different, though. Billings fought to keep from smiling. An isolated island, bad guys ashore, and nowhere for them to go. Between the airplanes aboard the carrier and the Marines and Special Forces aboard the amphibs, he could deal with anything. Absolutely anything short of an armored division in a forest, and even that could probably be dealt with if he had just a little more time.

The bow of the supercarrier cut smartly through the dark ocean westward. The sun was directly in Billings's face as he watched the progress of the ship. The wind had died down to five knots, so the ship was making up the rest of the thirty knots required to land airplanes by crashing through the ocean at twenty-five knots, effortless for

the USS *Constitution*, one of the fastest ships afloat.
Maybe *the* fastest now that the *Pacific Flyer* was at the
bottom of the Java Sea. Billings glanced at the nuclear
cruiser to the north of the carrier and the turbine-powered
destroyer off to the south. They were keeping up nicely.
He loved being at sea and watching the gray ships pound
their way through the ocean.

He climbed into his chair and squinted into the sun,
putting the bill of his baseball cap just below the orange
disk to block its direct rays.

Commander Beth Louwsma ran onto the bridge. "Couple of interesting developments, Admiral," Beth said, out
of breath from her climb to the bridge.

"Like what?"

Beth looked at a message in her hand. "By back channel message," she said looking around, "we're informed
that maybe these Islamic terrorists aren't all they claim to
be."

Billings frowned, confused. "Speak English."

"They claim to be the Front for an Islamic Indonesia,"
she said as she pulled some stray hair behind her ear.
"But nobody's ever heard of a group by that name, including Indonesia. That seems curious. You'd think
they'd know their troublemakers. Well, turns out, they do.
And these guys ain't them. The first intel report we got
implied they were tied to Iran. That Iran was giving them
arms and weapons, kind of the Islamic brotherhood
thing—fomenting revolution around the globe for a
worldwide Islamic solidarity. Good theory. Only it
doesn't hold together. We've been watching Iran like a
hawk for a long time. We know where they're trying to
stir things up. They're in touch with some people in Jakarta, some fundamentalists, but these guys who took our
ship don't seem to be among them. Indonesia confirms
it."

Billings stood up and began to pace the bridge. Forward, aft. Forward, aft. He stopped and asked quietly, "So
they're not some fundamentalist Islamic front?"

Beth shook her head. "We don't think so."

"Well then, why would they say they were?"

"I don't know . . ." Her voice trailed off.

"Whenever you do that, where you let your voice trail off, you have something else to say. Spit it out."

"I don't want to guess. . . ."

"Go for it. Guessing is good exercise for thinking. It can't hurt."

"My guess," she responded, contemplating whether she should speak freely, "is that they're using that as the bogeyman—they know we're spring-loaded to respond to Islamic fundamentalism. We're used to dealing with it, to attributing all terrorism to them immediately. It's like"— she stopped and thought—"like default logic in software. Whenever we don't know who has done something, we assume it's Islamic fundamentalists. We'll believe anything about them. It's a stereotype."

"So?"

"So if they *say* that's what they are, we'll believe them instantly. Nobody would claim to be fundamentalists if they weren't. It'd be like pretending to be a leper . . ."

"And?"

"And their real identity will go unexplored."

Billings studied her face for indications of how sure she was. "Well, who are they really then?"

"I don't know. I'm just saying they probably aren't the Islamic whatever of wherever."

"Well, that's not very helpful. That message tells us that much."

"Yes, sir. I just wanted to add my two cents' worth."

"I think maybe one cent's worth. If I'm generous."

"Yes, sir. Sorry."

"Find out who they really are and what the hell they're up to. If they murder people and then lie about why, something is going on."

"Yes, sir." Beth turned to leave.

"I want national assets over Bunaya. I want an overflight by photo bird and satellite imagery. We need to know what we're dealing with.''

"Yes, sir, but the President said we're not going after them.''

"That's for public consumption. You watch," the admiral said confidently. "We'll be in there within forty-eight hours. I'll bet you. I expect an order any time now appointing me as the joint task force commander. I'll need you and ops to get a list of JTF assets in the area—Air Force, Army, whatever there is.''

"Yes, sir. Never hurts to be ready.''

Billings was thinking hard, thinking ahead, the way he was paid to do. To anticipate every contingency. "We'll also need the beach studies, helicopter landing zones, the usual." He took his eyes off the active flight deck for a moment. "What intel can you give us about this place right now?''

"Frankly, sir, not very much. I didn't expect much because it's so out of the way, but it's also uninhabited—not much need to photograph uninhabited land. We've got enough to do—''

"Anything else?" he said, cutting her off.

"No, sir. I'll see what else I can dig up.''

"Not good enough," Billings said in a tone tinged with frustration. "I want you on-line with all the pinhead intel types you know in Washington or anywhere else. Get with the attachés in Jakarta, anybody who might know anything. Get it straight from the sources. As unfiltered as you can. We need to know what we're up against." As he finished talking, Captain Black walked onto the bridge. "Anything new?" he asked his chief of staff.

Black walked over to him. "Yes, sir. We just got a report from one of our EA-6Bs. They flew near Bunaya and picked up a fire-control radar." One of their ultrasensitive electronics airplanes had picked up the signal of a radar that was created for only one purpose—to guide a missile or a gun.

Commander Beth Louwsma flushed with embarrassment. This piece of information had made its way to the admiral without any intelligence analysis or any chance for her to research it. "From Bunaya?" the admiral asked, concern on his leathery face.

"They couldn't tell for sure. There are a lot of islands around there. Hard to pinpoint it to that island, but they think so."

"What kind of fire control?"

"That's the thing. Couldn't correlate it to a specific type. Right frequency range for fire control, but not from a platform they readily recognized."

"Beth, what do you think?"

Louwsma thought for a moment. "I don't know what to make of that at all, Admiral. Do these terrorists, or whatever they are, have surface-to-air missiles or antiaircraft batteries? Seems unlikely, especially something we don't recognize."

Billings looked out past the bow of the *Constitution*, then back at his staff. "What does Indonesia have in the way of SAMs?"

Louwsma blushed, immediately and painfully aware that this was a question she should have anticipated. "I don't know, sir, but I will sure find out," she replied weakly.

Billings looked at her with disapproval. "You should know the order of battle for every country within a thousand miles of us."

"I know, sir. I've concentrated on the countries I thought might be hostile to us. . . ." She stopped, seeing the look on Billings's face. He turned and looked down toward the flight deck.

He spoke with his back to them. "Everybody better be doing their homework. We could be going ashore within twenty-four hours. I want to know who the hell we're up against, what they have, and who, if anyone, is behind them." He turned to face them. "Is that such an unreasonable request?"

"No, sir," they said in unison.

"You all took off your packs because you heard the President say we weren't going to respond. I'm telling you, that was for public consumption only. I've got a feeling. I think we'll be going after these guys. Soon. I don't think we're going to let them get away." He smiled and the crow's-feet around his blue eyes wrinkled up. "Either the President's ruse will work, or if it isn't a ruse, Congress will pressure him into it."

Captain Black replied, "You think this Letter of Reprisal thing . . ."

"Letter of Marque and . . ."

"Latest thing on CNN is that the Speaker's calling it a Letter of Reprisal. . . ."

"Why? That doesn't make sense." The admiral seemed puzzled. "I wouldn't worry too much about that. We just need to be ready." He thought for a moment. "Bill, get a message to the rest of the battle group. I want a recon plan by 1500, and plans for attacking this island by sunset. We may have to hit them before they try to move again. We were lucky to catch them once. We might lose them if they go again."

"Yes, sir." Captain Black glanced sideways at the others. "How big a force do you plan to send in?"

Billings stared at Black, annoyed. He adjusted his ball cap down toward his eyebrows, as if putting on a helmet. "I'd tell the Marines to expect to send in all fifteen hundred. Every one."

"Aye, aye, sir."

🏴

"Bunaya?" Lieutenant Jody Armstrong said, staring at Tyler Lawson. "Where the hell is that?"

"I have no idea," Lawson replied. "But I've got the coordinates." Lawson indicated the chart in front of them. "It's supposed to be kind of near Singapore."

"What do you think these guys are up to?" wondered Armstrong.

They stared at the chart, alone in the planning room, as

the USS *Wasp* steamed westward with the rest of the battle group toward Bunaya. Neither of them had ever heard of the island. But then, neither of them had given Indonesia a second thought before leaving on this cruise for the Southern Pacific. Neither Lawson nor Armstrong cared very much about the politics or religion of their destinations. They had long since put behind them the idea that the military leaders who ordered them on their missions and the political leaders who were behind those orders should be questioned. Long ago they had decided such questions were rarely fruitful and often led to slowed response time. Now they simply did what they were told.

Armstrong's frustrations at the earlier two missions continued to mount. He had lost the *Pacific Flyer* and then stalked a deserted island like a fool, looking in vain for the terrorists. He leaned over and examined the chart. It showed Bunaya clearly, with the terrain outlined and graded for density of foliage and ground elevation. It appeared to be an unremarkable island with no high points above four hundred feet and covered with heavy foliage. Most islands that he had encountered in his time in the Navy were similar — arid on the coast and tropical inland. This island appeared to be tropical down to the water, a less common setup, but certainly not unheard-of. "Sure isn't very big," Armstrong remarked.

Lawson leaned over his shoulder.

He looked up at Armstrong. "The bad news is we don't have any beach studies of this place at all. We don't know anybody who's even been ashore at this island, and we've got no imagery."

"How are we supposed to do this?"

"On the fly."

"Let me guess. A night mission," Armstrong said, raising his eyebrows twice, mischievously.

Lawson smiled with the understanding of a comrade. "Only if we're lucky."

"You really think Admiral Billings would send us poor

boys in there at night without having any idea what this shoreline looks like?''

''Sure. What do you think you are, important?''

''I lost my head.'' Armstrong stood up and stretched his arms back, his large muscles pressing against the fabric of his shirtsleeves. ''Shouldn't really be much to this. There were only, what, thirty guys that went aboard the *Pacific Flyer*?''

Lawson squinted as he thought. ''Yeah, something like that, but we don't know that they didn't rendezvous with some other guys when they went aboard that mother ship.''

''Right, so maybe thirty or forty guys total. We could probably take care of them with one squad if we took them by surprise.''

Lawson looked worried. ''Don't assume anything. These guys may be highly trained. You know better than to assume anything—don't assume you're as good as you think and don't assume they're as bad as you think.''

''I'm not assuming anything. I'm just saying we should be able to handle this without too much difficulty.''

Lawson breathed deeply. ''If only we knew what 'this' was.''

Admiral Billings sat at the desk in his at-sea cabin near the bridge. He took time every day to read Shakespeare. No one on his staff knew. They simply knew he took thirty minutes every afternoon to be by himself in his at-sea cabin. Rumor had it that he was a religious fanatic and liked to read the Bible but didn't want anybody to know. But he cussed, and that threw his staff off. Maybe he was one of those unstable Bible readers, like Patton, who read his Bible every day and cussed like a sailor.

He didn't mind people believing that. He thought it was probably better if they believed that than if they realized he read Shakespeare. They wouldn't understand at all. What would they accuse him of, being a Shakespeare fundamentalist? He particularly loved the sonnets. He read them over and over again, reading three sonnets and part of a play every day. Occasionally he would read aloud, doing the different parts with different voices, which caused quite an underground conversation among his staff. He was reputed to talk to himself, but no one knew what about.

At home he had a bookshelf filled with a series of black leather–bound copies of Shakespeare's works. While at sea, though, he brought with him his single volume of the complete works of Shakespeare. It was well worn and the pages had absorbed some of the sea moisture, making them almost damp to the touch. It had been with him ever since he was a lieutenant commander in a squadron and had begun reading Shakespeare to avoid his commanding officer, who was a screaming, frothing-at-the-mouth lunatic. Everyone in the squadron had avoided that commanding officer in different ways. Some had watched every movie on the ship ten times. Others had actually done more work, getting to know the enlisted men they were supervising. Billings had done more Navy work but had also developed his affinity for Shakespeare. Now he couldn't do without it.

He sat hunched over the desk, using the reading glasses that he tried to deny he needed but was willing to endure to drink in the luxurious language and insight of Shakespeare. He turned to *Henry IV,* one of his favorite plays, and rolled the words over his tongue without pronouncing them aloud. The 1MC, the loudspeaker system for the ship, came alive quietly in the corner of his cabin. He could tell by the change in pitch of the electronic tone that a microphone had been keyed on the ship's bridge. He waited for the usual two seconds until the boatswain's mate of the watch hit the bell eight times with his small hammer to mark the passing of the afternoon watch. Eight bells. Four sets of two. Followed immediately by a knock on the door.

Billings sighed and took off his reading glasses. He put

his bookmark in the middle of *Henry IV,* closed the book, and put it in his desk drawer. "Come in," he said with something of an edge to his voice. In walked Beth Louwsma with an odd look on her face.

"Sorry to bother you, Admiral, but have you had the tube on?" she said, looking around the room to see what he had been doing. The admiral was simply sitting quietly at his desk with nothing in front of him.

"No."

"They're going to do it."

Billings stood up and put on his leather flight jacket. In spite of the stifling heat on the outside of the ship, the inside spaces were cooled by the air-conditioning. "Who's going to do what?"

"The House and the Senate are about to vote on the Letter of Reprisal. They think it's going to pass."

16

DURING THE LONG NIGHT OF DEBATE, THOSE OP-
posed to the Letter of Reprisal had become shrill, accusing
the Speaker of various crimes: treason, usurpation of presidential authority, dishonesty, general unconstitutionality,
and illegality. Those in favor of the Letter used the opportunity to accuse the President of cowardice, pacifism,
encouraging terrorism, and generally being frozen in in-
decision.

Stanbridge made no accusations. He argued that something needed to be done and the Letter of Reprisal was
the proper tool. Very simple. It was a historic power that
Congress had exercised in the past and should exercise
again. There was nothing that said it couldn't and plenty
that said it could. The only ticklish part from Stanbridge's
perspective was the idea of issuing the Letter to a Navy
ship instead of a private ship of war. There was some
historical authority to support that, although even he had
to admit it was something of a reach. But it was time to
reach. The Constitution had been mauled by his opposition his entire political life. It was barely recognizable.
The document and the words in the document had become
almost meaningless, being reshaped and molded to accomplish whatever policy the justices wanted. It had become legislation by a body of nine unelected justices.
Well, it was time for the interpretation to go his way for
once.

169

The night had gone better than he could have hoped. The President's earlier speech had galvanized those who supported Stanbridge and caused those who were against a strike to sound hollow. They had no explanation other than the President's stated reason of avoiding the "cycle of violence." After the first few repetitions of that concept, it had become threadbare. It had begun to sound like an excuse. Few, if any, accepted it in their hearts.

As the session of Congress continued deep into the night, the feeding frenzy of the press slackened and the debate tapered off. Stanbridge had his feelers out to begin taking straw votes. By 3:00 A.M., with members sleeping at their places and a few lying in the aisles, he realized he had enough votes to pass the Letter of Reprisal. Pete Peterson had given him the same indication from the Senate. The time had come.

John Stanbridge stood up in the Speaker's chair and cut off the last Republican congressman scheduled to speak. Stanbridge glared at him and he sat down quietly. Stanbridge looked out over the assembled members of the House of Representatives. He saw rage, excitement, fatigue, uncertainty, and fear. He swung the gavel down onto the wooden block that had received it so many times before. The loud bang shot through the Chamber like a rifle shot. "The time has come to call this motion for a vote. It's time for each of us to stand and be counted and tell our constituents where we are. I therefore am requiring a roll call vote so that each one of us is on the record as voting for or against this motion. Will the clerk please call the roll."

The Clerk of the House went through the roll as each member voted electronically. No one moved or spoke. The votes came in and by the first one hundred it was clear that he had a 3 to 2 margin at least. By two hundred it was clearly a 7 to 3 margin, and by the end of the roll call, of the 435 Members of the House of Representatives present, 302 voted in favor of the issuance of the Letter of Reprisal to the USS *Constitution* Battle Group. The

Senate's numbers were nearly identical. Stanbridge watched as journalists dashed out of the balcony seating to use their portable telephones in the hallway. The phone rang on the Speaker's desk and Pete Peterson confirmed the Senate's vote. The vote was on the identical document. No conference was necessary.

"Ladies and Gentlemen of the House, it is my honor to announce to you that the United States House of Representatives and the United States Senate have both overwhelmingly passed the motion to issue a Letter of Reprisal, under Article one, Section eight, of the United States Constitution." He watched as he let that fact sink in. "I promise that this Letter will be issued and signed as soon as practicable, and hand-delivered to the battle group in the Java Sea. I want the world to take note that the United States Congress will not stand by and have American lives taken and American property destroyed without holding accountable those who are responsible." Stanbridge moved his shoulders back in an involuntary swell of pride. He was overwhelmed by the new role he felt himself assuming, that of Statesman and Leader and International Figure.

"I will notify the President of our actions personally and will expect him to immediately sign the Letter of Reprisal for the issuance of the commission."

"May I be heard, Mr. Speaker?" said the Minority Leader of the House.

Stanbridge nodded at him. He stood up and looked around solemnly. "Mr. Speaker, you will not need to call on the President." He stared at Stanbridge, who stared back, not understanding the point.

"Perhaps you are right, sir," Stanbridge replied. "Since this is a power exclusively of Congress, I can see a valid argument that a presidential signature is not required, and in fact may be prohibited. Because to give him a signature implies that he could prevent us from . . ."

"Mr. Speaker," he replied. "You have misunderstood

me. You do not need to call on the President, because he has just arrived.''

The President of the United States entered and walked down the aisle of the House of Representatives toward the Speaker. Stanbridge stood frozen at the Speaker's podium, staring at Manchester.

Manchester stopped where the tables ended and looked at Stanbridge. "Mr. Speaker, may I be heard?''

Stanbridge tried desperately to recover his composure, which was leaking away. "Good morning, Mr. President. What brings you to the House this early in the morning?''

"You know very well what has brought me to the House, Mr. Speaker.'' Manchester spoke slowly and deliberately. Every eye in the House was on him. "You directed an intentional violation of the United States Constitution and I'm here to stop you.''

An hour later the Speaker sat back in the huge leather chair behind his desk, put his hands behind his head, and stared at the few staffers in his office, including Dillon, Chuck, and Rhonda. "We did it.'' The Speaker was smiling. "We did it!'' He shook his head. His bloodshot eyes were still filled with the triumph of the night.

"I've got to admit,'' he continued, "the President had a lot of nerve coming over here and vetoing that bill on the spot. If he had waited until we submitted it to him, some of the air might have gone right out of our sails. But he thought that by doing the big, dramatic, early morning veto, it would scare off enough people that we couldn't override it. And he was *wrong*!'' The Speaker laughed. "He was dead wrong!''

The Speaker stood up and walked around his desk. "Mr. Dillon, I have you personally to thank for this. It was your baby; you pushed it and it worked.''

"Thank you, sir.'' Dillon was feeling his own sense of accomplishment and triumph. He glanced at the other staffers, who were regarding him with a mixture of wonder and envy. He liked that.

"Chuck," the Speaker said, looking at the former Air Force pilot who still had his cropped haircut, "how do we get this thing delivered down to the battle group? Who's going to take it?"

Chuck looked at him in surprise. "I hadn't really thought about that, Mr. Speaker. I assumed that we would go through the Pentagon and they would have it messengered down."

"The Pentagon? How the hell can we trust them? Who do you think they work for?"

Chuck hesitated. "Well, I assume they work for the same person for whom the USS *Constitution* Battle Group works. I suppose, directly, the President."

The Speaker looked at him intently, "You think the Defense Department is going to just carry this Letter of Reprisal down to the *Constitution* Battle Group and say, 'Sure, happy to help'?"

"I don't know." Chuck looked around for help.

The Speaker pondered the new roadblock.

Dillon raised his hand. "Mr. Speaker, I'll take it down there myself."

The Speaker looked startled. "What are you talking about?"

"Like you said, I started this thing; I want to see it through to the end. I'll personally carry it down there and hand it to the admiral. If he has any questions, I'll answer them. It seems like the only way to do it." Dillon's heart was in his mouth.

"How would you get there?"

"Commercial air, I guess. There must be some way to get out to the ship from Singapore, or Jakarta."

The Speaker looked at the rest of the staff. He saw no objections and couldn't think of any himself. "That might be just the thing. The admiral may have some questions and you can respond to them. You know more about this than just about anybody right now."

"I'll go home and pack a small bag and leave as soon as possible."

The Speaker walked to the desk and opened the large maroon folder. He stood the Letter up on this desk so everyone in the room could see the fancy lettering with the seal and the appropriate signatures. He looked at Dillon. "You started it; now make it happen."

President Manchester threw his suit coat over the back of the couch and stared at Molly Vaughan, who was standing on the other side of the office. Arlan Van den Bosch sat on the other couch with his head back, eyes closed.

"Well, Ms. Vaughan," Manchester began, "frankly, I'm not in the mood for a meeting right now. I've been up all night, I've been to Congress, and I've watched and been the victim of a very unpleasant political process. Now, what is it that was so urgent?"

Arlan Van den Bosch sat forward and rested his forearms on his knees. "Mr. President, I tried to prevent this meeting from happening. I tried to get the White House Counsel on the phone, but he was not available. Ms. Vaughan would simply not take no for an answer. Said it was a matter of urgency and importance. She had to speak with you personally. . . ."

"Well then, get on with it," Manchester said irritably.

Molly had forgotten to put her suit coat on before coming to the Oval Office, something about which she was very self-conscious. She had worn her suit all night and had sweated through her silk blouse. She tried to remember to keep her arms down. "Mr. President, I don't think any of us really expected Congress to pass this bill, and certainly not with enough votes to override a veto. They've now done both."

Manchester grew cooler. "I know all this, Ms. Vaughan. Tell me something that might interest me. Please."

Molly nodded slightly. "At our office we've been trying to come up with some way to stop this process, some way to throw a wrench in the works if Congress did in fact pass this. I've also been on the phone with the attorneys at State and the Attorney General's office. I think I have a possible solution."

Manchester responded with instant interest. Van den Bosch turned and looked at her, his eyes widening.

"Let's hear it," Manchester said anxiously.

Molly spoke. "Every time a President has done something with which Congress was unhappy, either some member of Congress or a group of members has almost always brought a lawsuit against the President. Congress sued President Bush when he went into Desert Storm, for violating the War Powers Act—for conducting a war without a declaration of war by Congress. . . ." She evaluated the President's knowing nod. "President Reagan was sued by Congress when he sent troops into Granada. President Ford was sued when he sent a rescue effort after the *Mayagüez* in the South Pacific, not unlike this situation. President . . ."

"I get the idea," Manchester said. "But I haven't done anything."

"I know," she said. "That's the point. Congress has always sued when it's too late to do anything about it, almost as a matter of principle. But we have a chance to jump in before Congress acts on the Letter. Mr. President, I think that you should file a lawsuit on your own behalf as an individual, and as the President of the United States, against Congress for taking an action that is unconstitutional and usurping your powers as Commander in Chief."

"Are you serious?" Manchester asked.

"Yes, sir, I'm very serious."

"Have you discussed this with your boss?"

"Yes, sir, I have. We've discussed it with State, and the Attorney General. They're all in agreement."

"Where is Benison? This should be his deal."

"Yes, Mr. President, but you may recall that his wife is in labor."

"Yes, of course. Is he aware of this?"

"Yes, sir, he is. We've been up all night analyzing this from every conceivable angle."

"Well, why would it stop anything from happening?"

"Well, because we would ask for a temporary restraining order to keep Congress from enforcing the Letter of Reprisal."

Manchester looked at Van den Bosch, who looked pleased. "It's worth a try," Van den Bosch said.

Manchester looked into Molly's eyes. "How long would it take to prepare the lawsuit?"

"It's ready. I have it here. I think we should file it this morning."

Fifteen minutes after Molly returned to her office, the phone rang.

"Hello?"

"Molly?"

Silence. She immediately recognized Dillon's voice. "What do you want?"

"I tried your number at home. Then I figured you had worked through the night like I did. I want to see you if you're available." The direct approach. Couldn't fault him for ambiguity.

"For what?"

"Breakfast."

"I'm really busy."

"Look, it's only six-thirty in the morning. We've both been up all night. You need breakfast, like I do."

"What I need is for the Speaker of the House to get rational. That would make my life much easier."

"How about we don't talk about that right now?"

Frustration flavored her tone. "How can we not talk about it? It's the most important thing that's happened to this government in ten years." She sighed. "You act like this is some kind of routine event, Jim. It isn't. It's tearing the country apart. The cracks are starting to form. I'm going to do what I can to stop it. I don't have time for nonsense right now.''

"Okay. Just thought I'd ask. Sorry I bothered you." He rubbed his eyes, trying to get the sand out of them. ''I'm gonna run out to the Westside Café before I go to the airport.''

"You're leaving—going where?'' she asked, suddenly interested.

"I'm carrying the Letter of Reprisal to the USS *Constitution*.''

Her voice changed. "You're kidding. When are you leaving?''

"Ten A.M. from National.''

"To where?''

"Singapore.''

She hesitated, then asked, "When will you be back?''

"I'm not sure.''

"Couldn't you get out of it?''

"Probably. I volunteered. It's my thing,'' he said with pride. "I want to see it through.''

"Maybe I should see you before you leave. I'll try to get there in twenty minutes.''

"Great,'' he said, surprised. "See you then.''

17

DILLON DRANK FROM THE HEAVY WHITE COFFEE CUP and soaked up the spilled coffee in his saucer with a paper napkin from the holder. His head jerked up as the café door opened for the fourth time in five minutes, but it still wasn't Molly. He felt that his brain was starting to trick him. He was so tired he knew that he was skipping steps in his thought processes. He closed his eyes for a moment. His contacts felt as if they had been super-glued to his eyeballs.

He rubbed his face and felt the day-old growth. He grimaced. He had intended to use the electric razor he kept in his desk. He didn't have time for this breakfast. He had to pack for whatever the weather was like in Singapore, which he thought was always hot, but he wasn't sure. He made a mental note to check the weather channel.

The glass door opened and Molly entered. She looked around the small restaurant with its private booths and walked back toward him.

He waited until she had hung up her coat and sat down. "You know me," he said. "I like to be blunt. How is it that when I call you this morning you're so cool, to put it mildly, then you come here and you're all smiles?"

She shook her head slightly. "I don't know, really. I was thinking about how this is all going to play out, and I've basically come to the conclusion that, ultimately, this is going to make *Congress* look foolish, not the President.''

"So how is Congress going to look foolish? I can't wait to hear this," he said, sipping his coffee.

"No admiral of a battle group is going to obey some vague Letter of Reprisal that has *no* historic precedent. He's going to obey an order from his Commander in Chief.'' She shrugged, as if she had just stated the obvious. "And that will be the end of it. Your Speaker will then be left holding the bag and looking stupid.''

"And that makes you feel better about having breakfast with me?" Dillon asked. "This some kind of competition?''

Molly opened her mouth to reply as a waitress walked up and stood quietly waiting for their attention. Her black uniform was perfectly pressed with a starched apron over it. "Good morning.'' she said cheerfully. "Special is eggs Benedict and freshly squeezed orange juice.''

Molly shook her head. "I'll have half a grapefruit and an English muffin, no butter.''

"Waffle with powdered sugar and a large orange juice," Dillon said.

The waitress nodded and turned away, then stopped and came back to Molly. "Would you like coffee?''

Molly nodded, and the woman poured it immediately.

Molly looked down at the table as she pulled her hair behind an ear. She looked back up at Dillon. "Ever since we met in law school, since the first year, we've had this competition thing going on, haven't we?''

Dillon smiled, as if remembering ancient history. "Yeah, we kinda have. Why is that?''

"Because you worked so hard to beat everybody with the best grades in the first semester that you challenged the rest of us. So we tried to outdo you. Some of us came pretty close," she said pridefully.

He nodded.

"I was kind of hoping that the competition thing was over.''

Dillon chose his words carefully. "You know, Molly, I was also hoping that we could put the whole rivalry thing behind us. I kinda thought we could start dating again, this time...."

"So did I..."

"But," he continued, "this Letter of Reprisal thing seems to have charged you up like nothing before. And you're holding it against me."

Molly played with her coffee cup. "You're making a big political play. To make your splash in the world of politics." She looked hard into his eyes. "It feels like you're losing your judgment."

"That's unfair," he said, trying not to respond as harshly as he felt. "Isn't there some way we can at least try to go out?"

Her face showed warmth and regret. "I don't know. We'll have to wait until this political crisis is over. Whatever happens, I think it will be fast. Especially now that you're leaving..."

"So we're going to leave it like that? I won't know anything until I get back?"

She looked at him directly. "Call me when you get back, but remember, until then I'm on the other side. It's nothing personal, and it's not our rivalry or competition. It's my job."

The waitress returned and put their food in front of them. Dillon looked at his waffle for a moment, then started to eat. Molly cut her grapefruit expertly. She didn't glance at him as she quickly ate each section of the grapefruit. She drank her coffee and finished her English muffin before she finally looked up. She spoke, with obvious difficulty. "I have to ask you something," she said haltingly.

He noticed that she was troubled, "What?"

"Will you accept service of process?" She looked directly into his eyes.

"What?"

"As soon as the Court opens this morning, the President is going to file a lawsuit against the House and the

Speaker to declare the Letter unconstitutional, and ask for a temporary restraining order.'' She looked away. ''Will you accept service of process on behalf of the Congress and the Speaker of the House? Can I have them just deliver the lawsuit to you?''

Dillon stopped eating, put his fork down, and shoved his plate away. He tried to catch her eyes, but she was not cooperating. ''Molly, look at me.''

There was a hint of moisture in her eyes.

''What is this?'' he asked, trying to read her and not her words.

''You heard what I said.''

''Who put you up to this?'' he said insistently.

She shook her head vigorously. ''I've got to go.'' She began sliding out of the booth.

Dillon grabbed her arm. ''Who put you up to this?'' he demanded again.

Molly looked at his hand on her arm and into his face. ''I've got to go, Jim.''

''Tell me.''

''The lawsuit was my idea.''

He sat back and thought about the implications of the President suing Congress to have its Letter of Reprisal declared unconstitutional. It could bring the process to a screeching halt. ''And it was your idea to agree to have breakfast with me on a pretense, then ask me if I would accept service?''

Molly pulled her arm away slowly. ''It wasn't a pretense. I did want to see you.''

''*Who* put you up to this?''

''The Chief of Staff wanted me to ask you to accept service, but I wanted—''

Dillon smirked. ''Well, that figures, he's such a worm. . . .''

''He's just trying to do his job.'' Molly stood up at the end of the table.

''Just doing my job,'' Dillon repeated, mocking. He stood next to her, pulled his overcoat off of the metal rack, and tossed some money on the table. "Well, you can give him my answer. Tell him I said he can go screw himself."

Dillon packed, showered, and dressed, then returned to the Hill. He hurried down the halls of Congress to his office and dumped his bag on the floor.

Grazio wandered in and said, "So you're taking the Letter down to the Navy?"

"That's right."

"How come the Pentagon won't deliver it?"

"If you were the Speaker, would you give it to the Pentagon, controlled by the President? You don't think they could find the one guy who would take it on as a matter of principle to buck the House of Representatives? The Speaker doesn't trust the Executive Branch right now." Dillon sat down and began unplugging his laptop from the wires that connected it to his large monitor and keyboard. "He figures that the President is going to start issuing orders to keep us from pulling this off. It might get 'lost' at the Pentagon and never get delivered. Then where would we be?"

"So you have to go all that way and carry this thing by hand?"

"Yep."

He looked at his watch. "Anybody in there with the Speaker?"

"I have no idea. I was down there about an hour ago. This place is like an anthill with a whole new group of ants trying to get in. There's press everywhere, the phones are ringing off the wall, people are calling from foreign countries, it's a complete zoo." Grazio thought for a moment. "Kind of fun actually."

Dillon left and ran down to his boss's office.

Robin looked up and nodded toward the Speaker's door. Dillon needed no other words as he walked right in. Reporters were waiting in every chair in the exterior office as well as up on the wall outside. There were television crews with idle equipment, radio crews with recording equipment, and countless newspaper writers.

As he closed the Speaker's door behind him, he could hear them starting to approach the door, assuming the Speaker would now be out shortly.

Stanbridge had no pleasantries for his assistant. "Where the hell have you been, Dillon?"

"I had to stop by my apartment to pick up my stuff so I could be ready to go."

"Did you see anybody from the President's office?"

Dillon hesitated.

That was enough. "Who did you see?"

"I think you know, Mr. Speaker, I have a friend, Molly Vaughan. She's in the office of the Counsel to the President."

"No. I *didn't* know that. I knew you had a . . . friend . . . but I think you failed to tell me that she worked at the White House."

"I'm pretty sure I did tell you, Mr. Speaker. Maybe you just didn't see it as being very important. . . ."

Stanbridge stared at Dillon. "Why would I not think it was important if you were dating someone from the enemy's camp?"

"She's an old friend, sir. And I never realized that the President was the enemy, Mr. Speaker," said Dillon.

"He is now," said the Speaker. "You know who is out there in the outer office?"

"Well, there are about a million people from the press, but other than that, no."

The Speaker got up from his desk and began pacing. "There is a guy out there from the George Washington Attorney Service."

Dillon felt a chill run through him. He said nothing.

"Do you know what he is here for?"

"What?"

"He is here to serve me *personally* with a lawsuit."

"A what?" asked Dillon, feigning surprise. "From who?"

The Speaker turned and looked at Dillon from across the large office. The Washington Monument was bright in the background behind him. "Who do you think?"

Dillon said nothing, hoping the Speaker would answer his own question as he usually did.

"From the *President*. The President is suing me, the Speaker of the House of Representatives, and the Congress of the United States. As the Chief of the Executive Branch of the United States Government, *and* as an individual—a regular citizen—he is suing me."

"Have you seen it?"

"No, Robin saw it and told me what it's about. She refused to let the man into my office."

"Well, what's he going to do?"

"He said he's going to sit there until I leave the office and then he's going to personally serve me," the Speaker said, visibly agitated.

"I'm not sure that it makes much sense, Mr. Speaker, to try and dodge ser—"

"I am not trying to dodge service! Do you understand the implications of this?"

"I'm not sure . . ."

"This could kill the entire thing! It's a lawsuit for a temporary restraining order, and an injunction to have the court determine that our Letter of Reprisal is unconstitutional and unenforceable. How could they have known we were going to move this fast? How could they have known that you were going to be on your way this morning to the East Indies to deliver this to Admiral Billings—that is his name, by the way, that is the guy you are going to see. I checked."

Dillon's face had more color than usual. "Molly and I had breakfast together this morning. I told her I was leaving."

The Speaker stared at him, motionless for what seemed like an hour. "You did what? You had breakfast with someone from the office of the Counsel to the President and told her you were taking Congress's Letter of Reprisal to the South Pacific this morning?''

"Basically . . . yeah. I . . . she . . . yeah.''

"What the *hell* were you thinking about?'' asked the Speaker, his voice rising.

''I didn't think anything about it, Mr. Speaker,'' Dillon said defensively. "She's a friend of mine and I told her where I was going. This thing has been on the news for a day and a half, and they know we are going to give it to the Navy. I didn't know this was a secret.''

The Speaker waved his hand at him in disgust. "It's not. I just don't like getting outmaneuvered.'' He clenched his teeth as he put his head back and closed his eyes. "So what should we do about this lawsuit?''

Dillon filled his cheeks with air and looked at his watch. "Mr. Speaker, my plane is leaving for Singapore in less than an hour. I could get to National Airport and take off before you let him serve the papers on you.''

"I want you on that plane!'' He reached out and picked up the wine-colored leather folder. An imposing thick, rich leather binder that exuded importance and solemnity. The Speaker handed it to Dillon.

"Here is the Letter of Reprisal, Dillon. The original is to be delivered to Admiral Ray Billings in person by you. Do you understand that?''

"Yes, sir, I sure do.''

"Good. So what should we do about this *stupid* lawsuit the President has filed? Can he do that?''

Dillon looked mystified. "I'm not really sure, Mr. Speaker. I know there was a lawsuit filed by Congress years ago against President Reagan when he sent troops into Grenada, so I guess turnabout is fair play. There was one against George Bush for Desert—''

"But what happens, how does this work?''

"Well, they asked for a temporary restraining order. Right?''

"Right.''

"Did they give notice of a hearing?''

The Speaker walked to his desk and picked up a note in Robin's handwriting.

"Yeah. Tomorrow morning."

"Then you have to have somebody show up tomorrow morning to argue your case before whatever judge it's set before."

"What if we ignore it completely and say that it's none of the court's business?"

"You could do that, but then the court might rule against you and issue a restraining order against the use of the Letter."

The Speaker balled up the note and threw it across the room. "Get out of here. I'll let you know what happens."

"Yes, sir. I'll be in touch." Dillon turned and walked toward the door.

"Dillon," the Speaker said. Dillon turned. "Should we get the House Counsel to answer this thing?"

"I wouldn't, sir. I'd get the best lawyer in Washington."

The Speaker nodded. "I know just the guy." He looked up suddenly. "Does the process server know who you are?"

"I doubt it."

"I want to make sure you're out of the building before he serves me with this thing. Get your stuff from your office and head straight to the airport. Don't let anybody stop you. You got that?"

"Yes, sir." Dillon pulled the door open and walked quickly out of the Speaker's office.

He grabbed his computer, briefcase, and bag.

"You off?" Grazio said, passing him in the hall.

"Yeah."

"Good luck."

Dillon nodded, thinking luck was unlikely to have much to do with whatever happened after this. Things were under way, and neither he nor luck was in control. Other forces were.

18

THE USS *CONSTITUTION* BATTLE GROUP STEAMED west at twenty-five knots for Bunaya, two hundred fifty miles away. The most recent F-14 reconnaissance flights had confirmed the location of the mother ship in a covered cove, and infrared photography had confirmed at least two hundred people on what was supposed to be an uninhabited island. More troubling, though, was the existence of what appeared to be reinforced concrete buildings, and the synthetic aperture radar of an S-3 Viking had also shown outlines of trucks pulling what looked to be portable weapons systems.

The news of the photos, radar reports, and infrared imagery had spread quickly through the air wing on board the *Constitution*. The response had been nearly universal enthusiasm; they were in a real fight instead of a turkey shoot. The fighter squadrons were disappointed so far because no fourth-generation Air Force had shown up to defend the island. But they could always hope.

Caskey stretched out at his place in the CVIC, the intelligence center and nerve center of the air wing aboard the *Constitution*. All the squadron commanders were there with Captain Zeke Bradford. They all felt the buzz, that excitement from the anticipation of action. None of them was sure what lay ahead, but they all knew it would probably involve the expenditure of ordnance and flying fast, two of their favorite things to do.

Zeke Bradford, the air wing commander, turned and pointed to a large chart of an island that was taped to the bulkhead. The island was approximately one hundred miles from Singapore, and sixty miles from the Strait of Malacca. He looked around for a pointer, then found it and slapped the rubber tip against the center of the island. "Good evening, gentlemen. This," he said, emphasizing by hitting the chart again, "is where they are. As I am sure all of you know, our latest intelligence indicates that there are at least two hundred people, and maybe more, on this island. We will assume that they are all allied with the terrorists who attacked the *Pacific Flyer*. We hear they may not be regular old terrorists. We're not really sure who they are. . . ."

"How many of them are just regular old inhabitants of the island?" asked Caskey.

"Probably none. Until very recently, this island was uninhabited. Word we get from Washington is that Indonesia does not believe it has ever been inhabited permanently. Occasionally they've seen a transient fishing village there." He scanned their faces. "For the slow-witted among us, reinforced concrete is not typical of a transient fishing village."

They chuckled. "What's the plan?" asked Drunk Driver, the F-18 squadron commander.

"We're waiting to get the go-ahead from the President. But either the President is putting on a good show, or he has no intention of sending us in. The question then of course becomes whether this Letter thing, this—whatever Congress has done—will have any effect on what we do. That, of course, is up to the admiral. I have no opinion on that and don't expect any of you to have any opinion on that. If told by the admiral to go, we go. Is everybody with me? Any of you want to second-guess the admiral and tell him he's stupid?"

He looked at each of the squadron commanders, who gave him no response. "All right. Here's what I think will happen. This island is going to be as difficult a target as you will see for any kind of airborne strike. The buildings we've identified, at least those made of concrete, appear to be reinforced and sunk into the ground except for the top two or three feet. You won't see any of that fancy footage of one of us putting an LGB down somebody's smokestack," he said, referring to the laser-guided bombs made so famous in Desert Storm. "There aren't any smokestacks. We're going to have to use penetrating weapons to get through any of these bunkers. For all we know, the bunkers are empty and the real weapons and people are in thatched huts elsewhere on the island and the bunkers are there just to suck us in. We'll do the best we can to ferret that out, but assume we'll be hitting reinforced targets for now. We've had some electronic emissions that appear to be a fire-control radar—we have yet to categorize them—so they may have some SAMs, or antiaircraft. We are trying to find that out too—where they might have come from, and whose they are. It does appear that these folks are serious.

"It's my guess that within the next two days we'll launch a coordinated strike with the amphibious ready group going ashore." He breathed deeply and blew out through slightly pursed lips. "Whatever weapons they have, I'm sure they don't have any armor. They'll be hard-pressed to deflect an attack by the Marines. Our role will be generally one of support. Flak suppression, if there is any, striking the buildings, and close air support when the Marines land. Questions?"

There weren't any.

"All right. Tonight's missions are on the air plan. Self-explanatory. One other thing—we might try a supersonic overflight to see if we can get their AAA or SAM battery to light up to identify it. Any volunteers?"

Caskey and the F-18 squadron commander raised their hands simultaneously.

Bradford smiled, his teeth brilliant against his dark skin. "That's the spirit. I'll let you know if we're gonna to do that; otherwise go with the flight plan."

The SEAL leader, Lieutenant Jody Armstrong, and their intel officer, Lieutenant Commander Tyler Lawson, studied the same chart that Bradford had on the wall on the *Constitution*. The *Wasp* was humming with activity as the Marines prepared for the expected assault on Bunaya. The Marine Expeditionary Unit and the Special Warfare Task Unit, including the SEALs had gone from the routine boredom of preparing for the joint exercise in Thailand to the real thing. The difference was palpable. They had been told to be prepared to go ashore within twenty-four to forty-eight hours. Armstrong had been told that he would be the first ashore prior to the raid—to reconnoiter the beach, do some preliminary surveillance of the island, take out suspected missile launchers, and with a follow-on mission as snipers. He didn't like this at all. They were going against an unknown foe, of unknown strength, on an unknown island, with no intelligence. Welcome to the Navy. Unknown foe, unknown island, and no intel.

Armstrong looked at Lawson. "This chart sucks. Is this the best we've got?"

"Yup."

"Well, our Defense Mapping Agency is doing a lousy job."

"I certainly will tell them that at my earliest opportunity."

"Oh, shut up," said Armstrong, still looking worried. "You know, I'm always the first idiot to go ashore. Have you ever noticed that about us, Tyler—we are always the first idiots to go ashore?"

"Of course, that's our job."

"I know that's our job, but it's hazardous."

"I think it's part of our job description—what we do is hazardous," Lawson said with a twinkle in his eye.

Armstrong just looked at him with mock contempt. "Where is Colonel Tucker?"

"I don't know." Lawson shrugged. "He said he'd be here."

"I thought the idea here was to go over their landing plans so I can know which beach to take our unsuspecting SEALs into so we can get our asses shot at first."

"That's the idea."

"Well, how am I supposed to know which beach to get my ass shot on if he doesn't come here to tell me?"

"Did you get up on the wrong side of your rack this morning or something?"

"Nah, I'm just pissed off. I don't like the way this whole thing is falling out."

"Why not?"

"Because the President doesn't want us to go. He's our Commander in Chief, in case you haven't noticed."

Lawson visibly stiffened. "He's a dick," he said. "He's an idiot; he has no idea what he's doing. These guys come down here and pop twenty-plus Americans and sink a U.S. vessel and he says he doesn't want to get involved in the cycle of violence? What kind of bullshit is that? The cycle of violence is already under way. We're just on one side of it—the receiving end. I get so sick of these politicians pretending this is all some kind of game, like if we're just nice to everybody, everybody will be nice to us. What a bunch of *bullshit*. I remember . . ."

The door opened and Colonel Tucker ducked his head and stepped in. He was six feet three inches and wore Marine Corps camouflage utilities with the sleeves rolled up past his elbows.

"Sorry I'm late, gentlemen."

"No problem, sir," said Armstrong and Lawson together.

"I was meeting with my staff to finalize our plans. Lieutenant Armstrong, did you get the word that the beach we anticipate is the south-facing beach?"

"Yes, sir, that was the word I got," he said, glancing at Lawson, who knew he had gotten no word at all. "I've been looking at that beach, but as you know, we don't have any beach studies and not many people know much about this place. By the way, sir, how many people do you anticipate taking ashore?''

"We don't know how many people they have ashore, do we? My current plan is to take everybody.''

Armstrong looked surprised. ''All fifteen hundred?''

Tucker glanced up from the chart and nodded. ''What's your plan?''

Armstrong studied the chart. ''We'll be doing the underwater hydrographic survey of the beach, which we'll transmit back. We'll use our new CLAMS. He noticed Colonel Tucker's frown. ''The clandestine acoustic mapping device—it takes soundings and makes a picture from the returns. Anyway, then we'll do recon and surveillance. . . .''

☙

President Manchester sat in the rocking chair he preferred at the end of the rectangle formed by the two striped couches in the Oval Office. He had ordered his Chief of Staff, the Chairman of the Joint Chiefs, the Chairman of the National Security Counsel, the Secretary of Defense, and the Attorney General to appear. He looked at Admiral Hart. ''Who's the admiral of the battle group?''

The Chairman of the Joint Chiefs, a four-star admiral in a dress-blue uniform, spoke with trepidation. He knew where this was going, and he didn't want to go there. ''His name is Ray Billings.'' He pushed his lips out together as he tried to decide whether to go on. ''Naval Academy, former fighter pilot—F-14s, commanding officer of Fighter Squadron 84, the Jolly Rogers—former commanding officer of the USS *Constitution*. Hardcharger. Golden boy.''

''Is he reliable?''

''Absolutely, he's one of our best naval officers. But I suppose it depends on what you mean by reliable.''

''Can we count on him?'' the President asked.

Hart hesitated. "Count on him to do what, sir?"

"Count on him not to follow this stupid Letter of Reprisal."

"That's a tough question. Navy officers have a historical appreciation for the concept of Letter of Marque and Reprisal that most politicians don't," he said, looking around. "Frankly, I don't know how he will respond."

The President stood up and pulled his rocking chair back to the side of the room and began his customary pacing. "You mean to tell me that there's a chance he'll actually do it?" The anger in his voice was uncharacteristic. The others noticed.

"I would say it is possible."

"How can we stop him?"

"Well, I think the thing that we should do is order him not to do it," the admiral answered. "A straightforward order from either me or you, or both, ordering him to do something else and to disregard that Letter of Reprisal."

"Would he follow that order?"

The admiral paused and stared ahead. His mind worked as he evaluated his next comment. "Let me ask you gentlemen something. Which takes precedence, a direct order from a senior officer or a direct commission from Congress straight out of the Constitution?"

Van den Bosch blurted, "It is *not* straight out of the Constitution. It is out of thin air."

"I beg to differ," said the admiral. "The Constitution clearly has a provision in it for a Letter of Marque and Reprisal. The real question is whether what Congress has done fits within that power; I don't think there is any precedent to say either way."

"Whose side are you on?" demanded Van den Bosch.

"I didn't know we were picking sides," said the admiral. "I thought we were trying to sort this out."

The President stepped in with his calming voice, which sounded forced. "Okay, Admiral, what do *you* think we should do at this point?"

"Well, as I understand it, you've already put in motion

the legal challenge to this Letter. Am I right?''

"Right."

"Well then," the admiral said confidently, looking at the Attorney General, "if the legality is so clearly in our favor, this should be over quickly." He looked around at each of the others. "Right?"

The Attorney General sat quietly.

"Assume we're unsuccessful in getting an injunction, or order," Manchester said, "what do you recommend?"

"I think, Mr. President," the admiral began slowly, "the only thing we can do is order him back out of the area, say, to Pearl Harbor, and specifically order him not to follow the Letter of Reprisal or take any action against anyone without our authorization."

"How soon can we get such a message to him?"

"It's my understanding that the Speaker has sent a member of his staff down there with the letter in hand."

"We've got to get our message there before he arrives."

"That's no problem, Mr. President," said the admiral. "We can send a flash message five minutes from now if you want."

"That is exactly what I want, Admiral. What should it say?"

"Just what we have been talking about. Do you want it coming from you or from me?" the admiral questioned.

The President hesitated, then nodded at the admiral. "From you *and* me. I think he might respect that more."

"I will draft the order and get it out right away. Do you want to see it before it goes?"

"No. Just get it to him. I want him to have it in hand before that Letter arrives."

"Will do, sir."

The President looked around at his advisers. "Anybody got anything else to say?"

They sat silently in response. "Any new information?" he said, looking at Cary Warner.

"Only that we've gotten some more information back

from both the USS *Constitution* and the Indonesians.''

''What information?''

''The Indonesians aren't buying that these guys are from some group for an Islamic Indonesia. They know all those guys. None of the usual Muslim fundamentalists are part of this group. They think there's something else going on.''

''What about from the *Los Angeles*?''

''They followed the mother ship that craned aboard the three fiberglass boats and followed it to Bunaya.''

''Where's that?''

''It is sort of near the Strait of Malacca, south of Singapore.''

The others in the room looked puzzled. ''Why would they go there?''

''It's uninhabited. It would also put them in place to harass other traffic that might be headed toward the Indian Ocean through the Strait of Malacca.''

''Anything else?''

''Just that at least two hundred people on the island have been identified as being somehow associated with this group. There are indications they have surface-to-air missiles and hardened buildings or bunkers.''

''Surface-to-air missiles and bunkers?'' He looked at the CIA Director. ''What do you make of it?''

''Hard to say, sir, could mean a number of things.''

The President shook his head. ''Whatever it means, it would only make it worse if we tried to attack them. I don't want to get a bunch of Americans killed attacking some island fortress—''

''I wouldn't call it a fortress exactly. We only know of two bunker—''

''Anybody disagree?'' the President said forcefully.

Van den Bosch jumped in before anybody could possibly say anything. ''We've been through all this before; there is no significant change.''

The others exchanged glances and remained silent.

''One last thing,'' Van den Bosch said awkwardly. The

others looked at him. "I have it on good authority the Speaker's staffer is leaving from National with the Letter in less than an hour." He looked at Manchester. "I think the CIA, or maybe the FBI, should have someone on that plane. Maybe Mr. Dillon won't be able to deliver that Letter. Maybe it will get lost."

Manchester stared at the carpet, then stood suddenly. "That's all for now, gentlemen."

19

EVEN THOUGH HE HAD GROWN UP IN SAN DIEGO, Dillon had never been west of California. The Singapore Airlines Boeing 747-400 had stopped in Los Angeles before making the sixteen-hour overwater flight to Singapore. He knew he was crossing the international date line and it became the next day. He tried to think about when today became tomorrow, and how, and gave up.

After landing, Dillon realized he was on the other side of the world from Washington. Twelve hours and twelve thousand miles away. Northern Hemisphere to almost the Southern. East longitude to west. Cold to hot. Light to dark. He stood in the middle of the large modern airport in Singapore wondering what to do.

Chuck, the only one on the Speaker's staff with military experience, had reassured him that the message with his flight number had been sent to the *Constitution* and they would pick him up. What Chuck couldn't tell him, though, was how they would pick him up and how they would establish communications. Chuck just said not to worry about it. Easy for him to say.

Dillon picked up his suitcase and walked toward the main terminal. He and his suit were wrinkled and saggy. He had worn a tropical-weight suit rather than casual clothes. He now regretted his decision.

A small burly American walked behind him as Dillon strolled through the terminal. Dillon felt a tug on his brief-

197

case. He looked around. The man behind him was carrying a camera bag that had become entangled with Dillon's briefcase. "Sorry," the man said, relaxing the pressure, as two women stopped directly in front of Dillon.

The two Caucasian women looked almost like twins. They were five five or five six, and both had blond hair done in a French braid that was tucked up underneath. They wore green Navy flight suits with black-leather name tags. One of them spoke first.

"Are you Mr. Dillon?"

"Yes, who are you?"

"I am Lieutenant Karen Morris and this is Lieutenant j.g. Shana Westinghouse." The one speaking stuck out her hand.

He shook her hand and smiled.

"We're the pilots from the COD."

He stared at them blankly. "What does that mean?"

"Carrier onboard delivery, sir. We fly people and parts out to the carrier every day from various airports."

"So what's the plan?"

Morris looked at her watch. "We a have noon charlie time—we have to be overhead the carrier in two hours—so we need to launch out of here in about thirty minutes. Can you be ready then?"

"I'm ready right now," said Dillon, smiling to impress them without knowing exactly why, other than they were pretty and he had noticed. He tried not to notice, but he couldn't help it.

"Great," she replied.

"Let me help you with your bag," Westinghouse said, grabbing it from his hand.

He protested, but then stopped. They preceded him through the airport.

"So what brings you down here, Mr. Dillon?" Morris asked over her shoulder as they walked.

"Don't you know?"

"Not really, no. We know you're coming from Washington, but we're not sure why." She glanced toward Westinghouse.

"I'm bringing a letter from the Speaker of the House to Admiral Billings."

They both looked at him quizzically. "What's wrong with the mail?"

"A Letter of Reprisal. Do you know what that is?"

"No. What does it mean?" Westinghouse asked, a light in her eye.

He sighed audibly. "It's kind of a long story. Haven't you been following the news?"

"Nope," they said in unison.

"We haven't seen much news for a while," said Westinghouse. "We've been flying out to the carrier and back about every three or four hours for two weeks. If we get extra time, we sleep. They had some problems with the F/A-18's engines and we were the only ones who could get them the parts. Why, what's going on?" she said, shifting the bag to the other hand.

"Too hard to explain," said Dillon. "Congress issued a Letter of Reprisal to this battle group to go after the terrorists who sank that American ship."

"Sounds like a good plan to me," said Westinghouse. "Somebody ought to go mort those assholes."

Dillon raised his eyebrows at her language but said nothing.

"So what kind of airplane do we fly to the carrier in?" Dillon asked.

Morris looked at him as if at a child. "A COD."

"What is a COD?"

"A COD is a . . . COD. It's an ugly, gray, bugsmasher kind of an airplane."

She looked at Westinghouse, who picked up the theme. "They're definitely ugly, but they're slow and unreliable. We've had a lot of trouble with them lately. We've lost three CODs in the last twelve weeks."

Dillon's eyes got big. "What do you mean, *lost* them?"

"Lost, as in crashed. You know, pranged. They're really old. They were supposed to all be retired five years ago.''

''Was everybody okay?''

Morris and Westinghouse exchanged glances of mock concern. ''No. 'Fraid not. They've had some very bad results.''

Westinghouse continued, ''Don't worry, Mr. Dillon. We've had most of our scheduled maintenance. They expect to identify the problem any day now.''

Dillon didn't say anything as the pilots' eyes danced with the inside joke. A COD hadn't crashed in two years.

''Are there any helicopters going out to the carrier?'' Dillon asked.

''No, sir. Helicopters don't come this far. We're it. If you have to deliver your fancy letter, you have to take it out by the COD. Your choice. Are you coming or not?''

Dillon hurried as they continued to walk at a pace faster than he was used to. ''Yeah, yeah, yeah.''

They walked through an unmarked door, down a flight of stairs to the concrete tarmac near the tower, and out toward a Navy airplane. The heat surrounded him and tried to suck out all his strength. He was shocked by the humidity. It was much worse than Washington in the summer—something he'd thought impossible. He had noticed the heat as soon as he got off the plane, but only now did he realize that that heat was inside an air-conditioned terminal. This was the real thing—spirit-crushing heat with humidity.

Dillon breathed deeply as the moisture settled into his hair and lungs as he shuffled along the tarmac. He looked up at their destination and nearly passed out. It was the ugliest airplane he had ever seen in his life. A tall young sailor in a green Nomex flight suit walked toward them.

''Everything okay, Petty Officer Wilcox?'' Lieutenant Westinghouse asked.

''Yes, ma'am. Little bit of an oil leak from number-one engine, but I think it's the seal we replaced two weeks ago.'' He narrowed his eyes. ''I think it must have a little wrinkle in it. It's within acceptable limits though.''

Lieutenant Morris approached Dillon and said, "Now, sir, before we get going, a couple of things we need to be sure about.''

Morris continued, "Before you left Washington, were you given the password?''

Dillon looked really confused. "What *password*?''

"To get inside the island.''

"I didn't think we were going to an island; I thought we were going to the carrier.''

Westinghouse jumped in. "Not an island, *the* island, the superstructure that is above the flight deck of an aircraft carrier. In order to get inside the carrier you have to have a password. Otherwise you'll have to stand outside on the flight deck the whole time you're here.''

"Are you kidding me?" Dillon asked, beginning to panic. "Nobody told me that.''

"Don't worry, Mr. Dillon,'' Westinghouse said. "We'll try to cover for you.''

Dillon looked at Lieutenant Morris, who tried not to laugh as she turned quickly away.

"Wilcox,'' Lieutenant Morris said. "Help Mr. Dillon here get situated and stow his gear, and we can get out of here. We have a noon charlie time.''

"Roger that.''

Petty Officer Wilcox turned to Dillon and extended his oily hand. "Can I take that, sir?''

Dillon took his bag from Westinghouse and handed it to Wilcox without looking at it.

"This way, sir,'' said Wilcox. Dillon bent down and followed him into the airplane underneath the four vertical tails. Wilcox pointed toward an uninviting seat. The rest of the airplane was packed with boxes and airplane parts wrapped in bubble wrap. "Here you go, sir.''

"It's facing backwards,'' said Dillon.

"Yes, sir. But we don't really consider it backwards. It's facing *aft*—works better on arrested landings because the force of being stopped by the tailhook throws you into the back of the seat instead of splitting you in half with a seat belt.''

Dillon looked at him incredulously. "We're going to do an arrested landing?"

"It's either that," Wilcox replied, enjoying Dillon's face, "or run off the pointy end of the carrier."

Dillon sat down in the canvas-lined seat and pulled the lap belt tight across his wrinkled pants. Wilcox produced a flotation vest. "Let's put this on, sir," he said as he slipped it over his head. "You need to lean forward so I can get this strap around you." Dillon did so and Wilcox secured the vest. Wilcox knelt beside him and looked into his eyes, looking suddenly serious.

"If we go into the water, sir, whatever you do, *do not* inflate this vest until you are outside of the airplane."

Dillon swallowed hard. "Why not?"

"Because if you do, you won't be able to get out. You won't be able to swim hard enough to pull yourself down from the overhead to get out of any of the hatches."

Dillon looked at him with a frown, confused. "Whatever," he said, praying to God they didn't go "into the water."

Wilcox handed him a helmet made of hard plastic and canvas with ears like stereo headphones. Dillon put it on and tightened the chin strap.

He heard the two pilots climb into their seats behind him and heard Wilcox close the hatches. They began exchanging gestures, unknown words, and acronyms that made no sense to him at all. Before long he felt the airplane shudder as the engines came to life, filling the interior of the airplane with deafening noise. He was amazed at what an antique the airplane was.

They taxied to the runway and stopped. The engines ran up to what he guessed was full power; the airplane sat there and shuddered. The engines returned to their dull roar as they taxied onto the runway and took off, lumbering into the humid air like a salmon up a fish ladder.

The flight to the carrier was uneventful, though noisy

and bumpy. After nearly ninety minutes airborne and a feeling in his stomach of which he was ashamed, they began their descent toward the carrier. He unlatched his belt and peeked out of the window to see what an aircraft carrier looked like from the air. He had seen many aircraft carriers during his time in San Diego, but never from an airplane about to land on one. It looked like a dime on a big blue sidewalk.

He felt the airplane continue to descend slowly and noisily as it approached the carrier, then an explosive, shocking noise. He braced himself, waiting for the airplane to pitch over the side of the carrier and for the water to come rushing in. He found himself repeatedly taking large breaths of air, hoping to get a good one before the water rushed over his head. His back was pressed into the slat and his head jerked backward involuntarily. Instead of flipping over, the COD came to a halt with its engines roaring at full power, wanting to fly.

Dillon's eyes darted from one side of the aircraft to the floor to the ceiling, looking for some indication of what was happening. Finally, the engines slowed and the COD taxied off to the side of the landing area aboard the USS *Constitution*. He let the breath out of his lungs and tried to look casual.

Wilcox walked down the minimal aisle and reached for a button above the rear ramp door. He pushed the black ''down'' button and lowered the ramp to the flight deck. He motioned to Dillon to unhook his lap belt and stand up, which he did, slamming his head into the overhead. He winced as he ducked down and waited for the stars in front of his eyes to subside. His mouth felt dry and coppery.

Wilcox motioned for him to follow him and then walked down the ramp to the flight deck. The wind nearly knocked him off his feet as his loafers gripped desperately at the nonskid deck. He knew if he fell on it in his tropical suit, both the suit and his skin would be ruined.

Dillon looked around, wide-eyed. He had never been

anywhere so loud or so busy. For a ship that looked so small from the air, *too* small, it suddenly seemed immense and overwhelming. Jets taxied in all directions and men walked fast, leaning into the wind with helmets and goggles on. There was so much activity he couldn't assimilate it all and found himself stopping and staring. He felt a tap on his shoulder as Wilcox motioned again for him to follow. He walked toward the island on the carrier and stepped back as someone opened the large steel door and stepped through. Wilcox held the door and pointed for him to go in. He stepped inside the door and they closed it behind him. He was ushered into a small room inside the island where people were standing and conversing. Wilcox leaned over toward him. "I've got to get back to the airplane, sir. Good luck."

Dillon looked at him and nodded, unable to speak. A man in a white turtleneck shirt approached him. "You must be Mr. Dillon."

Dillon looked him over. "Yes, I am."

"We've been expecting you, sir; the admiral's aide is on his way. We were told to keep an eye on you until he got here. He called ahead and said that the admiral wants to see you as soon as you arrive."

🙰

Captain Clay Bonham looked around at his new setting. He was surprised they hadn't blindfolded him. He was glad, but that could mean they planned to kill him soon. The island was tropical—hot, dense, and humid. He longed for the seventy-two-degree bridge of the *Pacific Flyer*. He had been too casual. He'd left security arrangements up to others. Ford, the government, Indonesia. If it had been up to him . . . but it hadn't been. But he hadn't even taken his own security measures when he could have. He should have had security on the ship ready for any eventuality. He breathed deeply as he began to feel nauseated. He wanted desperately not to throw up. He hadn't been fed since being taken. They didn't seem to

care whether he lived or not. They gave him water when
he asked for it, but that was all.

He looked at the three guards escorting him to one of
the many huts in what appeared to be a village. Washington was beside him, personally supervising his transfer to
this new island.

"The Navy is going to come and get you," Bonham
said through gritted teeth to Washington.

Washington yelled something to the men that caused
them to stop. He turned toward Bonham and slapped him
in the face. "Do not speak to me about what will happen.
You know nothing."

"I know that you're a goner," Bonham said.

"Captain, your President has already said to the entire
world that he is not going to do anything about this. He's
going to leave it up to Indonesia."

Bonham looked concerned. "He said nothing like
that."

"CNN," Washington said, showing his teeth.

"I don't believe you," Bonham said.

"I don't care," Washington said. "They will comply
with our demands. The President is already doing so. The
Navy will be out of Java Sea within two days, you'll see."

Bonham shook his head. "I don't think so."

Washington looked at him and then glanced around
with his arms wide. "It doesn't matter. If they come, we
will be ready."

▨

"Thank you for coming in at this late hour, Mr. Pendleton." David Pendleton nodded, his silvery hair perfectly in place. His face was tanned, but less wrinkled than
one would expect from a man of sixty. He wore a double-
breasted glen-plaid suit with a maroon handkerchief in the
pocket. His French cuffs extended the perfect quarter inch
beyond the sleeves of his suit and the gold wraparound
cufflinks were barely noticeable.

David Pendleton had come to Washington when his

firm decided it needed an office in the nation's capital, especially since the Speaker of the House was from San Diego. They had almost waited too long, but Pendleton had made the office a success. He was a senior partner in the litigation department of San Diego's largest law firm, Blanchard, Bell and Martinez. He had tried over two hundred civil cases and had won an award as the best trial lawyer in California. Since coming to Washington he had specialized in representing California interests before regulatory agencies and Congress. He hadn't tried a case in five years.

"I've never heard of anything like this," said the Speaker. "Have you?"

Pendleton shook his head without speaking. He had a reputation for being slow to speak and slow to anger, but intense and efficient. "Not really," he said finally.

"Well, what do you make of the lawsuit?" the Speaker asked, always wanting to cut to the chase.

"According to some quick research of my associates, and after reviewing the memo of your staff member, Mr. Dillon, this is a very close question of constitutional law. It does not seem to be appropriate for a temporary restraining order."

"What's our next step?"

Pendleton sat still with his legs crossed. He had no emotion on his face at all. After a pause that was too long for the Speaker's comfort, Pendleton asked, "What is your objective?"

Stanbridge just stared at him. "What do you mean, my *objective*?"

Pendleton repeated his phrase. "What is your objective?"

"With what?"

"With the issuance of your Letter of Reprisal. What is it you want to accomplish?"

The Speaker sat down directly across from Pendleton. "I want the United States Navy, and the United States Marine Corps, to go down and find those terrorists or whatever they are, knock the hell out of them, capture them if possible, then return to the United States to the hero's welcome they'll deserve. *That's* what I want.''

"Do you believe that the admiral—Billings, I think—will accept the authority of the Letter?''

"I think so, but I'm not sure," replied the Speaker.

"You didn't have some communication with the admiral before issuing the Letter?''

"No." The Speaker felt uncomfortable, realizing that perhaps he should have taken more steps to prepare Billings rather than letting him receive it cold. "Maybe I should have, but I didn't. But I will tell you this. I was in the Navy and I know how these guys think. They would like nothing better than a change in the daily routine, to test their equipment and tactics. Whether they acknowledge it or not, given a chance, I think they'll take it.''

Pendleton let the Speaker's comments sink in. "Do you have any secondary objectives?''

"What are you *talking* about?" the Speaker replied impatiently. "I thought you were here to represent me and Congress in defending this unbelievable lawsuit that the President has filed. To get us out of this.''

"I'm getting to that," Pendleton said quietly. He started again, as if to a dull witness, "Do you have any secondary objectives? Is there anything else that you want to accomplish other than attacking the terrorists?''

"Like what?" asked the Speaker.

"Like challenging the President's authority," said Pendleton.

The Speaker looked at him without responding. "Not exactly. I want to challenge this President, but not the office. That's not my objective. If he wants a fight, I am perfectly happy to fight," he acknowledged, "but I didn't set out to challenge his authority, and I don't want to do it now.''

Pendleton nodded. "Good. Then we are clear as to what the objective is. That makes it easier to make decisions on how to approach this lawsuit." Pendleton uncrossed his legs and stood up. He walked to the window and looked out at the Washington Monument with his hands behind his back. He turned and addressed the Speaker. ''Do you have any particular instructions on how you wish this handled?''

''I don't even know what my choices are, David. Talk to me about what we can and cannot do.''

''The way I see it, Mr. Speaker, you and Congress have two choices. If you wish to make this a *cause célèbre*, then we can meet them on the merits at each step and attempt to prevail based on being right. The other choice is to delay the procedure as much as possible so that when this ultimately is decided, the facts and events will be behind us and the court will in all likelihood dismiss the case as being moot. Do you understand those two options?''

''Of course.''

''Do you have a preference?''

''I really have a preference for having this heard on the merits. I believe that Congress has this power, and that it should exercise it more often.'' The Speaker stood up, suddenly energized. ''For the last fifty years, ever since Korea, we've been fighting people all over the planet, and *not once* has Congress declared war against anybody. Not since World War Two. That's a scandal. It's a usurpation of power by the President, but it's also an *abdication* of power by Congress. They passed this lame War Powers Act trying to limit the President's ability to send troops abroad. That's when all this should have been decided. But it wasn't, so here we are. The power to make war must be decided. It is Congress's power—that's clear in the Constitution—and not the President's. This Letter of Reprisal is the next step.'' Stanbridge scratched his scalp, then rubbed his eyes. ''But,'' he said, fatigue overwhelming adrenaline, ''I don't want to lose. I want to get these guys in Indonesia, and if that means stalling so that it happens, then I'm all for it.''

Pendleton picked up his briefcase. ''I understand. I will

be attending the hearing at nine in the District Court by myself. I do not recommend that you come, nor do I recommend that you send any other member of the House.''

Stanbridge indicated agreement.

"I will be in touch directly after the hearing to let you know what happened.''

As Pendleton reached for the door handle, Stanbridge spoke. "David.'' Pendleton turned. "Let me ask you something. This is a question of constitutional law, isn't it?''

Pendleton nodded.

"The President is Commander in Chief of the armed forces. Right?''

Pendleton, acknowledged the obvious, but said nothing.

"What if the President of the United States is a pacifist?''

Pendleton's eyes narrowed as he tried to discern Stanbridge's thoughts.

Stanbridge rose and tucked in his shirt as he crossed the room toward Pendleton. "If the Commander in Chief of the United States armed forces had no willingness, and I mean *no* willingness, to use the armed forces or the nuclear defense under *any* circumstances, he wouldn't be *fit* to serve as President, would he?''

Pendleton looked back understanding but without answering.

Stanbridge finished his thought. "Wouldn't it be the obligation of Congress to impeach him?''

20

LIEUTENANT RICK REYNOLDS, ADMIRAL BILLINGS'S aide, led Dillon down the ladder to the 03 level, the deck below the flight deck and slightly less full of violent noise. They walked inboard onto the blue-tiled area and turned right, toward the bow. The lieutenant made an immediate left and rapped smartly on the door marked ADMIRAL'S WARDROOM. A Marine sentry opened the door and Reynolds stepped through. Dillon followed.

Reynolds stopped ten feet inside the door, facing a table full of officers. Dillon glanced around the room. It wasn't at all what he had expected. He had heard how cramped and uncomfortable Navy ships were, and even though carriers were much bigger, he assumed they weren't much more comfortable. But this room was huge. It had a table with ten chairs around it, nearly all occupied, a separate area with a couch and chairs and a coffee table, a kitchen nearby. The walls were covered with paintings, not the emergency instructions he had noticed elsewhere. He gazed longingly at the leather couch to his left and wished he could lie down on it and go to sleep. He noticed on the wall a framed, poster-sized replica of the United States Constitution. The ship's namesake. ''We the People . . .'' Right next to it was a painting of the original USS *Constitution, Old Ironsides,* the undefeated frigate that fought the English so gallantly and was still commissioned and sitting regally refurbished in Boston Harbor. John Stanbridge had sponsored a special act of Congress to allow two U.S. ships with the same name to be commissioned at the same time.

Dillon looked at the officers surrounding the table. His mouth went dry and his stomach jumped. He was accustomed to dealing with people in power, but he was out of his element with the military. It was a foreign world to him, full of people he had stereotyped, and an environment that made him very uncomfortable.

"May I present Mr. James Dillon, assistant to the Speaker of the House of Representatives." The lieutenant then turned to Dillon.

"Mr. Dillon, may I present Admiral Ray Billings, commander of the *Constitution* Battle Group, and his staff." Admiral Billings rose and crossed over to Dillon. He extended his hand.

"Good afternoon, Mr. Dillon. Welcome to the *Constitution*."

"Thank you, sir, I appreciate it."

"I hope your trip wasn't too taxing."

Dillon responded with a pained expression. "I had no idea how big the earth was until I traveled halfway around it in one day."

The admiral laughed. "Imagine how long it took to deliver such a Letter the last time one of these was issued. You would have been traveling six months to get here. If you got here at all."

Dillon nodded and smiled without speaking.

"Please, sit down. Join us. We were just discussing what to do about this Letter. The attack is scheduled for approximately thirty-six hours from now."

Dillon felt a cold chill.

"Coffee?" the admiral asked as he took his seat.

"What attack is that, Admiral?" Dillon asked as he gestured to the messman with the coffeepot.

"Well, the attack on these terrorists on Bunaya." Admiral Billings indicated a seat at the far end of the table. "Please sit there, Mr. Dillon."

Dillon looked around. "I seem to have misplaced my bag."

The aide spoke. "No, sir. That was taken care of. I gave it to Petty Officer Johansen, who put it in your stateroom."

"My stateroom?"

"Yes, sir. It is my understanding that you are going to be here at least a day, maybe two, and we have you in a stateroom on the second deck."

Dillon looked at him curiously. "Why two days?"

"It depends on the COD schedule, sir," the aide said, looking to see if he was speaking out of turn. "We have you scheduled on the COD ashore tomorrow evening, but it may not be until the day after that, and if we are involved in the attack it may be even later."

Dillon was taken aback by the thought of being aboard the carrier during the attack. It could be exciting to see his Letter of Reprisal in action, but it also brought the ramifications into sharp focus. Dillon sat down slowly, hoping to appear at ease. He tried to seem older and more sophisticated.

"Well," said the admiral. "First, Mr. Dillon, let me introduce my staff to you." He went around the table and introduced his chief of staff, his intelligence officer, his operations officer, and the rest. Dillon was surprised most by Beth Louwsma and had to force his eyes on to the next officer introduced.

"Mr. Dillon," the admiral asked as a messman poured Dillon's coffee into a porcelain cup with a blue anchor on it, "before we do anything else, I take it that you have brought the Letter of Reprisal with you." He looked at the leather folder lying on the table next to Dillon. "Is that right?"

"Yes, sir, it's right here," he said, tapping the folder.

"Mr. Dillon, would you please read aloud that letter?"

Dillon raised his eyebrows, slightly surprised at the request, and then opened the folder.

The rest of the room grew deathly quiet. No more stirring of cups, no sipping of coffee; even the inevitable shifting in chairs had stopped, as every person in the room gave him their undivided attention.

He read the language, taken almost directly from the Letter of Marque and Reprisal issued by Congress and signed by James Madison in 1812. The flowery language had been toned down, but the flavor was the same. When Dillon finished he looked around the table. No one spoke.

"Well," the admiral said, "there it is. Sounds like an op order, with timing, target, and objective. Any comments?" Some shook their heads gently; others did nothing. Beth Louwsma rubbed her finger around the top of her coffee cup without looking up.

"So the question for us, Mr. Dillon, is, should we do it?"

Dillon sat at the table and listened to the noises of the carrier: the loud aircraft directly overhead on the flight deck, the hum from the power plant somewhere below— the nuclear power plant—the air-conditioning, the conversations and rushed footsteps in the passageway on the other side of the thin metal door. Dillon felt the sweat under his arms, even though the wardroom was cold. He couldn't tell if the admiral's question was rhetorical, or whether he was truly expecting a reply. Was he looking for Dillon to say the obvious? To go over all his thinking, or the thinking of the Speaker? He finally spoke, hesitantly. "Yes, you should."

The admiral drank deeply and set his cup down with a loud clank. "Why is that?"

Dillon sat forward slightly, keenly aware of all the eyes on him. "Because it comes directly from the Constitution and was lawfully passed by Congress."

Billings nodded slightly, then reached for a folder that sat on the table. He opened it slowly and took out a one-page document. He began to read:

FLASH

F   072200Z FEB 01

FM   SECDEF WASHINGTON DC

TO   CTG SEVEN SEVEN PT ONE

INFO   WHITE HOUSE SITROOM WASHINGTON DC
         CJCS WASHINGTON DC
         CNO WASHINGTON DC
         CMC WASHINGTON DC
         USCINCPAC HONOLULU HI
         COMSEVENTHFLT

TOP SECRET // N03450 //

OPER / PACIFIC FLYER //
RMKS / THIS IS A MANDATORY ACTION ORDER //
1. YOU ARE HEREBY ORDERED AND DIRECTED
BY THE PRESIDENT OF THE UNITED STATES
THROUGH THE SECRETARY OF DEFENSE AND
THE JOINT CHIEFS OF STAFF TO CEASE AND DE-
SIST ALL EFFORTS TO LOCATE AND MONITOR
THE PARTICIPANTS IN THE ATTACK ON THE PA-
CIFIC FLYER.
2. YOU ARE HEREBY ORDERED TO WITHDRAW
FROM THE JAVA SEA AND PROCEED IMMEDI-
ATELY TO PEARL HARBOR.
3. YOU WILL NOT COMPLY WITH A REQUEST OR
ORDER FROM CONGRESS BY WAY OF LETTER OF
REPRISAL OR OTHERWISE TO LOCATE, ENGAGE,
OR ATTACK ANYONE. ANY STEPS TAKEN BY
YOU OR THE TASK GROUP UNDER YOUR COM-
MAND OR ANY OTHER OFFICERS SUBORDINATE
TO YOU WILL BE A DIRECT VIOLATION OF THIS
ORDER.
4. ACKNOWLEDGE RECEIPT OF THIS MESSAGE
AND YOUR INTENTIONS TO COMPLY. //
BT

Billings looked up and glanced quickly around the table as he finished reading the message. Nothing needed to be said. He sat up straight in his chair and rested on his elbows on the table. "Which wins? Your letter, or an order from the President and Joint Chiefs?"

Commander Mike Caskey and Messer Schmidt rechecked their switches as they turned the Tomcat toward the island. Caskey could see it clearly in the high afternoon sun. The objective was to get imagery so that the intelligence specialists could do mensuration on anything that was casting a shadow. One pass. That's all it would take.

"We got good radar paint on the island, skipper."

"Roger that. Anything unusual?"

"Nope. Not a thing."

"All right, here we go," said Caskey as he bunted the nose of the F-14B toward the horizon and went to full military power. The island was fifteen miles away. His objective was to pass by the island at six hundred knots, just under supersonic. There were no expected difficulties, but one lucky bullet from a ground-fired rifle could ruin their whole day.

Caskey loved flying the F-14. He had spent his entire aviation career flying F-14s and now was at his peak as commanding officer of an F-14B Squadron aboard the Navy's newest carrier and he loved it.

"Range," he asked Messer.

"Five miles."

"Okay. This island isn't very big so we ought to be able to get the thing in one pass. Remember to keep your RAW gear on to check for SAMs. Somebody thinks they may have some."

"Roger that," said Messer, looking to his left inside the cockpit to adjust the timing for the cameras.

"How does it look on the television?"

Messer adjusted the angle of the television sight unit,

TVSU, in a chin blister under the nose of the aircraft. Its magnification allowed him to zoom in on the island and examine it via his internal screen. "I don't see anything unusual at all, but this island is completely covered with foliage. I don't know that we would see anything."

Caskey said, "I'm going hot mike," as he flipped a switch in his cockpit to activate the microphone inside his oxygen mask. They could hear each other breathe and could speak to each other without pressing any buttons.

"Remember where those concrete bunkers are supposed to be?"

"South side of the island, couple of miles in from the beach."

"Keep your eye open in that direction."

"Will do."

"Camera on!" Messer announced.

Caskey went into afterburner to accelerate as they passed the island.

Messer heard a buzz in his headset and looked down at his indicator. "Skipper! SAM radar at one o'clock!"

Caskey looked at his one o'clock position to see any missiles coming their way. "Nothing in the air," he said, his breath coming hard, his hands poised to slam the stick in whatever direction might be necessary to avoid a SAM. "Any launch indication?"

"Negative," said Messer, his voice rising in pitch. "They're just tickling us."

"Roger that, keep your eyes open."

"Roger."

Caskey was thrown forward into the stick as the surface-to-air missile slammed into the F-14 just between the engines in the rear of the Tomcat. Sections of the engines and fuselage fell to the ground underneath the burning airplane. Their momentum carried them past the island and out over the dark blue ocean as Caskey fought the forces, leaned back, and pulled the stick back in a desperate automatic attempt to keep the Tomcat in the air. He traded some of his speed for additional altitude.

"You got it?" Messer asked, nearly panicked.

"Engines are overtemp. I'll keep them going to get as far out as we can!" Caskey said through clenched teeth. "All the systems are failing. I've got two solid fire warning lights!"

Messer wrapped his right hand around the ejection handle between his legs. "Go to idle on both engines, turn the air source off. Check the lights!"

"No chance! We're going to lose both engines—we just need to get away from the island."

"Let me know when you're ready! I'll punch us . . ." Messer said as they lost electric power and their internal communications stopped. The Tomcat suddenly rolled violently to the left and pitched over toward the occan.

21

"GOOD MORNING, YOUR HONOR," DAVID PENDLE-
ton said softly in the packed courtroom of the District
Court for the District of Columbia. The judge could barely
hear him and leaned forward as Pendleton spoke.

"Good morning, Your Honor," said Jackson Gray, one
of the senior litigators in the Department of Justice.
"Jackson Gray, on behalf of the United States." His
round gold wire-rim glasses gave his large black face a
look of intellectual intensity which was heightened by his
closely cut beard. He glanced back at Molly, who sat quietly in the back of the courtroom.

"Good morning . . ." began the judge.

"Excuse me, Your Honor, but I think Mr. Gray mis-
spoke," interrupted Pendleton. "He said on behalf of the
United States. I'm afraid in this case he is here on behalf
of President Manchester, *not* the United States."

"I am here on behalf of the United States," said Gray,
glancing at Pendleton.

"Good morning, gentlemen," said Judge Konopka, the
senior judge for the District Court and on senior status—
semiretired. He had volunteered for this case, which none
of the sitting judges wanted to handle.

Judge Konopka looked around the courtroom, which
didn't have room for one additional human being. "Ladies and gentlemen in the gallery," Konopka said quietly,
squelching even the light buzz of conversation. "The

218

courtroom is very crowded. This hearing is very important, and we all need to be able to hear. I am having difficulty due to the whispering and conversations in the back of the room." He adjusted his rimless bifocals. "If anyone in the gallery utters a sound, the marshal will escort that person into the hallway." He sternly scanned the journalists and political staffers in the gallery. He returned his gaze to the attorneys.

"Now, Mr. Gray, I believe this is your motion. I have read your application and supporting papers for a temporary restraining order, and your complaint for declaratory relief and a permanent injunction. It is filed on behalf of the President as an individual citizen, as well as on behalf of the President as the Chief of State and Head of the Executive Branch. Is that correct?"

"That is correct, Your Honor. I might add that service was effected in timely fashion and the Speaker of the House accepted service on behalf of himself and Congress—"

"Excuse my intervention, Your Honor," said Pendleton quietly. "The Speaker of the House did not accept service for anyone. He was served by a courier yesterday morning. He was handed two copies of the complaint. That is the extent of his participation."

"Thank you for that clarification, Counsel," said Judge Konopka.

"Now, Mr. Gray, why this extraordinary step? Why an emergency application for a temporary restraining order against Congress? A defendant is normally allowed twenty days to respond."

Pendleton sat down at the enormous table in the paneled courtroom. His closed briefcase rested on the floor. He had no papers in front of him. Jackson Gray had a notebook crammed full of cases that had been highlighted and tabulated. Gray was trim and tall, and nearing fifty. He was clearly nervous, but well in control of himself.

Gray continued, "I ask that the court take judicial notice of this morning's newspaper and yesterday's newspaper, in which it was outlined that Congress has issued what it has called a Letter of Reprisal to a Navy battle group in the Java Sea. It is Congress's purpose to usurp the authority given to the President in the Constitution as Commander in Chief, and order the Navy to attack certain people on an island of Indonesia, a country with which we are not at war. This is an intolerable situation which is clearly unconstitutional and must be stopped. The President has ordered the battle group out of the area, but as of this moment it is unknown whether that order will be obeyed. Although it is a remote possibility, the Navy battle group may choose to follow the Letter of Reprisal rather than a direct order of the Commander in Chief. Because of that possibility, and because of the stunning misuse of a very limited constitutional power by Congress, the President thought it necessary for this court to issue a restraining order and a declaration that the order is unconstitutional. Since the court has reviewed our papers, I will yield to the court for questions, if there are any.''

Judge Konopka looked down at the papers and flipped through a couple of pages. He then looked up at David Pendleton. ''Counsel?''

Pendleton rose and adjusted his suit coat. He waited for ten seconds, allowing the tension to build, and then spoke. ''May it please the court. This court cannot hear this matter today because there is an indispensable party not before the court.'' Pendleton paused. Those behind Pendleton began to murmur, which caused a sharp look from Judge Konopka. Silence again descended on the courtroom. Pendleton continued, ''Mr. Gray, on behalf of the Justice Department and the Attorney General, has come into this courtroom this morning and requested an order enjoining—prohibiting—Congress from issuing a Letter of Reprisal. That is impossible. The Letter of Reprisal has already been issued. He asks for a declaration that the Letter of Reprisal is unconstitutional. He may ask that, but it cannot be asked in the form of an injunction.

That too is impossible. Any decision on the constitutionality of an issue so deep, so full of history and implications, should be made only after Congress is given an opportunity to respond. No one could argue otherwise.'' Pendleton swallowed and began again in the same soft yet riveting voice.

"Most fundamental though, Your Honor, is the failure to join the party that the Attorney General and the President truly want to enjoin. The indispensable party to this case is the United States Navy. It is the Navy, according to Mr. Gray, whose acts may be contrary to the law. It is the Navy that has its battle group poised to respond to the murder of Americans. It is the Navy that will either regard, or disregard, the Letter of Reprisal issued directly out of the words of the United States Constitution Article one, Section eight. It is therefore the Navy that must be before this court.''

Pendleton paused again as there was the indrawing of breath in the gallery. He looked around, then continued. "As far as I can see, the United States Navy is not before this court, has not been named in the action, and has not been served with notice of this hearing. Moreover, this points out the fundamental conflict of interest that exists for the Attorney General to represent one branch of government against another.'' He glanced over at Gray and spoke to the judge while looking at Gray.

"What the Attorney General is truly here to do, Your Honor, is to enjoin the Navy, which by definition is part of the *Executive* Branch of this government, part of the government under the President of the United States, which is the branch bringing this case. They do not need an injunction to stop the Navy; they need only an order from the President. It is my understanding that such an order has been issued. It is therefore up to the Navy whether it will follow the order of the President, who does not wish to act in response to an attack on American citizens, or the constitutionally issued Letter of Reprisal from the Representatives of the American People.'' The back of the room erupted and several journalists dashed out of the room with their pads in their hands.

Gray jumped up at counsel table. "Judge, may I respond to th—"

Judge Konopka put up his hand. "Mr. Gray, I gave you your chance to speak, let's hear Mr. Pendleton out. I will give you a chance to respond."

Molly felt a sudden wave of panic as she watched Pendleton dismantle her plan. Judge Konopka *had* to issue the restraining order, or a catastrophe would result. It had to be stopped now before people were killed.

Pendleton returned his gaze to Judge Konopka and waited for the noise to subside. "It is clear, Your Honor, that Mr. Gray has a conflict of interest. He is here asking for an injunction by one part of the Executive Branch against another part of the Executive Branch. Mr. Gray has such a conflict of interest that he cannot possibly be here before this court asking for the relief requested. Thank you for your attention, Judge Konopka."

With that, Pendleton sat down and folded his hands on the table.

Gray sprang up, anxious to speak. Judge Konopka nodded to him. "Thank you, Your Honor. I am shocked by the bold approach of Congress to dodge this critical question of constitutionality. They attempt to throw this over onto the Navy, when in fact it is they who have issued this unconstitutional Letter. They attempt to use it to intrude in the relationship between the Commander in Chief and the Navy by ordering the Navy to do something that the Navy has been specifically prohibited from doing. This argument is a pure red herring. The court has the authority, and it must act. If this court does not act, then the events after the Letter of Reprisal was issued may spin out of control. The implications for the United States military, the foreign policy of the United States, the authority of the President, are nearly infinite, and the very foundation of the United States Constitution will be in jeopardy." Gray paused and stared at the judge. "You must act, Your Honor, and you must act *now*. I have prepared a proposed order enjoining Congress from issuing this Letter of Reprisal, and declaring it unconstitutional, pending further briefing and the determination on the permanent injunction. I would like to submit it to the court at this time.'' Gray passed a copy of the document to David Pendleton, who put it on the table unread, and handed the original to the court clerk, who walked it to the judge. The judge looked at it and put it in front of him.

"Anything else, Counsel?" the judge said.

"Your Honor," Gray continued, "I have a lot more to say about all of these issues, and am prepared to argue the merits of the declaratory relief action.''

Pendleton rose slowly. "Your Honor, I am not prepared to argue the merits of this case since Congress received service of this case only yesterday, although I have done some preliminary research and briefing on the merits. I am confident that Congress will prevail and that this act will be clearly constitutional because of the very clear language of the document itself. However, I am not prepared at this point to argue this very complex matter on twenty-four hours' notice."

"Mr. Pendleton," Judge Konopka said quietly, "is it your position that Congress took the step it did, by issuing this Letter of Reprisal, without doing the legal research necessary to justify it? And have they not shared that research with you? Can they issue it and then have you come before this court and claim not to be ready to answer for it?" Judge Konopka paused, then turned toward Gray. "Mr. Gray, I have read all of your papers, which I believe make most of your arguments, do they not?"

"They do indeed, Your Honor. In addition, though, I have read more cases and believe that I can provide additional support for our position, but the gist of our position is certainly in our motion.''

"Very well. Thank you, gentlemen," said Judge Konopka as he rose.

Gray addressed him with a quizzical look on his face.

"Your Honor, if I might, it is important that we hear something immediately. I don't mean to imply that the court is inclined one direction or another, but if the court is not inclined to grant this temporary restraining order, it is my intention to file an emergency appeal under section 1292(a)(1) to the Circuit Court for the District of Columbia this morning and ask to suspend the usual timing requirements under Rule 2. Might I ask the court for a ruling within an hour?"

Judge Konopka looked at Pendleton, who said nothing.

"This is a very serious matter, Mr. Gray. I find it remarkable that you expect a District Court judge who received these voluminous motion papers yesterday and opposition this morning to have read through them and be prepared to issue an order on an issue of enormous constitutional significance in an hour. Do you really expect me to do that?"

Gray took a deep breath. "Yes, Your Honor, I must insist."

Konopka looked at both counsel and the gallery, which was on the edge of its seat, and stood to leave the courtroom.

"All rise," the bailiff cried.

As Molly stood, she watched Gray for some indication of what he expected. She was reassured. Gray looked confident as he stood next to Pendleton and fought back a smile.

🖾

Admiral Billings looked at his staff as he drank his coffee. Dillon sat at the other end of the table. The admiral looked at his aide across the room and called to him, "Drano, get Lieutenant Commander Walker up here, ASAP. I want to get an answer back to this message right now. Mr. Dillon, I would like you here during the discussion in case you have anything to add."

Dillon raised his eyebrows. "Yes, sir."

The phone rang and the aide picked it up. "Admiral,

it's CAG. He says he must speak to you—it's urgent.''
The admiral walked to the coffee table. His aide handed
him the phone.

''Admiral Billings,'' he said and then listened. The rest
of the officers in the room watched his face as it changed
from its usual immovability to concern and then anger.

''When?'' he asked casually. ''Any doubt about where
it came from? When are they due to arrive? Do you have
an on-site commander? Okay. Keep me posted.'' Billings
put the phone down too hard and returned to the table.
Still standing, he picked up the silver coffee pitcher and
poured the steaming black coffee into his cup. He set the
coffee pitcher down with a thud and looked at his staff.

''We just lost one of our F-14s. CO of VF-143.'' There
were stunned looks and controlled gasps.

The chief of staff, Captain Black, finally spoke. ''What
happened?''

''TARPS run over Bunaya. Apparently got a SAM up
the ass. They don't . . .'' The phone rang again.

The admiral's aide picked up, nodded, and said, ''One
minute.'' He turned to the admiral. ''It's CAG again.''

Billings rose and received the phone. ''What?'' he
asked. ''What?'' he said again, incredulous. ''How is that
possible? Are you sure? Okay. Give me hard identification
as soon as possible.''

He turned again. ''Looks like it was a South African
SAM.''

Beth Louwsma was the most surprised. ''Excuse me?''
she said. ''South African? How do they know that, sir?''

''Apparently the EA-6B was airborne and picked up
the fire-control radar. They finally categorized the signal
as an SAHV-3. Never got a launch indication, so they
don't think that's what got them.''

Commander Louwsma spoke quickly. ''Admiral, South
Africa has an infrared version of that same missile, the
SAHV-IR.'' She gritted her teeth as she realized the failure of the entire intelligence community to pick up on this
transfer of surface-to-air missile technology to terrorists

or whoever these people were. "They might have tried the Vietnam trick—light up an airplane in front with a radar SAM and shoot from behind with infrared so that he never sees it coming."

Billings glanced at her and didn't respond.

"Did they get the crew?"

The admiral shook his head. "No, another airplane saw two good chutes and is the on-scene commander. He hasn't heard from them yet. They're twenty-five miles west of the island, which is one hundred fifty miles from here. They haven't seen anybody come off the island to get them yet."

The chief of staff nearly shouted his concern. "You think those guys would go after them?"

"It's certainly a possibility. We're going to keep somebody there to make sure that doesn't happen. CAG's going to keep an armed bird nearby to make sure those boats don't get anywhere near them."

The door to the wardroom opened and Lieutenant Commander Walker stepped in, breathing hard after climbing up five decks from the ship's JAG office, where he'd been researching the Letter of Reprisal. "Good afternoon, sir," he said to the admiral.

Without looking at him, Billings directed him to the table. "Sit down. Have you had time to look at this issue?"

The admiral's staff judge advocate had been thinking about nothing else since he heard about it. He knew the time would come when he would have to answer the question. His thinning hair had begun to stick up on his head as if his body were electric.

His mouth was dry as he began to speak. "Yes, Admiral, I've looked at it pretty thoroughly."

Admiral Billings held up his hand. "Excuse me. Let me introduce Mr. James Dillon, the Special Assistant to the Speaker of the House. He has also done a substantial amount of research on this issue. Isn't that right, Mr. Dillon? The Speaker of the House didn't go forward with this Letter of Reprisal without having done exhaustive research, did he?'' Admiral Billings's eyes burned holes through Dillon.

Dillon's mouth began to get as dry as Walker's. "No, sir. We looked at it very hard."

Billings turned to his JAG officer. "What's the answer?"

"Well, Admiral, unfortunately there is nothing out there that says either way." Walker read the admiral's displeasure on his face and continued, the words coming out faster in hopes of warding off disaster. "Nor is there anything within the Constitution that makes it particularly easy to answer that question. The Constitution clearly provides for Letters of Marque and Reprisal, but it doesn't say to whom they should be issued or what their limitations are. I suppose," he said, adjusting his glasses, "that the writers expected people to understand the term as meaning the historical Letter of Marque and Reprisal, which had been used by many countries for several centuries before that. That would be a letter issued to a private ship to act as a man-of-war against a foreign country. It allowed it to attack and take commerce and prizes. Sort of legalized piracy."

"What about issuing one to a Navy ship?"

"There is some limited authority that it may have been done, but not much and not for a long time."

The admiral sat back and looked at Dillon. "Mr. Dillon? Do you agree with that?"

Dillon swallowed. "Yes, sir, I do."

"Why did Congress issue this Letter of Reprisal to a Navy ship?" the admiral prodded.

Dillon fought through the dry mouth as his anger returned. He put his arms on the table. "Because they wanted the Navy to *act*. Because the Speaker believes it is within Congress's power to issue a Letter of Reprisal to whomever it wants. We have an obligation, not just a right, but an *obligation* to defend ourselves and our citizens from attack." He leaned forward slightly, his confidence growing, "What kind of country is it that builds a huge defense establishment, enormous ships with thousands of sailors, incredibly capable airplanes, missiles, and bombs, and then stands by and watches its own countrymen get murdered and its ships sunk? And if a Letter of Reprisal can remedy the situation, do we send a merchant ship with a bunch of untrained civilians with guns, or CIA agents? We don't even have armed merchant ships anymore. We used to, and it made sense to send them. Now we don't, so the only thing that makes sense is to send a U.S. Navy warship."

Billings nodded. "I agree with your sentiments, but this is a question of authority. I have a message right here"— he picked the paper off the table—"from the President of the United States telling me not to do it. I have a letter right here"—he picked up the folder—"signed by the Speaker of the House, voted on by the Senate and the House, with a presidential veto that has been overridden by the Senate and the House, that tells me to do *exactly* the opposite." He looked at the faces in the room.

The staff remained stonily silent, unwilling to contribute to the discussion for fear of going down in history for making The Big Blunder. Finally the chief of staff spoke. "Sir, do you think we should get the captain of the carrier, the commander of the airwing, and the squadron commanders here to go over this with us? If we go forward with this, they're the ones who are going to have to implement it. Perhaps they should be part of the decision. . . ."

Billings shook his head. "No. This is my decision. I don't want them to even be a part of it. If I'm wrong, I don't want them to take any of the heat."

Billings sipped his coffee as he evaluated his options. "Gentlemen," he said, rising, "Beth, this is one of those times where you simply have to decide. You may be proved wrong, but decide you must." He turned and looked at his staff, then the picture of *Old Ironsides* behind him.

Dillon spoke. "Sir, may I be heard?"

"Sure," Billings replied curiously.

Dillon crossed to the replica of the Constitution on the wall. "When the United States was founded, it wasn't because we had great men who were going to tell us what to do; it was because those men recognized principles that were binding on us all. We're not bound to men, we're bound to *ideas*. Ideas like equality, freedom of expression, freedom of religion." He paused and looked at Admiral Billings. "The thing that protects us from losing those freedoms isn't a person, it's a document. The document this ship is named after. Without it, we're just another country arguing about who wins, which is decided by who is in power. Is it up to the President to say what we are to do? Is he the Commander in Chief? Sure he's the Commander in Chief of the armed forces. But can he do whatever he wants with us?" He shook his head. "He is limited by the Constitution like everyone else."

Dillon paused to consider his words. What he was about to say could be perceived as a rude challenge by a young staffer. He proceeded cautiously. "Admiral Billings," he said slowly, sweat visible through his shirt, "when I was doing my research, I came across something that surprised me. I came across the oath of office that the President takes when he is sworn in. It's right there in the Constitution. Word for word. The oath for the Vice President isn't in there. And the oath for Cabinet members isn't in there, and your oath, the oath that military officers take, isn't in there. The oath that you took, Admiral, that each one of your staff members took"—he swept his hand around the table—"that the Vice President took, and that the Speaker of the House took, is the same oath. Everybody's oath is the same except the President's. And your oath is that you will support and defend the Constitution, 'against *all enemies*. . . .' All the President promises to do is preserve, protect, and defend the Constitution. He never swears to defend it against all enemies. But *you do*." Dillon realized he was speaking too loudly. He took a breath to slow down. "Against all enemies, *foreign* and *domestic* . . . that's what you swore to do, Admiral, and that's what you must do."

Dillon returned to his seat.

Billings looked around the table at his staff. Each one of them met his gaze. He recited from memory the oath he had taken as an ensign. "I, Ray Billings, do solemnly swear that I will support and defend the Constitution of the United States, against all enemies, foreign and domestic. . . .

"Our first allegiance, gentlemen, Beth, is to the Constitution. Our second allegiance is to obey the orders of those above us, but they must be *lawful* orders. An order directly contrary to the Constitution is not lawful. Seems to me," he said, the momentum of his words driving him, "that we follow our first allegiance, to the U.S. Constitution." He looked around at the picture of the square-rigged frigate, and then back at them. "And to the USS *Constitution.*" He paused and strode back to his chair. "Chief of Staff, prepare a message. Tell the Joint Chiefs of Staff and the White House: 'Have received your message. Since receiving your message, Navy F-14 shot down by terrorists with South African surface-to-air missile. Am proceeding against the terrorists with all due speed. Believe bound by allegiance to the United States Constitution and therefore will follow the direction of the Letter of Reprisal issued by Congress.' " He spoke to his staff again. "I am not even going to ask you if you are with me or against me—" the Admiral said.

"Admiral," the chief of staff interrupted. "May I say something?"

Billings hesitated. "I don't know. If I—"

"I think you're making a big mistake. The oath is right, but you're missing the point. The order of the President is right out of the Constitution too. He is the Commander in Chief. . . ."

Billings stared hard at him. "So *any* order of the President is automatically right?"

"Well, of course not every order, there would be—"

"And how can you tell the difference?"

"By the rules of war, the rules of law under which we operate, the UCMJ . . ."

"But what if his order was directly contrary to the Constitution?"

"Well, in that case, maybe . . ."

"Isn't that what we have here? He has given us an order that is contrary to the Constitution. And you've heard these two gentlemen"—he indicated Dillon and Walker—"and there's nothing out there, *nothing*, that says this can't be done." He continued to stare at his chief of staff, who had stopped looking at him.

Billings lowered his voice. "What if the President has lost his nerve? What if he won't do anything, no matter what? What if he's not fulfilling his obligation as President? Congress can't do anything about it?" He shook his head. "Looks to me like they can. And they have."

Pendleton and the Speaker of the House were in the corner of the Speaker's enormous office. Pendleton was shaking his head slowly. "That's really not my area, Mr. Speaker. I have never looked into impeachment at all. I know Johnson was impeached, but short of that . . ." He was interrupted as the door opened and they both looked up. Robin walked in hurriedly. "There is a phone call for Mr. Pendleton. It is urgent."

Pendleton looked inquiringly at the Speaker, who shrugged anxiously.

Pendleton picked up the phone on the Speaker's desk. "David Pendleton." He listened intently, then said, "What does it say?" He waited and listened.

The Speaker crossed over to stand next to him. He resisted the temptation to lean closer to the earpiece and attempted to appear calm.

After about a minute, Pendleton spoke again. "Thank you. Please fax it over to me at the Speaker's office immediately." Pendleton placed the receiver gently on the telephone. He turned to the Speaker, expressionless.

Stanbridge could not stand the suspense. "Well?"

"That was the associate I had waiting at the courthouse." Pendleton glanced at his watch. "Only forty-five minutes. The judge must have already had his decision in mind before we arrived this morning."

"Well, what does it . . . what happened?"

Pendleton looked at him and a glint appeared in his eye. "We won the first round."

"And what does that mean?"

"I argued that they did not have an indispensable party before them, specifically the Navy, and if they did, they would have a conflict of interest, as it would be the Executive Branch suing the Executive Branch. The court has said that there is an indispensable party not before them for the temporary restraining order. The court also said that the constitutional issue should not be resolved in twenty-four hours, but with both sides having a chance to be heard on the merits by submitting briefs. The court set a hearing thirty days from today to hear the constitutional question." The corners of Pendleton's mouth curled into the faintest smile. "I take it thirty days will give you sufficient time to accomplish your objectives?"

"Absolutely," the Speaker said enthusiastically.

"Very well, then," Pendleton said. "Now we wait for them to try to get to the Appellate Court before it's too late."

22

ADMIRAL BILLINGS STARED AT THE THREE ENORMOUS screens in front of him in the cold, darkened room. One screen showed the entire Pacific Ocean, a second showed the smaller Pacific area in which they were operating, and the third showed a smaller area still, with the ships and formation around the USS *Constitution*. Dillon stood behind the admiral and took in the displays. The countries were outlined in different colors, each ship and airplane was represented by a graphic, and there were various other symbols that Dillon could only guess at. It looked like a very complicated—and very enjoyable—computer game. For a moment he forgot he was on a huge moving ship.

"You ever seen anything like this, Mr. Dillon?"

"No, sir, I really haven't," Dillon said, understating the obvious. Dillon had been awestruck ever since setting foot on the aircraft carrier. He had seen movies, heard stories, even lived in a city that always had carriers present. But nothing had prepared him for the sensory assault that being on a carrier created. The activity around him moved at the speed of sound, especially on the flight deck. He had watched the launching and recovery of aircraft, which seemed to go on nonstop. Dillon felt out of his element. He was completely at home in Washington—knowing exactly when to snicker and roll his eyes. But here, people didn't roll their eyes if you screwed up; they

wrote to your parents and said what a fine person you had
been.

"Good thing your staff sent your clearance so we could
let you in here."

"Yes, sir. It was somebody else's idea; I sure didn't
think of it." Dillon knew that if any of this had been left
to him, it simply wouldn't have happened.

"Well, this is where I sit during significant operations," Billings continued. "The bridge is really more for
life as a spectator; this is where I operate."

Lieutenant Reynolds handed Dillon the cup of black
coffee he had requested. The dim light accentuated the
gold braid around Reynolds's shoulder, the mark of an
admiral's aide. Reynolds was clean-cut and sharp, as always, which mystified Dillon. He felt dirty, unkempt, and
out of sorts every minute he was on the ship. He couldn't
imagine how Reynolds stayed so . . . impressive.

"So, Mr. Dillon," the admiral continued. "As you can
see, we know where every ship in the area is, and where
we are in particular. All this information is fed to us from
many sources, which we consolidate and filter as necessary to give us the picture we want. It allows us to have
a tremendous amount of flexibility in decision making."
The admiral looked over his shoulder to his operations
officer. "Any word on those two downed F-14 crew?"

"Yes, sir. The helicopter's halfway there. On-scene
commander has both their strobes in sight. He has good
radio comm with both of them. They're sitting in their
rafts, fat, dumb, and happy." He added as an afterthought,
somewhat smugly, "And probably looking for sharks in
the dark."

"Nice thought," the admiral said.

The phone rang and the chief of staff picked up. "Yes,
go ahead." He paused. "How many?" he said suddenly,
anxiously. "When? Somebody over them? Okay,
thanks." The chief of staff turned to Admiral Billings.
"Admiral, the *Los Angeles* has just issued an emergency
unscheduled report. She's at periscope depth and saw

three boats pass at high speed. He estimated forty knots, headed in the direction of the two downed aviators. It's unclear whether the helicopter will get there before those boats do.''

Billings fired a question back at Captain Black. "Who's on-scene SARCAP?"

Dillon leaned over to Reynolds. "What's that?" he whispered.

"Search and Rescue Combat Air Patrol. Armed airplane over the downed aviators that will stop anybody who tries to harm them before they're picked up out of the water.''

Dillon thought for a moment. "Stop?"

Reynolds looked at him. "Kill."

"Who is it?" the admiral asked anxiously.

"It's Drunk Driver, the F-18 squadron commander."

"Does he know about these boats?"

"It's being put out through the E-2 right now, sir," Louwsma added quickly.

"Do we have the three boats on our screen?"

"Not yet, sir."

"Why not?"

"We don't have a radar signature on them, sir. They're probably fiberglass."

Billings spoke, to no one in particular. "Are they coming from Bunaya to get our guys?"

No one responded.

"Do we have any idea whether those boats are armed?"

"No, sir, we have no idea," Beth said.

Billings said nothing, then, "Send a message to Washington, flash priority. 'Cigarette boats believed to correlate to attackers of *Pacific Flyer* en route to downed F-14 crew. Request clearance to fire.' "

"Yes, sir."

"How long before they reach our aircrew at current speeds?"

"Approximately thirty minutes, Admiral."

"How far away is the helicopter?"

"Approximately an hour."

The phone rang again and Black picked it up. "Yes?" He frowned, a deep frown that started in his forehead but continued deep inside. He blinked and turned toward Billings. "Admiral, the communications nets seem to be down." He returned to the phone. "How long do you expect it to be down . . . what do you mean?" He looked at the admiral and put his hand over the receiver. "Admiral, they don't think it's the ship's communications that are down."

The admiral looked at him, a dark cloud forming on his countenance. "What are you talking about?"

Black paused, looked at the screens, then spoke softly. "They think Washington's cut us off."

"What?" the admiral asked.

Black continued, "The President has taken us out of all the comm links, Admiral. We're on our own."

≤

"I want the Attorney General, and I want him here now," President Manchester said with his eyes closed as he rubbed his temples.

"Admiral," he said, looking at Hart. "I thought you said that Billings would follow our order."

Hart tried not to wince. He had been waiting for this question from the President.

"I thought he would, Mr. President. Obviously we never know what somebody is going to do until they are in that situation, but I expected him to follow the direct order of his Commander in Chief."

"Well, apparently he is not going to." The back door to the Oval Office opened and Greg McCormick, the Attorney General, strode in quickly.

"Good morning, Mr. President," he said. He had been a corporate lawyer from Connecticut and Manchester's campaign manager. "I didn't know we were going to have this meeting."

Manchester stared at him incredulously. "Well, neither did I, Greg. I didn't know you were going to lose this wonderful motion on this more wonderful lawsuit that you agreed we should file against Congress. You want to explain that?"

McCormick's cheeks flushed slightly red. "I didn't expect to lose that hearing. I thought we had an excellent chance, and I have my best advocate on it. And if you recall, the lawsuit wasn't my idea, it came from your office of the couns—"

"What about this conflict issue?"

"We're dealing with it, Mr. President. Frankly, it hit us kind of sideways. We didn't anticipate it. But I don't think you need to worry about it."

"So what's the plan?" the President asked.

"We're going to be taking an emergency appeal to the D.C. Court of Appeals within the hour."

Manchester looked at the wall clock, which read 10:30 A.M. "What's the press doing?" Manchester asked his press aide hovering in the corner.

"Afraid there's a lot of confusion, Mr. President," he said quickly and forcefully. "Everybody seems to understand the idea of hitting back at the terrorists, but nobody seems to understand what is going on between you and Congress. There's a mixed bag of opinion out there, but for the most part, the people seem to be in favor of some kind of action."

"I feel like we've been pushed back into our own end zone," Manchester said. "We lost the motion, the admiral in charge of the battle group has decided to go contrary to our direct order, we're no longer in communication with them, and public opinion is not in my favor." Manchester stuck out his chin almost involuntarily. "But I will tell you one thing, I am not changing my plan." He turned his attention to the Chairman of the Joint Chiefs again. "Admiral, what do you make of those boats going after those downed pilots?"

"Sounds to me like the same boys that took over the *Pacific Flyer*, Mr. President. My guess is they intend to do to them the same thing they did to the crew of that ship. Billings did ask for permission to fire upon—"

"I know that," Manchester interrupted, "but they've disobeyed orders directly and completely. Admiral, can you explain to me how that airplane got shot down if they were not supposed to even be approaching into Indonesian airspace?"

"No, sir, I cannot. I'm not sure what kind of SAM it was. I'm not familiar with the South African system. Most SAMs, though, would reach into international airspace."

Manchester winced. "You mean they might have been in international airspace when they were shot down?"

"It's a distinct possibility, Mr. President."

Manchester shook his head. "Are they in international waters now? The two who were shot down?"

"Yes, sir, but that doesn't mean that's where they were shot."

"We just don't know, do we?" Manchester asked, frustrated.

"No, sir, we don't. Billings didn't say exactly where the shoot-down occurred, only that it did. We could certainly reopen communications and ask . . ."

"Oh, that's rich. 'Please, Admiral, give us more information so we can look even stupider than we already do.' No, he can just figure it out for himself. He seems to be quite willing to do that already." Manchester rose. "They brought this upon themselves, Admiral. Now they're going to have to deal with it themselves." He suddenly changed tack. "Where is the nearest carrier not under Billings's command?"

Those in the room focused on the admiral.

The Chief of Staff stood up. "Mr. President, may I speak freely?"

Manchester scowled at him. "What?"

"I think this has gone on long enough, Mr. President. We're driving a wedge between ourselves and the military, between ourselves and the people, between ourselves and Congress, and between ourselves and the courts. We are being fenced off. All of our decisions are going contrary to the way things are working out and . . ."

"You losing your nerve?"

"I am not losing my nerve, Mr. President. I am simply trying to arrive at the best decision for you and for the country, in that order."

Manchester shook his head. "No, Arlan. That's where you don't get it. That's where you've never gotten it. How can you not understand me yet?" His face burned with disappointment at his old friend. "My decision will be what is best for the country *without* consideration for my own political gain or future. I refuse to resort to killing dozens of people when there are other ways this can be dealt with! If Congress wants to fly off the handle and take a crazy position, we will fight them about that as well. I simply will not succumb to the idea that the only response to violence is more violence." He turned again to Admiral Hart. "Where is the nearest battle group, Admiral?"

Before the admiral could speak, Van den Bosch jumped in again. "Mr. President, the implications of what you are considering are enormous."

Manchester's eyes were bright and full of anger. "You think I don't know that? You think that I am stumbling through this without understanding the implications? How dumb do you think I am?"

"I don't think you are dumb at all, Mr. President, you know that, but this thing could spin out of control very fast."

"It is already spinning out of control!" Manchester's voice rose. "What we need to do is restore order, not allow disorder to rule."

"I don't think getting another battle group . . ."

"I didn't ask you what you thought. I asked the admiral where the nearest battle group is. That is the question I want answered right now. Please *sit down*."

Van den Bosch sat down and stared straight ahead, his sandy complexion reddening.

"Mr. President, the nearest battle group is in the Philippines."

"How long would it take them to get there?"

"To get where, Mr. President?"

"To get to where the Billings battle group is right now."

Hart considered the problem. His heavy breathing was the only sound in the room. "Sir, that battle group is about fourteen hundred miles away."

"How long would it take them to get there?"

"That would depend on whether you would want escort ships to go . . ."

"How long would it take for the aircraft carrier to get airplanes overhead the *Constitution*?"

The admiral played with one of the brass buttons on his double-breasted navy blues as he thought. "It would take about forty hours at flank speed."

"Send them," the President said softly.

"What do you want their orders to be, Mr. President?" the admiral said, pressing for a clear decision.

"To intercept the *Constitution* Battle Group."

The admiral was dumbstruck. His heart raced as he considered what the President was doing. "Mr. President, do you realize what this will say to the rest of the world?"

"What do you think it will say, Admiral?"

"That we have a rogue battle group. That we have to send our own military force to stop it. It looks like a civil war, with part of the military fighting for Congress, and part for the President."

The President looked around the room. No one dared to speak, or even move. "Isn't that exactly what we have?"

🔖

"Admiral, the F-18 has those three boats on its radar. They're approaching rapidly to the location where Caskey and his RIO are down. He requests clearance to fire!''

The admiral looked at the screens, which now had the three targets moving toward the location of the two downed airmen. "The White House is going to let us twist slowly in the breeze. They're not going to give us any advice, and in fact, they are making it hard on us. So be it." He spoke to his operations officer without looking at him. "Is the E-2 in communication with the F-18 and the downed aircrew?''

"Yes, they are.''

"Under no circumstances are those boats to be allowed to approach our pilots. Instruct the F-18 that if those boats approach, he is to take them out. These are boats that have already demonstrated a hostile act, and I hereby designate them as hostile. They are committing hostile intent, and you are free to fire on them if they approach. Does the E-2 have a good fix on the aircrew's position?''

"Yes, he does, sir.''

"Okay. Tell the aircrew to shut off their strobe lights and stop transmitting on their radios until the helicopter is in the area. We can't make this easy on those boats.''

◆

"MC, you up?" Drunk asked Caskey over the search-and-rescue frequency.

"Yeah, what's up?"

"Three bad-guy speedboats inbound from the island. Cut off your strobe until the helicopter is nearby. Leave your radio on. Don't transmit; they may have a direction finder.''

Caskey breathed in quickly in response to Driver. He sat in his black-rubber life raft and bobbed silently on the dark ocean trying to visualize, or hear, the coming boats. Even though it was over 80 degrees and the water temperature was in the eighties, he was cold. There was a slight breeze, which cooled his body faster than he would have liked. Being out of the water and in the raft helped, but he still felt chilled. *"Roger, copy,"* Caskey said into

his hand-held radio. He had plugged his helmet into the
external jack and could hear the radio transmissions
clearly in his helmet. He set the waterproof radio in his
lap and reached his hand up to the strobe light that was
attached to his helmet by Velcro.

He looked across the sea to Messer, six hundred yards
away. When they had initially hit the water and climbed
into their rafts, they had attempted to paddle closer together to hook up to each other. They soon discovered
that the amount of effort required to get together was not
worth the benefit and they gave up. The currents kept
them in the same location though, and they remained in
visual contact. But now, after nightfall under the star-filled
moonless sky, the two strobe lights that had been so reassuring were extinguished. Messer had heard the same
radio transmission that Caskey had. Good.

Caskey could see the F-18 circling above him at ten
thousand feet, its red anticollision light obvious against
the night sky. Then, just like his strobe, the F-18's lights
were extinguished. Good idea, Caskey thought. If those
guys in the speedboats have shoulder-fired surface-to-air
missiles, they could do some serious damage to an F-18.
No sense showing them where you are.

Caskey lay back in the raft as fatigue began to over-
whelm him. He yearned to be able to put his head against
the back wall of the raft, but he couldn't. His head bobbed
to the back involuntarily as sleep momentarily overcame
him. He jerked his head forward with that panic feeling
and grabbed a handful of seawater to splash on his face.
He shook his head to clear his mind and raged at himself
for nearly falling asleep. With his strobe light off, if he
fell asleep nobody would ever find him.

It seemed as if he had entered a different world, where
time was suspended. The stars didn't seem to move and
there was no sound except the lapping of the waves
against the side of his rubber raft. He saw no ships on the
horizon and began to wonder if the helicopter was in-

bound at all. He knew the CH-46 that was coming had no inertial navigation system and would need to be directed by the E-2. With his luck they would get more lost than he was.

Caskey sat up straight in his boat and his heart began to pound. He could hear engines: not the *wap-wap* beating of the CH-46 that he had hoped to hear; these engines were deep-throated high-speed engines. He sat up taller in his boat and strained to see across the water. On the horizon a mile or more away he thought he glimpsed three dark objects. He thought of the leverage these terrorists would get if they captured two American aircrew. What a fiasco. He thought of the 9mm Beretta in his survival vest and wondered if he should get it ready. He scanned the sky hurriedly but couldn't see the F-18. Nor could he hear it.

He decided to take the risk and picked up his radio. He pressed the transmit button. *"Hey, Drunk, you got these guys?"* he whispered, as if someone else listening on the frequency would not hear him.

"Yeah, I got 'em," Drunk said confidently. *"Shut up and stay off the radio."*

Caskey continued, *"They can't be more than a mile or two from me. If you are going to hit them, you better hurry."*

"Rollin' in on 'em now, MC. You got nothing to worry about." Caskey looked back at the forms racing toward him. High and to his right he could hear a jet engine going to full power. Out of a dark place in the sky, where the F-18 blocked out the stars, came a sudden short burst of flame. Guns, Caskey thought to himself. Exactly right. He waited but saw no indication of damage on the three racing boats. The engines increased their pitch slightly as they raced faster toward him. He heard the F-18 pull up at the bottom of its run and could visualize the dark night air vaporizing at the ends of its wings.

Again he saw the shadow and the flame. But this time there was an explosion on the horizon so bright that he

had to cover his eyes. Debris flew into the air backlit by
a burning hulk. "Yes," Caskey whispered. He waited to
see what the other boats would do. In the light of their
burning sister he could see them smashing over the waves
toward him at incredible speeds.

Another pass by the F-18, another burst of flame from
its hidden nose, and a miss. By now the cigarette boats
were less than half a mile away. He could clearly hear the
throbbing of their powerful engines and hear their bows
slapping the waves. *"One down, two to go,"* Caskey
transmitted.

"Roger that," his fellow squadron commander replied.
"Stay off the damned radio, MC!" He sounded aggravated. *"I got another F-18 inbound, but we better get this
done now."*

Caskey heard the engine race as the airplane accelerated
toward the ocean. Its shadow blocked more stars. Again
the flash in the nose and another blinding explosion as
the second cigarette boat burst into an infinity of pieces.
"Nice shot," Caskey transmitted.

Suddenly a missile flew off the third boat. *"Missile
airborne!"* Caskey cried into his transmitter. *"Shoulder
fired SAM!"* he finished.

"A shot in the blind," Drunk replied calmly. *"They
were off by about ninety degrees."*

He saw the cigarette boat make a broad sweeping turn
and fire off another missile. *"Another missile airborne!"*
Caskey yelled.

"They're not even close," came the reply.

A new voice came up on the radio circuit. *"Casper
903 is five miles out,"* the E-2 NFO announced.

"Tell them to hold off until this shooting is done,"
Drunk replied instantly.

The F-18 pitched up one more time and went back
down. Another missile flew toward the F-18 just as the
flash came from the Hornet's nose. The third boat exploded as the other two had. Caskey held his arms up
over his head as if signaling a touchdown. "Yes!" he

yelled, releasing the tension in his body. He reached up and hit the strobe light on the top of his helmet, showing that the last boat had been destroyed less than four hundred yards in front of him. His face was lit up by the reflection of the flames of the burning boat. He saw no movement or survivors. From behind the burning hulk he could see the rotating beacon as an H-46 approached, and above the H-46 he saw the lights of the F-18 come on and roll over in the darkness.

"*Nice shooting,*" Caskey transmitted, unable to control his relief.

"*Thanks, MC. Can you see the 46?*"

"*Yeah, I got him.*"

"*MC, this is Casper, we see you.*"

"*Then get in here and get me out of this raft.*"

"*Roger that,*" said the CH-46 as it slowed to a hover over Caskey, illuminated by the burning boats. One of the figures in the water began to swim toward him from a quarter mile away.

23

DAVID PENDLETON LOOKED OUT OVER WASHINGTON, D.C., from the windows of his immaculate law office on the corner of the eighth floor. One window faced the Capitol; from the other, the Washington Monument was visible. Pendleton marveled at the beauty of the government buildings and monuments. If only the government were as beautiful as its buildings.

The phone rang and he heard his secretary pick up.

"May I say who is calling? One moment please. Mr. Pendleton, Mr. Gray on the telephone."

Pendleton picked up the telephone slowly. "Yes," he said as if he were answering, rather than questioning.

"Mr. Pendleton, this is Jackson Gray. I wanted to give you notice that I have requested and obtained a time for an emergency appeal hearing before the D.C. Circuit Court of Appeals. The hearing will be this afternoon at three-thirty. I told them I would call you and give you notice."

Pendleton waited five seconds before responding. "You contacted the Court of Appeals without me being present on the telephone?"

Gray skipped a beat, then, "Are you trying to imply there was something *improper* in scheduling a hearing?"

"I asked you a question. You haven't yet answered it," Pendleton replied, his voice growing cooler.

"I called to obtain a hearing time. There was no discussion of the merits of this matter at all. And you know it.''

''What is it you plan on asking the court to do?''

''For the court to reverse Judge Konopka. Simple as that.''

''Very well,'' Pendleton said.

''Good-bye.'' Gray hung up without waiting to see if Pendleton had anything else to say.

Pendleton called to his secretary in a voice only slightly louder than the one he'd used with Gray. ''Maria, please get Rebecca in here immediately.''

Pendleton returned to the window until Rebecca appeared at the door two minutes later. ''Good morning,'' he said.

''Good morning, David,'' she replied, using his first name as the San Diego firm demanded in spite of the Washington tradition of calling partners Mr. or Ms.

Pendleton considered Rebecca as bright as attorneys got. She was slightly overweight and had a long face that would never be beautiful. But her mind was razor-sharp and was matched by her eagerness to solve difficult problems.

Pendleton continued, ''As expected, the Attorney General's office is going to the D.C. Circuit on an emergency appeal. Have you finished your memo?''

''Yes.'' She looked at him inquisitively. ''Do you really think the Circuit Court will stop Congress?''

''That's the point that the Attorney General's office continues to miss. It's not Congress they have to stop. The people they have to stop now are in the Navy.''

''But the court could issue an order declaring the Letter unconstitutional,'' she said eagerly.

''How?'' he asked, testing her research.

''Well''—she leaned forward slightly, holding the papers on her lap—''they could say the Letter is a usurpation of the President's power, or that it was a historical power that no longer applies with a modern military, or . . .''

"Based on what?"

"They could say it's never been done before, at least not like this, and . . ."

"Do you really believe the D.C. Circuit is going to declare an act of Congress unconstitutional because it's never been done 'like this' before?"

"It's possible . . ."

"Without our even having a meaningful chance to brief it? The President files his action, declares it's an emergency, and the court runs around in circles trying to satisfy him?"

"They may . . ."

"What would the order say? 'We hereby order that this is unconstitutional'?"

"I guess that's the question."

"Indeed."

Rebecca smiled, exhilarated. She admired Pendleton's calm.

Pendleton put out his hand, and she handed him the notebook she had prepared with all the relevant case law, both procedural and on the constitutional question. Without looking at her he began reading voraciously. He always found the key to a case between the lines. It was what the court didn't say that was of particular interest to him.

Picking up on the subtle way Pendleton was now completely ignoring her, Rebecca backed out of his office and closed his door.

He pored over the materials, including the memoranda brought by Rebecca, without stopping for lunch. Pendleton had an ability to commit virtually everything to memory. His objective on argument was always the same: to guide the court to the simplest possible solution in his favor. At three o'clock he glanced at the clock and closed the notebook.

He put it on the side of his desk, put the memoranda in a small briefcase, and headed out. Others in the firm hovered near his office but didn't try to distract him. They just wanted to *see* him, to be part of the great argument without actually participating. They just happened to be walking by, or chatting with the secretary next to his office, or waiting for the elevator with no button pushed. He walked by all of them without a word—his mind elsewhere.

The Attorney General's office had obviously called the press. The front steps to the court were thronged with television reporters—eager men and women with microphones. He walked straight into the group and continued walking as they opened before him like the Red Sea. They yelled questions during his entire approach to the court. He put his hand up in slight protest with a small smile on his face and a continuous shaking of his head. He didn't say a word. The door opened before him as one of the U.S. marshals saw him approach. He placed his briefcase on the conveyor belt for the X-ray machine and walked through the metal detector. Another group of reporters had beaten him there. The courtroom was overflowing with people. Their hurried looks toward Pendleton showed their excitement and anxiety.

Jackson Gray sat at one counsel table and Pendleton walked to the other one.

"Good afternoon, Jackson," he said cordially.

Gray looked up at him, surprised. "Hello," he said quickly, returning his gaze to his papers.

"All rise," said the clerk as the three Appellate Court judges walked in. Pendleton and Gray stood up with the rest. "The Circuit Court of the District of Columbia is now in session. Please be seated and come to order."

The presiding judge addressed them. "Would counsel please state their appearances?"

"Good afternoon. Jackson Gray of the Attorney General's office on behalf of the United States and moving party."

Pendleton stood up. "Good afternoon, Your Honors. David Pendleton on behalf of the Speaker of the House of Representatives and on behalf of the Congress of the United States.''

The presiding judge spoke first to Pendleton. ''Mr. Pendleton, have you had a chance to review the papers filed this morning by Mr. Gray's office?''

''Yes I have, Your Honor.''

''Very well. Mr. Gray, this is a very extraordinary procedure. Would you please explain to the court why there is such a critical need for this matter to be heard today rather than in the ordinary course?''

''Thank you, Your Honor,'' Gray said. He took a long breath and launched into the argument that he had gone over fifty times in his head. His hands shook almost imperceptibly. ''This matter, Your Honors, before this court on this day, is perhaps the most serious issue faced by a Circuit Court of Appeals in this century.'' A murmur went up in the gallery behind Gray. ''What Congress has done is tantamount to tearing up the Constitution. What Congress has done, Your Honors, is overthrow the authority of the President over the military, and take that authority for itself. Congress is attempting to overthrow the Executive Branch.'' He paused for effect, and looked at the faces of the three judges. ''This usurpation of authority and attack on the entire existence of the government cannot be tolerated. This court must act and act quickly to stop it before it careens out of control and ruins the democratic government of the United States.''

Gray stopped again, apparently having already rehearsed these pauses. ''There is currently a Navy battle group that has received a so-called Letter of Reprisal from Congress to attack citizens of other countries without the authority of the Commander in Chief of the military. In fact, the Letter is in direct contradiction to an order of the Commander in Chief, who was given that authority by the Constitution. It *cannot* be allowed to happen. The specter of a rogue battle group from the United States with a nuclear aircraft carrier and its supporting ships, a Marine Expeditionary Unit and its supporting troops, special forces and submarines, is a frightening thought. The District Court was unwilling to act. That is understandable,'' Gray said solemnly. ''This is a very serious matter, which must be dealt with at the highest level of the court system. If this has to be taken to the United States Supreme Court, we will go there.'' The murmur increased.

The presiding judge looked down at those behind the rail. ''Will those in the courtroom please refrain from expressing themselves? I would like to have a quiet courtroom to hear these arguments. Please continue, Mr. Gray.''

''Thank you, Your Honor. As I said, if we have to take this argument to the United States Supreme Court, we will do so. But the sooner the order is issued declaring this act of Congress unconstitutional, the sooner we will return to a normal state of affairs and the entire world can breathe more easily. I therefore ask that this court reverse the decision made this morning by the District Court denying our temporary restraining order, and mandate that the court issue such a temporary restraining order. Thank you.''

''Mr. Pendleton?'' the presiding judge said.

Pendleton sat motionless for ten seconds, his usual time to get the court's entire attention, then rose. ''Good afternoon, Your Honors.'' Pendleton glanced over at Gray, then back at the justices. ''Mr. Gray makes several interesting arguments, which the court may certainly consider at some point. When this issue is joined on the merits, the Congress of the United States is confident that it will prevail. It acted on language in the Constitution based on the power *directly* given to the Congress and *never* amended or modified.''

He paused. ''For the Attorney General to come before this court and make such sweeping statements about the unconstitutionality of this power is disingenuous and inappropriate. The only issue before this court is whether the district court abused its discretion in failing to issue a temporary restraining order. I do not need to cite to the court all the authorities on the criteria for the issuance of a TRO. But one of the rather obvious and critical elements is that the President must clearly demonstrate a likelihood of prevailing on the merits. That the President cannot do. The Letter, specifically authorized by the Constitution, was passed by both Houses of Congress, vetoed by the President, and then the veto was overridden. There is simply no question that it was properly passed and issued. The only conceivable constitutional question is whether or not it is proper to issue a Letter of Reprisal to a U.S. Navy vessel. There is no direct legal authority, and certainly no case law, forbidding the issuance of such a Letter. It will be an argument from history brought forward to modern times by regarding the Constitution as a 'living document.'

"The United States Supreme Court holds dear the concept that the Constitution must yield and change based on modern circumstances and cannot be held to a strictly historical interpretation. So be it," Pendleton said, letting that thought sink in. "That is exactly what Congress has done. The question, then, is who will decide whether what Congress has done fits within that interpretation of the Constitution, in other words, whether Congress is right? That is a very large issue that Congress must have an opportunity to brief and argue. To have it declared unconstitutional in a hearing before this Court of Appeals on five hours' notice is impossible. It would stop a legitimate exercise of congressional authority."

Pendleton continued, cautiously, but firmly. "But even if the President could convince the court he is likely to prevail, he has failed to bring before that court or this one the necessary party—the Navy. The injunction he seeks is to prohibit Congress from doing something. That is an impossibility. Congress has already done it. He cannot ask you to restrain the past." A slight snicker rose in the gallery.

"The President has the power to order the Navy to do whatever he chooses within legal limits. By coming to this court and asking for an order to enjoin the Navy, the President is admitting that the Navy, another part of the Executive Branch, disagrees with his interpretation of the Constitution. Otherwise the Navy would simply follow his order.

"Thus, the true request by the President is for the Court to *give him a hand* in getting the Navy to do what he wants." Pendleton stopped, then continued. "It could be argued that the Navy is before this court because it is part of the Executive Branch. But that would require the President to request an injunction against himself, which I doubt even he would do." The gallery erupted in laughter and applause. Pendleton waited until the noise had subsided in response to the scowl of the presiding judge. "Thank you for the opportunity to be heard." And with that Pendleton sat down.

Gray stood up quickly. "May I respond?" he demanded of the judges.

The presiding judge nodded. "Quickly," he said.

"Your Honor, Mr. Pendleton has set up a classic red herring, a head fake to throw Your Honors off the real issue in this case. The jurisdiction over the Navy is a false issue. We are not asking you to enjoin the Navy, Your Honor. We are asking this court to enjoin *Congress*. You do not need the Navy here to do that. If this court declares the Letter of Reprisal unconstitutional, at least through a temporary order pending further briefing, then the Navy would follow any such Letter at its own peril. The issues are whether we have a likelihood of prevailing and whether there will be permanent irreparable injury, in the absence of the court's actions. There will certainly be permanent injury if the Navy follows the Letter and people are *killed* as a result."

Gray paused and breathed deeply. "The issue here is whether *Congress* can decide what the words of the Constitution mean. Whether *Congress* can decide, for example, that a Letter of Reprisal would allow it to issue an order to the National Guard of California to take over the state house and overthrow the governor of California. Obviously it cannot. Can Congress say the Letter of Reprisal means . . . anything? Do they have the sole power to define its content? That cannot be. It is up to the *court* to set the limits on the language of the Constitution.

"So, can it be this court's position, as Mr. Pendleton apparently requests"—he glanced at Pendleton—"that Congress can make it mean whatever they want, and can do whatever they want, and the court is powerless to stop them until briefed? Until months pass? Until Mr. Pendleton and his firm have stalled long enough for the damage to be done?

"There is no authority in history for issuance of a Letter like this to a U.S. Navy warship. It has never been done before—"

The judge interrupted Gray. "Sir, but there is no authority saying that it cannot be done either, is there?"

"No, sir, but the historical context in which it has been issued before—"

"Don't you have to show a likelihood of prevailing at trial before the trial court can even consider issuing a restraining order?"

"We believe it is clear that we will prevail, as we showed in our papers. Moreover, the risk of injury is so great—"

"Thank you, Counsel. That will be all," the judge said, cutting him off. The judge shuffled papers momentarily, then looked at Gray. "I take it that you want our decision immediately. Am I right?"

"Yes, Your Honor, as soon as possible. It is already four o'clock on Friday afternoon, and if the court could get the decision out before the end of the day it would be much appreciated. We need this action stopped right now. Waiting until tomorrow or, even worse, until Monday would be disastrous."

"Very well. We will give you our decision within the hour."

"Thank you very much."

Pendleton stood up. "Thank you."

"All rise," said the clerk as the judges stood and the three of them filed out through the door at the front of the courtroom.

Gray walked over to Pendleton as Pendleton picked up his briefcase and began to leave. "I think I've got you this time, Mr. Pendleton."

Pendleton looked him straight in the eye. They were of equal height. "Then why are you sweating?" he asked, his gaze steady.

"You know what really gripes me about all of this?" Gray moved closer so that his voice could not be heard by the gallery. "This whole thing started because the Speaker of the House is simply trying to protect his own turf. The *Pacific Flyer* was built in his home state and Stanbridge has a lot of friends in the shipping industry. One of his cronies owns the Stewart Shipping Line. Before he was Speaker, Stanbridge supported the President's proposal that would mandate that fifty percent of all goods shipped into and out of the United States be shipped on U.S. flagged vessels."

"Do you have a point?" asked Pendleton stonily.

"So, he gets this bill passed, fifty percent of all shipping has to go through American-built and -flagged ships, NASSCO goes nuts because they now have more ship-building contracts than they can shake a stick at, and suddenly one of Stanbridge's primary campaign contributors, Mr. Jack Stewart, has a shipping line with his name on it that is going to take advantage of this new legal requirement. Sure enough, he comes up with a new ship design built by NASSCO in San Diego, starts a new automobile-shipping facility in San Diego—which the Port Authority loves of course—and the Stewart Shipping Line convinces Ford to ship through them to Indonesia with their brand-new cars on his brand-new ship, and these guys go and blow the whole thing to bits. They humiliated *your guy.* That's why we're here,'' Gray said with a patronizing tone at the end of his sentence.

Pendleton stared at him. ''Where did you go to college?'' he asked him.

''What difference does that make?'' Gray responded hostily.

''Did you ever take basic logic?''

''No, why?''

''Have you ever heard of the logical fallacy of *post hoc, ergo propter hoc*?''

''Of course. Because B followed A, it was caused by A,'' Gray said proudly.

''Exactly. Now, if you will excuse me, I have other things to do.''

Gray frowned, confused. ''And do you know who the two largest contributors were to John Stanbridge's last congressional campaign?''

''No, but I have a feeling you're going to tell me.''

''That's right. Jack Stewart and Bryce Dabny. Do you know who Bryce Dabny is? President of NASSCO. Isn't that a surprise?'' Pendleton began to turn. ''And you know who else is on his list of big contributors?'' Pendleton kept walking. ''Your law firm.'' Pendleton excused himself and made his way through the mob of reporters in the back of the room and down the hallway.

Gray came out into the hallway. ''I think I'll talk to some of these reporters around here,'' Gray said loudly. ''I'll bet they're more interested. . . .''

24

THE COMMUNICATIONS OFFICER RAPPED SMARTLY ON the door to Admiral Billings's at-sea cabin. "Come in," Billings called loudly.

The officer stepped into the cabin empty-handed. "Well?" Billings looked at him with questions in his eyes as he buttoned his khaki shirt with the two stars on each collar.

"No messages, Admiral," he said, chagrined but not embarrassed. "Not a one. I thought maybe one of our systems was down or maybe one of the comlinks in the satellite had failed. But the satellites are working fine. Their locator signals are intact. We can hear the signals coming down. We've definitely been cut off, Admiral. I think they have sent out a modification of the encryption schedule so that we're off it and everybody else is on it. They sent the message to everybody but us. There are signals flying all over the place; it's just that nobody is talking to us and nobody is acknowledging our signals. Even the HF radio signals. We can hear people talk in a clear voice, but they won't acknowledge us. You want my opinion?"

Billings just looked at him as he tucked his shirt into his pants.

"I think the word went out, Admiral, that we're a pariah. Nobody is to communicate with us in any way whatsoever. Even if they receive our messages, they're not to acknowledge or respond to them.''

Billings head jerked up suddenly. ''What about the other ships in our battle group? Are they responding?''

''Yes, sir. We have normal comm with them, but they're in the same fix we're in. They're not getting anything from the outside either.''

Billings looked at his brass wall clock and saw that it was 0400. ''This is going to be an interesting day.''

The communications officer smiled weakly. ''Yes, sir. I have a feeling you're right.''

''Thank you for your efforts. I'd like to keep our communications lines open. I want to continue sending situation reports, and all other messages that we would normally send, as if nothing had happened. If they don't want to acknowledge us and pretend we're not here, that's their business. We'll continue to do what we have always done. They can at least know what we're doing, even if we don't know what they're doing.''

''Roger that, Admiral.''

''That'll be all.''

''Yes, sir.'' The communications officer spun around and left the stateroom, closing the door behind him. Billings finished dressing and walked to SUPPLOT. Beth Louwsma was staring at a chart.

''Well, Beth, looks like you're out of a job.''

''I will never surrender, Admiral.'' She grinned in response.

''Get any intel on those South African SAMs before they shut us off?''

''No, sir, we're going with what we've got and that's it.''

''Where is that Dillon fellow? I wanted to pick his brain about a couple of things.''

''I expect he's still racked out—he traveled a long way yesterday.''

''I guess he did.''

''It's only 0400,'' she added.

Captain Black walked in. "Morning, Admiral. Beth."

"Good morning," they chorused. The admiral drew coffee from the urn bolted to the countertop.

"You over your tantrum from last night yet, Chief of Staff?"

"I'm sorry, Admiral. I thought we were supposed to speak freely. I hope I wasn't out of line."

"No, you were just saying what you thought, which is your job." His eyes narrowed slightly. "But I have to know if you're onboard. Are you going to be against me now, or are you with me?"

"I think you made the wrong decision, Admiral, but it's your decision to make. I'm with you."

Billings blinked and went on. "What do we need to do between now and tomorrow morning?"

"Well, Admiral, I was checking the ship's track just now," Captain Black began, clearly preferring the new topic. "It's my understanding from the planning we did last night and from talking to Colonel Tucker that they want L hour and H hour to be 0540 tomorrow—fifteen minutes before sunrise," he said, referring to the time the landingcraft and helicopters touched the island. "They think the only way to achieve any type of surprise is to hit the beach before the bad guys wake up."

"I agree. What's our current position?"

"Currently one hundred twenty miles east/southeast of Bunaya. We're scheduled for a light flight schedule, about seventy-five percent of the usual cyclic ops. The Amphibs are ready to go. The Marines say they could go today if they had to, and will be more than ready by dawn."

"Okay. Ops O up yet?"

"Yes, sir, he is. I saw him at the wardroom."

"Get him down here. I want to go over a couple of quick things."

"Yes, sir," the chief of staff said, going to the phone located on the admiral's desk.

"So, Beth, what do you think? We going to get any additional intel?"

"No, sir." She shook her head. "That's why it's crit-ical we get the SEALs ashore tonight. Our last planned TARPS run was shot down—we haven't even had any imagery since yesterday afternoon."

"So, for all we know, they could be reinforcing the island with hundreds of troops teeming over the sides of mother ships from all over Southeast Asia?"

"That about sums it up, Admiral. I seriously doubt that's happening though—I don't think anybody has that kind of force outside of Vietnam, and I don't think these guys are working for *any* country—wait a second," she said, brightening. "We may have an option after all. Ad-miral, remember our special guests for the Cobra Gold exercise?"

"The Army contingent?"

"Yes. Remember what they had with them?"

Billings looked puzzled.

"The Predator, sir."

"I'm not following you," Billings said.

"Admiral," Beth said, moving closer to him, "it's the newest remotely piloted vehicle in the inventory. It's pretty small—they'll never see it or hear it on the island. Remember those tests they did, where it flew at fifteen thousand feet and sent live video to the *Lincoln*? It works!" She tried to control her excitement. "It can be our eyes. It's the answer to our lack of satellite coverage, or any other intel. The Predator can do it all for us."

He looked at her, curious.

"It was set up to be launched from the shore, but I'll bet the catapult guys can rig it for a launch from the cat as a dummy load."

"What else can it do?"

"IR, radar, and live video link. And it can be up for hours."

"You think you can make it work?"

"I'm sure we can."

"Make it happen," the admiral said enthusiastically.

"But wait—if we use it tonight, can we use it tomorrow morning during the strike too?"

"I wouldn't count on it. We should probably use it for only one launch."

Billings sat back and considered his options. "Send the SEALs in tonight, and launch the Predator before the attack in the morning."

"Roger that, sir," Beth said.

"The close air support . . ." The door opened while he was speaking and the admiral's operations officer rushed in.

"Good morning, Admiral," he said, out of breath.

"Morning, Ops. How are you doing?"

"Frankly, Admiral, I'm getting a little uptight. The idea of being cut off from the entire United States and Washington is a bit spooky. You couldn't drive a pin up my butt with a ballpeen hammer."

The admiral smiled slightly and sat down. He turned away from his screens to look at the other three officers. The two sailors in the background, who were accustomed to moving plastic ships around on the board, were sitting idly. With no additional intelligence on updated positions for the ships, they stayed where they had been twelve hours before. "Let me ask you guys something. What do you think the President is up to? What do you think his plan is?"

No one answered.

"No opinions?"

No one dared speak. They didn't want to be wrong. The admiral looked at the chief of staff. "Call Drano. Tell him to wake up Dillon and get him up here. He's the most political guy we've got. I'll ask him."

☙

Dillon sat up and hit his head on the bunk directly above his. Someone was banging on his door. His mind raced to gather data, to tell him where he was and what he was doing there. He looked at his luminous wristwatch:

4:15 A.M. *Bam, bam, bam. What in the world?* He put his feet over the side of the bed and stood up. The tile was cold under his feet. *What happened to my carpet?* He located the source of the knock and walked toward it. He felt movement. Ship. *I am on a ship.* He shook his head to clear it and reached for the door handle. Bright light from the passageway streamed in.

"Good morning, Mr. Dillon," said Lieutenant Reynolds.

"Good morning. What's up?" Dillon asked, less confused.

"The admiral would like to see you right away, sir."

"What?" Dillon asked. "Oh. Right. Um, let me . . . let me get dressed. Do you want to come in?"

"No. I'll wait out here, sir. I'll just escort you there when you are ready."

"Okay. Give me five minutes."

Dillon reached for the switch and turned on the overhead lights. He had never been this tired in his life. He felt as if he had lost 30 percent of the knowledge he'd had two days ago. He walked to the steel-doored closet and opened it. *What do you wear on a ship?* He had brought his boat shoes, thinking that they would work just fine since he would be on a boat. He had never realized that an aircraft carrier is related to a cruise ship only in that they both float. It was a very serious place with some very serious corners and sharp things that would break your feet if you weren't careful. Your feet might even break if you *were* careful. Most of the officers and sailors wore black hard-soled shoes or boots, most with steel toes.

He pulled out a white shirt that had gotten wrinkled in the around-the-world flight, and put it on with his gray suit pants. He tied a red and blue striped tie and combed water through his hair. He ran the toothbrush quickly over his teeth and went out the door. "Okay, let's go," he said to the lieutenant.

The lieutenant nodded and led him down the passageway. Moments later they entered SUPPLOT and Dillon tried to remember whether he had been in this particular space before. He recognized the large color screens and the admiral.

"Well, good morning, Mr. Dillon."

"Good morning, Admiral. How are you today?"

"Fine, thank you."

Dillon stood in front of the admiral and his staff, not knowing what to say. He had been summoned, but had no idea why. "Is there coffee anywhere?" Dillon asked hesitatingly.

"Absolutely. Fowler!" the admiral yelled across to a sailor. "Get Mr. Dillon here a cup of coffee."

"Yes, sir." Fowler grabbed a porcelain cup off a rack next to the pot. He filled it and gave it to Dillon, who sipped it gratefully.

"Mr. Dillon, sit down here," the admiral said, pointing to a chair near his. "Just talking here with my staff . . . we wanted to discuss the political implications of . . . what's going on. We thought that you might be better placed than anybody else to deal with that question."

"I'll try, sir," Dillon said, listening to the hum of the air-conditioning and the equipment. It was cold in SUPPLOT and Dillon felt a chill.

"You ever been to Israel?"

Dillon looked at him puzzled. "No, sir. Never."

"Speak any Hebrew?"

"No."

"When I was commanding officer of VF-84, the Jolly Rogers—you may have seen them, skull and crossbones, black tails . . ." Dillon shook his head. "Well, anyway, when I was the CO of that squadron on the *Nimitz*, we pulled into Israel once. Haifa. Great city. On a hill, pretty. Anyway, they have a saying over there that I love. I've used it ever since. If something is really screwed up, a fiasco, they say it is a *balagan*. If it's *really* screwed up, it's an *eza balagan*. A real fiasco. Good word, huh?" he asked.

"Yes, sir."

"Well, Mr. Dillon, what your boss has given us, this Letter, has put us in a position that could really turn out to be a *balagan*. My job is to make sure it doesn't. You understand?"

"Yes, sir."

"As you may or may not know, the President has cut us off."

Dillon squinted as he drank. "What do you mean?" he asked.

"Cut off our communications. They can still receive ours in all likelihood, but they're not sending us any information. They've also taken our identifier out of the transmissions and we believe have instructed all other commands and ships not to communicate with us at all. We're on our own." He waited for the information to sink into Dillon's obviously foggy brain. "What do you make of it?"

"Well, I assume he's trying to get you to change your mind or trying to make it so that you can't go forward with your attack even if you want to."

"He's got to know that if we want to go forward, we can, and there's nothing he can do about it." The admiral shook his head.

"Mr. Dillon, do you think the President would do something drastic?"

"I'm sorry, Admiral, it's too early. I'm just not following you."

"Do you think he has the nerve to send another battle group down here to try and stop us?"

Dillon's eyes got big as the thought sank in. "Is there one nearby?"

"There's a battle group in the Philippines, and another one in the Indian Ocean near the Persian Gulf. He could send one or both toward us if he chose to do that."

"What would they do?" Dillon asked, trying not to breathe too quickly.

"That's the question. Would he have them come and

try and intimidate us, or would he actually send them after us with orders to attack?''

Dillon sat silent as the implications of everything that had happened weighed on him.

The admiral addressed everyone. ''Do you think the President has the nerve?'' He lowered his voice as his staff hung on every word. ''Would he be willing to tell the world that the United States of America has a battle group with its supporting ships, submarines, and amphibious group with Marines onboard that's out of his control? And not only to tell them that, but do you think that he is prepared—by sending other battle groups toward us—to imply that we're on the verge of civil war?''

Dillon bit his lower lip as he tried to think. ''Admiral, these are very big questions and I don't know the answers to them. Perhaps I could call the Speaker and find out.''

''I don't think you heard me, Mr. Dillon. He's cut us off. Even our normal communications of high-frequency radio communication and the like have been cut off. No one is responding.''

''I have my MI phone, though, Admiral. Couldn't I just call? These new Motorola Iridium satellite phones are supposed to work anywhere in the world.''

The admiral looked at him with enthusiasm, ''It may be just the thing. But if everyone is under orders to cut us off, it won't do us much good to call anyone in the chain of command.''

The phone rang and the admiral's aide picked it up. He talked quietly, then looked at Dillon and said, ''Okay. I'll tell him.'' He placed the receiver back on its cradle. ''I guess you're going to be here for a little while longer.''

''What do you mean?''

''The COD is grounded in Singapore. Port engine ate a bird.''

Dillon grimaced. ''Okay. Thanks,'' he said, not very thankful. ''So do you want me to call the Speaker?''

The admiral spoke into another phone and nodded at him.

Dillon stood on the flying bridge outside the admiral's bridge on the 08 level. The admiral sat on his chair inside the bridge and Beth Louwsma stood next to him. Dillon took out his Motorola Iridium phone. It was linked to a network of sixty-six Motorola satellites that allowed him to make and receive digital calls anywhere without interference. He had owned the phone for only a month and hadn't used it once outside Washington. He dialed the Speaker's private number. His heart pounded as he waited. He heard clicking, and then the phone suddenly started ringing. Dillon breathed in expectantly, wondering what phone in the world was actually on the other end of this connection.

"Hello, office of the Speaker of the House, may I help you?"

Dillon blurted, "Robin!"

"Mr. Dillon, is that you?" she asked.

"Yes, it's me," he said, amazed at the clarity of the connection. It sounded as if she were down the hallway. "Is the Speaker there?"

"Hold on."

Dillon waited for three seconds.

"Dillon! What are you doing?" the Speaker asked.

"Good morning, Mr. Speaker."

"It's almost the end of the day here. Why are you calling?" Then with an anxious tone. "Did the admiral get the Letter?"

"Yes, I delivered it to him yesterday afternoon as soon as I arrived."

"What did he say?"

Dillon looked over his shoulder to see if anyone was listening. He was by himself on the flying bridge of the *Constitution* as it steamed westward in the dark morning at twenty-five knots. The wind whipped around his head, making the conversation on the telephone difficult. He stepped behind a large steel screen, which broke the power of the wind momentarily.

"You should have seen it, Mr. Speaker. People here were sweating bullets all over the place. They didn't know what to do. There was a big argument between the admiral and his chief of staff on whether the Constitution or the order of the President would win."

"Did the President send him an order?"

"Sure. Didn't you know? He sent him a direct order from the Joint Chiefs of Staff and the President telling him not to obey any Letter of Reprisal and to immediately evacuate this area and return to Pearl Harbor."

"Stupid son of a bitch," he growled. "What'd the admiral do with that order?"

"He hesitated long and hard. Frankly, I thought that because of what his chief of staff said he was going to ignore the Letter, and if he did, there would have been nothing that we could have done about it."

"Oh, I don't know about that, but in any case, what did he finally decide to do?"

"He's going to go for it, Mr. Speaker. H hour and L hour, whatever those are, are tomorrow morning."

"Outstanding," the Speaker said.

"What is going on with that lawsuit filed by the President?"

"David Pendleton was the right guy. He's already been to two arguments. They had a hearing at the District Court and it was *denied*, so they asked for an emergency appeal to the Circuit Court. We're waiting to hear from them now. If they deny it, I'm sure these clowns are going to try to go to the Supreme Court. We'll have to see how this plays out."

"One thing I wanted to ask you, Mr. Speaker. Do you know why the President has cut us off?"

"What do you mean?"

"We're not getting any communications. They can't get any intelligence updates, they can't get any current photo intelligence, they can't even get the normal Navy routine messages over the satellite. We're blacked out.''

"You're shitting me," the Speaker said.

"No. The admiral said we can't get anything. We're sending out our messages just like usual, and they may be listening to them, but they sure aren't talking back. The admiral thinks the President may be sending another battle group after us. Do you think that's possible?''

"That pantywaist?" the Speaker responded with contempt. "Send another battle group after you? Not in a million years."

"Anyway, could you check on that?''

"You bet," the Speaker said. "I absolutely will find out the answer." He hesitated as he considered the logistical difficulties and the actual implications of having a battle group cut off from Washington. "How do I get it to you?"

"Call me on my cellular phone number. You just dial like I'm in Washington. It'll ring here. We'll probably have to have a set time though, because I think if I'm down inside the ship, it won't work. So let's say one hour from now, at five-thirty Washington time, you call me back or I can call you . . . I'll just call you then."

"Fine," the Speaker said. "And tell the admiral I want to talk to him then."

"Sure will." Dillon said. "See you later." He ended the phone conversation and placed the phone in his pocket. He looked out over the ocean at the two or three ships that he could see accompanying the carrier as they smashed westward toward Bunaya. He felt a sudden sense of pride. He breathed in the salty air as he watched the power of the ships, the power of the Navy, and the power of Washington coming together in one act. One act to exact retribution against the murderers of innocent Americans.

25

THE PHONE RANG AND MARIA PICKED IT UP IMME-
diately. With barely a pause she yelled across the hallway,
"It's Rebecca. The Circuit Court's decision is out."

Pendleton swiveled around quickly and hit the button
on his speakerphone. "Yes?"

Rebecca began with no introduction, "It's half a page
long, David. It reads as follows: 'In the case of *President
of the United States* v. *John Stanbridge et al.*, Petitioner
Edward Manchester, as President of the United States and
Chief of the Executive Branch, and as a citizen, came
before this court this day for a writ of mandamus. Having
reviewed the pleadings, heard oral argument, and given
due consideration, petitioner's request is denied. Circuit
Court of the District of Columbia.' That's it, David."

"Perfect. They didn't give the Supreme Court any hint
of what they really want to do. So," he said, satisfied,
"now we wait for the Supreme Court. I'm going to sit
here until five-thirty, then I'm going home. Keep your
fingers crossed that the Supreme Court doesn't feel like
handling the biggest constitutional bomb it's had in decades this afternoon. Why don't you come back here and
review these Supreme Court rules with me?"

"I'll be right there," Rebecca said.

Pendleton sat back in his chair, rubbed his eyes, and
smiled. With his eyes closed, he spoke loudly to his sec-

retary outside his door. "Get the Speaker of the House on the telephone, please."

A moment later she called back, "He's on the line."

Pendleton picked up the phone. "Mr. Speaker, good news. Circuit Court has denied their request."

"Good," the Speaker said distractedly. "Pendleton, I want you over here right now."

Pendleton sat forward in his chair. "What for? I need to be here in case they take this to the Supremes tonight."

"Get *over* here. Have somebody else stand by there and call if something comes up with the Supremes."

"Okay, I'll be right there."

☙

As Pendleton walked into the Speaker's office, he saw several people he didn't recognize seated on couches and chairs around the coffee table. They were all clearly waiting for him. The Speaker was the only one to rise as he walked in. "Afternoon, David, glad you could make it. Nice work on the President's lawsuit. Looks like that thing is dead in the water."

"Not completely dead, Mr. Speaker. The Supreme Court might accept an application for emergency stay to hear it tonight. We'll have to wait and see. They'll probably give this the same consideration they would give a death penalty case for expediency."

"Well, let's hope not." The Speaker chuckled with no humor in his eyes. "David, let me introduce you around. You know Rhonda, my staff historian; you know Chuck, my staff member for military affairs; you know Frank Grazio, my assistant; and these two gentlemen over here are the head legislative assistants for the Majority Whip and Bart Rutledge, my good friend and the congressman from South Carolina. Please, sit down," he said, motioning to them all.

"David, we were just talking about the articles of impeachment."

Pendleton's eyes opened wider than he intended. "What?"

"I want to impeach the President."

Pendleton hid his reaction. He leaned down and picked up the cup of coffee. He raised it to his mouth and sipped slowly. "On what grounds?" he asked.

The Speaker returned his gaze and paused. He spoke softly, deliberately. "Has any President ever been impeached?"

Pendleton looked to see who would answer the question and realized they were all looking at him. "Yes," he said.

"Right," the Speaker responded. "Who was it?"

"Andrew Johnson." Pendleton responded. "Abraham Lincoln's vice president. He became president after Lincoln was shot."

"Right," the Speaker said. "Were you around during Watergate?"

Pendleton nodded gently. "It's my recollection that articles of impeachment were voted out of committee and were to be voted on by the entire House of Representatives when Nixon resigned in 1974."

"Exactly!" said the Speaker. "Any other big impeachments?"

"I don't follow you."

"Any Supreme Court justices ever impeached?"

Pendleton thought hard, wondering why any of this mattered. "I think one, but I don't remember who."

"Rhonda?" the Speaker said.

"Justice Chase," she said.

"Was he convicted in the Senate?" the Speaker prompted.

"No, acquitted by one vote. So was Andrew Johnson."

"Exactly. And how long ago was it that either of those things happened?"

"More than a century."

"Right," the Speaker said, nodding. Approving of his student. "Do you think that because the power to impeach hasn't been exercised in a long time against a president, anyone could argue it doesn't exist?'' he asked rhetorically. ''Of course not.'' Stanbridge began walking around the office, fueled by his ideas. ''It's another power left *exclusively* to Congress. Just like the Letter of Reprisal. And we are going to exercise it again.''

No one spoke or looked at anyone else. They all looked at the Speaker.

Pendleton spoke. ''On what grounds?''

''Incompetence,'' Stanbridge said, sitting heavily in a chair next to Pendleton. ''Incompetence, *and* a refusal to act as Commander in Chief to fulfill his obligation as President.''

Pendleton shook his head. ''That would be politics. You can't impeach somebody for not doing as good a job as you think they ought to do.''

''I'm not talking about a good job or a bad job. I'm talking about inability and unwillingness or refusal. And I'm not talking about just any kind of inability.'' The Speaker stood up again, walking behind his chair and leaning against it. His eyes were alight. ''I'm talking about inability as in a fundamental inability, an''—he searched for the right word—''incapacity. It's like. . . . it's like''—he struggled to articulate the clear idea in his head—''being on a jury in a murder case. If they're going to ask for the death penalty, you as a juror, you *have* to be willing to vote for the death penalty. Right? They ask you whether or not you are opposed to the death penalty as a matter of principle—if you are, then you can't sit on the jury even to determine if the guy is guilty of the crime.'' Stanbridge stopped and looked at the others in the circle. He saw mostly blank looks.

Pendleton asked the question. ''So how does that apply?''

''The President of the United States is the Commander in Chief of the armed forces, right?'' he asked. They nodded. ''What if he is a *pacifist*? A genuine, committed, deep-in-his-heart pacifist?'' He let the thought sink in for several seconds. ''What if he is unwilling, under any circumstances, to employ the armed services of the country of which he is the president?'' Stanbridge lowered his voice and looked around the room. ''Wouldn't that automatically disqualify him as president? Wouldn't he have just lowered the nuclear defense umbrella completely? Wouldn't he have just done in one fell swoop what the entire Soviet Union or Russia and everybody else in the world was unable to do? Wouldn't he have completely emasculated our defense and left us vulnerable and exposed?''

''What does that have to do with Manchester?'' the legislative aide for the Majority Whip asked.

''Because he *is* a pacifist.''

Nearly everyone looked at him with shock.

Pendleton asked, ''Why do you say that, Mr. Speaker?''

''Because I think that is the reason he wouldn't send the USS *Constitution* after those terrorists. Think about it!'' he said, waving his hand. ''Where is he from?''

''Connecticut,'' Pendleton answered.

''No, before that. Where did he grow up?''

They searched their memories and Rhonda spoke. ''Harrisonburg, Virginia.''

''Right. And what church did he grow up in?''

''The Mennonite Church. Why?''

''Do you know anything about Mennonites, Rhonda?'' the Speaker asked.

''A little, why?''

''How do they feel about the military?''

Rhonda nodded her head. ''They are pacifists.''

''Right. And where did he go to college?''

''Goshen College in Indiana,'' Rhonda answered.

''Right. Who owns and runs Goshen College?'' the Speaker asked.

Nobody replied. The Speaker answered for them. ''The Mennonites. Do you remember, during the presidential campaign, when Manchester was the governor of Connecticut, what he said when asked about his faith? He said he still 'held to the tenets of the Christian faith.' " Stanbridge held up two bent fingers on each hand to indicate quotation marks. "Remember that?"

Rhonda replied, "But he said he isn't a member of the Mennonite Church anymore, doesn't attend, and hasn't in a long time. Not since college. He said he isn't a Mennonite anymore." Rhonda smiled slightly. "Just like Nixon, who was a Quaker, or a former Quaker, and Quakers are pac—"

"Exactly!" said the Speaker. "It doesn't necessarily tip you off. Nobody accused Nixon of being a pacifist. . . ."

Pendleton shook his head. "I don't know where this gets you, Mr. Speaker. Even if he is a *member* of the Mennonite Church, surely in running for the office of president he understood that it carried with it the obligation to serve as Commander in Chief."

The Speaker leaned over and looked at Pendleton, "*Exactly*. That's it exactly. What better opportunity to put into place a policy of pacifism than to run for the office of president of the United States? He never served in the military, never served in the National Guard. Even while governor of Connecticut, he never called out the National Guard even when they had that flooding several years ago. The National Guard was not employed *once* during his tenure as governor there. I *checked*. And with him as President of the United States, U.S. forces have not been deployed anywhere around the globe in any hostile activities, even though there have been several opportunities. Granted," he said, building up steam as he went along, "those decisions could have gone either way politically. But isn't it curious that none of them resulted in sending U.S. forces into action? And then this one, the one that we're here about today, the one that *we've* been *sued* about, is the clearest example of an attack on American citizens in the last ten years. And what does he do about it? He dodges the issue and says we're going to let the Indonesian police take care of it. The police! You've got to be kidding me!" He looked around.

"None of you were there," he continued, lowering his voice for effect. "The night this broke—when he announced to the public that he wasn't going to do anything about it—I went over to the White House and met with the President. Nobody else was in the room. I asked him straight out if he was a pacifist. You know what he said?" He paused. "He didn't answer. He did *not* deny it. So the question I have for each of you is whether or not it is sufficient grounds for impeachment, if the President of the United States is truly a pacifist and unwilling to use the American forces. Anybody have any comments?" He waited. "And to give you more food for thought, what about plain old failure to defend Americans—general incompetence as Commander in Chief?"

Nobody said a word. They sat there in stunned silence, not believing what the Speaker was saying. Two or three of them were sure the Speaker had lost his mind. They looked at his eyes, expecting to see either humor or a crazed, lost-touch-with-reality look. Pendleton, however, fought back the slightest smile, amazed at the cleverness of the Speaker. He just might be right.

The door opened and Robin hurried in. "Mr. Speaker, I just got a call from Rebecca from Mr. Pendleton's office. She wanted to speak with him right away."

"Okay, David, go ahead."

Pendleton crossed to the Speaker's desk. Robin said, "She's on line one, Mr. Pendleton."

Pendleton picked up the phone, "What is it?" he said curtly. He stared at the others and listened to Rebecca without saying anything else. He nodded and looked grim. "Okay, thanks. I'll meet you back at the office." He set the phone down. "They've made their application to the Supreme Court for an emergency stay. We'll know within an hour whether the court is going to hear the motion this evening. If you will excuse me, Mr. Speaker, I need to go back to my office and prepare in case they decide to hear this."

The Speaker walked over and stood directly in front of

him. He gazed into Pendleton's eyes with a worried look. "Think the Supreme Court will listen to this tonight?"

"I really don't know. They've never faced anything like this before. I can't think of any time they've accepted a civil application in this short a period and heard it . . . maybe in one of those biomedical cases when someone was dying . . . anyway, we'll know in an hour. Are you going to be here?"

The Speaker nodded. "I'm not going anywhere." He turned to the others. "In fact, I'll be here pretty late, I think. We're keeping Congress in session tonight to vote on articles of impeachment."

"Mr. Speaker," the legislative assistant from Rutledge's office said tentatively.

Stanbridge looked at him in surprise. "Yes?"

"This is . . . I don't know how to say it. This is . . . *crazy*. We could bring down the presidency; the whole reputation of the government is at stake. First the Letter of Reprisal, now this. I'm just . . ." He ran out of words.

"It is *not* crazy!" Stanbridge said too loudly. "Why is it everyone wants to give the President the benefit of the doubt? That's the last thing we need to be doing. We need to smoke him out. I sure as hell don't want to find out if I'm right when we get attacked."

"We might look ridiculous, or vindictive. . . ."

"I don't care how we look. And if it spells the end of the President," he said enthusiastically, "then so *be* it. Maybe we could get someone in there who knows what the hell he's doing."

26

DILLON STOOD ON THE FLYING BRIDGE IN HIS DRESS shirt and suit pants. He had long since abandoned the tie and his sleeves were rolled up. He had undone the second button of the shirt to give him some additional cooling. Sweat pooled at the bottom of his back where it had rolled down from his shoulders. He looked at his watch again as he had every half minute for the last fifty minutes. 5:29 A.M. He waited a little longer, then turned on his phone and dialed the Speaker's private number. As before, the phone quickly rang and Robin answered. "Morning, Robin," he said, trying to sound more cheerful than he felt. "Speaker available?"

"Yes, he is. He was watching the clock, and waiting for your call. I'll put you through."

Two seconds later the Speaker picked up the phone. "Dillon. Great to hear from you. Everything all right?"

"Fine, Mr. Speaker. How are things in Washington?"

"Oh, we're doing great. I'll tell you what though, it's starting to pop around here."

"Why's that?"

"I told you they lost their appeal with the Circuit Court. Well, they're taking it to the Supreme Court. We're going to hear very shortly whether the Supreme Court will hear this fiasco tonight, or at some other time, or not at all."

Dillon swallowed hard. "You know, Mr. Speaker, this thing has taken on a life of its own. . . ." Dillon glanced up to the array of lines, antennae, and masts above his head. He looked at the flag flying over the ship, snapping briskly in the wind high above him. He noticed it wasn't the American flag at all. It was an old American Revolutionary War flag: red and white stripes with a rattlesnake on it, and the words 'Don't Tread on Me' in black underneath. It gave Dillon chills. He looked for the American flag that he thought always flew over American ships—maybe this is a special battle group flag, or a ship flag. There was no American flag anywhere above him. He interrupted the Speaker's thought. ''You're not going to believe this, Mr. Speaker.''

''What?''

''Somebody has replaced the American flag on the ship with the American Revolution flag. You know, the one with red and white stripes, a rattlesnake, and 'Don't Tread on Me.' ''

The Speaker paused, then said, ''I like that. Don't Tread on Me. That's *exactly* how I feel. Does the admiral know that flag is up there?''

''I don't know.''

''Well, there's more news here. I've told the House we'll be in session again tonight.''

''What for?'' Dillon asked, confused, staring at the flag above him.

''To pass articles of impeachment against the President.''

Dillon's head came down instantly and his mouth flew open. ''What? For what? What'd he do?''

''He's not fit to be President, Dillon. I am absolutely convinced he won't use the military under any circumstances. At least not in a way that would require them to hurt anybody. He's a pacifist. He might use the military to distribute rice cakes somewhere. . . .''

''How do you know that?''

''Trust me.''

''Do you have anything that shows that, or is this just political?''

The Speaker lowered his voice. "You think I'd do this for political gain?"

"I sure hope not. Do you have anything or not?"

"I'll spare you the details, but I'm not going to make a fool of myself. I don't make this charge lightly. Believe me."

"When's that going to happen?"

"Tonight."

"Washington must be about to explode."

"I've never seen anything like it, Dillon, not in my entire political career. People are on edge, they'll bite your head off, and everybody has an opinion on everything." He sighed. "Let me talk to the admiral."

"Hold on. He's over here." Dillon walked to the hatch to the bridge and stuck his head in. "Admiral, the Speaker would like to talk to you." The admiral climbed down from his bridge chair and walked out onto the flying bridge.

"This is Admiral Billings."

"Good morning, Admiral Billings. This is John Stanbridge, the Speaker of the House."

"Yes, sir. Nice to meet you."

"Nice to meet you as well, Admiral. How are things going with the battle group?"

"Doing fine. Everything's in order, except, as I'm sure Mr. Dillon told you, we had an airplane shot down."

"What?" the Speaker said excitedly. "When?"

"Yesterday, late afternoon. Doing a final reconnaissance run by an F-14. Photos. We were trying to get some imagery on Bunaya to see what we're going to be up against. We encountered South African SAMs. They lit them up from the front with radar and shot them from behind with an infrared missile. At least that's what we think happened."

"South African? Why are the South Africans there?"

"No, not owned by South Africa, manufactured by South Africa. It's a South African system. We don't know who these guys are."

"Is the pilot okay?"

"Yes, the pilot and RIO were plucked out of the water. But that was pretty hairy too. Those three fiberglass cigarette boats that they used when they took the *Pacific Flyer* came out and tried to pluck them out of the ocean."

"What happened?"

"Our F-18 strafed all three of them and sank them."

"Unbelievable," the Speaker exclaimed. "These guys started firing on us? This needs to get out."

"Yes, but"—the admiral hesitated—"that F-14 may have been flying over Bunaya, which he probably wasn't supposed to be doing. We were trying to stay in international waters and not overfly. I was hopeful that the TARPS would be able to get some imagery from a side look, but I think he might have decided to fly directly overhead."

"Yeah," the Speaker said, "but that would give Indonesia a right to go after us, not a bunch of terrorists."

"That's true," said the admiral.

"Why haven't we heard anything about this in Washington?"

"Well, we notified Washington by message, Mr. Speaker. We have been doing our usual reporting; the problem is we've been cut off, as Mr. Dillon told you. We are incommunicado, if you will."

The Speaker thought for a moment. "So nobody else knows this? Nobody else knows that they shot down one of our airplanes?"

"Well, somebody knows, but I don't know what they've done with the information. It hasn't changed the way they've been dealing with us."

"Just for your information, Admiral, I have already told Mr. Dillon that the President has brought a lawsuit against Congress trying to get this Letter of Reprisal declared unconstitutional. They took it to the District Court, who denied their request for an order, went to the Circuit Court this afternoon, who also denied it; they are trying to get it before the Supreme Court right now. I'll make sure that we get word to you through Dillon if there is some change.''

''Yes, I would appreciate that.''

The Speaker paused for a moment, trying to decide whether to ask the next question. Finally he plunged ahead. ''What exactly is your plan, Admiral?''

''In what regard, Mr. Speaker?'' Billings asked, playing with him ever so slightly.

''In terms of these . . . terrorists . . . what do you plan to do?''

''H hour and L hour are tomorrow morning at first light, Mr. Speaker. We'll be conducting preliminary reconnaissance and intelligence work today, and then tomorrow morning we will begin with air strikes. Marines will go ashore in the first half hour of daylight.''

''How many Marines?''

''Fifteen hundred.''

''Isn't that a bit of overkill?''

Billings responded sharply, ''Well, Mr. Speaker, can you tell me how many men there are on that island? Can you tell me how they're armed? If they have South African surface-to-air missiles sophisticated enough to shoot down an F-14 that is flying at five hundred-plus knots, can you tell me what else their capabilities are? We have *no* intelligence, no imagery, no beach studies, no idea who these guys are or where they got their armament, and nobody is telling us. So, yes, it might be overkill, but I've never seen a combat operation where a military commander regretted having too much force.''

''Do you expect to take casualties?'' the Speaker asked.

''Yes,'' the admiral replied immediately. ''And I'm sure that you do, too. I am sure Congress wouldn't have sent us this Letter of Reprisal *instructing us* to go after these guys unless you had already considered the risk of casualties and expected to take some. Am I right? And we're supposed to go in even though they're holding the captain of the *Flyer*. Right?''

The Speaker replied, ''Well, I think that we expected

some minor casualties, but I certainly don't want there to be many. And just be careful. I don't know where the captain is, or even whether he's still alive.''

"Mr. Speaker, I believe Mr. Dillon mentioned that I think there is a remote possibility that the President is sending another battle group down here. Have you been able to find out anything?''

"I'm doing my absolute best to find that out. I will let you know. Now give me back to Dillon. By the way, Admiral—good luck.''

"Good-bye, Mr. Speaker. I'll talk to you again.'' He handed the phone back to Dillon and turned into the bridge. He stopped suddenly and squinted at the flag snapping above him.

Molly's fingers hesitated over the buttons on her telephone. She looked at the name on her Rolodex, then back at the phone, then back at her Rolodex. She stared at the phone, picked up the receiver slowly, then dialed the number. She glanced at her clock. End of the business day for most Washington bureaucrats. When Bobby answered the phone on the first ring she said, "Hi. This is Molly.''

A pause. "Molly? Hey.''

"Just wanted to call and say hello.''

"Oh,'' he said, not quite sure how to respond. "What's up?''

"Oh, I just thought that maybe we could get together and do something this weekend. There aren't any Virginia games on, but maybe we could . . . uh . . . do something else.''

"Come on, Molly, get serious. You called because the Chief Justice—my boss—is considering whether to accept this application for emergency stay on this Letter of Reprisal thing. Right?''

"Well, now that you mention it, I was curious about the timing, when we might hear . . .'' She tried to sound nonchalant.

"Don't tell me you didn't call about that. I wouldn't believe you, and then I'd think less of you," he said angrily. "Don't screw with me. Did your office have anything to do with that case being filed?"

"The Attorney General's office is representing the President, not my office."

"Right," Bobby said with disgust. "You're as bad as Dillon."

"What are you talking about?"

"Never mind. Look, I have to go. If I get any time this weekend, I'll call you. Bye."

"So that's it?"

"Yeah, that is it. This is serious, Molly, and you know it. Don't be a fool." He waited for some response, some explanation that would restore her to the lofty position she had held in his mind, but he heard nothing. "Goodbye," he said finally and hung up.

She kept the receiver up to her ear without really knowing why. She was *ashamed*. She knew she shouldn't have called him but simply couldn't resist. This was the most important constitutional issue in her lifetime. The Supreme Court *had* to come out the right way on it. It would be catastrophic for the existence of the government if it didn't. It had to act *tonight*. She tightened her lips and put the receiver down.

The phone rang immediately. Her heart jumped. Bobby had changed his mind. She picked it up quickly. "Hello?" she said enthusiastically.

"Hey, Molly!" Dillon asked.

"Jim! What are you doing?" she asked. "Where are you?"

"I'm standing outside the admiral's bridge on the USS *Constitution*. I'm about"—he looked down at the ocean—"a hundred feet above the water."

"Is the Navy letting you use their sophisticated telephone or something?"

"I'm using my new Motorola satellite phone," Dillon said with a serious tone. "Your boss cut off the ship's communications. He won't talk to them or let them talk to anyone else."

"What do you mean?"

"Messages can go out but nothing comes in."

"You're it, then? Your phone is the only way they have to communicate with anyone off the ship?"

"Well, I guess so."

Molly changed the subject. "I'm a little surprised to hear from you. I didn't expect to until this whole thing was over."

Dillon suddenly began to regret having called. "Yeah, I just wanted to . . . I don't know. I'm not sure why I called. I guess I just wanted to . . . hear your voice. I'm not quite sure why, since last time I heard your voice it was telling me that you wanted to serve me with a lawsuit. Even in the middle of all this, just don't let it completely die. Maybe when it's over . . ."

"We just don't know how this is going to affect us in the long run. We need to wait and see what happens."

"I know. We'll see. That's all I really wanted—"

Molly asked recklessly, "Is the admiral really going to do this, Jim?"

Dillon hesitated. "Yeah, Molly, he is, and you know it. He sent a message to the President telling him he was going forward with the Letter. That's why the President cut off our communications. Don't act like you didn't know that."

"I had *heard* it, but I didn't *know* it. Don't get so accusatorial."

"I wasn't accusing you of anything. It's just that there's not much trust of Washington on this ship right now."

"There's not much trust of that ship in Washington right now either."

"All the admiral's done is follow the law . . ."

"I gotta go," Molly said. "I'm not enjoying this conversation."

"That's the whole point," Dillon said. "Don't hold all

this against *me*. Keep your mind open until all this is history.''

"It's not a matter of timing, Jim, it's a matter of integrity and honesty. I just don't know what I think right now. I've got some serious concerns—"

"Really, and how's your character doing right now?" Dillon asked. "You're the one who came up with this lawsuit to throw a wrench in the works of Congress, aren't you? Are you holding yourself to the same standard you're holding *me*?"

Molly hesitated and immediately thought of her call to Bobby. She didn't know what to say.

"Well, are you?" he pushed.

"I always hold myself to the same standard."

"Are you meeting it?"

"Well, we'll see what happens, and then we'll talk. When are you coming back?" she asked.

Dillon breathed deeply, regretting he had called her at all. "Couple of days anyway. The airplane I need to get out of here broke down. This whole thing is gonna happen before I get back."

"What whole thing?"

Dillon perceived her heightened interest and its implications. He stopped himself from saying what he had been thinking. "Never mind. Sorry I bothered you. See you later."

"The admiral's going forward with the attack? When?" she asked directly.

"Gotta go. See ya." He pressed the "end" button on his phone and headed into the admiral's bridge.

🏴

Dillon walked into SUPPLOT and looked around for Lieutenant Reynolds as his eyes grew accustomed to the low light. Dillon could find only three locations on the ship, his stateroom, SUPPLOT, and the admiral's bridge. Unfortunately, they were separated by eight stories. His legs were killing him. His eyes felt like four eyelashes had been floating in each eye for two days. His hair was greasy and stuck to his scalp, and his new gray suit pants looked like pajamas as they hung loosely on his legs with no remnant of a crease. He was grateful for the air conditioning in SUPPLOT, which felt like forty degrees but was actually set at seventy-five.

Beth Louwsma was drinking from a heavy coffee cup with her name on it, studying an official-looking yellow publication three inches thick. She looked up and smiled. "Morning again," she said. "How are you doing?"

"Okay, I guess." He scanned the large screens and recognized Malaysia, Indonesia, and the Strait of Malacca. "Well," he said, half looking at Beth and still looking at the board, "at least there aren't as many ships out there today as there were yesterday."

She looked at the board and then at Dillon. "Actually there are probably more."

"There don't seem to be as many."

"Exactly. That's because a lot of the information we get on ships and their positions is from other aircraft, other ships, satellites, all kinds of sources. We're able to put information from all those onto our screens automatically. But we're not getting information anymore. The computer will keep a track that it doesn't have new information on for only so long; then it will drop it. So all we can see now are the ships and airplanes that we detect with our own radars. Just like the old days."

"Does that matter?"

"Sure. One of the critical things you want in any kind of naval operation is the best information possible. This means that we won't have it."

"Think it will make a difference?"

She shrugged. "We'll have to see."

"When is this big thing supposed to happen?" Dillon asked tentatively.

"Tomorrow morning, dawn."

"Do you think the admiral will really go through with it?"

Beth looked at him for several seconds with a curious expression, to see if Dillon was joking, and seeing he wasn't, said, "Absolutely."

27

THE REQUEST FOR AN EMERGENCY STAY HAD BEEN submitted to the Supreme Court over an hour ago. The clerk's office usually closed at 5:00 P.M. It was now 5:30 and Pendleton hadn't heard anything. Rebecca, who was at the Supreme Court building, had told him that the clerk's office, while closed to the public, was still occupied. All the Supreme Court law clerks were there with the justices. It was her impression that they were deciding right now whether to hear the application. If anyone understood the implications, they did.

But Rebecca hadn't called in over twenty minutes. Finally the phone rang. He tried not to leap at it. He walked to the phone and stood by it, letting it ring three times before lifting the receiver. "David Pendleton," he said slowly.

"Mr. Pendleton, this is Earl Compton, clerk at the Supreme Court."

"Yes, Mr. Compton. What can I do for you?"

"I believe that the Justice Department informed you they were filing an application for emergency stay to the United States Supreme Court, am I correct?"

"Yes. I have a copy of their application."

"The Chief Justice asked that I call you directly to inform you that application has been accepted."

"Will there be a hearing?" Pendleton asked, forcing his heart back down his throat.

"Yes, sir, there will be a hearing."

"When do you expect that hearing to occur, Mr. Compton?"

"Sir, I don't believe they have decided. My understanding—this is rather extraordinary in a civil case, you understand—is that the Chief Justice is going to have a preliminary review tonight without a hearing and will contact you either tonight or tomorrow to let you know they've ruled without a hearing or to set a specific hearing date. I therefore need to have numbers where I can reach you throughout the evening and tomorrow as well."

"Very well," said Pendleton as he recited automatically his work, home, cellular phone, and Rebecca's numbers. His mind was already planning his strategy and drafting the brief that he hoped he wouldn't have to write. This was absolutely the last thing he wanted, a Supreme Court review of this question before it was moot. "I will look forward to hearing from you, Mr. Compton."

"Thank you, Mr. Pendleton. I have already called Mr. Gray of the Justice Department and he is aware."

"Thank you for calling," said Pendleton as he heard the clerk say good-bye to the air while the telephone was on its way to his desktop. He took one deep breath. He didn't allow himself more than one. He turned toward his door and said in a voice louder than his usual secretarial instructional voice, "Get the Speaker on the line!"

Pendleton dialed four numbers quickly and got Rebecca's voice mail. He remembered he had stationed her at the Supreme Court and wondered what had happened to her. He hit a button to skip her greeting and said into his speakerphone, "Rebecca, call me as soon as you get back. The Supreme Court is going to hear this matter tonight privately, then perhaps set a hearing date. We need to convert our Appellate Court brief into a Supreme Court brief overnight. Call whatever other associates, paralegals, and staff you need. This will be a maximum effort." He hit the button for his other line as soon as it lit up.

"Mr. Speaker?" he said, assuming that his secretary had gotten through.

"Yes, David. What's up?" The Speaker sounded harried. "I have to get onto the floor. Word's out that we're going to be considering articles of impeachment. The press is double swarming," he chuckled slightly. "They were already swarming; now they are double-swarming. You get the implic—"

"Yes, I get the implications, Mr. Speaker. I just received word from the Supreme Court that they are going to be hearing the emergency application tonight. I can't tell if it's only some kind of preliminary look or whether they're going to hear it on the merits. The clerk was unclear. I need to be prepared to brief this and go before the Court tonight or tomorrow morning." He looked at his watch. "I'm going to stay here, so if you need anything, call me. Are you going to be where I can reach you if I need anything from you?"

"Not really. I'll be on the floor, it'll probably be pretty late, but get word to me somehow if you need to hear from me. I can always call a break."

"Okay. I'll be in touch," Pendleton said as he reached for the release button on his phone. His finger stopped in midair as another thought occurred to him. "Mr. Speaker?"

"Yes?"

"Do you have any . . . how should I put this . . ." Pendleton said hesitatingly, ". . . influence on the Supreme Court? And I don't mean improper influence. I mean do you know anybody who knows anybody over there who could give us a feel, not so much for what they plan on doing but how they plan on doing it and when—timing, that sort of thing?" Pendleton was forming the idea in his mind as he spoke.

The Speaker thought for a moment. "Not really, no. I knew one of the justices many years ago, but it would be completely inappropriate for me to call him. He would also probably take it the wrong way."

Pendleton interrupted. "No, I didn't really have that in mind. Is there anything else?"

The Speaker hesitated. "Well, I know that Dillon gets together with the clerk for the Chief Justice all the time. I think they're friends. He's the only one that I know of."

"That may be just the thing." Pendleton paused, considering. "See if you can convince Mr. Dillon to see how his friend is doing."

"That will be tough. Dillon's down on the *Constitution* and they are incommunicado. But I do have his cellular phone number. He has one of those fancy new satellite phones. I can try it."

"Please do, we need to use whatever . . . tools we have."

"I hear you," said the Speaker. "I will be in touch."

"Thank you," Pendleton said, hanging up.

Dillon stood on the 0-10 level, Vulture's Row, overlooking the flight deck. He watched the sailors scurry around preparing the planes for the early morning launch. The fact that people could take off and land from an aircraft carrier to him was still just short of miraculous. People had been doing it for a long time, and the United States had nearly perfected the art, but it still impressed him much more than he expected. He was also surprised that he was jealous of the officers on the carrier. Many were his age, had similar educational backgrounds, and shared many of his values and ideas. Yet they had more of a mission than the average Hill staffer. He wanted to identify with the pilots in the airplanes and be part of them, to share in their camaraderie and sense of mission. It was like watching a football team from the stands.

Dillon thought of himself back in his small office in the Capitol building. The thought was singularly unattractive to him. He compared himself sitting in an office in Washington, one of a sea of staff members for the House of Representatives, to the active, thriving men and women aboard the USS *Constitution*, who were actually *doing* something. Dillon argued with himself. He *was* doing something: He was the one who came up with the whole idea of the Letter of Reprisal, he was the one who brought it down here and gave these people their mission. But still, he would rather be taking off in an airplane right now than getting a muffin with Grazio.

It was a spectacular morning in the South Pacific as the carrier battle group and the amphibious ready group, as he had learned they were called, raced toward Bunaya. The sun was just above the horizon, casting a golden glow on the Americans through the cloudless blue sky. The wind whipped past, invigorating him. His fatigue receded as he thought of what lay ahead.

He felt a vibration in his rear pocket and heard an unusual sound. It took him a moment to realize his phone was ringing. He had never heard it ring before, and its ring was different from the cellular phone he had carried before. He opened it up. "Hello?"

"Dillon!" the Speaker exclaimed. "I'm glad I caught you. Can you hear me okay?"

"Yeah," Dillon said surprised. "Boy, am I glad you called."

The Speaker stopped, interrupting his own thoughts. "Why are you glad I called?"

Dillon tried to stop himself, but he had always been aware of his compulsion to say exactly what he thought. "Mr. Speaker, ever since we spoke a few minutes ago, I've been thinking about this impeachment thing."

"Isn't it a great opportunity?" the Speaker asked enthusiastically. "Finally, we can bring this pointy-headed President of ours down to earth."

"That's what's been bothering me," Dillon said. "This feels very political."

"What are you talking about?" the Speaker said impatiently.

"I think this is a big mistake, Mr. Speaker. I've got a

real strong feeling about this. I think you definitely should not go forward with the impeachment.''

''Why the hell not?''

''Because it looks vindictive. It looks like you're after the President personally, like you want to run him out of his job.''

''I *do*.''

''But that's not the right motive. If it's not done for the right motive at this point, we shouldn't do it at all. It looks too personal.''

''It's not personal. The President doesn't deserve to be president. It's as simple as that. He's unfit.''

''This is really about your Purple Heart, isn't it?'' Dillon asked pointedly.

The Speaker hesitated. ''You mind explaining that?''

''You ran riverboats in the Delta, got shot at, got wounded. Purple Heart. You're pretty proud of that. . . .''

''Yes, I am. What's the matter with that?''

''Nothing. But Manchester managed to avoid serving in Vietnam.''

''Yeah, avoided is the right way to put that. Four-F, physically unfit, flat feet. What a bunch of bullshit. He jogs three miles a day.''

''What I'm saying here, Mr. Speaker, is that I think you've got it in for him. I think you should consider whether your impeachment is personal or not.''

''It is the right motive. He's unfit to be President.''

Dillon ran his hand through his hair and held it back from his forehead. ''Mr. Speaker, you cannot go forward with this. It could kill the whole thing. It could turn public opinion against us, could put the whole Letter of Reprisal into question; it could be a disaster.''

The Speaker stopped. Instead of responding automatically as he wanted to, he listened. ''Why do you say that?''

''You know politics a lot better than I do,'' said Dillon. ''We've already got a two-front war, Mr. Speaker. The last thing we need is another front. People are going to start thinking Washington has just lost its mind.''

''I've already got this thing under way. The articles of impeachment have been drafted, the committee's considering them, I don't know . . .''

''Well, it's your decision, but that's my input,'' Dillon said.

''I'll think about it, but you've got to do something for me,'' the Speaker said ominously.

''What's that?''

Stanbridge spoke quickly. ''Can you call . . . I can't remember his name . . . your friend over at the Supreme Court?''

''Bobby?'' Dillon responded.

''The Supreme Court has agreed to hear some kind of motion about the President's lawsuit against me . . . I don't know the details. Pendleton called. They're going to consider it tonight.''

''You're kidding me,'' Dillon said. ''On what grounds?''

''I don't know, they aren't saying. Just that they're going to hear it. They're probably going to set a hearing date, but we don't really know. Pendleton is handling it.''

''So what do you want me to do?''

''Call Bobby, find out what the plan is . . . see if it wouldn't be better for them to hear it on, say, Tuesday. . . .''

''I can't do that,'' Dillon said, his stomach churning.

''What do you mean, you *can't* do that?'' the Speaker asked with anger in his voice. He paused.

Dillon listened to the silence on the phone as the sounds of the ship filled the void.

The Speaker continued, ''You mean you won't.''

Dillon's heart pounded.

''Find out what's going on. When they're going to set the hearing.''

''I don't know, Mr. Speaker . . .'' Dillon said, his voice trailing off, the panic of being cornered tightening his gut.

The Speaker of the House was quiet on the other end of the phone.

"Dillon, I've never asked you to do anything for me that I didn't think was appropriate. Call this friend of yours, see if it isn't in the Supreme Court's *best interests* to hear this matter next week and not tonight." The Speaker paused again. "Are you following me?"

"Yes, Mr. Speaker, I *follow* you."

"Call me back in an hour," the Speaker said.

"Yes, sir," Dillon said and ended the call. He put his phone back in his rear pocket and looked out over the water. His jaw was tight as he thought of the Speaker's request. He looked at his watch.

The crisis sparked by the attack on the *Pacific Flyer* was putting every relationship he had at risk. Why couldn't the President just do what he should have done in the first place?

He pulled out his phone and dialed. The phone rang and Bobby picked it up on the first ring.

"What?" Bobby said, agitated.

"Bobby," Dillon said, trying to sound friendly.

"Who is this?" Bobby barked.

"Dillon."

"Where the hell are you?" Bobby said.

"On the USS *Constitution* in the South Pacific. I am surrounded by Tahitian women who are trying to get me to eat this really cool fruit—"

"I don't have time for this, Dillon. What do you want?"

"I was just calling to say hi. Calling to show you the magic of technology. Here I am sitting in the middle of nowhere on a Navy ship and I'm talking to you in Washington on my new little portable phone. I don't know, I just thought it would be neat."

"You got any idea what's going on here?"

Dillon hesitated, "Yeah, I pretty much do."

"Are you aware that your boss has got a case in front of me right now? Right this second while you called and *interrupted* me doing research on whether your boss ought to be enjoined?''

"Yeah, I kind of did know that.''

"Then what the hell are you doing calling me? Is this about basketball? Are you going to use that ruse again?''

"It wasn't a ruse. I'm not trying to do anything, Bobby. Get off your horse.''

"I'm not on a horse, man. What I *am* on is a short time schedule. What do you want? If it's not about this, what's it about?''

"I just wanted to see how it was going. Do you have any idea when this thing is going to be resolved?''

"Dillon, you just said it wasn't about this. The timing is *the whole question.*'' Bobby suddenly changed his tone. "Did you say you are on the USS *Constitution*?''

"Yeah.''

"Isn't that the ship that this is all about?''

"You're awake!''

"What are you doing down there?''

"I'm the one who delivered the Letter of Reprisal to the admiral, Bobby. I was the delivery boy.''

"You're unbelievable . . . How'd you get that job?''

"I don't think they wanted to send anybody from the military. I can't really get into it,'' Dillon said, cutting himself off, regretting he had said anything at all.

"Then you can answer a question for me. Maybe you can make my job a lot easier.''

"What's that?''

"This big thing with the aircraft carrier and the Marines, *when* is it going to happen?''

"What big thing?''

"The big attack. When is the carrier going to go after these guys, if they are going to. Has the admiral even decided whether he is going to follow the Letter?''

"Yeah, he's decided.''

"So? What's he going to do and when is he going to do it?''

"What if I told you? You gonna use that information?''

"I wouldn't do that. It would be *inappropriate*." He paused to make sure Dillon didn't miss his point. "Wouldn't it?"

Dillon stood and listened to the phone connection. He thought about what to do, how hard to press it, how hard to work for his boss, how hard to lean against the ethical line. He imagined Bobby staring at the photo of their study group, which they both had on their desks. "Hey, Bobby," he said.

"Yeah, man?" Bobby said.

"Do what's right," Dillon said.

"You got it," Bobby said. "But there's one thing I gotta know. . . ."

"What?" Dillon said. He waited for Bobby to respond but heard nothing. He continued to wait, wondering what it was that was so hard for Bobby to say. "Hello? Bobby?" There was no response. His phone connection was dead.

28

JOHN STANBRIDGE HELD UP A STUBBY HAND TO STOP the questioning. "... I'm not here to talk about that. I'm here for one reason, and one reason only. I wanted to tell you something that your President hasn't told you."

The members of the press corps were pushing each other out of the way to get the best position for what might be the biggest story of their lifetimes.

Stanbridge held up his hand again and moved back from the microphone. He wasn't going to continue until they got control of themselves. The noise subsided slightly, and he stepped forward.

"First," he said, "the President has cut off the USS *Constitution* Battle Group. The Navy is no longer talking to them—the ships in the battle group are still transmitting messges but our Commander in Chief has had the coding of messages changed and instructed all military units not to communicate directly with the most powerful battle group in the world. ..."

The reporters began shouting like schoolchildren.

Stanbridge signaled for them to quiet down. Then continued, "Thus, not only has the President failed to go after the terrorists, he has impeded Congress's ability to do so by disabling the communications of the battle group on the scene and depriving them of critical intelligence.

"But it's worse than that! These terrorists have not only murdered innocent Americans and sunk a valuable ship,

they have now attacked the military directly." He paused
for effect. "Yesterday, about five o'clock P.M. Jakarta
time, the terrorists fired surface-to-air missiles at one of
our F-14B aircraft—clearly flying in international airspace—hitting it and shooting it down. . . .

"This direct attack on our military was well known to
the President SECDEF, and the Joint Chiefs, because the
Constitution Battle Group sent them a message. As the
airplane was burning and falling to the ocean, two aircrew
ejected from the F-14 and parachuted into the water."
Stanbridge sensed the intense fear and interest of his lis-
teners, as if he were telling a good ghost story to children.
He lowered his voice and slowed his pace. "As night fell
they were sitting in their rafts waiting for rescue. Shortly
after the shootdown, three boats raced from the island to
the downed airmen and got there before the rescue helicopter could arrive. The three boats were going to do the
same thing to those pilots that happened to the crew of
the *Pacific Flyer*. Thankfully," he said with relief, "Admiral Billings saw fit to post an F-18 over the downed
airmen, and the F-18 fired warning shots and, when ignored, shot and sank the three cigarette boats before they
could get our men. For that we are grateful. . . ."

One particularly tall and loud reporter shouted a question from right in front of Stanbridge, "Mr. Speaker, have
you talked to the Presid—"

Stanbridge ignored him. "Those three high-speed boats
that were trying to get our airmen were the same three
boats on which the men that shot our citizens on the *Flyer*
escaped."

"How do you know it was them?" the loud reporter
demanded.

"How do we know? How do we know? Because we
followed them to one island and then another by submarine, that's . . ."

Manchester's face looked as serious and grim as any of them had ever seen it. A vein on his forehead stood out. It was usually only visible when he was on the verge of fury. "Can somebody explain to me how this happened?"

The President had called yet another unscheduled meeting. Only this time it was in the Situation Room on the ground floor of the West Wing of the White House. Electronic boards and world situation maps covered the walls.

"We don't know for sure, Mr. President," said Central Intelligence Director Warner. "We have to assume he got all his information from Dillon before we cut him off. Unfortunately, we had no idea he was communicating through one of those mobile satellite phones until he called Ms. Vaughan here."

Molly sat in a chair in the corner, not comfortable being at the main table where all the others were sitting. She felt out of place and exposed.

"Didn't you think someone on board might have a cellular phone? Didn't that even occur to you?"

"We were monitoring everything, sir. That's why we were finally able to locate his signal when he called her."

"It was kind of a good thing he called, actually," Molly said, uncrossing her legs and sitting forward in her chair. "He confirmed the admiral is in fact still planning to go forward with the attack and is *not* going to comply with your order."

"Now there's some big news."

"He also confirmed that he was the ship's only communication link to the outside. My guess is that anything the Speaker knows, he learned from Jim Dillon, no other source."

"He's a friend of yours?" Van den Bosch demanded.

"Yes, we went to law school together."

"You're not giving him information that you're gathering from these meetings you're sitting in on, are you?"

Molly flushed red down to her V-neck suit coat. "I'm surprised you even asked that question."

Van den Bosch stared at her. "Well, what's the answer to that surprising question?"

"No. I haven't told him anything, nor would I. That would be inappropriate."

Van den Bosch returned his gaze to President Manchester.

Manchester turned to Admiral Hart. "Where's the other battle group? The one that was in the Philippines?"

Admiral Hart crossed the Situation Room to a large chart of the Pacific. He studied it for a moment. "Right here," he said, pointing to an area southwest of Manila.

Manchester looked at the Attorney General. "What about this impeachment thing?"

The Attorney General was surprised by his change of subject. He weighed his response. "This is a clear attempt to try to knock you down, to defeat you. It's pure politics. The Speaker clearly has it in for you. The Letter was just one step, but now he's shown his colors. He's going to try every means possible, even *arguable,* to try to destroy you."

"I know that," the President said with a wave of his hand. "I know that. My question is: Is there any chance he will actually get this through?" Manchester clenched his jaw. He looked at his Chief of Staff. "Arlan, I want the Speaker stopped."

The Chief of Staff studied his boss. He glanced around the room at the others, who were equally confused and concerned. "What do you mean by 'stopped'?"

Manchester stared straight ahead. "He's trying to destroy me. Why?"

Van den Bosch looked around again. "Political. Obviously. He wants your job."

Manchester shook his head. "No. There's more to it than that. Everybody in the House and the Senate wants my job. This feels personal."

"Well, Mr. President," Van den Bosch continued,

"could be the old military thing. He served and you didn't. He's held that against you since you first met him fifteen years ago."

Manchester rubbed his eyes. "Could be. But I don't think that explains it. I think it's time *we* got personal." He looked at Van den Bosch again. "How can he be stopped?"

Van den Bosch waited for the words to come. "Well, Mr. President," he said haltingly, "there are several things that we, uh, could do. Do you have in mind using the press?" he asked, testing the water. "Or did you have in mind just political . . ."

Manchester looked at him with his steel eyes. "Whatever it takes. It's either him or me. I know that now."

"Hold on here," the Attorney General chimed in. "I'm starting to feel a little uncomfortable about this. Let's not have a John Dean conversation about what we're going to do to the Speaker of the House."

"I'm not talking about anything illegal," the President said with a look of disgust on his face. "I'm simply talking about something effective. So far everything we've done has been made to look ridiculous. Including this lawsuit that your shop is in charge of, *Mr.* Attorney General. We've lost two rounds; the third strike and we're out. What are our other alternatives, not only to stop this craziness but to take the Speaker out of the picture."

"Well, our political alternatives are really quite limited," Van den Bosch continued. "I can call the Minority Leader and ask him to stir things up a bit, make it hard for the Speaker, make sure that they don't agree to anything and that he tries to make the Speaker look bad, but he's not really in a position to do that much. The Speaker runs the House. But if you're thinking of simply reducing the Speaker's credibility with the public, there is that one little gem that we've been saving for quite a while."

Manchester understood him. "Try," he said. He looked at the Attorney General. "So, any chance of this impeachment thing succeeding?"

The Attorney General sucked in his breath. "Well, Mr. President, that really depends on you. Is there any truth to the charge that you are a pacifist?"

Suddenly the room was filled with electricity. All eyes were riveted on the President's face for any sign of anger or indication of the truth of the accusation. Every one of them had been involved in his campaign indirectly, except Hart. They had all studied his position papers, his speeches, his campaign promises. And they all now realized that they didn't know whether the President was, deep in his heart, a pacifist. It was a shocking thought to each of them and they wanted to hear him answer the question directly.

"My goal," the President started slowly, "is to prevent the unnecessary death of American servicemen. Congress can attempt to avoid my decision in this matter in whatever way it chooses, but this decision has to stand on its own merits." The President was no longer fully with them. He was somewhere in a moral universe where they weren't welcome, or which they couldn't understand. He continued with an air of superiority. "Whether it is moral or immoral for the President to decide not to pursue terrorists when the country of their origin, or the country in which they are currently found, has given us assurances of pursuit—"

"As to the terrorist angle, Mr. President," Warner interrupted, unmoved by the President's speech, "I'm afraid we have some new information in that regard."

The President looked at him and raised his eyebrows. "What new information?"

"Remember the videotapes they sent earlier?"

"Sure."

"It was a bunch of crap. The content was nonsense. But the photographs, or rather the tape itself, helped us finally track down who these people are. We think we've identified them."

The President looked at him with wide eyes. "Are you serious?"

"We think so."

"I thought we already knew—the Front for Islamic Indonesia. The country has been in turmoil, everybody hates the military dictator, so it all fit." He finished his sentence with something of a questioning tone.

Warner seemed almost apologetic, as if he understood the President's confusion. "That's right, Mr. President, it does all fit. That's why I don't think anyone was looking real hard to find out whether their story was true. We just accepted them at their word—not always the smart thing to do when dealing with terrorists, I must admit—but the Indonesians smelled a rat; they knew every Islamic fundamentalist group in the country. They've infiltrated most of the movements. They've had all of their intelligence and security police review the tape. They even showed it to every undercover operative they have. Nothing."

"So?" the President asked impatiently.

"One of the Indonesian intelligence officers took a look at the ring on the head terrorist's hand." Warner held up his ring finger. "It was only visible for a moment in the corner of the videotape. When he hit Captain Bonham. We slowed the tape and enhanced the image. It's a very common ring, and we didn't notice anything remarkable about it at all. He did. He recognized one of the symbols—it is a Thai symbol. You see it elsewhere now and then, but it is used almost exclusively in Thailand."

"And?" the President asked.

The director strung out his explanation, relishing it. "The ring from Thailand, Mr. President—that was what made him look elsewhere. They finally talked to their Navy Intelligence people and they think they have put it together." He paused and looked around the room. Admiral Hart was riveted, annoyed that he had paused. "They think in fact, Mr. President, it is an Indonesian group working with a Thai group to form an international piracy ring to control the Strait of Malacca."

"What?" the President asked clearly shocked. "Pirates?"

"It all fits. They didn't sink our ship because they wanted us to stay out of Indonesia for the freedom of an Indonesian Islamic front. They wanted us to stay out of the Java Sea and the Strait of Malacca so they can jump on foreign ships. They don't like the U.S. Navy presence because ours is the only Navy left that is much of a threat to them."

The President scratched his forehead. The Chairman of the Joint Chiefs sat up on the edge of his chair and looked into Warner's face. "How sure are you about this?" Manchester asked.

"The Indonesians feel pretty sure, but I haven't seen enough to be sure myself."

"Does it makes sense to you?"

"Yes, sir. We also got a copy of that message about the F-14 getting shot down. If they have that kind of sophisticated weaponry, they may have surface-to-surface missiles as well. They are apparently on this island called Bunaya, which is strategically located. It's not near much else and it's within missile range of a lot of the shipping that goes through the Strait of Malacca."

The President fought to keep his temper. "How could the idiotic Indonesians not know that some of their own people are working with the Thais, building SAM sites, and nearly closing the strait?"

"Well, they're not exactly closing them, Mr. President, but I get your point. We asked them that very question. They got kind of angry with us, said they have seventeen thousand islands, half of them uninhabited, and they can't go around checking them all the time. It's hard enough to keep track of the ones that are populated with two hundred million people. They've got a lot of problems and not a big navy. They weren't surprised at all. In fact, they're now starting a check on the rest of the islands in their control, but say it will take months just to put a human being on each of the islands. And they are not anxious to do it. They're afraid of running right into another nest of these pirates and not making it back. So they want to check them out with their navy ships and air cover and . . . it's going to be a long, tedious process. They've even thought about asking for assistance, but haven't decided yet.''

''This is unbelievable,'' the President said. He looked at Hart. ''Admiral, what do you think about this?''

''I had always thought that the Islamic terrorist bit wasn't very convincing, Mr. President. It was too . . . I don't know, it was just unpersuasive. The idea of them trying to close the strait is pretty amazing. Usually pirates don't try and close straits. What they may do is threaten every ship through there and then take money from them—extortion. Just like the Barbary pirates in the days of Thomas Jefferson.''

''This is great,'' President Manchester said, leaning back and closing his eyes as he rubbed his face. ''The Speaker of the House is going to jump all over this. I can hear it now: 'Just like in the days of Thomas Jefferson, the Congress has issued a Letter of Reprisal against pirates. . . .' '' He stopped, anger rising in him. ''I cannot believe this!'' he yelled.

''Actually, it was James Madison who issued the last Letter of Marque or Rep—''

''I don't care who issued the last one, Admiral.'' He looked around the room. ''Does this change anything?''

Van den Bosch immediately jumped in. ''It sure does! We're not going after terrorists who are fighting for freedom of religion in their own country, or actually purity of religion in their own country, we would be fighting *pirates*. Everybody hates pirates; this country has a long history of fighting pirates. You just have to squash them. Like bugs.''

The President looked at Warner. ''Are they or are they not Indonesians?''

''From what I hear, we're not sure, but it seems . . .''

''And this island, Bunaya, is it an Indonesian island?''

''Yes, it is.''

The President was recovering his cool. ''So we are talking about Indonesians conducting illegal activity, on Indonesian soil, and launching missiles from Indonesia?''

"That's right,'' Warner echoed. "That's all correct,'' he said, implying that it didn't matter.

"Well, I need to think about that. What is the status of the application before the Supreme Court, Mr. Attorney General?''

"There's more,'' the Director said.

"What?''

"We don't think they're operating alone.''

"I can't wait to hear this,'' the President said. "Let's have it. Tell us everything.''

"Well, sir, when we heard there were South African missiles involved, we began doing some digging into the international arms trade we keep track of. We initially thought Iran was involved. The international pariah. Our early intel, our early indications, all pointed to Iran. Their favorite sport is supporting fundamentalist Muslims who then wreak havoc on secular Arab states, or anyone else that isn't die-hard Muslim. It fit nicely. Plus, Iran is a major player in international arms sales. But the South African connection threw us. We don't have any indication of South Africa dealing with Iran. . . .''

"Get to the point,'' the President muttered.

Warner stopped, stung, and said suddenly, "China. That's the point. China.''

"You've lost me.''

Warner shrugged, almost smug. "You didn't want all the in-between stuff,'' he said. "The end of the analysis is China.''

"They're behind this? Why?''

"Behind it may be too strong. We think, though, that China at least 'encouraged' it, and probably financed it. Over the last few years China has been building up its military. They're trying to build up their navy, but it's slow going. *Their* primary objective is certainly to get us out of the Southwest Pacific. We're the only ones left who have any influence there. If we're not around''—he shrugged, as if stating the obvious—"China fills the void. And one way to get us not to be around is to encourage others, like these idiots, to hurt us. Maybe we'll go away. Kind of a Vietnam-writ-small theory."

"Why do you say China is involved?" Van den Bosch broke in.

"Because a few months ago China sent another shipment of Silkworm missile crates out. We thought they were going to Iran. We tracked the arms carrier to the area around the Strait of Malacca, but then we lost them. We expected them to go to Iran, but weren't ever sure if they did. It was such a fungible ship; it could have been repainted in a million ways and we'd never know where it came from. But no new Silkworm sites were set up in Iran, and none received new missiles." Warner looked around. "We think those crates contained the South African SAMs, and maybe other things we don't know about. Maybe even Silkworm surface-to-surface antiship missiles."

"Have we told Indonesia about this?" the President asked.

"Yes, sir. I discussed it with them. That's what clinched it for me," Warner said.

"What?"

"The biggest hitters, financially, in Indonesia are of Chinese descent. Most of them have no ties to mainland China and in fact despise the communism China stands for. But a couple do have such ties. Secret ties, which we have learned about. Two Indonesians in particular. The two, Mr. President, whom you know. The two who know you."

Manchester seemed puzzled.

Warner continued, "The two who opened a bank in your hometown in Connecticut. Whom you've met."

"What does that have to do with it?" the President said with concern.

"They may have been the ones who told China you

wouldn't do anything about it. They may have said you didn't have any nerve—''

"Who said I don't have any nerve?''

"Nobody. This is hypothesis, Mr. President. But it is a curious coincidence. They are thought by some to be positioning themselves to have influence when China extends its tentacles into Indonesia, Malaysia, Singapore, and Thailand, which some think will happen in the next five years if . . .''

"This is all conjecture,'' the President finally said, waving it off with his hand. "When you have some facts, come tell us about them.''

Warner sat back, hurt by the sudden dismissal of what he thought was magnificent intelligence work. "There's one additional development, Mr. President.''

"What?'' Manchester said angrily. "Make it fast.''

Warner spoke quickly, "A missionary family has been kidnapped.''

"Where?''

"Irian Jaya,'' Warner said, then, seeing the lack of recognition, continued, "an island in eastern Indonesia.''

Manchester frowned, "Is it related to the rest of this?''

"We don't know. We don't know anything except that they vanished. The natives say it wasn't them. Somebody came and got them.''

"What can we do?''

"We're already doing everything we can. . . .''

"Keep me posted,'' Manchester said, turning to the attorney general.

Manchester didn't want to hear any more about it. "So, Mr. Attorney General, Ms. Vaughan, where are we on the emergency stay before the Supreme Court?''

"Well, Mr. President,'' McCormick said, "it has been accepted for emergency review by the Supreme Court, but it is such an extraordinary circumstance that nobody knows what it means. They're handling it like a death penalty case, keeping counsel on standby on the telephone and talking to everybody in the process, but they are not telling us what their plan is. We don't know if they want to hear it on the merits tonight, or issue a temporary order or stay pending ultimate resolution, or when they are going to set a hearing. These are uncharted waters."

"Nice analogy," the admiral said.

The President glanced at the admiral, unamused, then turned back toward the Attorney General. "When do you think we'll hear anything?"

McCormick shrugged. "We've got our best attorney on it—there is really nothing to do. We're just waiting to hear from the Supreme Court, and we have no idea when they're going to call. If I were personally going to guess, I think we would hear something from them in the next couple of hours, but"—he shook his head—"I don't have any feel for how accurate that guess is."

Manchester looked at Molly, sitting quietly. "You still think it's a winner?"

"The restraining order?" she asked. "Yes, I do. It would solve everything by freezing it—maintaining the status quo. And the court could decide the merits at another time."

The President looked at his Chief of Staff. "Arlan, is there any way we can derail this rubbish over at Congress—this impeachment stuff?"

"Yes, sir. You can restore communications with the *Constitution* and order them to go after these pirates."

"I told you I needed to think about that. What else?"

"I think you should let it fall of its own weight." He leaned forward and spoke to the President in a tone he usually saved for subordinates. "Unless you are prepared to go before the press and deny that you are a pacifist and tell them how eager you are to send troops if necessary. I would recommend you do that. Short of that, I'd let others come to your defense for you and make it look like the Speaker is just trying to cut your head off."

"May I speak?" the admiral said.

"Go ahead," Manchester said grudgingly.

"Is anybody going to tell the battle group down there

that the people they're going against aren't a bunch of wackos? That maybe they're backed by China and have sophisticated weapons, possibly including Silkworms? And that they may have a missionary family as hostages?''

"They're cut off," the Chief of Staff said.

"That's the point. They're our Navy, and we cut them off, and we know what they don't. Don't we owe it to them to at least tell them what we know?"

"They're not authorized to do anything, Admiral. When you operate against orders, you take risks."

"Sure, but . . ."

"No 'but' about it," Manchester said, cutting him off.

The admiral sat back in his chair red-faced, fighting with himself. "At the risk of being accused of insubordination, Mr. President," he said with quiet dignity, "your decision could get people killed. Americans. Sailors."

"Not if they obey their orders," the President shot back.

"One last thing about that Supreme Court hearing, Mr. President," Warner said cryptically.

Manchester looked at him quizzically. "What?"

"The last person Dillon was talking to when we located his signal? His friend on the Supreme Court. The clerk to the Chief Justice."

Colonel Brandon Tucker had made his way from one Marine company to another aboard the *Wasp*. The best amphibious ship in the United States fleet. It carried Harriers, the vertical takeoff and landing jets the Marine Corps loved and nobody else wanted, as well as the helicopters the Marines had flown for years—the CH-53E and the CH-46, and up to sixteen hundred Marines.

Tucker had met with each company commander and discussed with him the tentative plan. Tentative because they really didn't know where they were going. Final approval would be based almost entirely on the reports they would get back tonight from the Navy SEALs.

Tucker had called all the company commanders together for an afternoon brief after he had inspected each one, and they were now before him, anxiously waiting for that most precious commodity: information. Lieutenant Jody Armstrong was there along with the colonel's staff.

"Does everyone understand the plan?" Tucker began severely. "Let me say it again. In less than twenty-four hours we are going to be standing on the island of Bunaya. I have to tell you, in all the landings that I have done, I have never felt more uneasy." He hesitated. "This should be a cakewalk. We should be going in against a bunch of terrorists with limited experience and probably not many substantial weapons—although they apparently have SAMs. It is unlikely that they have any antitank weapons. It is unlikely that they have armor-piercing shells, howitzers, land mines, or an ability to prevent our landing. However, we will assume that they have all of those. We are going to treat this as if we are going against the Russian Army and we are walking ashore in Petropavlosk." He put his hands on his hips. "We are going to assume that these people are defending their homeland and we are coming to take their wives. We will assume that these are the greatest fighters ever trained in the history of warfare. We will assume that they have weapons that are more advanced than ours, and that they can shoot better than we can. We will assume they have armor, armor-piercing ammunition, satellite intelligence, and video data link of our entire landing. We will assume CNN will show them a live shot of us commencing our landing." This brought a laugh from the gathered officers.

He looked around. "Most of which is probably *not* the case, but if you assume the enemy is stronger than he is, you will take additional precautions and live longer. Don't get me wrong. This does not mean that we are not going ashore hard. This means that we are going to go ashore twice as hard and twice as fast with twice as many forces.

Frankly, gentlemen, we are going to beat the shit out of them. This is going to be their worst nightmare. They picked on the wrong people. And for those of you who don't yet feel the need to do this, just remember those twenty-five merchant sailors, who were simply trying to carry goods to the people of Indonesia, and the SEAL off *this ship* who was murdered in cold blood.'' He paused for effect. ''The people we are going against can call themselves Islamic fundamentalists or a convention of Bozo the Clowns. Doesn't matter to me. If they abduct, shoot, and blow up my countrymen, they better dial 911, 'cause they're gonna need all the help they can get. Any questions?''

There weren't any. They had gone over the plan a dozen times and were simply waiting for the updated information.

Tucker looked back at Armstrong. ''Your men are ready, right? When are you off?''

Armstrong looked at his watch. ''Eighteen hundred.''

''When are you ashore?''

''Twenty-three hundred,'' Armstrong said.

Tucker looked at him hard. ''Do you have everything you need?''

''Yes, sir. I could use some more imagery, but I guess we're not getting that.''

''Not happening. We're not risking another TARPS bird to get another set of pictures. The satellites are out of our control and we're on our own. You're gonna have to get the information for *us.*''

Armstrong nodded. ''Roger that. We'll get it.''

Tucker's enormous arms bulged against the rolled-up sleeves of his camouflage uniform. ''Let's go kick some ass.''

29

DILLON WATCHED CNN, THE ADMIRAL, HIS AIDE, and the ocean all at once. His stomach felt queasy. He had heard that aircraft carriers were so big that you couldn't even tell they were moving. He could definitely tell this one was moving. Most of the movement was because of the ship's speed—about twenty-five knots. But he could also feel it rolling just slightly from one side to the other. He looked at others around him and could detect no sense of movement or queasiness from them. He wondered how much of his current unease was due to the forces that had been set in motion by the Letter. *His* Letter. His idea, his research, his enthusiasm for an obscure constitutional concept. He couldn't think about it without a rush of battery acid into his stomach.

He watched his boss, the Speaker of the House, on TV, answering questions posed to him in a press conference in the hall outside his office. A reporter said, "So, Mr. Speaker, there is a rumor on the Hill that you are going to request the House approve articles of impeachment against the President for being a pacifist. Is there any truth to that?"

"On the night the President gave the speech declaring that we would not go after these terrorists, I went over to the White House—I think most of you reported on that. I asked the President directly whether he was a pacifist, and he refused to deny it."

314

Stanbridge watched the reaction of the reporter.

"So are you going to pursue the articles of impeachment?" Another reporter repeated the question.

"As you have reported, this issue has been under consideration by some members of the House. I have considered it myself, so I think frankly that the President should put this issue to rest by answering the question. However, he does not seem willing to do so. That gives me pause. It also makes me think that maybe there is some truth to it. However, after meeting with my colleagues, it is our considered opinion that now is not the time to go into this. The President has already shown that he has no intention of protecting American citizens against vicious attack, and he can answer for that later. Right now, the ones who need to answer for this are the terrorists in the Southern Pacific."

Stanbridge raised his hand and shook his head indicating that he wasn't answering any further questions. He walked to his office and turned around. "That's all I have for now. I may have more for you on this later, but right now, I have other things that are pressing. Thank you." He closed the door behind him as the reporters turned to the cameras to close.

Dillon smiled. Nicely done.

Lieutenant Reynolds stood beside him. "This is unbelievable. You ever see anything like this?" indicating the television hanging from the overhead.

"Never," Dillon said.

"You think the Speaker means this? Do you think he's really gonna lay off trying to get the President canned?"

"Sure looks like it. The press is frothing at the mouth. They haven't had this much to write about in decades. This is better than war, because it's all right in front of them. The reporters can sit in their little offices and write all kinds of things; then when they want to stir it up a little more, they go and get a bunch of quotes from some politician, roll those words into a sharp stick, and poke some other politician in the eye with them. Works great."

Reynolds spoke softly so he wouldn't distract Admiral Billings, who was glued to the television. "You like working in Washington?"

Dillon looked out over the ocean, at the sun glistening on the water. He breathed in deeply, trying to suppress his nausea. "I used to. Sometimes it gets tedious with all the infighting, the backstabbing, and the self interest—that's probably the worst of it. Everybody looking out for himself and not enough people caring about what's really going to happen. Still, if you want to actually change anything in this country, politics is about the only way to do it. But I don't really see myself as a politician."

"So, do you like it?"

"I like it sometimes, sometimes no." Dillon shrugged. "How about you, do you like being out on the ocean, do you like being in the Navy?"

The aide smiled. "Sometimes yes."

"This is unbelievable." The admiral shook his head. "Washington has gone mad. Funny thing is, the country may think that I'm the only one who is out of control and I'm probably the only one that's *under* control."

The aide and Dillon watched the fiasco on the House floor as the admiral looked around. Billings saw his ops O standing across the bridge. "Hey. Are the Marines ready to go ashore?"

"Yes, sir, they're ready—L hour is 0540."

"Perfect. Everything else all set?"

"Yes, sir. Everybody's briefed and ready to go."

The admiral stood and leaned back, stretching. "Pass the word. Mission is a go."

"Aye, aye, sir," the ops O said, as he turned on his heels and headed off the bridge.

≱

The speaker walked enthusiastically back into his office and removed his suit coat. He had closed the outer door behind him to exclude the teeming press. Only his staff members were allowed in at this point.

Robin looked at him. "Need I tell you, Mr. Speaker, that the phone is ringing off the hook, and about two million people want to see you?"

"Nope. I assumed that would be the case. Anything that can't wait for forty-eight hours?"

"I don't know, sir." Robin stopped him. "But before you go in there, sir, that's what I wanted to talk to you about."

The Speaker turned and gave her a confused look. "What?"

"While you were on the floor, the President's Chief of Staff came to see you. He's waiting for you in your office."

The Speaker looked mystified. "Does the press know he's here?"

"No, sir, came in when the press was covering the floor."

"What does he want?"

"I don't know. He just asked if he could wait in your office and it seemed the only appropriate place, so . . ."

"Of course. Well, this is something, isn't it?" He stood a little taller. "This should be interesting."

He entered his office, closing the door carefully behind him. Van den Bosch was sitting on the sofa by the coffee table, sipping from a china cup. He looked calm, relaxed, and confident.

"Well, Arlan," the Speaker said, extending his hand, "good evening."

Arlan stood up. "Good evening, Mr. Speaker. I'm sorry for intruding without being announced, but I just wanted to have a chat with you."

"Not a problem at all," said the Speaker, trying to read his enemy's face. He didn't dislike Van den Bosch; in fact, he had always respected him. He perceived him as the only adviser to the President who had his head screwed on straight. He seemed to understand the concept that strength was respected in foreign affairs, and weakness was preyed upon. That was the foreign policy the

Speaker believed the United States should always have, but rarely did. Too often the United States would degenerate into misty-eyed wishful thinking, which resulted in disastrous decisions and a lot of dead people.

Van den Bosch seemed to grasp that. In some ways Van den Bosch was an ally on the President's staff. That's probably why he's here, the Speaker thought to himself. Because he's the only one I'd listen to for five seconds.

"Please sit down, Arlan," he said, using the Chief of Staff's first name again in a forced attempt at familiarity. The Speaker reached behind him for the silver coffeepot and poured himself a fresh cup. "So, what brings you to this side of the world?"

Van den Bosch leaned toward the Speaker with forearms on his knees. "Mr. Speaker, these are trying times."

"Agreed." The Speaker sipped his coffee.

"I don't know that in my entire thirty years in politics I have seen anything that remotely resembles the past couple of days. I have never seen so many forces at work in so many directions, with people unable to foresee the outcome and plan accordingly. I *know* we are plowing new ground when *The Washington Post* sounds confused." Van den Bosch stopped for a moment to see if the Speaker was going to respond. Then he pressed on. "As you know, we have a substantial disagreement on the issue of the Letter of Reprisal. It's remarkable to me that Congress believes it has the right to order a U.S. Navy battle group around when the President is the designated Commander in Chief of the armed forces. That to me is a remarkable usurpation of—"

The Speaker inclined toward Van den Bosch and narrowed his eyes as he interrupted, "Did you come here to lecture me? I don't need a lecture. I know what your position is and it's wrong. We have historical precedent on our side, we have the lack of action on the . . ."

Van den Bosch raised his hand. "No," he said, "I'm not here to lecture you. I didn't even mean to raise that issue on the merits as such. I simply wanted to frame where we are to date.''

"I know where we are. Go on."

"The Letter of Reprisal is with the Navy, as I understand it?"

"That is correct; the admiral has accepted it."

"Do you know what the admiral is going to do?" Van den Bosch asked directly.

The Speaker sat back. "Well, if the President is the Commander in Chief, he should be asking the admiral that himself, shouldn't he? With all of our technology, the President could ask that question in about two seconds. Has he done so?"

"I am not at liberty to discuss the communications between the battle group and the President. Let it be said that the admiral's intentions are currently unclear."

"Well then, what makes you think I would know?"

"We are not sure, Mr. Speaker. You seem to have ways of getting information."

"Well, you certainly didn't come over here to ask me the admiral's intentions. Let me ask *you* a question. What are *your* intentions? Are you in fact sending another battle group down toward Admiral Billings's battle group to stop them? Is it your plan to start a friggin' civil war?"

Van den Bosch's eyes showed surprise momentarily but he recovered. "Where did you hear that?"

"Is it true?"

"Well, if it were, that would certainly weigh against the President's being a pacifist, wouldn't it?" Van den Bosch said, smiling slightly.

"Maybe. Why don't you have the President go on national television and announce that he is sending a battle group down to attack another U.S. Navy battle group, and that he in fact intends to attack them, and therefore he is not a pacifist. Let him make that statement before the American public that the proof of his manhood is his willingness to kill other Americans."

"I didn't say he had sent a battle group down there," Van den Bosch replied quickly.

"Do you deny it?" Stanbridge pressed.

"I am not at liberty to discuss the President's intentions concerning Admiral Billings," Van den Bosch said with a tone of finality.

The Speaker was annoyed with the direction of the conversation. He lowered his voice. "Then why are you here? I've got a lot to do."

"Because I want to see if we can lower the stakes a little." Van den Bosch placed the cup on the table and looked intently at the Speaker. "This whole thing is now to the point where instead of one constitutional crisis, we are dealing with two or three simultaneously. I don't know if the country can stand it. I don't know if the government can stand it. What you have done, Mr. Speaker, could cause severe and lasting damage to the United States, not only by way of reputation with other countries but to the confidence people have that their government will be in existence a year from now. You're attacking the Constitution itself."

Stanbridge mimed his disgust. "If the President simply had the *sand* to do what he was obligated to do, none of this would have happened. Don't try to blame this on me."

Van den Bosch sat back. "I am not saying this very well. I am not here, Mr. Speaker, to accuse you of anything. I am not here to make our case on any of the major issues that have been raised. I think we have a case, I think our case is the right case, and I think we will prevail in every respect." He saw the Speaker's expression and raised his hand again in defense. "But I am not here to make that case before you; I am just here to see, as I said, if we can lower the stakes a little."

"What do you mean?" the Speaker asked quickly, looking at his watch.

"Your threat to bring articles of impeachment before the House of Representatives was an insult to the President, Mr. Speaker. Accusing him of pacifism is unfounded. It was clearly a political move which you have now wisely abandoned.''

''Really?'' the Speaker said angrily. He stood up. ''Let him go before the people and tell them he's willing and ready to employ U.S. troops as necessary, that he's willing and ready to use our nuclear defense umbrella if called upon to do so. Have him make that statement, Arlan. You think I made that accusation lightly? You think I didn't do my homework? You think I didn't realize the implications? I had my staff review every speech he made in the presidential campaign. I looked at every debate, every written question he responded to, every publication he has made. He has *never* said that he will use nuclear weapons if called upon to do so, and he has *never* said he would employ U.S. troops to defend our interests. Oh, sure, he talked a lot about defense budgets, and increasing percentages of defense budget as a percentage of gross domestic product, blah, blah, blah. He said all the political things.''

''It's not your place to challenge the President to respond, like some kind of a carnival dog.''

''Fine. Then why are you here?''

Van den Bosch waited for the atmosphere to clear. ''Here's what I am prepared to propose. If you withdraw the Letter of Reprisal, the President will withdraw his lawsuit for an injunction.'' He looked for a reaction. ''It's as simple as that, one for the other. That way the Constitution will not be put on trial, and neither side can really claim victory.''

The Speaker stared at Van den Bosch, shocked. ''You think this is all political, don't you?''

Van den Bosch raised his eyebrows. ''Everything is political.''

''But not everything is *completely* political.''

Van den Bosch shrugged. ''Are you interested, or not?''

''Not,'' the Speaker said immediately. ''I am really surprised the President sent you over here. That really burns my shorts. What this shows, Arlan, is that your President is on the ropes. You have realized that you are going to lose now and you're trying to scramble to limit the damage. You've lost twice in the courts and the third test is ahead. You know what happens when you lose that. The Admiral has already shown he's going to follow the Letter of Reprisal and the President is going to look stupid. That's why you are here.''

Van den Bosch shook his head, as if saddened by the comments of the Speaker. "This is not good for the country, Mr. Speaker. We do not need to test the war powers in this way. If there is any damage, you will be the cause of it.''

The Speaker stood up quickly. "I'm sorry, I've got a lot to do. I can see this isn't very productive.''

"Sit down, Mr. Speaker.''

"I'm really not interested in sitting down—''

"Trust me, sit down.''

The Speaker sat back down quickly, impatiently. "What?''

"We want you to withdraw the Letter of Reprisal.''

"That's it? Just . . . withdraw it? And why might I do that?''

"For your own sake.''

"My own sake? What are you talking about?''

"You've taken great risks to get where you are, Mr. Speaker. I found it particularly curious that someone like you, someone who hails the free market system as the solution to all economic problems, would jointly sponsor the President's proposed bill requiring fifty percent of all shipping into the United States to be done on American-flagged carrier ships. Such a position is, almost by definition, anticompetitive. It will certainly increase the price of goods to consumers in the United States.'' Van den Bosch sat back. "So I asked myself why. Why would the Speaker of the House propose such a bill? The answer, of course, is obvious. The only ones who would benefit from such a law would be the American shipping industry.''

"Do you have a point?"

"Oh, I definitely have a point."

"The American shipping industry was almost completely gone," Stanbridge said. "I did it to save the industry."

"You did it to save *one* participant in the industry, which may have benefited others."

Van den Bosch stood up and walked to the window overlooking the Washington Monument. He turned to Stanbridge. "Turns out that your good friend and constituent, Mr. Jack Stewart, president of Stewart Shipping Line, was within thirty days of filing for bankruptcy. I have located the attorney who prepared the bankruptcy filing papers."

Stanbridge's eyes showed his surprise, which he immediately tried to hide. "So what?"

"So, he didn't file for bankruptcy. In fact, he seemed to take on political participation as his new hobby. From what I've learned, he had never donated more than fifty dollars to any political candidate until he decided to come to Washington and visit his congressman, John Stanbridge. What did he tell you?"

"What are you getting at?" Stanbridge said defensively.

"I can't expect you to admit this. Well, obviously, Mr. Speaker, you and he entered into a very nice agreement. You had proposed the law that would save his company and the American shipping industry, and he would ensure that you got reelected."

"I won with sixty-five percent of the vote. I didn't need anybody to help me get elected."

"I believe that's the same defense Richard Nixon used as to why Watergate was unlikely to have happened. He was going to crush McGovern anyway."

"Oh, please . . ."

"Let me continue. I won't take up much more of your

time. The point is this—I have now been able to trace approximately two million dollars that made its way from the shipping lines and Stewart's friends into your campaign. He donated money to your campaign through employees, family, friends, subsidiary corporations, and a myriad of other ways. Mr. Speaker, from what I can tell, you've violated somewhere between five and twenty campaign-financing laws. I also learned another piece of this puzzle recently," Van den Bosch continued. "Your pretty young secretary is very nice."

"What does she have to do with this?"

"Well, I didn't think anything, until I learned that her last name before she was married was Stewart. Is she related to Stewart Shipping Line?"

Stanbridge did not respond.

"I think you need to tell the admiral that he should hold off until the courts have decided this issue. I can make sure he gets your message. That's not too much to ask, is it?"

Stanbridge remained silent.

"Well, I really should be going." Van den Bosch headed for the door. "Please consider what I've said. I've prepared the information that I've shared with you, plus substantially more, in a memo that lists names, dates, amounts, and other tidbits I have not shared with you. If this Letter of Reprisal goes forward, that memo will be faxed anonymously to every newspaper in the country." He looked at Stanbridge, who had balled his hands into fists. "Consider your next move very carefully. Now, it's my understanding you need to get back on the floor. I'm simply going to wait here, and after you have gone, and the press with you, I will walk quietly out of this office and no one will know that I was here."

Stanbridge walked to the door and began to open it. He stopped and turned back toward Van den Bosch. "I used to have respect for you. I thought you were the only one over there who had any brains. I was wrong. You're just another sycophant. That's too bad because I want you to take a message back to President Manchester from me. Tell him I said he can shove it up his ass. Be sure you get the words correct, shove-it-up-his-ass,'' he said slowly, as if he were about to spell it. ''And one other thing—I'm going to *get* him. He will not be President for long,'' Stanbridge declared as he jerked the door open and slammed it behind him.

30

REBECCA LEANED ON PENDLETON'S DOORJAMB. "Nothing yet?" she asked.

Pendleton shook his head. "I'm going to call. Come in." He hit the speakerphone and the dial tone filled the room. He punched the buttons to the private number for the clerk of the Supreme Court.

A woman answered, "United States Supreme Court, clerk's office."

"Good evening. This is David Pendleton, representing the Speaker of the House and the Congress. Is the clerk of the court, Mr. Compton, available?"

"Hold, please," the woman said warmly.

After about a minute Compton came on the phone. "Good evening, Mr. Pendleton," he said in his distinctive voice.

"Good evening, Mr. Compton. I was about to go home. I wondered if you could give me a feel for whether I should continue to stand by here in my office or call it a night. It's not my intention to put any pressure on . . ."

"No pressure felt, Mr. Pendleton. I understand. I can tell you that the Chief Justice has the emergency stay in front of him, and he is considering it. I frankly don't know what his intentions are."

Pendleton thought. "Why are *you* still there?"

"Because as long as he is deliberating, I have to be here to make the calls if a decision is reached. The rules require us to notify counsel by reasonably expeditious means. That is the telephone for the parties. Later the public information office will notify the press and whoever else is interested.''

"Well, since we don't know anything, I guess I'll just hold fast.''

"If it were me?'' Compton asked.

"What would you do?''

"If it were me, Mr. Pendleton, I would go home. I've got your home number and I can call you there just as easily. It is extremely unlikely that you will have to do anything; it will simply be me telling you what the result is.''

Pendleton considered. "Okay. I think I'll take your advice. Is it possible, Mr. Compton, that the Chief Justice will stop deliberating and go home?''

"Very possible,'' Compton replied immediately.

"Would you be so kind, Mr. Compton, if in fact the Court is going to call it a night, to give me a call and let me know that so I can get some sleep?''

Compton laughed. "Yes, sir, Mr. Pendleton. When I go home, I'll give you a call.''

"I sincerely appreciate that. I look forward to your call.''

"You are quite welcome. I will extend the same courtesy to the attorney general's office.''

Pendleton smiled. "I would expect no less.''

"Good evening, Mr. Pendleton.''

"Thank you. Good night.'' Pendleton hung up.

He looked at Rebecca. "Well, Rebecca, the Chief Justice is backing himself into a very tight corner.''

Rebecca looked confused. "How?''

Pendleton's eyes sparkled. "He is the justice for the circuit for the District of Columbia.''

"Right . . .'' she said, uncomprehending.

"That means that he's considering this emergency stay by *himself*. He can refer it to the Court, of course, if he chooses to under Rule 38, but typically a justice will handle an emergency stay by himself."

"Right." Rebecca agreed.

Pendleton glanced down at the phone, then back at her. "As Manchester's appointee, does he dare decide for him alone?"

"I see what you mean."

"They claim to be nonpolitical, but they're not."

"So he'll refer it to the rest of the Court?"

"That's my bet." He drank from a glass of water.

"How could he do anything else?" she asked with less confidence.

"But what will the Court do?" Pendleton asked. "And when?"

The air wing commander, Zeke Bradford, stood in front of them in his flight suit. His black-leather name tag had gold Navy wings and one word: CAG. The air wing commander. The head guy. The one who decided how, when, and where the air wing went. He looked at his squadron commanders. "Well," he said, "I'm sure you've all heard by now, the operation is a go. Tomorrow morning, 0540 H hour and L hour."

The commanders nodded.

"I'm sure you all feel just as strange and awkward about this as I do. This is the most bizarre circumstance I have ever found myself in as a Navy officer. And I suppose we each have our thoughts about whether we ought to be doing this or not." He looked around but nobody responded. "Frankly, I am more than happy to go and beat the shit out of anybody who kills Americans by shooting them in the head. I think we ought to return the favor. I just wish they had some airplanes so we could have a fair fight. That doesn't look like it's going to happen. They do seem to have surface-to-air missiles, though, I hear. Anybody here got any more information on that?" he asked, looking at Caskey with a wry look. Caskey put his hand over his eyes, as if in shame. "You all right, MC?"

"Yeah, I'm fine, just embarrassed."

"I don't know how you could have known they had South African SAMs and knew how to use them *and* would give you a head fake in the shot."

"I'm still embarrassed," MC replied.

"Don't worry about it, it's only a forty-million-dollar airplane. I'm sure the taxpayers understand," CAG said. "What I was saying was, I'm sure you guys feel as awkward about this whole thing as I do. I'm just not sure what we can do about it. Seems to me that we do whatever the admiral tells us." The squadron commanding officers on board the USS *Constitution* murmured in agreement.

"Anybody got any problem with that?" CAG asked.

They shook their heads in unison, almost enthusiastically. "Okay. As you know, we still have part of the flight schedule to complete, then at 1600 we'll knock off flying so that we can do final maintenance and get the ordnance loaded on the airplanes. There will be some birds airborne for SSSC, EW, et cetera, but most will be standing down."

"You got any better idea what our targets are going to be?" asked Drunk Driver. "We've heard about hardened concrete bunkers and jungle over the island. Do we have any more information?"

"Negative," CAG replied. "We're supposed to get some updated intel from the SEALs tonight, but I wouldn't hold my breath. I don't think they're going to give us much good target info. I think basically we're going to be flying close air support and overhead protection. Our current plan is to lob some SLAMs into the bunkers we've identified, and be ready with some HARMs if any of their radars show up. We've tweaked our ESM to be triggered by those South African SAMs, but other than that, this looks like a bullet fight to me. We don't know enough to be after them with any big ordnance. This is going to be mostly fighting by the grunts, and they'll have to look out for the captain of the *Flyer*. More power to them. Anybody got any questions?''

MC raised his hand and lowered it as soon as CAG looked at him. "What's Indonesia gonna do about this? Isn't this an Indonesian island?''

"Yeah, it is, but it looks to me like they've abdicated it to these Islamic terrorists. Anytime you let a bunch of guys have a mother ship and bring their attack boats ashore, build some concrete bunkers and surface-to-air missiles unchallenged, I think you're waiving any claim that nobody else can go smack them.''

Drunk responded, "Yeah, but wait a second, I thought the President said that we were just going to tell Indonesia where these guys were, and then let them take care of it. Have we told Indonesia that these guys are on this island?''

CAG looked at him curiously. "You know, I don't know. Since they cut us off we've been telling Washington everything we know, but what we don't know is whether they're passing that information on.''

"So Washington may have told Indonesia that these bad guys are there, and that we are going in, but they're not telling us?''

CAG shrugged. "Last we heard, before they cut us off, Indonesia was talking to Washington every hour. They were with us. But we don't know the current status 'cause nobody's telling us. All *I* know is that the admiral is telling us we are going in hot tomorrow morning at first light, that we're flying cover and shooting anything that moves, and they have SAMs. That's about the extent of everything I know. Let's not get into political speculation and wondering the who, the what, and the when. You copy?''

"Sure, I copy. I just don't want us to run into somebody or have somebody come after us because they think we are going to do something they don't know about.''

"I hear you," CAG replied. "There's nothing we can do about that right now.''

Drunk looked dissatisfied. "I just don't know, CAG. It

seems to me if the admiral's driving us off a cliff, we'd be better off not going.''

The other squadron commanders watched him closely. He continued, ''I mean, we are sworn to obey orders, but only *lawful* orders. We're supposed to use our brains.''

CAG let his impatience show. ''So what do you suggest we do, Drunk? Convene a committee and sit around and make some kind of ultimate decision on whether the admiral's order's lawful, whether his interpretation is right? And then what—we decide not to do as he has instructed and order people below us not to go? Then maybe all your department heads and pilots wonder whether *your* orders are lawful? How far down does this go? What if each level of the chain of command questioned whether the guy directly over him is 'lawful'?''

''That's what Nuremberg was all about, CAG.''

Caskey intervened. ''So now we're war criminals? Ordering Jews into the gas chamber? Come on!''

''No, I don't mean it's like that.'' Drunk sat up a little straighter. ''Every one of us has an obligation to obey only lawful orders.''

''And what if it's not *clear-cut*?'' Caskey asked, perturbed. ''I hear what you're saying, Drunk. I just don't think we can get into it right now. This isn't one of those clear-cut 'shoot the prisoners' kind of orders. This is a question of authority, and whether our admiral has it. I would say that it's his problem, not ours.''

Driver looked relieved. ''Yeah,'' he said. ''I'm not saying I'm not going to do it, I'm just saying that we ought to think about the implications. Sounds to me like we have.'' He paused. ''I'm in, CAG.''

CAG's face brightened. ''All right. Fair enough. Anybody got anything else they want to get off their chest?''

When there was no response, he concluded, ''Okay. Get your birds in one hundred percent up status, get your men up and ready, line up the bullets, get your bombs and missiles ready, and get your crews some rest. We're going to be up early.''

Beth Louwsma pushed the steel door open after the magneto released the lock. A tall, lanky lieutenant in a flight suit stepped through the door right behind her. She glanced over to make sure he was still with her and proceeded directly to Admiral Billings.

SUPPLOT was a frenzy of activity with the final preparations for the dawn attack. Billings and his staff were poring over the operational orders and flight plan.

Beth approached the admiral. "Excuse me, sir."

Billings did not hear her. The lieutenant looked at her, then at the admiral, and then back at her, feeling awkward.

"Excuse me!" Beth said loudly.

Billings stopped his conversation and looked up at her. "What?"

"This lieutenant has some information that I think you'll need to know immediately."

Billings stood up straight. "Good evening, Lieutenant."

"Good evening, Admiral."

"What is it, Beth?" Billings asked, impatience in his tone.

"I happened to be in CVIC for the debrief of the last recovery, sir," she said, "when I heard the debrief of the E-2 crew. This lieutenant was giving the debrief. He said he was listening on the HF radio and overheard a conversation. I'll let him tell you."

Billings looked at the lieutenant. "Well?"

The lieutenant began, uncertain why he was being questioned. "There really wasn't much to it. I was spinning through the HF frequencies and listened in on a conversation between a man and I believe his wife. I'm pretty sure it was an E-2 guy, but he obviously wasn't from our squadron since we were the only E-2 up. It was clearly an HF patch into the U.S. phone system."

Billings looked at him and at Beth. "How do you know he was from an E-2?"

"Well, I could tell he was using a lip mike, and not talking into an oxygen mask."

"How do you know it wasn't a helicopter?" Billings asked.

"You can usually hear the rotor vibrations in a helicopter transmission, and I don't know for sure, but I don't think the H-60 has an HF."

"Good point," the admiral said.

"Well, he was talking to her and they weren't saying much of any substance; he was being careful not to tell her anything classified. And then when she asked where they were going, he said, 'Well, I can't tell you, but we're heading south like a bat out of hell.' "

"Could you tell where he was?" Billings asked, immediately interested.

"No, sir. I had our DF on the signal, but all I got was a strobe. It was northeast of us, but it could have been anywhere from a hundred miles to a thousand miles. I couldn't tell."

"What do you make of this, Lieutenant?" Billings asked.

"Well, I don't make much of it, sir. Commander Louwsma seemed to think it was pretty significant, but I'm afraid I frankly don't see it."

"You think it was an E-2?"

"Yes, sir, I'm pretty sure it was."

"Whose E-2?"

"Well, the only one that I could think of that would be northeast of us would be the *Truman* Battle Group somewhere around the Philippines. But that's just a guess."

"Anything else?"

"Well, sir, I'm not sure, but I really think it was a lieutenant that I know."

"You know him?" Billings raised his eyebrows.

"I think so. The E-2 community is not that large and I think it's a lieutenant that I went through training with. His name was Eric Stone. He's a real little guy with an iddy-biddy voice, and it's so distinctive that we recognized him all the time. In training we used to call him Chirp, and that's pretty much stuck with him. I'm almost positive it was Chirp.''

"And what do you take it to mean?'' Billings asked.

The lieutenant shrugged. "That's what I'm missing. I don't see the significance of that conversation.''

"Do you think that when he said he was heading south like a bat out of hell, he was referring to the E-2?''

The lieutenant laughed involuntarily, struck by the humor. "I've never heard anybody say that an E-2 with its big radome on top is flying *anywhere* like a 'bat out of hell.' Certainly not those of us who ride in them.''

"Exactly,'' Billings said, smiling as well.

"So you think he was referring to the *Truman* Battle Group?''

The lieutenant shrugged again. "I guess he is.''

Billings looked at Beth. "They're on their way.''

David Pendleton sat in the deep leather chair in his family room with his suit pants and white shirt on, his tie loosened. The fire burned low as he waited for word from the Supreme Court. He drank deeply from his glass of water and waited.

The telephone rang and Pendleton glanced at the clock: 2:10 A.M. He lifted the receiver. "Yes.''

"Good very early morning, Mr. Pendleton,'' said David Compton. "I told you that I would tell you when I was leaving the office and when their deliberations, if you will, were over for the night. Well, I am going home.''

"And what is the status of the emergency stay?'' Pendleton asked cautiously.

"Mr. Chief Justice Ross considered it and decided to have it considered by the entire Court. It is going to happen tomorrow, actually later today. Saturday.''

"Nothing more tonight?''

"No, sir. They will be back to it first thing in the morning. Seven A.M."

"Very well. Thank you for calling. Do you have any idea when they might have an actual decision?"

"No, Mr. Pendleton. They don't tell me those kinds of things."

"So he referred it to the entire Court, did he?"

"Yes, sir, he did."

Pendleton paused. "Good night."

"Good night, Mr. Pendleton."

Pendleton set the phone down and smiled. He quickly downed the rest of his water, waited five minutes, and dialed.

The Speaker of the House picked up his private line.

"Mr. Speaker, this is David Pendleton."

"Have you heard anything?"

"Yes, sir. The Chief Justice has referred the application for emergency stay to the full Court."

"What does that mean?"

"The Chief Justice, Justice Ross, is responsible for any emergency stays out of the D.C. Circuit. This application came from D.C. so the Chief Justice could hear it himself. But according to Rule—"

"Spare me the rules; what does it *mean*?"

"If the justice hearing the emergency application wishes to, he can refer it to the entire Court. That's what Justice Ross did. And the clerk of the court said they'd get together on it early this morning, this being Saturday."

"Hmmm." The Speaker seemed to be considering.

Pendleton pressed. "How much time do we need, Mr. Speaker?"

"I don't know. I think their intention is to go in—according to our time—tonight about six P.M."

Pendleton looked at his clock. "Just over fifteen hours from now?"

"Right."

"This could be close," Pendleton said. "I'll call you as soon as I hear anything, Mr. Speaker."

"Okay. I, for one, am going to go home and lock myself in the house, turn off all the radios and televisions, and sleep as long as I can."

"Okay, but make sure you have a phone where I can get to you."

"Oh, yeah. You have my private home number, don't you?"

"Yes, I do."

"Well, David, it's been quite a day. Don't know that I have ever seen one like it. Don't know that we'll ever see one like it again. Thanks for your help. I'm sure we'll be talking later on. Good night."

"Good night, Mr. Speaker." Pendleton hit the button on his portable phone and set it down. He couldn't relax yet. The Supreme Court could still upset the cart and impose a stay on someone and wreck Congress's plans. But in the meantime Pendleton was going to enjoy himself as much as he could. And if he succeeded, he would earn his place in history.

31

JIM DILLON WAS STILL OVERWHELMED BY THE EXPE-
rience of being on an aircraft carrier. Every new thing he
saw or learned amazed him more. Lieutenant Reynolds
showed him around the ship, explaining how everything
worked—no doubt out of a sense of duty—but Dillon was
unable to retain any of it. Reynolds used acronyms and
terms that were completely alien to him. He would nod
knowingly and hope that his responses were appropriate,
like an immigrant in a foreign land.

At every opportunity he would try for a glimpse of one
of the many televisions on the carrier broadcasting CNN
live. He pretended he was paying attention to Reynolds
while his ears strained to hear the news of any developments.

He had been with the lieutenant at air wing meetings,
squadron briefs, ordnance loading of aircraft, and tele-
vised briefs by the intelligence officers, who continued to
claim that they knew very little about the situation as a
result of the information cut off.

As he stood in CATCC, the Carrier Air Traffic Control
Center, he listened as a twenty-five-year-old enlisted man,
prompted by the ever-helpful Lieutenant Reynolds, explained how he would communicate with airplanes landing aboard the carrier at night, and "talk them down."
Dillon was sure this made sense to someone, but his mind
was pulled away by the images on the television visible

over the sailor's shoulder. It was bolted to the wall and was, of course, tuned to CNN. The President was holding a press conference. Dillon strained to hear him, but the sound was not turned up. He saw the President step up to the podium.

Dillon suddenly longed to be back in Washington in the midst of the turbulence. Washington was never more fun than when political hand grenades were going off. Dillon put up his hand, stopping the monologue of the sailor. "Excuse me. I'm sorry to interrupt, but do you think we might hear what President Manchester has to say?"

The lieutenant and the sailor both looked up at the television. "Yes, sir. No problem." The sailor turned around and yelled to a shipmate across the room who was polishing a brass electrical cover, "Green! Turn up the tube!"

Dillon walked slowly toward the television as Manchester began what appeared to be a prepared statement. The President looked exhausted. He was wearing a dark blue suit and a red and blue striped tie. "I have just been informed by the Attorney General that the United States Supreme Court has agreed to hold a hearing on whether the stay requested in our lawsuit should be granted. As you know, as an individual citizen and also as President and Chief of the Executive Branch of this government, I filed an action against Congress attempting to get a quick declaration of the inevitable, that the Letter of Reprisal issued by Congress is in violation of the United States Constitution. I am quite confident that the Supreme Court will agree and am very pleased that they have agreed to hear this matter."

Manchester stopped and gave the reporters the opening they had been waiting for. Every single one leaped to his feet and began yelling for attention.

Dillon shuddered. If the Supreme Court ruled the Letter unconstitutional, the entire plan would fail and the Speaker of the House would look like a fool.

Manchester held up his hand. "I had hoped that the hearing would be today, even though it's a Saturday, but I have just been informed that the Court has met and the earliest time the Court can consider the matter, based on its calendar and workload, is Tuesday morning. I expect they would have heard it Monday, but as you know, Monday is a federal holiday—Presidents' Day. The hearing is therefore set for seven-thirty A.M. on Tuesday at the Supreme Court."

"Tuesday?" Dillon's eyes opened wide. In Washington time that was two or three days from now. It was at least two and a half in Indonesia. Nothing was going to stop the attack now. Dillon's brain spun as he considered the implications.

Manchester continued, "As you know, I disagree with the entire approach of the Letter of Reprisal. We should leave it to Indonesia and allow them to deal with their own criminals. We and Indonesia know where they are, and who they are. Indonesia is prepared to take appropriate action. I fully expect the forbearance of the Navy in waiting until there is a ruling by the Supreme Court on this issue. To act before such a decision would be imprudent, but I have full faith that our armed forces will follow their Commander in Chief."

Manchester relaxed and took a breath. "That's all I have to say at this point. I, for one, am hopeful that our country can ride out this storm caused by the Speaker of the House and allowed by Congress. Thank you."

The President turned and walked off the stage. Without warning, a shrill voice from the front row yelled out, "Are you a pacifist?"

The room fell silent as the question thudded into the podium, its echoes resounding for all to hear.

The President turned around. He sighed heavily. "I will not respond to accusations by the Speaker of the House simply because he makes them. I am not a trained dog, and I will not sit up and beg for a bone."

"Don't the American people deserve to know—"

The President spun quickly and walked off.

Dillon stared at the television in disbelief.

Reynolds walked up and smiled. "Well, looks like the Supreme Court isn't going to stop us."

"Nothing is," Dillon replied with enthusiasm in his eyes.

The aide looked at his watch in the dim light of the windowless room. "Did you notice what the President said, though?"

"What?" Dillon said, assuming he must mean something other than the obvious.

"He just announced to the world, including the terrorists, that it's known who they are and where they are."

Dillon immediately understood the implications.

Reynolds continued, "Nice of him to tell them we know where they are. Now they'll be waiting for us, or heading to another island like they did last time. But you'd think he'd at least tell us the rest—who it is we're going after." Reynolds had a look on his face that Dillon hadn't seen before: cold, hard. "Petty Officer Meehan, you want to go on?" he said, looking again at the controller who had followed everything that had been said.

"Yes, sir." He pointed to a radar screen. "You can see right here, the last launch of the regular flight schedule before we arm up for the attack."

❧

Caskey and Messer turned right off the bow catapult and headed north past the Riau Archipelago, a long string of islands of which Bunaya was one. It was the hottest time of day and the sun was a large white ball beating on them through the thick Plexiglas canopy. It was the first time they had flown since being shot down and rescued. Caskey, like most squadron commanders, was a believer in the falling-off-the-horse wisdom—get right back on. If a pilot had an accident or was scared by something, he had to get him right back in the cockpit before he lost his edge. Once that edge was lost, it wouldn't be recovered.

They passed through five thousand feet and leveled off, slowing to three hundred knots.

"Another exciting SSSC mission, Skipper."

"Hey, you should be thanking me for getting us on the schedule."

"No, you're right, Skipper," Messer said tongue-in-cheek as he started a radar search of the horizon for aircraft and shipping. "I was being ungrateful."

"See anything?"

"Just the usual ten million ships. Plus fifty airplanes, most at flight level 350 and probably airliners."

"Roger. Let's take a look at a few ships since we're out here. You can sure see 'em lined up to go through the strait."

They descended to two thousand feet and headed toward the first large ship on the radar.

"You think this attack is really going to happen tomorrow morning?" Messer asked.

"Sure do."

"How can we go in if the President has said not to?" Messer studied the radar picture.

"Yeah, we had quite a discussion about that among the squadron COs."

"Come port ten," Messer said, redirecting them toward the target.

Caskey slowed to 250 knots and lined up with the ship they were approaching. "How did we get to do all this SSSC anyway?" he muttered. "What happened to intercepts?"

"Of what? Airliners?"

"Sure. Anything in the air. I'm sick of looking at ships. Coming up on the port side."

"Roger," said Messer as he looked at the approaching ship over the nose of the Tomcat.

"You gonna take a picture?"

"Sure. I haven't won photo of the week for months."

"Okay. Here it comes." Caskey gently banked the

plane and flew down the port side of the ship. As they passed, Messer took three quick photos.

"Got it," Messer said, as Caskey pulled up hard into a three-G climb away from the ocean. "Hold it." Messer looked back at the ship between the Tomcat tails. "Holy hell, hold it!"

"Hold what?" Caskey eased back on the stick and leveled off at seven thousand feet.

"That ship looks awfully familiar. Let's take another pass."

"What for?" Caskey said.

"Remember the mother ship they photographed from the submarine, the one they followed to Bunaya?"

"Yeah?"

"Looks just like that. Same superstructure, same crane amidships . . ." Messer groped through his helmet bag for the photo he had been carrying around. "Here," he said into his mask. "I've got that photo. Let's go take another look. Yeah, the *Sumatran Star*. This might be it."

Caskey pulled into a hard left turn to bring the nose of the Tomcat back around onto the ship, suddenly interested. "Where is Bunaya from here?"

"About seventy miles west southwest."

"Wouldn't the *Los Angeles* have told us if the *Sumatran Star* had sailed?"

"Probably, if they knew about it."

"Well, let's check it out," Caskey said as he descended rapidly to five hundred feet, five miles aft of the ship. They approached quickly and were within a mile. Caskey looked at the rounded fantail for the ship's name and registry. He couldn't make out anything at all. He slowed.

"Let's not get too close," Messer said, remembering the missile from a doorway on the *Pacific Flyer* and the "SAM from nowhere" on Bunaya.

"I hear that." Caskey turned gently to his right to move outboard of the ship. "Name's been painted over. I can see where it was. No flag or registry either. Very suspicious." The ship was now at their side half a mile away.

Messer took ten more photos, then compared the ID photo he had with the ship to their left. "Either it's the *Sumatran Star,* or it's a sister ship. Either way, we'd better report this pronto."

"Concur," Caskey said, pulling up quickly and away from the ship. "Call the E-2. Give them a posit on this ship. Could be full of weapons, more troops, or nothing important at all. Either way, they're going to want to know about it. He's heading directly toward the island."

32

DILLON STEPPED THROUGH THE LAST KNEE KNOCKER—
what seemed like the hundredth—and opened the flimsy
metal door to the wardroom. He paused and looked for
anyone familiar. Even though he had been on the ship
awhile and was being treated as a congressman might be,
he recognized a finely defined pecking order, mostly by
the obvious—rank—but there were other forces at work
that he was just beginning to pick up on: air wing versus
ship's company, fighter versus attack, Navy versus Marine
Corps. At first he thought it was actual animosity, but then
realized it was family squabbling and rivalry. He also realized he wasn't part of the family.

Dillon wasn't even sure why he was still awake. It was
probably because he was excited. An attack was about to
take place that *he* had put in motion. As an individual.
Not as a government, not as a committee. Just one person
sitting in an office and discovering a power everyone had
forgotten. He hadn't foreseen it becoming so momentous,
but he was glad it had. He hadn't foreseen it driving a
wedge between Congress and the President, and he regretted that—but that was President Manchester's choice,
not his. If Manchester had seen this for the opportunity it
was, he would have signed the Letter and gone after these
terrorists.

"You're up late," Beth said to Dillon as he looked
around, deep in thought.

"Yeah, I'm kind of wound up. I feel like a fish out of water."

"What are you looking for?"

He thought for a moment. "I don't know, I guess for the operation to be in the open and approved by the President . . ."

"No. I meant do you want ice cream or a hamburger— a slider as we call it?"

He was embarrassed. "Ice cream, I guess."

"You know where the auto dog is, don't you?"

"The ice cream thing? Yeah."

He got a glass of ice cream and sat down at the long metal table. There were several maintenance officers and aviators in the wardroom. More than he had expected this late—it was well after midnight. He could smell the cheeseburgers cooking on the grill around the corner. Someone had anticipated an unusually high turnout on a nonflying night. Some of the officers were joking quietly, but most of them seemed subdued.

"Lots of people here for one A.M."

Beth looked around. "More than usual."

"What are you doing up?" he asked.

"Trying to get the best intelligence picture I can so I can pass it on to the morning launch."

"What more can you find out since we've been cut off?"

"We have an alternative plan we're about to put in place."

"What's that?"

"We'll be launching the Predator soon."

"What's that? That thing from the Schwarzenegger movie? *That* ought to take care of those terrorists." He was enjoying her presence more than he thought he should. She was three or four years older than he was, but he didn't care. He thought of Molly and felt a pang of guilt, which surprised him. "So what's a Predator?"

"A drone. A very capable drone. Only problem is, they've never launched one off a ship before. I thought it would be a good idea, and said we ought to try it. So . . . the admiral told me to make it happen. I've been trying to convince the Army men who control it. They remain unconvinced. They feel like prisoners of war on a lunatic carrier. So, we'll see. It will be taking off shortly. If it works, we'll have a lot to do very quickly. If it goes into the ocean, I'll probably get an opportunity to go to the admiral's at-sea cabin with my dancing rug and explain what happened.''

"Rug?'' he asked.

"Figure of speech,'' she said, as she studied his face. "It means you're in big trouble, and you'd better start entertaining your superior *fast,* because he is currently *not* amused.''

"That's good.'' Dillon paused. "Can I ask you something?''

"Sure.''

"How old are you?''

"Why do you want to know?''

"My friend and I have a theory that the entire country is run by twenty-nine- or thirty-year-olds who come up with all the ideas, all the strategy, and just hand it over to the old guys.''

She laughed. "Well, I hate to disappoint you, but I'm not twenty-nine or thirty. I'm thirty-five.''

Dillon raised his eyebrows. "I'm surprised. I figured you for thirty or thirty-one.''

"It's the skin. I don't wrinkle, at least not yet.''

Dillon shifted his eyes away from Beth, afraid that she might read too much in them. He forced his thoughts back to business. "You seem calm. I figured everybody would be pretty anxious.''

"I'm not calm at all. I'm just good at looking calm.''

"Nice skill to have.''

"Are you ready?''

"For tomorrow? Nothing much I can do now.''

"I don't know,'' she said. "You have a pretty rare opportunity for a politician. You get to see the action firsthand. And if the Predator doesn't crash, you may get to see it in real time."

"Real time?" he asked, confused.

"As it's happening. The Predator will send us live video."

Dillon thought about that, then heard what she had said before. "I'm not really a politician . . ."

"Of course you are," she laughed. "What do *you* think you are?"

"I'm just a staffer."

"You mean you're not an *elected* politician."

"I guess that's what I mean," he said defensively.

"So you get to do what every politician does when a big decision is made, sit back and watch the results on television."

Dillon wasn't sure whether she was being hostile or playful. "Why are you teeing off on politicians?"

"I wouldn't call it that. It's true, isn't it? They send people to war; they don't go. They send us away on cruises for six months at a time; they never go on a cruise for six months. They might come for a day, but not six months."

Dillon's face reddened. "I don't know that it's like that at all. It's just different responsibilities. And they go overseas sometimes."

Beth chuckled and shook her head. "Right." She glanced at her watch. "Well, I need to get going; don't worry about your little Letter of Reprisal. Now it's up to us." She looked at Dillon, who was lost in thought. "Predator launch is in fifteen minutes," she announced. "Want to come out on the flight deck and watch?"

"Isn't it dark?" He envisioned himself falling off the flight deck into the black ocean, never to be seen again.

"You have no idea how dark it is. You'll have to put on a white safety flotation jacket, helmet, and goggles, but I'll watch out for you. Want to come?"

"Sure," he said excitedly.

The two dark RHIBs dashed across the ocean well south of Bunaya. Armstrong anxiously watched the coxswain study the GPS receiver for the rendezvous point. They had made good time. Armstrong scanned the horizon quickly and saw nothing but water reflecting the faint light of the moon amid wispy black clouds.

The coxswain reduced the throttles of the boat and went into a gentle starboard turn. "This is it, Lieutenant. We're fifteen minutes early."

Armstrong nudged up next to the coxswain. "You got a good read on the GPS?"

"Yes, sir."

Armstrong compared the coxswain's GPS to his own portable set and saw that their fixes were identical. "Looks good to me. Let's go DIW," he said, instructing the coxswain to go dead in the water.

"Yes, sir."

The other RHIB had fallen in fifty feet behind them and expertly came alongside the lead RHIB and joined up over the gentle swells of the glassy sea.

What a beautiful night, Armstrong thought, as he took in a deep breath. Almost immediately, he saw a periscope break the water immediately in front of him. "Periscope," he said pointing.

"Yes, sir, I saw it," the coxswain said. "We're okay here."

The periscope moved slowly toward them. Armstrong could make out a lens or glass top on the periscope, which seemed to be examining them from no more than one hundred feet away.

Suddenly, the periscope disappeared below the surface and seconds later the sail of a submarine emerged.

The USS *Los Angeles* rose out of the ocean depths directly in front of them.

Armstrong looked at QMC Lee standing next to him.

"That would be a rather troubling sight if we hadn't been expecting it."

Lee added, "Or if it was somebody else's submarine."

They watched the *Los Angeles* rise to its full surfaced height. The two coxswains gunned the engines of the RHIBs and headed toward the sail. As they did, four sailors in flotation vests climbed out of the sail, down the ladder, and stood on the forward portion of the *Los Angeles*. They caught the lines that were thrown to them and pulled the two RHIBs to the submarine.

The captain of the *Los Angeles* looked grimly on from the top of the sail, unhappy at having to bring his nuclear submarine to the surface for *any* reason. He looked down to the bow of the *Los Angeles* and his senior chief petty officer. "Hurry it up, Senior Chief," he muttered.

"Yes, sir," the senior chief responded without looking up. "Come on, men. Hustle up," he said to the SEALs as they clambered on board the *Los Angeles* and up the sail. As soon as all the SEALs were below, the senior chief threw the lines of the RHIBs back onto the boats and went below himself.

"Take her down," the captain said as he descended into the interior of the sail.

The *Los Angeles* immediately began submerging and heading toward Bunaya.

After only a few hours, the *Los Angeles* hovered silently off the island. It stopped and settled slowly into the sand, resting on the bottom to check for currents and stability. Bubbles began to rise from the bow as an indiscernible hatch opened in the dark Pacific waters. Four SEALs emerged from the *Los Angeles* and inflated a buoy which lurched upward, pulling a line behind it toward the surface of the ocean seventy feet above. Two of the divers followed the line up to the surface, propelled by bags that gradually filled with air.

Four more divers followed the first two, taking several satchels of gear up with them. Automatic weapons, a sniper rifle, explosives, several MUGRs—Miniature Underwater GPS Receivers—and several CLAMs—Clandestine Littoral Acoustic Mappers. Armstrong and Lee stayed by the *Los Angeles* as they watched the rest of the platoon lock out, swim to the surface, and wait for them in a swimmer pool at the buoy. When everyone was out and all the gear had been taken up, Lee and Armstrong gave each other a thumbs-up and followed the line up to the buoy, exhaling all the way. After the gear was distributed, the platoon divided into swim pairs, attached their buddy lines, and initialized their CLAMs with a GPS fix. They turned toward the shore of Bunaya and began swimming.

They swam slowly but steadily twenty feet down, breathing through their Dräeger LAR Vs. There were no bubbles and no lights, just millions of bioluminescent particles trailing behind each swimmer.

Knowing their position was critical to map the approach. Chief Lee was responsible for operating the CLAM that had only recently been acquired by the SEAL platoon. By sending out doppler acoustic signals and reading the returns, they could precisely navigate and record a hydrographic survey chart of the ocean bottom. This was the road map that would tell the Marines where to land. Without it, the landing would be a crapshoot, the craft subject to running ashore or getting stranded on coral reefs as they had in Tarawa. The SEALs weren't going to let that happen.

The SEALs continued silently toward the shore, then, on Lee's signal, dispersed to their prebriefed lanes to clear the two-hundred-yard-wide approach corridor for the amphibious landing. They swam the assigned grid pattern in to the shore, looking for any obstacle, natural or manmade, that would threaten the shallow-draft boats that were to bring the Marines ashore in a few short hours.

After an hour of difficult underwater labor in the dark, the SEALs rendezvoused at the center point of the corridor. Armstrong took out his mouthpiece. "Anything?"

Lee nodded. "Coral head, sir, about fifty feet in from the left perimeter a hundred yards out."

"Can you blow it? Is it a factor?" Armstrong asked, breathing a little harder than he would have liked.

"Yes, sir. We'll put a little extra charge on it," Lee said mischievously.

"Two swim pairs enough?"

"Yes, sir."

"Take swim team six with you; place the charges on the coral head and set the timers."

"Yes, sir," Lee said. He nodded at his buddy and swim team six, who followed him with their haversacks toward the coral.

The rest of the SEALs treaded water in a swimmer pool, scanning in every direction for any signs of life.

Ten minutes later, "All set, sir."

The SEALs moved toward center beach and fanned out in the shallows.

Armstrong crawled up farther until his entire head was out of the water. He pulled his mask off and held his monocular night-vision goggle to his left eye. He turned it on and scanned the shore three times. He signaled all clear and the platoon removed their fins and crawled slowly onto the beach in a line, watching for any signs of defense or opposition.

They entered the jungle and removed their underwater gear.

Armstrong looked at his men and each gave him a nod. He moved closer to Lee, who hooked up the CLAM to a laptop computer he produced from a waterproof bag.

"Did you get a good download from the CLAM?" Armstrong asked.

"Yes, sir."

"Go ahead and data-burst it back to the *Wasp*."

"Wilco," Lee said, pulling out his radio to transmit the data for the amphibious group. "I *hate* doing this insecure. Sure hope to shit they don't have a DF. Here goes."

"Snake," Armstrong said, "you and Rodriguez set up

your sniper post five hundred yards from the concrete bunkers. You got a good fix on our waypoint?''

"We're all set, Lieutenant."

"If compromised, hotfoot it to waypoint Echo and call for hot extraction."

"Wilco." Snake had no intention of getting caught.

"Lee and I are heading for those rails that the radar identified. We'll blow them at L hour. As soon as we blow 'em, we'll head toward you and rendezvous at your sniper position at 0600."

Armstrong looked at Lee. "You done?"

Lee was folding up the antenna line. "All set, Lieutenant. The landing is still a go."

"Let's do it." Armstrong adjusted his night-vision goggle and headed into the jungle.

⬛

The catapult officer stood back from the group that worked busily around the shuttle. The frenzy of activity was slowing, as a consensus emerged that they were ready to go. The long, dark Predator was attached by a Rube Goldberg system to the catapult. The catapult officer had been opposed to the idea from the first.

Maintenance men worked all around the quiet flight deck to get the airplanes ready for the morning strike. The intense anticipation of the coming day was heightened by the mysterious presence on the catapult.

The Army men, the ones responsible for delivering the Predator to Thailand for the upcoming Cobra Gold exercise, were apoplectic. They didn't want anything to do with flying the Predator off the carrier, especially attached to the catapult. It had never been done. They knew the ship would break their toy, and they would be responsible. The captain had to intervene. He had done so because of Beth Louwsma.

She had refused to take no for an answer. She had been adamant because the battle group had no eyes, no way of monitoring activity on the island, no way of detecting movement or threat, other than the men on the ground and ·their usual sensors. No satellite, no intelligence, no communication with the outside world. The President had seen to that.

Beth stood back behind the jet-blast deflectors in a white safety-officer flotation vest and watched the activity. She didn't venture onto the flight deck very often, and felt uncomfortable there. Especially at night. Those who worked there all the time knew where most of the dangers were. Those who didn't, didn't. She continually glanced around for something that was going to blow her over the side or crush her. Dillon stood by her side, twice as uncomfortable as she was.

One of the sailors pulled away fast from the Predator. He shook his hand for a second, trying to ignore the burn he had just received from the hot engine, and crawled toward the center of the deck, giving a thumbs-up.

The catapult officer surveyed the bow to make sure it was clear, then looked at the Predator.

Its propeller spun at full power as it strained at the line holding it to the deck, a line calculated to break at just the right time for the Predator to be pulled off the deck. The engine looked good; the straight wings were ready; the black drone awaited its first combat mission. With its oversized head it resembled an alien space ship. Its operating lights went on, just like an airplane's.

The catapult officer reached down and touched the deck. The petty officer on the side catwalk determined that the way was clear and pushed the launch button.

The Predator was pulled forward, the line broke perfectly, and the drone began its run toward the bow. Beth held her breath as the small drone was thrown off the bow and sank toward the ocean. It suddenly pitched up and headed for the sky, but too steeply. It had begun to stall when suddenly its nose pitched forward and it settled into level flight through the darkness toward Bunaya.

Dillon rubbed his eyes. He had gotten half an hour of sleep—about average for the officers he was with. He sat in CVIC and watched the early morning brief, live. The rest of the air wing watched via closed circuit television. Dillon stood next to the cameramen and tried to stay out of the way.

The lights came on, brightening the room dramatically. The cameraman waited for the exact time, then pointed at the air wing intelligence officer. Pinkie stood behind the podium with a chart behind him. He became instantly animated, even though it was two o'clock in the morning. "Good morning, Pulau Bunaya!" Pinkie said in his best Robin Williams imitation. "Of course, I am not actually talking to them, I am talking to you, but that's where you're headed. For those of you who don't know exactly where it is, join the rest of the world. Nobody has ever heard of this island and the reason is, it is uninhabited and unimportant. And another reason is, it is one of a zillion islands that make up Indonesia."

Dillon whispered to Reynolds next to him, "Is he always this flippant?"

"Yep. He's famous for it. He gives the best briefs in the air wing, the best information, and they all remember it because he delivers it in his own way."

"He makes it sound like he's kidding."

"Look at his eyes," the aide said. "He's not kidding."

"This is the brief for Event One. The event in which we are going to go and beat the shit out of a bunch of people who shot Americans in the head and sank their ship, and killed a frogman from this battle group. As you know, we are now considered a renegade battle group. I don't know about the rest of you, but I kind of like the way that sounds. In fact, in case some of you haven't noticed, the battle group has been flying the new group flag." He removed a large piece of white butcher paper from the board next to the chart and exposed a hand-drawn red and white "Don't Tread on Me" flag. "Thanks to IS1 Alvarez for her rendition of this old Navy Battle

Flag used in the Revolutionary War. For those of you who graduated from high school in the last ten years and therefore by definition don't know *shit*, the Revolutionary War was when we fought England for our Independence and kicked their *asses*. This flag said how we felt then, and I think''—he posted it behind him—''it still does.

''I've been thinking that as a newly established renegade battle group, there is a whole list of places we should go after Pulau Bunaya. But they'll have to wait.

''Event One will go as follows: We will have two F-14Bs from VF-143 flying CAP over the amphibious group which is right now''—he paused and pointed at the chart—''about thirty miles offshore. We don't expect any air threat, but your CAP station is ten thousand feet over the amphib group. We will be operating in situation Alpha. So Bravo Whiskey will be aboard the *Ticonderoga*.''

''What's Bravo Whiskey?'' Dillon asked.

Reynolds whispered, ''The officer in control of the air defense. Usually a commander, and usually on a cruiser.''

''We will have two F-14Bs from VF-11 that will be CAP in support of the amphibious landing. As you know, the takeoff for the first launch is 0500. You'll be airborne before L hour. Two F/A-18Cs from VFA-131 will do close air support. They'll have five hundred-pounders. Two other F/A-18Cs from VFA-136 will be HARM shooters, and the last two F/A-18s from VFA-131 are going to be lobbing their SLAMs into the concrete bunkers that we have confirmed. The ES-3A from VQ-6 Det Charlie will be orbiting east of the island and the EA-6B from VAQ-140 . . .''

Dillon's attention drifted as he realized he wasn't understanding most of the brief and was tired of asking the aide to translate for him. He looked at the camera pointed at the flight deck. The deck was bathed in the usual nighttime red light and showed mechanics and ordnance men doing last-minute checks and preparation. The reflective tape on their vests was obvious in the haunting light. He could see them darting in and out of the airplanes, underneath the airplanes, around the tires, looking at the missiles and bombs.

Dillon leaned to the lieutenant. "Shouldn't we try to reach Washington one last time before going through with this? I could try my phone again."

The aide shook his head. "They'll find out soon enough." Trying to read his suddenly serious face, Dillon's stomach churned. "Drano," he said to Reynolds.

Reynolds looked at him, surprised at hearing his call sign from Dillon. "Yes?"

"I've got to see the admiral."

Reynolds looked concerned. "This would not be a good time, Mr. Dillon."

"It doesn't matter. I've *got* to see him."

"Do you mind if I ask what it's about?"

"I want to go ashore."

Reynolds tried to keep from smiling. "I think you heard the admiral say that the COD is down. We can't get you out of here until probably late tomorrow or the next day. If you don't want to watch this . . ."

"No, I mean I want to go ashore with the attack."

"What do you mean?"

"I want to go ashore with the Marines."

🏴

Dillon and Lieutenant Reynolds stood behind Admiral Billings in SUPPLOT. Billings was clearly busy with the preparation for the attack. Dillon felt like turning and running.

"Admiral," Reynolds said, trying to interrupt.

"Not now." Billings raised his hand as he spoke with someone on the telephone.

Reynolds turned toward Dillon and held up a finger. They stood there awkwardly. Billings finally put down the receiver and he turned his head toward Reynolds. "What?"

"Admiral, excuse us, but Mr. Dillon has something he'd like to ask you."

Dillon could tell that Billings was not amused. "What is it, Mr. Dillon?"

"I'm sorry for interrupting," Dillon started. "I would like your permission, Admiral, to go ashore with the Marines when the attack commences."

Everyone in SUPPLOT had been listening with one ear and most now looked at him. Billings turned completely around in his chair, stood up, and sat on the desk. He cocked his head as if examining a lunatic. "Excuse me?"

"You let journalists go ashore with combat troops, don't you?"

"Sometimes."

"Photographers are allowed to go ashore, aren't they?"

"Sometimes."

"I don't want to be just another politician who watches something happen on television, Admiral. I want to see it firsthand."

Billings glared at Dillon. "Do you have any idea what you're asking?"

"I know I could be putting myself in danger, but I'm willing to accept . . ."

"This isn't some kind of a game. This isn't a demonstration we're putting on for the benefit of politicians."

Dillon closed his eyes momentarily to avoid the penetrating gaze. "I know that, Admiral. I'm not implying that it is. All I'm asking is for special permission. I'm asking you for a favor."

"A favor? For the special assistant to the Speaker of the House to go ashore and get his ass shot off? These are real bullets, Mr. Dillon. They will kill people. People are going to die this morning, I promise you. I don't want one of them to be you."

"I don't either, Admiral, but if I go ashore with the Marines, and stay toward the back, I shouldn't be in too much danger."

"There is no 'back' in an amphibious assault, Mr. Dillon." Billings looked at Reynolds and jerked his head slightly. "You put him up to this?"

"No, sir. He asked me about it and I said that you would have to make that kind of decision."

Billings stood with his hands on his hips considering the implications of letting Dillon go and the implications of not letting him go.

"Ops!" the admiral yelled.

"Yes, sir?"

"Any helos going over to the *Wasp*?"

The operations officer considered the idea of Dillon's being helicoptered over to the *Wasp* so he could go ashore. "No, sir. We'd have to put on a special flight."

"Could that be done?"

"Well, my guess is that the flight deck of the *Wasp* is about as busy as a one-legged man in an ass-kicking contest, but I suppose if it were directed to happen, it would happen."

Billings looked at Dillon. "You sure you want to do this, Mr. Dillon?"

"Yes, sir, I'm sure."

"You realize you might be killed?"

"Yes, sir."

Billings turned to the operations officer. "Make it happen. Call Colonel Tucker and tell him Mr. Dillon is en route, and that he is to take Mr. Dillon ashore with him as an observer."

⌖

Admiral Jack Blazer stared at the three large screens. The screens on the USS *Harry S Truman* were exactly like ones that Admiral Billings was looking at, only these screens had complete information. Admiral Blazer was short and stocky, a burly man with no noticeable waist, but no obvious fat either. His personality and voice were both larger than life, but right now he was subdued. At first he had been afraid that he wouldn't get to the *Constitution* Battle Group in time. Now he was afraid he would.

"How long till sunrise?" Blazer spoke to the room at large.

One of the enlisted men checked the flight schedule. "Three and a half hours."

Blazer glanced quickly at the circular clock on the bulkhead. He paused. "Ops?" he said suddenly.

Commander Hugh Morrison lifted his head from a chart. "Yes, Admiral?"

Blazer pointed at the three screens with his chin. "Look at the formations."

Morrison stared at the electronic symbols on the projected screens. The blue half circles indicated friendly surface ships. "Look at them," Blazer commented. "The amphibious group has broken off. They're in position. They're going in at dawn." He looked at Morrison to see if he agreed.

He stared at the screens and back at his boss.

"I concur, Admiral, this is it."

"Are we at flank speed?"

"Yes, sir, we have been."

"We're still out of range for the F/A-18s to get there before dawn."

"Well, they could get there, but they wouldn't be able to get back. They'd have to refuel. We can send an S-3 with—"

"Well, that's not going to work." Blazer stared at the symbol representing the USS *Harry S Truman* Battle Group that had been charging south from the Philippines at flank speed since receiving the President's order. He had been ordered to "intercept" the USS *Constitution* Battle Group. He had asked for clarification. None had been forthcoming. Intercepting them might be possible, but then what?

"Do we still have two F-14s in alert five, and two in alert fifteen?"

"Yes, sir."

"They all have tanks?"

"Yes, sir."

"If we launch the F-14s now, and they head toward the *Constitution* Battle Group at military power, can we get a tanker to meet them on the way back so they don't go in the drink?"

Morrison stared at the symbols, then measured distances by latitude lines on the chart. "It would be close, but I think so. Worst case, if they ran out of gas, they could land aboard the *Constitution*, I suppose."

Blazer shook his head. "No, they couldn't." Blazer's mind turned to his Naval Academy classmate Admiral Ray Billings, one of his best friends during their long careers in the Navy. They had been in the same fighter squadrons, had been on the same carriers, and had dated the same women. He respected Ray Billings as much as any man he'd ever met. But he had his orders—whatever they meant.

Blazer looked at the overhead quickly, then at Morrison. "Launch the alert five F-14s, and prepare to launch the alert fifteen F-14s. Vector them to the *Constitution*."

"Aye, aye, sir."

Blazer turned to him. "And if they get there? Tell them only to intercept. They are *not* to interfere. Without specific orders to the contrary, we wouldn't want to interfere in ongoing combat operations, would we?"

33

DILLON WAS WHISKED OUT OF THE ISLAND ON THE USS *Constitution* to a waiting SH-60F helicopter from HS-5. He had been robed in a white flotation vest, uninflated of course, and the same odd helmet with headphones that he had worn on the COD. It was still pitch-dark on the flight deck; the only lighting was from the red floodlights overhead. Two people took his elbows and walked him briskly from the island to the helicopter. Dillon immediately experienced sensory overload from the noise, light, sensation of moving, and general confusion. He felt the men lifting up on his elbows as they stepped up into the passenger/cargo area of the helicopter.

As soon as he was seated with an odd seat belt around him and over his shoulders, the four blades of the helicopter began spinning. A man approached him, checked Dillon's helmet, his chin strap, his flotation vest, the CO_2 cartridges in his flotation vest, his shoulder straps, and his lap belt, looked him in the eye, and gave him a thumbs-up with a grin. Dillon wanted to return the thumbs-up, but instead sat there frozen by anxious anticipation. Moments later his head was pulled down involuntarily as the helicopter lifted away from the flight deck, dropped over the edge toward the black water, and moved quickly away from the lights. The red floodlights from the ship were far behind them, and the illumination in the helicopter was barely enough for the aircrew to see what they were doing. Dillon swallowed and squeezed some saliva down through his pinched throat. There was no overhead reading light, flight-attendant call button, or adjustable air vent. He had failed to notice the relative location of the *Wasp* to the *Constitution* and therefore did not know how long a flight he was in for. He hadn't gone to the head since before he'd seen Beth Louwsma in the wardroom; he had a sudden rushing fear that he was about to wet his pathetic pajama-like gray suit pants. The pants seemed to have gotten shorter. The legs bunched up in his crotch under the lap belt, leaving the bare skin of his lower calves feeling cold. Dillon closed his eyes and tried to ignore the vibration. He hoped desperately that he had made the right decision and that his mother was not about to get a letter describing his stupidity.

Without warning, the helicopter flared and the nose came up dramatically above the horizon. *Oh no,* Dillon thought. *We're gonna crash.* He supposed the same instruction applied in the helicopter as the COD, not to inflate his life vest until he was outside. He imagined himself gasping in some air pocket of the helicopter as it descended thousands of feet to the ocean bottom.

Suddenly the helicopter was engulfed in red floodlights as it settled onto the deck of the *Wasp.* Dillon sighed in relief as the weight of the helicopter was transferred to its landing gear and the blade rpm decreased rapidly. Two men stepped into the helicopter, unbuckled him, grabbed his elbows, and led him toward the door. As he slowed to step off the helicopter, they lifted him up and set him down on the flight deck. They all moved rapidly toward the island. As they approached, the steel hatch swung open and he stepped to the inside of the ship. The hatch was closed behind him, the long handle dogged down.

They removed his vest and indicated that he should take his helmet off. He did so and handed it to a sailor standing next to him. The two men who had taken him off the helicopter were wearing camouflage uniforms, mostly green and brown. The shirts with large pockets hung over the belts and the sleeves were rolled up past their elbows. They had close-cut hair and serious looks. They introduced themselves. "Good morning, Mr. Dillon, I'm Corporal Luther. This is Corporal Gordon. Welcome aboard the *Wasp*."

"Thank—"

"We've been asked to escort you directly to Colonel Tucker. Please follow us," they said, turning on their heels.

One led and one followed as they descended the ladder to the next level. They turned sharply and headed down the passageway.

Luther opened a gray door and indicated for Dillon to go in. Luther and Gordon followed behind him. Luther spoke loudly. "Colonel Tucker, Mr. Dillon. Mr. Dillon, this is Colonel Tucker, Commander of all Landing Forces, commonly called the CLiF, the one in charge of the landing."

Dillon crossed the small room and extended his hand to the colonel, who was at the head of a table with eight or ten other people in cammies. Colonel Tucker looked him in the eye. "Welcome aboard the *Wasp*, Mr. Dillon. I must tell you that I'm not very glad you're here."

Dillon tried not to look surprised or disturbed. "I understand your concern, Colonel, but I will not get in the way."

"I'm not really concerned about your intentions, Mr. Dillon, I'm concerned about your safety."

"I'm prepared to take that risk, sir." Dillon faced the colonel squarely.

"You have no idea what you're talking about, Mr. Dillon. Have you ever heard a rifle fired?"

"No, sir," Dillon said.

"You ever heard a hundred rifles fired at the same time?"

"No."

"You ever heard a hundred rifles fired at the same time at you?"

"Well, obviously not."

"So what is it that has caused you to want to experience that today?"

The other officers looked at Dillon with impatience. He had obviously arrived in the middle of a final briefing.

"I feel responsible for this whole thing."

Tucker's eyes narrowed. "What whole thing?"

"The Letter of Reprisal was my idea—sending it to a Navy battle group and going after these terrorists."

"It was a good idea. Now you need to let us execute it."

"That's my intention. I just want to watch."

"This isn't a spectator sport, Mr. Dillon."

"I know that, sir. I just want to go along. I don't want to be accused of being a politician who watches the results of his actions on television."

"This is my staff, Mr. Dillon. I'm not going to introduce you to save time. We're in the short hairs of our preparation here and what I'd like you to do is get ready to go. If it were up to me, you wouldn't be going at all, but it's not. So I'm going to take you ashore *with* me. I want you to listen carefully. You will be with me the entire time. You will do exactly as I say. You will go where I say, do what I say, and you will do it without questioning and without hesitation. Do you understand that?"

"Yes, of course."

"That may not be so easy. Do you promise you'll do exactly what I say?"

"Yes, I do."

Tucker blew out a breath. He looked at Luther, who was standing behind Dillon. "Corporal Luther?"

"Yes, sir?"

"Go check out some cammies that will fit Mr. Dillon. I would assume a large. What size shoe do you wear, Mr. Dillon?"

"Eleven."

"Get him some combat boots, utilities, helmet, flak jacket, utility belt with two canteens, and whatever else he needs. Mr. Dillon, I want you to go with Corporal Luther, and when you get your gear, I want you to change."

"Yes, sir."

"Corporal Luther, show Mr. Dillon the nearest officers' head. Mr. Dillon, I want you to report back here after you've changed."

"Yes, sir." Dillon turned and began to follow Luther.

"And, Corporal Luther . . ."

"Yes, sir?"

"Get some adhesive tape. What's your first name, Mr. Dillon?"

"Jim, James."

"Corporal Luther, put adhesive tape on the back of Mr. Dillon's helmet, with 'Jimmy' on it, so nobody shoots him in the ass. Mr. Dillon," Tucker said finally, "I can't put a dog collar and leash on you and have someone watch over you. Your safety is going to be up to you as much as it is up to me. Are you with us?"

"I'm with you, sir."

"Go get him changed, Corporal Luther."

Commander Mike Caskey couldn't see the deck at all in the pitch-darkness, nor could he see the edge of the deck, on the other side of which was ocean. The two nosewheels straddled catapult 1 on the bow of the *Constitution*. He and Messer were to be the first Tomcat airborne. He kneeled the airplane. The nosestrut compressed and the launch bar lowered itself slowly to the deck. The yellow shirt standing in front of him moved his lighted wands together slowly. Caskey watched him carefully, keeping his feet on the brake pedals which were above the rudder pedals. The nose of the airplane was light, making it easy to turn the nosewheel. But too much turn, and the plane could start to slide and skid across the slippery flight deck.

Caskey inched his Tomcat forward. As he approached the shuttle, the yellow shirt slowed his lighted wands. Caskey could feel the launch bar push up the metal shuttle and drop on the forward side. The yellow shirt immediately crossed his wands and Caskey stepped on his brakes. The yellow shirt looked down at the sailor attaching the hold-back fitting. He ran out from under the F-14 and gave him a thumbs-up. The yellow shirt moved off to the left and transferred control to the catapult officer who would launch the aircraft from the flight deck itself instead of from inside the glass bubble recessed into the flight deck, as he usually did. He's probably just excited and wants to feel like he's part of this strike, Caskey thought. The catapult officer quickly rotated the flashlight in his right hand, telling Caskey to run up his engine to military power. Caskey jammed the throttles forward with his left hand and began checking his instruments. "Everything looks good, Messer," he said quickly.

"Roger that. Controls."

Caskey slammed the stick to the left side. "Left."

Messer looked quickly to the left with his flashlight shining on the left wing spoilers. "Good."

Caskey moved the stick to the right and Messer checked the right-hand spoilers at the same speed. "Good."

"Aft," Caskey said.

Messer turned himself tightly in his seat and looked at the horizontal stabilizers evenly deflected with the aft ends up toward the sky. "Good."

"Forward," Caskey said.

Messer watched the horizontal stabilizers shift to point their forward edges toward the sky. "Good."

"Rudder," he said, moving the rudder pedals from one stop to the other.

"Good."

"Caution, and warning lights are out. Engine instruments look good."

Messer checked the warning panel and quickly scanned the hundreds of circuit breakers. "I'm good."

Caskey flicked the switch on the throttle to turn on the airplane's exterior lights, indicating they were ready. The catapult officer saluted, looked down the flight deck, and looked back at the Jet-Blast Deflector as the F-14B's powerful engines forced the burning air into the JBD and up into the sky. He leaned forward and touched the deck. The catapult petty officer pushed the launch button and the F-14 was jerked down momentarily, then raced toward the bow of the ship. The acceleration was exhilarating. Zero to one hundred thirty-five knots in less than three seconds. The shuttle ended and the plane was hurled off the deck and into the black sky seventy feet above the water. The small amount of light on the flight deck disappeared entirely as they climbed away from the ocean.

Caskey raised the landing gear and climbed straight ahead, away from the carrier.

Messer checked in with strike control on the radio. *"Strike. Park Bench 104 airborne."*

"Roger, Park Bench, proceed directly to cap station and report in. Switch button 9."

"Roger. Switching 9." Messer looked at his TACAN needle and his tactical information display to get a good heading to their cap station.

"Come port to 263," he said to Caskey.

Caskey gently turned the F-14 to a heading of 263—nearly due west—and continued his climb to 10,000 feet. The rest of the launch for Event One continued flawlessly in the dark behind them. "Cold mike."

"Ditto," Messer said turning off his microphone.

The airplanes from the *Constitution* streaked toward their assigned positions as adroitly as ballet dancers finding their places onstage. They left their lights on to avoid midair collisions until they approached the island; then they would go dark. Almost all the commanding officers

of the squadrons were airborne, not wanting to miss this
chance. The voices were a little higher on the radio frequencies, the turns more precise, the checklists more en-
thusiastic.

Within thirty minutes they were all at their assigned
posts. Caskey and his wingman took up their position over
the amphibious group heading for the beach. There were
two other F-14s northeast of the amphibious group. The
other fighters were F/A-18s—two west of the island, two
east, and two south. The electronic EA-6B flew southeast
of the island, out of sight, listening carefully for any
surface-to-air missile activity or other unusual electronic
signals. The ES-3A patrolled southward from the island,
listening for any radio communications. So far there had
been nothing.

The night was dead quiet. The moon was about to set
in the west, but was still bright enough to illuminate the
horizon for three hundred and sixty degrees in the warm
night. Caskey and his wingman flew in a general circular
pattern covering the amphibious group. They were on opposite sides of the circle and their radars pointed in opposite directions. The E-2C Hawkeye was airborne east
of the amphibious group, and had the island, the carrier,
and a two-hundred-fifty-mile area covered like an electric
blanket. There were no other airplanes in the sky.

There were ships scattered over the sea, but all but three
had been previously identified as merchant shipping.
Those three were being watched by an S-3B.

Caskey looked down at the *Wasp:* its flight deck was
aglow with AV-8B Harrier jets and helicopters preparing
to take off. The *Wasp* had a well deck in the back that
flooded so landing craft, LCUs and LCACs, could drive
out with their complement of Marines and equipment. The
LCUs were loaded and were circling behind the large amphibious carrier. He could barely make them out in the
early morning as the sun started to light the sky. One after
another, then another—a long train of boats circled, waiting for the chance to turn toward the beach.

Caskey and Messer made another circle around the Amphibious Group, two hundred fifty knots, ten thousand feet. Just a cruise. But with each circle the tension increased for everyone in the amphibious operation. Someone was going to die soon. The only question was who.

The amphibious group and the Marines hadn't had time to do a rehearsal, one of the required elements of any amphibious landing. Go somewhere else, similar to your destination, and rehearse the entire operation. Get the Marines in the boats, get the helicopters airborne, turn everyone in toward shore, and even land if you have time. Then, when the real landing comes, the bugs will be worked out of the plan, and everyone will be fresh and ready to go. But not this time.

Caskey glanced to the north and could clearly see the island in the early-morning light, its greenness visible in the heat.

"Fifteen minutes to L hour," Messer said, sounding slightly bored. "Must be a real challenge for those Marines, to send fifteen hundred of them against a couple of hundred pinhead terrorists."

"Easy, Messer. They probably think it'd be easy to do a TARPS run over this island."

"Touché," Messer said.

"Are we still outside the SAM envelope?" Caskey was looking at the chart on his kneeboard.

"You bet," Messer said. "I'm not going anywhere near that guy."

"What did they say the max range was on that thing?"

"12.5 clicks, about seven miles."

"Okay."

"Are we going to roll in hot and strafe?" Messer asked hopefully.

"Only if they need us, and there's nothing else to do up here."

"Cool," Messer said, trying to cover the dryness in his mouth with enthusiasm.

Suddenly the circling boats below them straightened

out and headed toward the beach. The LCAC—Landing Craft, Air Cushion—that carried Colonel Tucker and Dillon led the rest of the craft. It was an enormous hovercraft that rode on a cushion of air, generating a cloud of saltwater from the black skirt that contained the air pressure. From the back, its huge airplane-like propellers pushed it toward the beach at twice the speed of the LCUs. It projected an air of menace.

The helicopters hovered low behind them, over the horizon from the island. The Harriers flew low, farther out than the helicopters, ready to pounce.

The FA-18s lined up to soften the beach. Two Spruance-class destroyers began shelling with their five-inch guns. One orange flash after another exploded on the beach as the automatically loaded guns slammed their shells into the vague target.

The one obstacle the SEALs had found in front of the beautiful south-facing beach suddenly blew up with a huge tower of water as the timer marked five minutes before L hour. The explosion reassured the Marines that they would hit the beach on time, in stride.

Two F-18s streaked from the southeast and popped up to their right. They rolled in one after the other and dropped bombs on the treeline just beyond the beach. Caskey could see the concussion spread through the trees and then black smoke rising as the bombs leveled two-hundred-foot areas.

The F-18s pulled up and the Harriers streaked in underneath Caskey to begin their own close air support. They began a racetrack pattern, bombing and strafing the beach line as the boats made their way in. Caskey saw no return fire from the trees.

"I wonder if they're bombing a bunch of sand crabs," Caskey remarked.

"I haven't seen any resistance at all down there. Have you?"

"Not a thing," Caskey said. "You know, I nearly shot you the other night."

"Where, in my bed?" Messer asked sarcastically as he adjusted the scan of the radar.

"No, when you came swimming toward me after Drunk got those three boats."

"Thanks. See if I come to you for help again. Some shrapnel tore my raft. I didn't think Drunk could see me— he hit the last boat about fifty yards from me. I could feel the explosions, and next thing I know I'm sitting in the water with my raft sinking underneath me. I just swam toward you so I'd get picked up."

"Yeah, I know, but I never told you I had my gun out and was pointing it at you while you were swimming toward me. I thought you were one of the bad guys—"

Suddenly the radio crackled and Caskey recognized the E-2 naval flight officer in control of fighters. *"Park Bench 104. Bogeys inbound bearing 260 for 25 miles!"* Caskey felt an adrenaline surge. "You hear that, Messer?"

"Yeah, I got it." Messer said, then stepped on the microphone button under his right foot. *"Roger 260 for 25 miles say angels."* Then to Caskey, "Come port hard to 260."

Caskey threw the stick to his left and pulled hard to drive the Tomcat quickly to 260. He instinctively accelerated through 300 knots heading toward 450.

"Angels unknown. Appear low."

"Roger low. Where'd they come from?"

"Unknown."

"Roger. Are they squawking?"

"Affirmative. Squawking mode 3."

Messer switched to transmit on the front radio to talk to his wingman. *"Mario, set combat spread."*

"Roger" came the reply as the wingman took his position a mile and a half to the south, their left, heading west and slightly above them.

Messer immediately found the bogeys on his radar. *"Contact 260, 21 miles angels four,"* Messer said, finding the planes at four thousand feet and climbing.

"That's your bogey."

Messer transmitted again. *"You sure those aren't the F-18s?"* he asked, making sure the captain in charge of air intercepts was available.

"I'm sure," the E-2 replied.

Messer transmitted, *"Do you have Bravo Whiskey on the line?"*

"Affirmative," the E-2 replied.

"Any change in the rules of engagement?" Messer demanded.

"Peacetime ROE," came back the immediate reply.

"Shit," Messer said on the internal communications system as he went hot mike.

"Combat checklist," Caskey demanded. Messer immediately ran through the list with Caskey responding properly. They reached the final item.

"Master arm on."

"Hold that," Caskey said. "I don't want to shoot anybody down by accident."

"Roger that, but if these guys are out to get us, I don't want to be shooting blanks."

"I hear you."

Out of the corner of his right eye Messer saw the smoke trails of two SLAM missiles that had been fired by F-18s at two concrete bunkers on the island. He wanted to watch the burning smoke trail as the missiles streaked toward their targets, but he had other things to do. Messer flipped his microphone switch to the front radio again and called Meat. *"You got these guys, Meat?"*

"I got them. Which one do you want?"

"I got the guy on the right, looks like line of bearings stacked right. You take the guy on the left."

"Got him."

"I got them," Messer told Caskey. "They're doing 550 knots and climbing. Geez, who are these guys?"

It was almost light as they accelerated through 450 knots.

"Buster," Messer said, telling Caskey to go to full military power. Caskey pushed the throttles all the way forward, short of afterburner.

"11 miles, 4 degrees low, 1,000 knots closure," Messer said to Caskey.

The E-2 NFO spoke again. "*258, ten miles . . .*"

"*Judy,*" Messer transmitted, cutting off the E-2 and taking control of the intercept.

"Who are you?" Caskey said to no one in particular as he strained through the windscreen to see the bogeys.

"I'm gonna lock him up," Messer said. "I don't see any other airplanes." Messer transferred the radar to single-target track and the radar instantly locked on the trailing bogey, slightly behind the lead. He slaved his TVSU—TeleVision Sight Unit—to the radar and switched his tactical information display to show the television picture. Although the light was dim, he could make it out. "It's a fighter," he said to Caskey. "I can't make out the type yet."

"The sooner the better," Caskey said.

"9 miles, 1,100 knots closure."

"Give me an ID, Messer," Caskey insisted.

Messer switched back and forth from the television picture to the radar picture, running the intercept and trying to identify them simultaneously.

Messer transmitted, "*These guys are coming awful fast. Request clearance to fire.*"

"*Stand by,*" the E-2 replied.

"*I don't have time to stand by!*" Messer said. "*These are fighters. They are doing almost 600 knots!*"

"*Roger. Stand by.*"

"It's an F-16," Messer said suddenly. "Definitely an F-16," he told Caskey. "*F-16, confirm F-16,*" he said to the E-2.

"*Roger Fox One Six,*" the E-2 replied.

"*Request instructions,*" Messer said.

"*Roger, stand by,*" the E-2 said yet again.

"Shit!" Messer said. "We're going to get our asses shot!"

"If a missile comes off the rail of one of them, I'm going to smoke him," Caskey said. "Switching master arm on."

"Good AMRAAM solution. Ready to fire," Messer replied tensely.

"I've got a good Sidewinder tone. What the—" Two missiles suddenly rose up from the island off to the right and streaked into the sky. "Messer!" Caskey called.

Messer looked up and saw the SAMs coming toward them.

"Not again!" Caskey said as he pushed the nose of the Tomcat hard over toward the ocean.

"They're not headed for us!" Messer said. "Throttle back!" They watched as the two missiles streaked toward their targets. "Throttle back!" Messer repeated. Caskey immediately retarded his throttles to idle and began to climb. The F-16s came up toward them.

"Tally-ho!" Caskey said. He could see the dot-sized targets six miles ahead.

"They don't see them," Caskey said to Messer, his voice full of confusion. The two missiles raced toward the F-16s and hit them from the left almost simultaneously. Caskey saw two bright orange fireballs directly in front of him. He then saw two other small bright orange flames behind the F-16s as two missiles flew off rails of unseen airplanes in the distance. The missiles climbed high into the sky and headed down toward the island. "HARMs," Caskey said. "F-18s got a fix on the SAM site when they lit up the F-16s. Unbelievable."

Messer transmitted to E-2, *"Splash two F-16s."* His heart beat like a hamster's. He switched to the television picture and saw pieces of the airplanes drifting down into the ocean. The radar had broken lock, but the television was still locked on the contrast.

The E-2 NFO came back in a panic, *"You never received clearance to fire!"*

"We didn't splash them," Messer replied in an annoyed tone.

"Say again?" the E-2 replied.

"We didn't splash them."

"Who did?"

"SAMs."

"Off the island?"

"Affirmative."

"Are you sure it wasn't one of our Aegis ships?"

"Positive," Messer said.

"Roger that," the E-2 replied. *"I see no other bogeys."*

"Where do you think those guys were from?" Caskey said.

"I don't know. Singapore has F-16s, I know that, or maybe Malaysia."

"Singapore? You think they're in on this?"

"I have no idea, but I bet we find out."

"Does Indonesia have F-16s?"

"I think so."

"Great, we've really got it narrowed down."

They turned quickly back toward the amphibious group and scanned the skies with their radar.

"You got anybody else out there yet?" Messer asked the E-2.

"Negative."

Colonel Tucker stood in front of Dillon in the LCAC as they made their way to the beach. He surveyed the line of landing craft behind him and the AAV-7s, the Amphibious Assault Vehicles, in front of him. The AAVs, Amtracs as they were called, were essentially armored personal carriers that motored in like boats, then crawled up on land like tanks, and carried a platoon of Marines inside the armored protection. The most heavily armed and protected, they went ashore first. Tucker wanted to touch the shore in his LCAC right after them. He looked at the other amphibious assault boats behind him.

Fifteen hundred Marines heading ashore. He loved it.

But he also knew how badly these things could get screwed up. That was why he was in the LCAC. He had seen it too often. *Mayagüez,* the Iranian hostage rescue, Grenada, Panama, Beirut, Somalia—he had been at every one of them. He had seen people die each time. These quiet little political missions, not the full-on wars where you got to use tanks and fighters as they were meant to be used, but the little political wars, they were the ones that got you. The Marines were always the first ones in and the first ones to die. And the last ones to get any credit.

It wasn't going to happen this time. He would go ashore with his troops and make sure. This was the first landing he had been in charge of. Every "i" had been dotted, every "t" crossed. *This one would be different.* He had been pleased by the lack of resistance thus far. They hadn't seen one shot fired from the island with the exception of the SAM, which hit somebody. He couldn't see who or what, but he assumed it was the F-18s. These guys were playing for keeps. That's fine, Tucker thought. So are we.

He flinched and pushed Dillon down as bullets suddenly slammed into the front of the LCAC with the characteristic *ping* that he had heard before. Small-caliber machineguns, he thought to himself. Probably AK-47s. Black market specials. Available by the truckload at a discount. He watched the other Marines as they scrunched down farther into the landing craft and looked at each other. None looked terribly frightened, but he knew better than to take this too lightly. Any bullet fired by anybody—including a stupid terrorist—could kill you very dead. He pulled his chin down to test the tightness of his helmet strap. Overhead the Harriers and F-18s raced in to strafe the line of palm trees just inshore from the target beach.

Suddenly the LCAC was at the beach and climbing up out of the water. It drove right across the sand on its cushion of air and stopped just short of the treeline. Its engines screamed and rattled. Tucker stood up. "Let's go!" he shouted. The other Marines charged down the ramp and fanned out to left and right. Several LCUs hit the beach behind them and Marines charged ashore by the dozen. No rebel yells, no screams, just the deadly efficient silence of trained Marines going about their business.

Dillon ducked down and ran awkwardly behind Tucker. His helmet bobbed on his head and was heavier than he had expected. He stepped onto the sand and was immediately thrown down by Luther, who had been assigned to look out for him. "Don't stand up when people are shooting at you," he yelled at Dillon. "Bad idea."

Those ashore first threw themselves down and began returning fire, trying to walk behind the AAV. A bullet suddenly hit the sailor driving the nearest LCU. He was wearing a flak jacket, but he was hit in the neck just above the flak jacket. Blood spurted as the sailor fell to the deck. A petty officer standing next to him immediately jumped to the wheel and continued the throttle pressure to keep the LCU pushing against the shore. A Navy corpsman quickly placed a battle dressing on the wound. When all the Marines were finally off, the petty officer backed the LCU off the sand and turned it back toward the fleet.

The first Marines ashore had reduced the fire from the treeline to a weak smattering of resistance. The terrorists were clearly backtracking into the dense foliage. Tucker knelt on the sand and monitored the radio reports from the Marines at the far ends of the beach. All the reports were the same. Minor resistance retreating into the jungle. *"Secure the beach and hold until further orders,"* he transmitted curtly. The objective was to get to the probable headquarters, near the concrete bunkers, before a defensive perimeter could be set up.

The second wave of LCUs jammed into the beach and the ramps came down. Just like D-day, Tucker thought. Not much advancement in getting ashore in the last fifty years. After two more assault waves the beach was overflowing with fully armed Marines and maneuvering armored vehicles looking for paths into the jungle. He could see two bodies lying on the beach, but no other casualties.

Overhead the powerful CH-53E helicopters headed for the scheduled landing. They're late, Tucker thought to himself. They flew directly toward the hill that had been identified as the LZ, the landing zone. He had picked it himself. It was a clear knoll a mile and a half inland, directly on the other side of their objective. Three hundred Marines would be dropped on the hill and twelve hundred on the beach. They were to converge on the target from both directions simultaneously. Tucker grabbed the radio transmitter from his radioman and personally called all the company commanders. When they were on their receivers, he gave the coded signal to turn inshore.

34

THE ENORMOUS THREE-ENGINED CH-53E DESCENDED
quickly toward the landing zone. The Marine captain pi-
loting the beast from the right seat scanned the nearby
trees quickly for any signs of life. He couldn't give the
scan as much time as he would have liked, though; he
was concentrating on settling the 53 onto the knoll without sinking too fast and breaking the aircraft's back.

The copilot in the left seat and the crew chief in the
back were much more diligent in scrutinizing the forest
around them. Their eyes darted back and forth as their
hearts pounded. Neither had been in combat before, and
although they were excited, they were nervous.

Despite their heightened awareness, they never saw the
bullets coming from the woods. As the 53 settled onto the
knoll, bullets slammed loudly into the helicopter. The Marines in the back bent over to minimize their exposure but
they were restrained by their belts. They scrambled to free
themselves and shuffled toward the back and side doors.

They could see white flashes from the woods and
quickly began to return fire. A couple of anxious Marines
began firing from inside the helicopter until a master gun-
nery sergeant slapped their helmets to stop them. They
poured out the back, formed a circle on the ground around
the helicopter, and continued returning fire in the general
direction the shots seemed to be coming from. The 53
lifted off and quickly pulled away, nosing down imme-

diately from the knoll once airborne. It skipped over the trees back toward the ship. The next 53 hustled in as soon as the landing zone was clear.

The second 53 tried to be smarter. The crew knew it was a hot landing zone, not a simple dropoff. The pilot came in hotter—faster and steeper. The Marines in the back felt themselves being lifted from their seats as the helicopter dropped quickly to avoid the gunfire from the trees. But bullets slammed into the sides of the ship. The men felt helpless, unable to return fire, and most leaned over and ineffectually covered their helmeted heads with their hands.

The 53's nose came up as the pilot slowed over the landing zone. The smoke from the three engines began to catch up with the helicopter and surrounded it with a haze of dark hot exhaust.

Suddenly three shoulder-fired heat-seeking missiles screamed up at them out of the woods. The missiles headed directly toward the hottest spot—and hit the engines just below the rotor blades. The engines burst into flame as the wounded helicopter settled the last fifty feet onto the ground and crashed. Fire broke out from the top of the helicopter and soon the entire aircraft was engulfed. Marines from the first helicopter ran back to help but the flames were too intense. Although some of the men were able to crawl out of the fire and run away, several were trapped on board.

Admiral Billings sat back in his chair, his eyes glued to the large screen where he watched the live, real-time video link from the Predator flying quietly fifteen thousand feet above the island. Its zoom television camera was fixed on the smoking helicopter. The Predator had done its job: Billings and his staff had been able to watch the entire landing. The Marine intel officer was able to forward information to Colonel Tucker and it had been relayed in time to make a difference to the troops on the ground. But Billings hadn't anticipated the impact of seeing the death of his men firsthand. The Predator's camera remained fixed on the burning hulk of a helicopter.

Billings turned to Captain Black. "We need a casualty report as soon as possible."

"Yes, sir." Black picked up the radio to call the *Wasp*.

Tucker and Dillon watched the advancing line of Marines penetrate the trees and head inland firing sporadically at anything that moved. But now there was mostly silence, although to Tucker's left, at the west end of the beach, there were two loud unidentifiable pops. Tucker, Dillon, and the men strode cautiously but steadily inland until they were surrounded by deep foliage. The ground was wet and slippery, but firm. They picked up speed as they realized that the foliage was not impenetrable. Tucker checked their position on his GPS receiver against his rough chart of the island.

Dillon watched over his shoulder, completely confused, just trying to stay out of the way. He still felt sick after watching the Navy coxswain take a bullet in the neck. He tried to view the experience with detachment, but he couldn't get the image out of his mind, the image of the sailor falling backward with blood spurting out of his neck.

Dillon was in good physical shape. He ran almost every day. But just coming ashore and going a few hundred yards exhausted him.

Tucker slowed and listened. He motioned Dillon to stay down while the Marines checked the trees for snipers and the ground for booby traps. Black smoke rose in the distance, and they walked slowly toward it. Their line was as straight as he could hope for as they worked their way silently through the jungle.

Suddenly the leaves were torn by bullets and machine-gun fire. The Marines threw themselves onto the green moist ground and fired back. Bullets and tracers flew in both directions.

Tucker had heard fire like this before. This wasn't twenty or thirty people; this was one hundred, or two hundred. It was the sound of constant, sustained firing of automatic weapons. The central company commander was right next to Tucker. Tucker yelled at him, "Call in the Harriers. Call them in on the smoke."

The company commander grabbed the radio while Tucker signaled for the platoons on the left and the right of the bunkers to advance cautiously.

A second radioman handed Tucker the receiver. "Otter Seven is calling."

"*Otter Chief,*" Tucker said.

"*Otter Chief. Otter Seven,*" the captain from the first helicopter said loudly over the radio. "*We're taking heavy fire on the north end of the perimeter. We have the smoke in sight, which we believe to be the bunkers. We've lost one helicopter and an estimated fifteen men, over. The smoke behind is from the downed helo.*"

Tucker grimaced. "*Roger. We're on the other side of the same smoke. I'm calling in the Harriers. Don't advance until I give you the signal. After the Harriers roll in, we're in hot.*"

"*Otter Seven, copy, out.*"

Tucker handed the receiver back to his radioman and looked up. The Harriers were two miles away. Tucker could hear them coming—a screaming jet noise. The Harriers popped up over the horizon from his left and climbed to about three thousand feet. They rolled in and Tucker could see for the first time how fast they were going—at least five hundred knots. The Harriers' cannon was audible above the general din of the firefight. The first one pulled up sharply and Tucker heard, then felt, an enormous *whump* as two five-hundred-pound bombs exploded half a mile away. The second Harrier followed right behind and then two more. The shooting slackened. Tucker stood and gave the signal.

The Marines doubled their pace through the jungle, almost running. They were nearly reckless as they headed for the spot where the bombs had just landed. Their hunger for a fight increased. Some of them shot wildly as they moved, while others stopped to fire from their shoulders.

Suddenly the lead platoon broke into the clearing with Tucker right behind. Dillon ran hard to keep up. They threw themselves on the ground as they were met with a hail of bullets. The Marines stopped on the edge of the clearing and began encircling the area. Then, behind the firing came the sound of a rocket motor igniting. A large missile flew out of an area carved into the side of a hill. The fat, ugly missile flew over their heads, picking up speed as it went, a huge piglike projectile headed for the fleet.

The EA-6B prowler electronic warfare plane saw the electronic guidance signals from the Silkworm anti-ship missile about the time Tucker heard it launch. *"Silkworm airborne!"* the NFO from the Prowler warned the fleet on guard frequency. The pilot could see the smoke trail coming from the island. "You got a bearing for the HARM?" he demanded.

"Affirmative!" his NFO in the right seat answered. "Come starboard ten."

As soon as the EA-6B was lined up it launched its HARM, the high speed anti-radiation missile, at the Silkworm site. It was faster than the Silkworm, but had gotten a later start.

"Park Bench 104, this is Long Bow, over," the E-2 transmitted to the Tomcat.

"Go ahead," Messer replied instantly.

"Vampire airborne!" came the immediate reply. *"Vector 338 for ten!"*

"104 coming port to 338. Say angels."

"Angels unknown, but thought to be low."

"Roger. Looking," Messer transmitted. "Keep your eye out, MC. Should be twenty-five left. Low. Cruise missile. Headed out. We've got about a minute to find it and shoot it down. Shit!" Messer searched for the missile with his radar. "Why can't the stupid Aegis take it?"

"Because the only Aegis ship is still with the carrier, and we're in the way," Caskey replied calmly. "Stay cool, Messer."

"Sorry. Okay." He leaned forward against his shoulder straps to look closely at the radar. "I got it! He's headed straight for the *Wasp*. It's really hauling, but subsonic. Come port to 291."

Caskey slammed the stick to the left to bring the nose of the Tomcat in front of the Silkworm, a huge anti-ship missile the size of a small airplane.

"Master arm still on?" Messer asked, his breathing loud in the ICS.

"On," Caskey replied as he watched the fast-moving speck that was the missile coming from the right. "We gonna try a forward quarter shot?"

"Yep. Buster," Messer said, calling for maximum power without afterburners.

"Roger."

The Tomcat picked up speed, but not fast enough. "Burner," Messer demanded. "There's too much drift. Come port hard! Hard as possible!"

Caskey wrapped the Tomcat into a ninety-degree left-hand turn to try to catch the missile.

"Descend to two thousand," Messer said as they leveled their wings. "We've got a beam shot. I'm going to take it anyway." He reached for the launch button by his left knee to fire an AMRAAM.

"Park Bench, new Silkworm airborne. 360 for 14."

"Roger," Messer replied. He pushed the red-lighted launch button with enthusiasm. The rocket motor on the AMRAAM missile fired and tore ahead of the Tomcat toward the Silkworm. Messer—like Caskey—had learned to fly intercepts with the AIM-7 Sparrow missile. If this

had been a Sparrow, they would have been required to keep their radar trained on the Silkworm until missile impact. But not with the AMRAAM, a "fire and forget" missile. As soon as it was off the rail, Messer yelled to Caskey, "Come starboard to 360, MC."

Caskey brought the Tomcat around hard, heading back north toward the island, which had smoke rising from it in several locations.

"Got it," Messer said quickly. "Come out of burner. Set 500 knots."

"Roger that. I'm going to check the other one," Caskey replied as he quickly dipped the left wing to check the AMRAAM they had just fired. Caskey watched the missile approach the Silkworm, then go stupid and fly by the target and into the water. *"Long Bow,"* Caskey transmitted to the E-2, *"missile failed to guide. Warn the* Wasp *that that Vampire is still inbound."*

"Wilco. Do you have the second?"

"Judy," Messer said, annoyed.

"Tally-ho!" Caskey called as he saw the missile ahead, still below them.

"Good target aspect," Messer studied the intercept on his radar. "Good solution." He waited. "Port five degrees," he asked. The Tomcat streaked toward the smoking island at five hundred knots and two thousand feet.

"Any signs of those SAM radars again, Messer?"

"No," he replied. "Stand by . . ." Messer pressed the launch button and the second AMRAAM came off the Tomcat and screamed toward the Silkworm. Caskey and Messer strained to watch as it guided directly to the Vampire and hit it squarely in the face. It was only four miles from their Tomcat when it exploded in a huge fireball and fell toward the warm ocean.

"Splash one Vampire," Messer called, then lifted his head and looked around for other bogies or missiles. "Come around south, MC. Let's get out of their SAM envelope."

As they headed south again and climbed back up to a

more comfortable altitude, Messer asked, "Who are these guys? They have fancy speedboats, SAMs, good tactics, and now surface-to-surface missiles? What the *hell* is going on here?"

"These aren't your average terrorists," MC answered. "They may not be very smart, but one thing is clear—they are well financed. I just hope that first Silkworm doesn't get through to the *Wasp*."

The first one was trying to do just that. There were no other air defenses between it and the *Wasp*. The Silkworm had unwittingly flown right down the corridor of least resistance.

The *Wasp* had been trying to clear the helicopters out of the area since being warned of the incoming cruise missile. Their best—and last—defense was the Phalanx, the point defense system—a Gatling gun with a radar mounted on the side of the ship to shoot down cruise missiles with good old-fashioned bullets. A lot of them. It was the same gun that the F-14 and F-18 had, but with a different radar. This radar was hungry for metal: it would find anything metal and shoot it. No discretion, no thinking. If it's metal, shoot it. Which required that those in charge of the system clear all friendly metal out of the way before shooting. And that's exactly what they had been trying to do.

The last helicopter cleared the deck of the amphibious carrier to the south as the *Wasp* went to automatic on its missile defense system. Robo-gun. It looked like a white R2D2 on the side of the ship. Its radar had a good return from the Silkworm and turned the six barrels of the Gatling gun toward the cruise missile as it closed on the *Wasp*. It jerked a couple of times, raised the barrels, and began firing. A steady stream of 20mm bullets ripped through the air toward the incoming missile. When the Silkworm was a mile away, small pieces of the tail began to fall away. Seconds passed as the bullets drew closer to the missile and finally caught up with it. The bullets tore the missile apart. It blew up and fell into the sea in thousands of pieces well short of the *Wasp*.

On the island, in the three minutes since the Silkworm launch, the Marines had advanced cautiously. They approached what they thought was the clearing Tucker had been heading for. They entered the perimeter carefully. Some knelt on the ground while others continued walking. Two smoking bunkers with thick concrete roofs stood on the left side of the opening, bigger than expected.

It looked like a small village, with dozens of huts. It was eerily quiet. There were several bodies, but no visible opposition. Yet there had been only minutes before.

"They must be in the huts," Tucker said to the Marine to his left. "I don't like this at all." He glanced around with the skeptical look he had developed watching rash men die. "Check every hut. One by one. Watch for booby traps!" he said.

The Marines advanced toward the village with their rifles swinging left and right, while Dillon stood on the perimeter trying not to look as scared as he felt.

35

TUCKER STUDIED HIS CHART. HE WAS CONFUSED, and he didn't like it. There was no place for the terrorists to have gone, but they had vanished. One minute there was furious automatic weapons fire from this village, and the next, it was empty. The Marines had the entire perimeter surrounded; the terrorists couldn't have gone through the Marines undetected. And the company that had been dropped by the helos on the other side of the clearing had arrived and reported no activity in their direction at all.

Tucker looked up suddenly. His staff surrounded him, waiting for instructions and wisdom. He breathed a little harder, trying to understand his sense of danger. Something was wrong. He knew in the back of his mind the answer was obvious; he just couldn't figure it out. Then he remembered the stories he had heard from Marines who had been in Vietnam. "A tunnel!" he yelled, starting to move quickly. "Check the floors of the huts!" he bellowed as he headed for the largest hut himself. Dillon trotted behind him.

The Marines approached the hut carefully with their rifles pointed at the door. Tucker gave the officer the sign to go in *right now*. They proceeded more quickly, but still with caution. One finally threw open the bamboo door and pulled back, waiting for some response. He was met with more silence.

Tucker wasn't waiting any longer. He strode through

the door with his 9mm handgun, ready for any movement. He noticed a bamboo floor mat over a large section of the dirt floor. The rest of the squad was in the hut, waiting anxiously for something to happen. Dillon instinctively pulled back as Tucker tugged gently on the bamboo mat to feel for any resistance: any wires, lines, or booby-trap triggers. He didn't feel anything as he slid it slowly to one side. Tucker grimaced at what was underneath. He peered down the dark mud stairway and examined the wood supporting the sides. He noticed several wires in the darkness across the wide mouth of the tunnel. Nearly every step was booby-trapped.

"This isn't even worth trying to clear," he said to those in the room, who were relieved. Tucker stooped down to examine something on the third step. It was a strange device. It was sitting on a steel plate. Very odd, Tucker thought. He had never seen anything like it. Round, no markings on it, and about five inches high. It looked like a UFO.

A faint bell of recognition sounded in the deep recesses of his memory. He had read something about a device like this in the op report of the attack on the *Pacific Flyer*. "Everybody out!" he screamed. "Out!"

The Marines, hearing his tone more than his words, were out of the hut before he was. They ran for the trees. Others, standing in the clearing, sensed the problem and began running themselves. Dillon was slower to react. He made it out just in front of Tucker and Luther. The hut erupted behind them in an enormous explosion that splintered the bamboo walls. Dirt and debris were thrown a hundred feet into the air as the concussion threw the Marines still in the clearing to the ground. Dillon, Luther, and Colonel Tucker were slammed down onto their faces and lay still as rubble and splintered bamboo covered them.

"Commander Louwsma . . ." Admiral Billings said in that tone that made people cringe. He stopped as the video image on the screen erupted and the hut from which Tucker had just run exploded. "What the hell . . . ?" Billings said, sitting forward. The Army officer in the corner turned a dial to back the video image from the Predator away from the burning hut so more of the island could be seen. The screen showed a large number of Marines looking at their colonel and several other Marines who were lying on the ground in the clearing. Those on the ship watched in horror as the situation became clear. The terrorists had disappeared, the main hut had been booby-trapped, and the central Marine force was either dead or wounded. Billings growled to Captain Black, "Get the colonel on the radio. I sure hope Dillon wasn't in there. That's all we need."

Beth Louwsma stared at the screen in amazement. What had seemed like a walk-through was becoming a disaster. Her throat was dry. She stared at the small images of the Marines lying on the ground.

🖾

Colonel Tucker stirred and staggered to his feet. He knelt down to examine Corporal Luther, who got up as well. Next to them was a body with white tape on his helmet. The tape was slightly singed and blackened, but "Jimmy" was clear enough. "Oh, hell," Tucker said as he dropped to his knees. "Corpsman!" he yelled. He put his face next to Dillon's. "You okay? Dillon!" he yelled as the hut burned behind them.

Dillon's eyes opened and looked around wildly. He turned his face and saw Tucker. As he swung his left arm up to defend himself from some unknown threat, Tucker grabbed it. "Dillon! You're okay. Can you hear me all right?"

"Yeah, I hear you fine."

"Can you get up?"

"Yeah, I think so. What happened?"

"The place blew up. We got out just in time."

Tucker and Luther hauled him effortlessly to his feet. Dillon's knees bowed involuntarily, but he recovered his balance quickly. He took a deep breath and tried to rub the dust off his face, but his sweaty palms smeared it, giving him a muddy look.

Tucker put his 9mm back in his holster. "This looks clear," he said to no one in particular. "They've gone somewhere else. Now we've got to find them. It's a small island." He began to walk toward his radioman and stopped to look at Dillon's face. "You sure you're okay?"

"Yeah, I'm sure." Dillon scanned his body to look for any signs of injury.

Tucker smiled slightly. "Well, now you look like a real Marine. We don't like pretty boys running around with clean uniforms.

"Come on, Corporal Luther. Bring Mr. Dillon and let's get on with this." The radioman walked up and Tucker grabbed the receiver.

"Beth," Billings continued, "can you explain to me how these terrorists had Silkworm missiles and we didn't know about it? And they actually *launched* two of them and almost got one of my ships? Can you explain that to . . ."

"Colonel Tucker on the radio, sir." Captain Black handed him a telephone receiver.

"Brandon, what's going on there?"

"Admiral, things are under control. We've captured the entire area, and the SAM launch sight and the Silkworm sights. Everything is disabled."

"Good. So where are the terrorists?"

"Several killed," came the reply, *"but the rest apparently escaped through a tunnel. We can't tell which way it leads—it was booby-trapped, as you can see."* He looked over his shoulder at the smoldering remains of the

hut. *"But we'll find them. It's a small island."*

Louwsma stared at the video image, which covered nearly a third of the island. She thought she saw some movement in the upper left-hand corner of the screen, but wasn't sure. She leaned forward and looked harder. Something was definitely moving. She looked around the room. No one was looking at the screen except to watch Tucker talk to the admiral on the radio—they were treating it like a video telephone.

She got the attention of the Army officer and motioned for him to skew the image so they could look left and up. He watched as the image pivoted slightly until Tucker was in the lower right-hand corner and the area of movement was closer to the center. He zoomed the image in slightly, and the movement became a line of men hurrying down a trail at the bottom of a hill. "We've got them!" Beth blurted out. "Sir."

Everyone grew suddenly quiet.

"In the middle left," she said, pointing.

"Brandon, they're coming out of a tunnel northwest of you. About half a mile away," Billings said quickly.

Beth whispered to the Army officer. The image moved left until the men emerging from the hill were in the right-hand corner. There were more in front of them, walking rapidly in single file toward the coast. Two smaller figures in lighter clothes were with the lead group.

Why head toward the ocean? Beth wondered. They're just backing themselves into a corner. She looked past the moving figures to the waterfront. Taking an unconscious step closer to the screen, she could make out more detail. She focused on a triangular shape, a shape that doesn't occur in nature. It seemed to be protruding from a tree-lined inlet set deep into a hillside.

"The *Sumatran Star!*" she exclaimed. "Admiral, they're heading for their ship. It's backed into an inlet and virtually invisible. There!"

Billings looked at the image, then signaled to the Marine intelligence officer. He immediately got on the radio with Tucker.

In less than a minute four Cobra helicopter gunships appeared out and flew down the line of figures. The nose gun of the lead helicopter fired steadily from five hundred feet above. The other three followed. The men on the ground returned fire and ran to find cover.

Above the helicopters came the scream of a Harrier as it rolled in on the position of the *Sumatran Star*. It dropped its two five-hundred-pound bombs and pulled up in a high G maneuver, its wings leaving thick vapor trails. The bombs missed the ship and slammed into the ground beyond it. Another Harrier rolled in behind the first and released its two bombs even lower. These found their target, hitting the ship in the bow.

A CH-53E rose over the horizon from behind the hill and settled onto the beach south of the damaged ship. It unloaded its Marines, cutting off the line of advancing men. The helicopter lifted off as a company of Marines on foot came up behind the line of men, who were now in disarray. The two groups exchanged fire. The enemy leader realized they were outmanned and surrounded and yelled to his men over the din. They stopped firing.

Colonel Tucker came over the hill at a run with Dillon and Corporal Luther in tow. "Hold your fire!" Tucker yelled as he came down the incline. He turned to his radioman. "Pass the word to hold fire."

"Stay here!" Tucker said to Dillon. He looked at him hard, as if pinning him in place, and hurried to the front of the Marines.

Breathing hard, Dillon glanced around to get his bearings. Luther was holding his M-16 in a businesslike manner and scanning the jungle for any sign of danger. They were on the west side of the base of the hill, near the path that wound toward Tucker. Behind them was an indentation that implied water or a promising brook. Corporal Gordon strode up next to them with his M-16.

"Everything okay?" Gordon asked.

"We're all set here," Luther replied. He motioned with his head to Colonel Tucker at the front. "Look's like this thing is wrapping up. I think we've got them cut off."

"I sure as hell hope so." Gordon adjusted the chin strap of his too-tight helmet.

Luther looked at Dillon. "You okay, Mr. Dillon? You about got your ass blown up back there."

"I'm okay," Dillon said. "I was just surprised."

"Surprised?" Luther tried not to laugh. "You were *unconscious.*"

"No, I really wasn't." Dillon was denying it more to himself than to the others. "I was just stunned."

Luther smiled mischievously. "I think we'll just stay right here, Mr. Dillon. I don't see any bad guys, and if the shooting starts again, we'll be better off here."

"I'd kinda like to go up front and see what happens."

"Mr. Dillon, I have a very clear recollection of the colonel's words. There were only two of them. 'Stay here.' Here means"—he looked around—"here. This oughta be over pretty quick," he added.

Colonel Tucker thought the same thing as he walked toward the front of the line.

The enemy group was much closer than he would have liked. Still armed and exuding menace, they were concentrated in a nearby clearing. A white woman and young girl stood beside the leader, a small stout man who was holding the woman's arm. "Tell your men to put down their guns," Tucker demanded as he walked slowly toward them.

"No!" the man said. "You leave island. Leave us alone or they will die."

"Who are you?" Tucker asked the woman.

"Missionaries. They . . ." She was cut off as the man slapped her face.

"No talk!" the leader yelled. He turned his attention to Colonel Tucker again. "Get off the island or they die!"

Tucker tried to control his anger. "Just take it easy," he said. He turned to his lieutenant. "Get Lieutenant Armstrong up here, and tell him to get Snake in place. We may need him to interpret.''

The lieutenant reached for the radio transmitter.

''You need to lay down your weapons before more of you are killed,'' Tucker said to the terrorist leader.

''You attack us! We did nothing to you.''

''Just put your weapons down, and we won't hurt you.''

''You get off island.'' The man looked desperately around.

Tucker hesitated. He was trained in amphibious attack, not hostage negotiations, and now he was faced with a standoff between the Marines and the terrorists. Tucker took the radio. *''Admiral, you following this?''*

''Yes.''

''Can you see what's happening?''

''Clear as a bell.''

''I'm going to call for Snake. You agree?''

''I'm with you, Colonel.''

Just then Lieutenant Armstrong, the Navy SEAL, came running up. ''Yes, sir,'' he said, quickly assessing the awkwardness of the situation. ''What would you like us to do?''

''Is Snake ready?''

''Yes, sir.''

''Seems to me,'' Tucker said, ''the one we need the interpreter for is the one holding the woman. If we convince him, the others will follow. Agree?''

''Yes, sir. I don't think we have any choice. We can't abandon the operation because of two hostages.'' The two exchanged knowing glances. Armstrong evaluated the vulnerability of the enemy's position and knew it was only a matter of time. ''Any sign of the captain of the *Flyer*?''

''No. Look, when I take my helmet off, that would be a good time for Snake to begin interpreting.''

''Yes, sir.'' Armstrong ran back toward the hill.

"Let her go, *now,*" Tucker repeated, then "What is your name, ma'am?"

She shook her head, not wanting to anger the terrorist leader.

Tucker walked slowly toward the three. The terrorists had their rifles trained on him. He held up his hands to show he wasn't armed. "Let them go," he said.

"No! You get off island."

"I think we need an interpreter. I can't really understand you."

"You understand fine. You stall."

"No, we clearly need an interpreter," he said. "Let me call him up here." He got down on one knee fifty feet from them. As he did so, he unstrapped his helmet, slowly so the leader could see his hands. He took it off and reached for a radio.

The leader was suddenly knocked back as a bullet slammed into his chest from Snake's long-range Remington 700 sniper rifle. The woman screamed. Tucker ran forward and pulled the woman and child down as a firefight broke out. The terrorists were no match for the Marines, who had taken the time to sight in with their M-16s and were firing with deadly accuracy.

"Get down!" Luther yelled at Dillon. They threw themselves to the ground just to the side of the path.

Fifty feet away there was a sudden explosion. The undergrowth was shredded as another explosion occurred twenty feet closer. Luther raised his head carefully. "Mortar!" he yelled. "Get away from the path!" Corporal Gordon scrambled toward Dillon and Luther in a crouched position. Each Marine grabbed one of Dillon's arms and dragged him toward the hollow in the hill, as another shell hit. They ran toward the hill as far as they could, then hugged the ground and lay still as shells landed around them. They could hear other Marines running up and down the path screaming instructions.

"Shit!" Luther said. "We've got nowhere to go."

The next shell went deeper into the soft ground, almost

exploding underneath them. Suddenly the ground gave way. Dillon felt himself falling into the earth. Luther and Gordon were falling with him into a massive crater in the side of the hill.

They fell ten to fifteen feet, surrounded by dirt, mud, dust, and brush. A gasp, almost a scream came from Dillon's mouth.

They hit the ground in a tumble as the noise of the firefight receded. Dillon lay on his back and stared at the sky. "Luther!" he yelled.

"Yeah?" Luther struggled to get to his feet. "Shit."

"What the hell . . ." Gordon said as he rolled over and moaned.

The three stood and looked around. They were in the middle of a natural cave. It was the size of a large room, but there was no indication of human improvement other than a tunnel coming in from their left and exiting to their right.

"You all right?" Luther asked.

"Yeah," Dillon said. "Where are we?"

Luther looked around for an escape route. "No idea. We could try one of these tunnels, but who knows where it leads."

"Maybe we should just stay here," suggested Dillon. "Wait until this thing is over."

"Not a bad idea," Luther said. Then they heard voices coming from the tunnel on the left.

"Move back!" Luther whispered as he pushed Dillon into the darkest spot. Five Indonesian terrorists burst into the room and stopped. They were dragging a bound and blindfolded white man in tattered and filthy clothes.

Dillon, Luther, and Gordon stood motionless against the wall, hoping their camouflage utilities were doing their job. The leader of the Indonesians looked up at the hole in the cave. The men began poking through the rubble and dirt beneath the hole, then spun around and caught sight of the Americans. The Indonesians pointed their rifles. The Marines did likewise, but no one fired.

''Drop weapons!'' the leader yelled as he placed his Chinese Type 64 silenced machine pistol against the temple of the white man. The image was identical to the Polaroid left on the bridge of the *Pacific Flyer*. The leader and the hostage stood directly beneath the hole. The light illuminated them clearly. Dillon could see a dried streak of blood underneath the blindfold.

''Drop weapons!'' the man repeated.

''Why should we?'' Luther asked in a controlled strong voice.

''I will shoot!'' the man said.

''Who the hell is he?'' Luther asked.

''Captain of ship,'' the man responded.

''Who are you?'' Dillon asked, surprising himself.

Luther looked at him.

''George Washington. I fight for freedom of my country, too!''

''From who?'' Dillon asked.

''From you and your Western imperialism,'' the man said. ''Put down weapons!''

''Let him go,'' Dillon said as he stepped away from the wall, walking slowly toward Washington.

''I shoot him first, then you.'' Washington remained calm.

''I'm unarmed,'' Dillon replied, holding his hands out so that Washington could see him clearly.

''Easier for me,'' Washington said, his voice rising in pitch slightly. The other Indonesians stood behind Washington with their guns trained on the Marines and Dillon.

Dillon took another tentative step toward Washington.

''Careful, Mr. Dillon,'' Luther whispered.

''Stop!'' Washington said icily.

In an instant all eyes were fixed on the mouth of the tunnel on the left. They could hear American voices. Someone yelled, ''Watch out for booby traps. Check for offshoots; we have to run them all back.'' They could hear the footsteps of many men.

"They're clearing this tunnel," Dillon said. "There's no way out."

"Oh, yes, there is!" Washington looked toward the exit tunnel. "You come with us!" he said. "More hostages the better." The Indonesians began moving toward the other tunnel.

"Come!" Washington yelled.

Dillon, Luther, and Gordon stood still.

Three Marines came into the cave holding M-16s. "Stop right there!" the lead Marine yelled as he saw the Indonesians.

Washington swung his gun from Bonham's head and shot at the lead Marine. The three Marines hit the ground and began returning fire.

Dillon ran toward Bonham and grabbed his shirt. "Fall to the ground!" he yelled.

Washington let go of Bonham and ran toward the exit tunnel. As he did, he trained his gun on Dillon. He fired. The first bullet hit Dillon in the chest and spun him toward Luther.

Another Indonesian fired at Gordon, hitting him in the thigh. Luther returned fire and that Indonesian fell.

Washington fired again and his second bullet hit the back of Dillon's helmet, right between the two *m*'s in "Jimmy." Dillon lurched forward and fell to the ground.

Six more Marines rushed into the cave and began firing. The terrorists vanished into the darkness of the escape tunnel and the Marines pursued, but a loud explosion rocked them backward. Dust engulfed the cave as the Marines hugged the dirt floor.

As the dust settled, Luther rose to his feet. The tunnel opening no longer existed. "Shit!" he said.

The Marines who had been at the mouth of the cave were uninjured. They rose and dusted themselves off.

"Looks like like they ran into their own trap," one of them laughed.

Luther ran back to Dillon. He turned him over slowly. "You okay, Mr. Dillon?"

Dillon tried to sit up.

"You got shot," Luther said. "You okay?"

"I don't know," Dillon said.

"Let me look at you." Luther checked the Kevlar helmet. Despite the bullet indentation over his taped name, there was no penetration there. He felt the back of Dillon's head and found a bump starting to rise.

"Ouch!" Dillon said as Luther probed with his finger.

"No blood," Luther said happily.

He looked down at Dillon's chest and examined the dent in the Kevlar jacket over Dillon's heart. "You owe Mr. Kevlar a case of Scotch, Mr. Dillon."

☙

Back out on the path, the result of the firefight around Tucker became clear. The remnant of Indonesians threw down their weapons and put their hands over their heads.

Tucker stood. "Cease fire!" The deafening noise subsided as the remaining terrorists were thrown down on their stomachs and their hands placed behind their heads. He held out his hand to his radioman. *Bravo, Bravo, Otter Chief. Island is secure. We have them all. Estimate one hundred fifty dead and fifty prisoners. We have minor casualties. . . ."*

Tucker crossed to the woman and girl and helped them sit up. The woman was in her thirties, slim, tan, and blond. She wore Western khaki clothing; the girl, probably nine years old, wore denim bib shorts and a T-shirt. The woman sat quietly, her short hair framing her face. The girl leaned her head against her mother.

Tucker touched the woman's shoulder. "I'm Colonel Tucker," he said. "Do you speak English? What's your name?"

She looked up at him, tears in her eyes. She was unable to speak. Tucker knelt next to her. "What's your name?" he asked again, gently.

She tried to get her breath. "Are you American?" she asked in an American accent.

"Yes. I'm Colonel Tucker of the United States Marine Corps."

"What are you doing here?" she asked.

"That's what I wanted to ask you," he said. "What's your name?"

She responded almost inaudibly. "Mary Carson."

Tucker waited and watched her. "What are you doing here?" he asked again.

"They brought us here."

"Who?"

"These men," she said, realizing for the first time that she wasn't being watched by the men who had brought her there.

"How long have you been here?"

"Two days."

"Where were you before that?"

"Irian Jaya."

"Where's that?"

She looked up at him and got to her feet. She wiped the tears off her cheeks. "Indonesia. It's one of the eastern islands of Indonesia—the other half of New Guinea."

"How did you get here?"

"Airplane," she said. "A float plane." She squeezed her eyes closed as if resisting horrible memories. "We are missionaries. My husband and I, and our daughter. We've been in Irian Jaya for five years. . . . We're with Wycliffe Bible Translators. We live with the people, learn their language, which isn't usually even written down, then translate the Bible into their language so they can read it. My husband is a Bible translator."

Tucker looked around. "Where is he?"

Her voice cracked. "He was in one of those concrete buildings. He's dead."

"What happened?"

She hesitated. "We had just gotten up . . . for breakfast. They told us to come, and he went back to get his Bible so we could have our morning devotions. This bomb hit it. . . ." Her voice trailed off, then stopped altogether as she looked for something to distract her, to give her an image different from the one that was seared into her mind. "So why are you here?"

"These are the men who attacked an American ship, murdered the crew, and sank their ship just north of Jakarta. We came to get them. Why'd they bring you here?"

She shook her head. "They never told us anything. They just told us to do what they said."

"Did they harm you, did they touch your daughter?"

She shook her head. She turned and looked at her daughter and stroked her face.

Dillon tried to ignore the throbbing headache and the bruise on his chest as he led his group up the path to find Colonel Tucker. Luther was with him. Gordon had stayed behind to have a battle dressing placed on his leg wound by a Navy corpsman who had responded to the radio call from the Marines clearing the tunnel.

"There's the colonel," Luther said.

Dillon looked at Bonham. "You going to make it or should we get Colonel Tucker to come here?"

"No, I'll make it," Bonham said curtly, trying not to slow them down.

Dillon hailed the colonel from twenty-five yards.

Several of the Marines turned to glance at the trio. "Dillon!" Tucker said, walking toward him. "Where the hell have you been?"

"A mortar shell went off right next to us and blew in the side of the hill. There's a big cave there. We fell in."

"What?" Tucker said looking at Luther for confirmation. "Well, what are you . . ."

Dillon put up his hand. "Colonel Tucker, this is Captain Bonham of the *Pacific Flyer*."

Tucker extended his hand, "You're the captain of the ship that got attacked?"

Bonham looked at Tucker and examined the Marines

around him. His face displayed shock and confusion. "What is all this?" Bonham said.

"We came to get you and take care of these assholes," Tucker said. "Are you all right?"

Bonham sighed. "More or less."

Tucker looked around at the Indonesians lying face-down near the edge in the jungle, their hands being tied behind them. "These the men that took your ship?"

"Yeah. The head guy that calls himself Washington was just in the tunnel."

"Did you get him?" Tucker asked Luther.

"No, sir," said Luther. "He took off through an escape tunnel and it blew up on him."

"That's too bad," Tucker said, feigning pity. "Well, Captain Bonham, I think we're about done here. We'll get you back out to the *Wasp* and get you cleaned up. You can write down what's happened to you 'cause I'm sure somebody is going to want to know about it." He suddenly remembered Mary Carson. "Did you know they had a missionary family here as well?"

"No," Bonham said. "They kept me blindfolded mostly. I knew something was going on, but I sure didn't know what."

The group walked toward Mary Carson. "Captain Bonham, this is Mary Carson and her daughter."

"Hi," Bonham said awkwardly.

Mary stood silently.

Tucker, sensing the awkwardness, turned toward Luther. "Corporal Luther, you're relieved from birddogging Mr. Dillon. I'd like you to take care of Mr. Bonham and get him back out to the *Wasp*, next available transportation."

"Yes, sir."

Tucker looked at Bonham, "I'll catch up with you out on the *Wasp*. I'd like to hear all about this."

Bonham scratched his head. He looked around at the hundreds of Marines and the dead Indonesians, unsure what to say.

Dillon's gaze followed Bonham's and for the first time he noticed the dozens of dead men lying within a hundred feet of him, flies around their eyes and their bodies beginning to swell. He fought back a sudden surge of nausea.

Luther led Bonham toward a waiting CH-53E.

Tucker picked up his discussion with the Marine captain. Dillon walked over to Mary Carson. "I'm Jim Dillon," he said, extending his hand.

She took his hand passively. "Hello."

"How did you end up on this island?"

"Missionaries. We were kidnapped from another island." Her face was full of pain.

"I'm sorry to hear that. I think we've taken care of these men, though. They won't be kidnapping anybody else."

She examined his face without speaking.

"You said we, you and your daughter?"

"My husband and my daughter and me."

"Where's your husband?"

"He was killed in the attack. By one of your missiles, I think."

Dillon went slightly pale. "I'm sorry, I didn't know."

Mary's daughter came over to them. Mary put her hand on her shoulder.

"I'm Special Assistant to the Speaker of the House of Representatives."

"How did this happen?" Mary asked.

"How did what happen?"

"This attack. Did the President declare war on Indonesia?" she asked.

"No," Dillon said. He studied her face. He couldn't tell if she was looking for someone to blame or congratulate. "Congress ordered this. I found a power in the Constitution that hadn't been used in a long time, and Congress ordered this battle group to attack."

"This is *your* doing?" Mary asked, tears welling in her eyes.

Dillon felt a huge burden shifting to his shoulders. "I guess so," he said.

Mary took her daughter's hand and turned toward the path to the helicopter.

Dillon watched her go, knowing that nothing he could say would make any difference.

≈

Admiral Billings stared at the display screens in front of him. The Predator showed the image of the woman and child clearly as they spoke with Tucker and Dillon. Tucker had just reported by radio what Mary Carson had told him about her husband. He looked at Beth and saw the deep pity in her eyes for the wife of the missionary. "These things never go like you expect them to go, do they?" he said.

"No, sir, they don't," Beth replied so quietly most couldn't hear her.

"We smoked a missionary. I can read the headlines now."

"No way we could have known that, sir."

"Yes, there is," Billings said, angry. "If we had been in communication with Washington." He looked at her. "I bet *they* knew about it."

"I bet we will find out whether or not they did. And if they did, and didn't tell us, they may have something to answer for."

"There's going to be plenty of answering done by a lot of people in the next few months," Billings declared.

≈

The helicopters cycled back and forth from the clearing, ferrying people back to the *Wasp*. They moved efficiently, taking the wounded Marines first, then the wounded Indonesians, and then Marines with the Indonesian prisoners.

Dillon watched the procession by himself, uninterested in speaking with anyone. After a few minutes, he sat on a fallen tree. Its leaves were green and perfect. Its trunk was intact, except where it had been severed by an explosion. Dillon stared at it. The tree was already dead as a result of the battle; it just didn't know it yet. Dillon sat on the ground and leaned against the fallen tree.

Dillon removed his helmet. His hand unconsciously went to the back of his head to feel the bump that was growing larger by the minute. A corpsman had already pronounced him fit, but told him to get medical attention, including an X ray, when he returned to the *Wasp*.

A Marine sergeant ran up to him. "You're on the next helicopter, sir," he said. As Dillon leaned forward to rise, he felt a searing pain in his chest. He took a deep breath and noticed a pungent, unpleasant smell. Then he realized it came from him. It was more than just a dirty smell from camping, it was sharper, more metallic. He realized he had never been this dirty in his life. He turned his head to the side to take a deep breath of fresh air and walked toward the helicopter.

The marine sentry opened the door and Dillon stepped through into SUPPLOT. Admiral Billings was waiting for him. Dillon had his Marine utilities on; the patch over the pocket read USMC. He hadn't even washed his face. He had come directly from the *Wasp* to the *Constitution*'s helicopter to return to the carrier. Another special trip, not originally on the flight schedule, about which numerous people were bent out of shape. But Dillon was tired of thinking about the burden he was to this operation. He was thinking more about how glad he was to be alive. The Marine closed the door behind him.

Admiral Billings looked up from his lunch. "Well, Mr. Dillon, you made it."

"Yes, sir," Dillon said, reaching for the chin strap to undo his helmet.

Beth Louwsma, who was eating with the admiral, as well as Captain Black and the operations officer, stared at him. "Are you all right?" she asked as she noted the dirt streaks on his face and his obvious fatigue.

"Yeah." Dillon nodded.

Billings watched Dillon. He spoke with laughter in his voice. "Colonel Tucker radioed that you about got your Jimmy shot off."

Dillon removed his helmet. He pointed to the dent left by Washington's bullet, right between the two *m*'s in his name. "Right here," Dillon said.

"You got shot?" Beth asked, incredulous. "You have a cut, by your ear. You're bleeding."

"It's not much." He touched the crusted blood.

Beth looked at Billings. "Can civilians get Purple Hearts?"

Billings smiled. "Don't know. Find out." He looked at Dillon.

Dillon sat down heavily in the leather chair. "It was my first time getting shot."

"What happened?" Beth pursued.

"I'll tell you later," he said, exhaustion oozing from each word.

"Well, Mr. Dillon, do you think we did the right thing?" Billings asked.

Dillon finally sat up. "That's really not for me to say."

Billings looked directly at Dillon. "I think it is for you to say, Mr. Dillon. If you can't form an opinion now, you never will." He pressed him. "Are you doing the political thing of waiting to see all the implications before you decide whether it's 'right' or 'wrong'? We don't have that luxury here. We have to act." He waited for a response from Dillon. "You're not under my command. Let's hear what you have to say."

Dillon rubbed his eyes. "I don't know, Admiral. I thought from the beginning that the right thing to do was to go hammer these guys. Now we've hammered them. I guess the part of it that surprises me is that I always thought it would feel good once you did it, but it doesn't . . ."

"No, Mr. Dillon. Despite the tough rhetoric, killing is killing."

". . . and now that I hear an innocent American missionary got killed by this and I *saw* people get killed . . ." His voice trailed off. "You just wonder if it was all worth it."

"You should always wonder that, Mr. Dillon. We look at everything we do in that same light. *Everything*. But now that you have, what's your conclusion?" He studied Dillon's face and saw the clash of emotions.

"Even knowing what I know now, it was the right thing. I'd do it again."

Billings nodded. "By the way, Mr. Dillon, I've got some bad news for you."

"What?"

"The COD's back up. It should be here in a couple of hours; then you can get out of here."

"That's not bad news," Dillon said, flooded with relief.

"Oh, I figured now that you've done your John Wayne imitation, you'd want to stay here for the rest of the cruise like us."

"Well, Admiral, I'm sure if I were in the Navy, that's exactly what I'd want, but frankly I'd like to get back to Washington. I'm interested to see how all of this plays out."

"So am I. But first, you'd better get down and have the ship's surgeon check you out." Billings glanced around. "Corporal Knight, escort Mr. Dillon to sick bay."

"Aye, aye, sir."

"Chief of Staff, have you gotten a message off to the Joint Chiefs telling them about the action?"

"Yes, sir, long gone."

"Admiral, I think you better look at this!" Beth was looking at the screen with the biggest picture.

"What is it?" the Admiral asked.

"A formation of ships, looks like about eight of them, heading toward us from the northeast."

"There are dozens of ships out there."

"Yes, sir, but the radio chatter indicates these are high-speed contacts."

"What do you mean 'high-speed'? Are they high-speed patrol boats?"

"The E-2 doesn't think so, sir. They're doing over thirty knots."

"Thirty knots? Formation?"

"Yes, sir."

"Get somebody out there to take a look at them."

"Yes, sir. They're on their way right now, but we don't have any report on who they are yet."

Billings listened to the E-2. As he looked at the screen, he noticed the numerous airborne contacts near the Navy formation headed their way.

"What the hell are all those airplanes doing?" Billings asked.

"They're not sure. They're sending fighters to check it out right now."

"How fast are they going?" the admiral asked.

"Six hundred knots plus."

Dillon looked from the admiral to the chief of staff and back to the admiral. They listened as the E-2 directed a section of F-14s toward the oncoming airplanes. There were six of them 150 miles to the northeast.

Billings asked, "Are they squawking mode 4?"

"We can't tell, Admiral. The mode 4 code changeover message was due yesterday. We're out of sequence."

"Great," the admiral said.

They waited and watched as the targets closed on each other. The closure rates of the targets increased to nine hundred knots, then one thousand.

The admiral spoke confidently, "Only one country would fly fighters this far from land. Those are our friends from the *Truman*. Let's see what they have up their sleeves."

▰

On the admiral's bridge aboard the USS *Harry S Truman*, Admiral Blazer examined the message and queried his communications officer. "When was this sent?"

"We just intercepted it about two minutes ago."

He looked at the display in front of him, showing every airplane and ship within three hundred miles. "How close are our fighters to the *Constitution*?"

His operations officer studied the numbers on the screen. "Under two hundred miles."

"Did you see this?" Blazer asked him, handing him the message.

"Yes, sir, I got a copy."

"Looks like we're too late," Blazer said, vacillating between frustration and relief.

"Yes, sir. Their message says it's all over. The rest of the report is to follow, but the result is in."

Blazer stared at the screen. "You think that message was for our benefit?"

His operations officer shrugged and studied the admiral. "I don't know, sir, could be. Admiral Billings probably knew we were coming."

"Our F-14s are one hundred fifty miles out from the *Constitution*, sir," the enlisted intelligence specialist reported as he studied the displays in the dark room identical to the one Billings was sitting in. "The E-2 says the *Constitution* F-14s are outbound and are running intercepts on our fighters."

Admiral Blazer smiled slightly, understanding the irony and difficulty of the situation. "Tell them to let the *Constitution* Tomcats rendezvous on 'em. Tell them to smile and wave. The fight's over down here. The way I see it, our mission is over." He looked around. "Anyone disagree?"

No one said a word.

"Set a course to rendezvous with the *Constitution* Battle Group. Send a message to Washington informing them of our intentions and requesting further instructions."

"Aye, aye, sir."

36

DILLON STOOD ON THE STACK OF *WASHINGTON Posts* in the hallway, fished in his pocket for his key, and unlocked his apartment door. He stumbled into the apartment, dropped his bag on the floor, and kicked the door closed behind him. His answering machine blinked frantically. He bent down and unplugged it. He took off his trench coat, flung it onto a chair in the kitchen, and lay down on the couch in his living room, wincing as he jarred the bump on the back of his head. He turned reluctantly onto his side. He lay there for five minutes without moving, trying to think about the last few days, but his brain refused to replay the tape. It was a blur, like an auto accident in which he had been a passenger.

He swung his legs over the edge of the couch and sat up, rubbing his face. He knew he should try to sleep, but while his body was exhausted, his mind wasn't. He grabbed his portable phone and dialed the Speaker's private residential number. The Speaker's wife answered the phone.

"Mrs. Stanbridge, Jim Dillon."

"Jim, how are you? Where are you?" Her voice was perpetually pleasant even when announcing natural disaster or political reversal.

"I'm back. I'm in my apartment. I feel like I fell out of an airplane, but I'm here."

"Hold on. I'm sure that John wants to talk to you."

I'm sure he'd like nothing better, Dillon thought, especially now that he knows how many Americans died. . . .

"Jim, you're back!"

"Yes, Mr. Speaker. Sorry it took me longer than I expected, but the airplane . . ."

"It doesn't matter at all. You didn't miss a thing."

Very funny. "I've got to tell you, Mr. Speaker, from over there, it looked like . . . well, like a zoo."

Stanbridge laughed gruffly, "It looked like a zoo because it *was* a zoo."

"Yes, sir. It sure was. Things weren't exactly routine on the Java Sea either."

"Yes, I know. Somebody at the Pentagon leaked the gist of the report to the press, basically saying we killed an American missionary, killed a bunch of terrorists, and killed a bunch of Americans. Not presented very flatteringly."

"What do you think the spin on this whole thing is going to be?" Dillon asked.

"Hard to say. Unless we get your story out ASAP, telling exactly what happened and how our men saved the captain of the *Flyer*, took care of those terrorists, and rescued a missionary, the President is going to have the high ground." The Speaker hesitated, not sure when to say it, but knowing it had to be said. "I want you to have a press conference tomorrow afternoon to tell our side."

Dillon felt a chill. "What do you mean, *our* side?"

"The side that proves it was the correct decision. You know how this works, Jim. Everything can be presented to look good or bad. *Everything.* They've got their side out—making the Navy look stupid—and me, by the way—and now you've got to put out what really happened."

"I don't know. It may have been classified," he said, not knowing whether to tell the Speaker he had actually gone ashore.

"Oh, nonsense," the Speaker replied. "As soon as I

heard you were inbound, I set a press conference for tomorrow afternoon at four P.M. Do you think you can make it?''

Dillon grimaced. Hard to avoid something the Speaker had set up already, just for you. ''Yes, sir, but tomorrow is Tuesday. I wanted to go to that Supreme Court hearing.''

''You'd *better* be there. Grazio said he's going to camp out all night or do whatever it takes to get a seat and he is going to save you one. The hearing is at seven o'clock A.M. I want you to be there. It should be fun.''

''Yes, sir, I wouldn't miss this for anything.''

Dillon's body was out of sync with day and night, and his hygiene was out of sync with clean and dirty. He had lost weight on his quick trip to the Southern Pacific but still wasn't hungry. He dressed in his best suit and put on a crisply starched white shirt and a navy blue tie with small gold diamonds. This would be practically the first day he walked out the door without a briefcase full of papers since he moved to Georgetown.

As he was leaving he again noticed the stack of *Post*s. He hauled them inside and took off the top one. Bold black letters in an unusually large headline read: ROGUE CONGRESS? SUPREME COURT TO HEAR THIS MORNING. Dillon scanned the other front page stories. Below the fold were various stories on the Letter of Reprisal, the actions of the battle group, Admiral Billings, and the Indonesian terrorists. He put down that day's paper and quickly scanned the front pages for each of the days he had been gone: ''ROGUE CARRIER F-14S SHOOT DOWN TWO INDONE- SIAN F-16S, INDONESIA SAYS.'' ''MARINES STORM ASHORE ON INDONESIAN LAND WITHOUT PERMISSION.'' ''19 MA- RINES DEAD IN ATTACK ON ISLAMIC FUNDAMENTALISTS PRIVATE ISLAND.'' The word of the week seemed to be *rogue*. A *rogue* battle group, a *rogue* admiral, a *rogue* Congress—*rogue*, occasionally interspersed with *rene-*

gade. The *Post* must not approve. Otherwise it would use words like *bold,* or *courageous.* He folded the papers and threw them back on the floor.

He walked out the door, locking it behind him. He rode the Metro to Union Station, the station nearest the Supreme Court, and walked the rest of the distance. It was just becoming light. Six o'clock in the morning, but he still hadn't beaten a large crowd to the steps. The camera crews were already set up; the journalists were poised, looking for someone they recognized.

He pulled up the collar of his blue wool overcoat to partially conceal his face without looking as if he were hiding. He made it into the courtroom with very little opposition. He was surprised, though, that virtually all the seats in the gallery were already taken. The clerk had opened the doors at 5:30 and journalists and other interested people had poured in. He saw Grazio sitting midway down the left side. Grazio saw Dillon at the same time and his face lit up. He waved at Dillon, who quickly made his way to the chair Grazio had saved for him.

"Hey!" Grazio said, lifting his hand to receive a high five. Dillon slapped his hand. "You made it!"

"Of course I made it. I wouldn't miss this for anything."

"No, I mean you made it back from the big war."

"Yeah, a big war. Fifteen hundred Marines against two hundred terrorists."

"Yeah, but they were *bad* terrorists. And most important, we kicked some ass."

Dillon was not particularly big on bragging about the operation right now. He could tell that a few journalists had recognized him, but he quickly glanced away so they wouldn't be encouraged.

Grazio was bouncing his legs up and down. He prodded Dillon. "So what was it like?"

"What was what like?"

"The carrier, the war, the whole thing?"

"It was pretty amazing." Dillon shrugged, trying to

downplay the strike. "I saw a lot I never thought I'd see."

"That must have been really cool," Grazio said enviously.

"It was pretty cool, but then you realize that real people were getting killed and suddenly it brings it . . ."

"Yeah, but they *deserved* it," Grazio said.

"Yeah, well, nineteen Marines got killed too."

"Yeah. I heard. What happened? They got a helicopter shot down?"

"Yeah, shoulder-fired surface-to-air missiles."

"Where did those guys get all those weapons? South African surface-to-air missiles? Silkworm anti-ship missiles? Shoulder-fired missiles? What is *that?*"

"It's unbelievable. One of the dead guys was Chinese," Dillon said. "He was their expert arms acquisitions guy. He knew every arms merchant in the world apparently."

"I guess he did," Grazio said. "What exactly did they have in mind?"

Dillon thought about it. "I think this is the new terrorist," he said. "Terrorists for money and power, not political gain. The scary part is, they fake the political agenda so they can use other people."

"So why go after an American ship? That's kind of stupid, isn't it?"

"Maybe, maybe not. If they'd pulled off the bit about the Islamic terrorists, maybe they really could have gotten an Islamic movement going in Indonesia and forced the U.S. out of there. We're the only ones who might actually go down there and try to clean out the terrorists—actually do something about it. So they insult us and try to get us to go home."

"I don't know. I don't think they thought that one out very well."

"They would have pulled it off, except for the—"

"Hey, that reminds me," Grazio interrupted. "When we leave, check out the Capitol building."

"What are you talking about?"

"Just do it. Think high," he said cryptically. Grazio continued to scan the audience for anyone he knew. "Hey, check it out. Here comes the big man."

Dillon turned around to see the Speaker and his wife enter the room. One of the Court officials escorted them to the front row immediately behind the bar and indicated two seats by the aisle. Dillon looked at Grazio. "What's he doing here?"

"Why wouldn't he be?"

Dillon shrugged uncomfortably. "I don't know. I talked to him last night and told him I was coming; he didn't mention he was."

"Guess who else is . . ."

President Manchester strode purposefully from the back of the courtroom escorted by Secret Service agents and his wife. Another Court official indicated the front row on the right as his group walked and took their seats.

"*Manchester,*" Dillon breathed.

"Holy shit. This is going to be good," Grazio said excitedly. "I'll bet it's never happened before. I'll bet the Speaker of the House and President have *never* attended an argument before the Supreme Court."

"This is incredible."

"Notice how the Speaker is sitting on one side and Manchester is sitting on the other," Grazio said with a smirk. "It's kinda like friends of the groom, or friends of the bride. I could sure tell you which one of those guys is wearing the dress. . . . Hey, don't look now . . . Molly's here, looking for a seat."

"So let her look; she can sit wherever she wants."

Grazio disagreed. "Nope, the seats are all gone. Tell you what, she can sit on my lap." He looked sideways at Dillon.

Dillon stared straight ahead without saying anything.

Grazio stood up. "Molly! Over here."

Molly walked toward him until she saw Dillon. She stopped.

Grazio motioned for her to come over.

"We don't have any room," Dillon said softly.

"She can sit on half of each of our chairs, right between us."

Dillon looked straight ahead again, trying to decide what to do and what to say.

Molly said, "Excuse me," and stepped across his right leg, then his left leg. The back of her thighs rubbed against his knees and he looked up at her. He knew it was a mistake as soon as he did it. He saw her hair bouncing against her shoulders and he could smell her perfume. Grazio moved over, giving Molly about six inches between them. Dillon slid over to his right. The person next to him gave him a dirty look.

Molly squeezed uncomfortably between the two of them. "How have you been, Frank?" Molly asked, shaking his hand.

"Primo," Grazio said in reply.

"Hi, Molly," Dillon said.

"Hello, Jim."

The three sat there in silence and stared at the Supreme Court justices' leather chairs. But the chairs could stand only so much examination. After a while, Dillon and Molly had to look at something else. She turned and looked Jim in the eye. He tried not to look at her, but was unable to stop himself. He tried to read her gaze. There was no anger, no hostility.

The back doors to the courtroom opened and David Pendleton and Jackson Gray walked in together. Each indicated for the other to go through the bar first. David held the railing open for Gray and followed him through. Pendleton looked ice-cold. Gray looked angry and frustrated, but hopeful.

Dillon looked for Pendleton's associate, but no one was with him. He had nothing with him: no briefcase, no papers, no notes, nothing. That's probably a first, Dillon said to himself.

Gray pulled out two large black three-ring binders and set them on the counsel table. He then pulled out a smaller black notebook which probably had his notes for his argument and opened it in front of him. I'll bet he's been reviewing it all night, thought Dillon.

Pendleton sat on the edge of his chair with his back straight and his hands folded on the table in front of him. He didn't look to the left or the right, nor did he review anything.

Dillon let his leg rest against Molly's as he watched Pendleton.

The conversation in the gallery died down as the minute hand rose. Finally, at exactly 7:00 A.M., the nine Supreme Court justices walked through the large curtains in the middle of the room behind the Chief Justice's chair. The clerk of the Court preceded them. "All rise," he said.

37

ADMIRAL RAY BILLINGS SAT ON THE ADMIRAL'S bridge and watched the flight operations on the deck beneath him. Two F/A-18Cs sat on the bow catapults ready to take off as the arresting-gear crew prepared the flight deck for the last daylight recovery of the long flight schedule. Airplanes circled the carrier in sections at their designated altitudes. Billings watched the fighters enviously and thought of the hundreds of times he had flown that circle. The air was clear in spite of the high humidity. Visibility was excellent and the sea sparkled with a silver blueness.

Billings's communications officer handed him a clip board stacked with messages. Commander Beth Louwsma stood next to the admiral and read the messages over his shoulder. "Nice to be back up on the message circulation list," she said absently.

"Yeah," the admiral said, "except now we have to read them."

"Yes, sir, the burdens of leadership."

"Had a chance to interrogate the prisoners yet?"

"We aren't really interrogating them, sir," she said facetiously. "We're interviewing them, checking for spies and the like."

"Of course."

"One of our cryptologists speaks Indonesian, Thai, and Malay."

"Excellent. Get anything?"

Her eyes narrowed slightly, the subtle indication she was moving to a higher level of mental activity. "It's very interesting. They seem to want to perpetuate this idea that they are Islamic fundamentalists, yet they aren't Islamic at all. At least not in any serious way. We found all kinds of drugs and alcohol on these guys and not a Koran in the bunch."

The admiral's eyes sparkled. "What else?"

"Seems they had big ideas. We've gotten one of the lower-level guys to sing. All the leaders are mum, but this one guy—we promised him immunity''—she looked at him questioningly but didn't see any response—"was ready to talk. They had set up this island which they hoped to build into a fortress. They were going to put in surface-to-air missiles and surface-to-surface missiles from about any country you can name. Their idea was to take their speedboats out into the strait of Malacca and threaten the ships that went by. If the ships agreed to pay extortion money, they'd let them go; if they didn't, they'd either take the ship or sink it with one of their missiles."

"I get that, but what I don't get is why they started off by attacking a U.S. ship. Did they really think we wouldn't do anything about it?"

"That's *exactly* what they thought," Beth said. "If they did the terrorist bit, the U.S. would be forced to withdraw from the Java Sea. We wouldn't come back here very often because Indonesia wouldn't want the U.S. Navy stirring up their Islamic fundamentalists. It was actually a pretty good plan."

"I believe that is called a miscalculation."

"I don't know," Beth said, "seems they knew our President better than we did."

The admiral glanced up at her.

She went on. "If Congress hadn't passed the Letter of Reprisal, they would have pulled it off completely. I don't think Indonesia would have been able to touch them."

"Sure they could have. They have a large enough air force to take these guys out."

"They'd have to find them first. We never would have found these guys if our submarine hadn't followed them."

"That's true enough."

"Admiral," Reynolds said from the other side of the bridge, "Admiral Blazer is on the radio; he wants to talk to you directly."

The admiral walked to the radio receiver. He looked at his aide. "Is it secure?"

"Yes, sir."

"Admiral Billings here."

"Ray!" said a deep booming voice, which everyone on the bridge could hear over the loudspeaker.

"Blazer, you lunatic, what's going on?" Billings asked, smiling.

"You read your message board this afternoon?"

"I'm working through it now. They cut me off for several days, so I'm playing catch-up."

"I don't think you knew I was sent down here to 'intercept' you."

"And what did that mean?"

"Nobody ever told me. But unfortunately, when we got here, all the fun was over. Hell, I'd probably have been tempted to join you. Did you get the recent message from the White House?"

"Negative. What does it say?"

"It says that you and the entire battle group are to report immediately to Pearl Harbor."

"Roger that. Hurt me. Send me to Paradise. You call me just to tell me that?"

"No. The interesting part is that I have been told to escort you."

Admiral Billings's neck reddened. *"Escort? For what?"*

"Don't know. Just said to escort you back to Pearl." Blazer's tone was enigmatic. Billings saw that all those

on the bridge had heard Blazer. *"Well,"* he said, *"how about that?"*

"So," Blazer continued more enthusiastically. *"Consider yourself under escort."*

"Escort aye," Billings said, trying to sound chipper. *"What do you want me to do?"*

"Think you could helicopter over here for dinner tonight? Maybe we could play some ace deuce."

"Not a problem."

"1800 okay?"

"Perfect."

"Okay. See you tonight." Blazer signed off.

Billings put the receiver back and returned to his chair. He stared ahead of the ship as it plowed through the beautiful blue ocean, northeast toward Hawaii. He looked at Beth, who avoided his gaze. "Sounds like a setup. I don't think they're telling us everything."

Reynolds spoke first after the awkward silence, "Hard to say, sir. Maybe they're going to put you in for a medal," he said without conviction.

"We'll see."

"I mean," Reynolds continued, trying to comfort him, "they should . . ." His voice trailed off.

Beth spoke. "Admiral, you did the right thing."

Billings looked at her with warmth. "Whatever comes of this, it was worth it, Beth."

"Yes, Admiral, it was."

❧

"Oyez, oyez, oyez. All persons having business before the honorable, the Supreme Court of the United States are admonished to draw near and give their attention for the Court is now sitting. God save the United States and this honorable Court. You may be seated." Silence filled the room. You could hear the wheels of the chairs on the wooden floor and the squeak of the leather as the justices sat down. The Supreme Court clerks sat to the right near a large marble pillar. Bobby was in front. He looked at

Dillon and Molly, who both smiled a friendly greeting. Bobby turned away.

The Chief Justice wasted no time. He looked over his reading glasses at the attorneys. "Call the calendar," he said to the clerk.

David Compton, the clerk to whom Pendleton could now assign a face, read loudly, in his court voice, "Number one on the special calendar, Edward Manchester, as a citizen of the United States and as President and Chief Executive Officer of the United States versus John Stanbridge as an individual, and as Speaker of the House of Representatives of the United States of America, et al. Please state your appearances."

"Good morning, Your Honors. Jackson Gray on behalf of the United States . . ."

"I'm afraid you are going to have to be more precise," David Ross said with a very serious face.

Gray looked at him. "Yes, sir. Jackson Gray on behalf of the Justice Department, representing the President and the Executive Branch."

Pendleton paused until he had the attention of all the justices. "David Pendleton on behalf of Mr. Stanbridge and the Congress, Your Honors."

"Thank you," Ross said. "Please be seated." Ross looked at the papers in front of him and then at Gray. "I believe this is your application, Mr. Gray."

"Yes, sir, thank you. May it please the Court," he said, then, nodding to Pendleton, "Counsel." He paused and took a deep breath. "We have reached a time where the Supreme Court must act, or risk the government falling." The gallery gasped audibly, but it was unclear to Dillon—who hadn't gasped—whether the gasps were due to the gravity of the situation or the audacity of Gray's statement. Gray continued, "Congress directed a Navy battle group that is wreaking havoc on citizens of foreign countries—and those of our country, I might add—without the authority of the President or the Executive Branch. All because the House of Representatives and the Senate adopted a Letter of Reprisal in a way that has never been done in history, and has used it as its own tool, *defrauding* the citizens of the United States. They have put forth disingenuous arguments based on history—''

Ross interrupted Gray. ''Mr. Gray, am I correct in noticing, and I do hereby take judicial notice, that the attack you are attempting to preclude by this stay, to which you refer to in your application papers, has already occurred?''

Gray pulled back visibly, as if he had been hit in the chest. ''There has been one attack, yes, sir.''

Ross continued, ''From the way I read your papers, that is the attack you were trying to prevent by this emergency application. Is that correct or not?''

''It is correct, Your Honor,'' Gray said as if talking to someone who wasn't completely clued in, ''that we were trying to stop that attack, but we also want to stop any *subsequent* attacks. We want to prevent this battle group from rampaging through the South Pacific at the whim of Congress.''

Dillon watched the back of the Speaker's neck, which had turned noticeably red.

Ross's face took on a sour, displeased expression. ''On what do you base your fear that the battle group is intending to do anything other than what it has already done? There is no evidence before this court that anything else is likely to happen.''

''On its past behavior, Your Honor. It has directly disobeyed orders of the President of the United States, and we have no indication yet that it doesn't intend to keep doing just that.''

''Well, that may be, but the question is whether you think any such disobedience or lack of control will be based on this Letter of Reprisal on which you have based your application. Will you be bringing actions against all battle groups, or only those to whom a Letter of Reprisal has been issued?''

Dillon grinned involuntarily. He had always thought of Ross as President Manchester's pawn, appointed to the position of Chief Justice of the United States from the Supreme Court of Connecticut, where he had served for ten years and where Manchester had met him. His appointment had caught the Court watchers off guard. He was unknown. Considered a moderate Democrat, he had graduated from Boston College Law School after college at Amherst. But no one knew what he stood for. His opinions were unremarkable in Connecticut. Most thought he would be Manchester's man on the Court. Apparently not, Dillon thought, as he watched Ross's face and Gray's back.

Gray answered, "The Letter is a factor, and we want that factor to be removed as a reason or grounds or justification for *any* action."

Ross said, "Before you go on, Mr. Gray, I would like to hear from Mr. Pendleton on this point. Mr. Pendleton."

Pendleton stood up. "Your Honors, whether the President can control the Navy under normal circumstances is a question that one might ponder on any given day. Why does the military obey the President?" He paused for effect. "Because of the direct constitutional authority of the President. This application is about whether the Letter of Reprisal should be stopped immediately by this Court." He shook his head gravely. "That was impossible even when this misguided action was filed in the District Court—Congress had already passed it. The only entity that could be enjoined was the Navy, and the Navy was not before the Court. But more important, as the Court properly points out, this action is moot. The only action that the President was attempting to forestall has already occurred. For the Court to issue an order now would be a meaningless gesture. It does not benefit the reputation of this Court to issue orders on matters that have already occurred. This Court was not appointed to issue futile orders." Pendleton let his voice travel off. "Thank you."

Gray, still standing, began again, "Mr. Pendleton continues to divert the Court's attention from the real issue—"

The Chief Justice raised his hand. "Mr. Gray, we were

willing to hear this issue at this early hour because it seemed to us an issue of critical importance. However, it is now out of our hands. The actions you were attempting to forestall have occurred. The application for stay is denied. The application is moot. The matter is remanded to the District Court for consideration on the merits.''

''Thank you, sir,'' said Pendleton, standing to go, a subtle way to encourage the Court not to change its mind.

Gray stood dumbfounded. He tried to hold his tongue. He was seething inside, angry at a system that waited too long to hear something and then refused relief, claiming it was too late. He forced himself to nod at the justices as they rose from their chairs. Then he couldn't contain himself, ''But *you're* the ones who decided not to hear this until today. This was in your hands Friday night. This *Court* has *made* it futile!''

Justice Ross ignored him. ''Court is adjourned.''

''All rise,'' Compton said as the justices prepared to leave the room.

Gray stared after them. He finished putting his notebooks away and, without saying a word to Pendleton, walked out of the courtroom. He avoided Manchester's gaze, refused to speak to any of the reporters in the gallery, and left the building. Pendleton lingered behind the bar and surveyed the room, which was in pandemonium. Several journalists fought to get out the door, and others fought to stay to savor the historic moment.

Dillon worked his way to the end of the aisle and then up through the crowd to David Pendleton. Molly followed and turned right to head out the door. Grazio stood at the end of the aisle watching Dillon. Dillon went through the bar and extended his hand to Pendleton. ''Good morning, sir. Jim Dillon. I don't know if you remember me . . .''

''Of course.'' Pendleton took his hand. ''You're the one who started all this.'' Pendleton looked at the crowd and realized he'd have to wait to have any hope of leaving. ''It was your idea, wasn't it?''

Dillon was unsure what to say. "You think it was a bad idea?"

Pendleton shrugged. "It was a high-wire act without a net." He looked into Dillon's eyes with a superior air. "Our government may *look* strong, but it really isn't. Our government is a set of *ideas,* not buildings or people. Its continuity depends entirely on the respect people give it. Congress and the President, the Court, are like banks. If people lose faith, the banks fail." His eyes glowed. "But there's no Federal Stability Insurance. There isn't anything that guarantees the government will still be around if people lose faith. If you push too hard, the structure could come crumbling down, even if you're right. It was a fun ride though, and I'm glad I helped John Stanbridge."

Dillon didn't know what to say. "You don't think the Speaker should have done it?"

"What do you think?" Pendleton asked. "Knowing all that you know now, seeing everything that has happened because of it, what do *you* think?"

Dillon looked around the emptying room, at the Speaker, who was being congratulated by many, and President Manchester, who was standing surrounded by Secret Service agents. Dillon thought of Admiral Billings, and Reynolds, Caskey and Drunk, Colonel Tucker and Lieutenant Armstrong, all the people who put their lives on the line. But mostly he thought of Captain Bonham's swollen face and the dead Marines in the burning helicopter, and Mary, and her daughter, and her dead missionary husband. "Yes, I would still do it," Dillon said finally. He squinted at Pendleton, bolder than usual. "And I think you're wrong about the government. It isn't fragile at all. It is built on *eternal* principles. It is the *people* who are weak and fragile."

Pendleton listened carefully. "Perhaps," he said.

Dillon turned toward the rail. The observers in front of him were still backed up. He pushed the small gate open.

Grazio was waiting for him. "So. Got to shake hands with the big guy, huh?"

Dillon kept walking.

"What's with you? You've been weird all morning. What's eating you?"

"Nothing, I just thought he'd be excited about his great victory. He didn't care at all."

"Not care? That could be one of the biggest arguments in the history of the Supreme Court!"

"I don't know," he said, as they shuffled forward at the end of the bulge of people waiting to get out. "He just doesn't seem to have any passion." Dillon suddenly looked up. "Where did Molly go?"

"I don't know. When you went to the end of the aisle, she headed out of here like a bullet."

"I've got to talk to her."

"Aren't you going to come to the office?"

"Yeah, as soon as I talk to her."

"Well, you better hurry," Grazio said as Dillon started hurrying forward.

"Excuse me!" Dillon said loudly, pushing his way through the crowd and out the hallway of the Supreme Court building.

A couple of journalists recognized him, but he was past them too quickly for an interview. Journalists stood throughout the hallway with cellular phones jammed to their ears; television reporters had their lights on and cameras rolling. Dillon knew how to look unimportant. He broke out into the bright sunshine in the cold February morning. He saw Molly at the bottom of the steps with her collar turned up as she turned and headed toward the Metro station. He ran down the steps and yelled her name.

In the courtroom the crowd thinned, except for those with Stanbridge and Manchester.

President Manchester walked over to the Speaker.

"Can I have a word with you?" he asked in a fairly loud voice.

John Stanbridge turned and looked into Manchester's eyes. "Certainly, where?"

"Here." Manchester turned to the Secret Service agent next to him. "I want to have a talk with the Speaker, here in private. Would you clear the room?"

The Secret Service agent said in a controlled yet commanding voice, "Would everyone clear the room, please, immediately." A dozen or so remaining people were escorted quickly to the enormous double doors, which were closed behind them. Secret Service agents guarded each entrance, yet stood back far enough that they could not overhear the conversation.

Manchester and Stanbridge looked at each other from three feet apart. Manchester began. "This has been a very . . . unfortunate series of events for this country." He waited to see if Stanbridge was going to respond. Stanbridge simply waited. "You and I have an obligation to do what is best for the country. Do you agree?"

"Absolutely," Stanbridge said.

"I hope that you noted that the Supreme Court did not decide the issue. It is still open. It now goes back to the District Court, where they may in fact determine that this entire Letter of Reprisal is unconstitutional."

Stanbridge spoke with confidence. "Mr. President, I'm sure you've read the cases. You know how these things go. The courts do everything in their power to avoid deciding political issues, questions of the balance of power between Congress and the President. They'll never touch it. Since the Supreme Court has already decided it's moot, I'm sure the District Court will do likewise. Mr. Pendleton has given me great confidence that this decision by the Chief Justice—whom you appointed—will end it." Stanbridge's eyes lit up with the irony of Justice Ross being the executioner of the President's lawsuit. "Your lawsuit was simply a bad idea."

"I think your Letter of Reprisal was a bad idea, Mr.

Speaker. I think you took great risks with the structure of our government and may have caused substantial damage. . . .''

"No, Mr. President, you're the one who was damaging the reputation of the presidency and causing the legislative branch of the government to take steps it would not normally need to take if you simply did your job." He pointed at Manchester for emphasis. "A long time ago you assumed that I was prepared to exercise the War Powers Act to stop you. Nothing could have been further from the truth. You had to comply with it, sure, but I wanted you to go down and take care of this, Mr. President. When you *refused,* I had to do your job for you. The Constitution gave me the tool, and I used it. You don't have to worry about me, if you'd just do your job. And just last evening I received a fax that *you* should have received. It was from the President of Indonesia, thanking me for taking the action we did."

"I didn't refuse to do my job, I just did it differently from the way you wanted. It is when you're trying to do my job that you are the most dangerous, Mr. Speaker, because you lack *judgment,* you lack proportion, and worst, you are driven by ambition. It's not right or wrong that makes your decisions, it's your *lust for my job.*"

"All politicians want to be the top dog," Stanbridge responded.

"But only one can have it," Manchester replied, "and you're not the one."

"Not yet," Stanbridge said. "Is there anything else?"

"Yes, one other thing. My real reason for stopping you," the President said with intensity in his voice. "Public opinion is against you. Too much death was caused by your wild scheme. You've lost in the arena of public opinion, and that could be fatal to you—" Manchester held up his hand, seeing Stanbridge starting to interrupt. "Hold on, let me finish." He paused, then spoke quietly. "I admit we have both sustained political damage to a degree each of us can determine on his own." He sighed.

"But what the country needs now, more than anything, is peace between our two branches of government. They cannot take any more fighting within the government." He looked straight at Stanbridge. "Can we go outside, in front of this building, right now, and tell the world that we will work together? That even though we have our differences, we will work within the structures of the government to solve them?"

Stanbridge smiled wryly. "Mr. President, that is *exactly* what I have been doing the entire time."

"Then agreeing to keep doing it should be of no great moment," Manchester said with the hint of a victory smile. "Can we shake hands, in front of all out there?"

"I'm still going to get your job."

"Take your best shot."

"One thing I need to know."

Manchester waited.

"Your Chief of Staff mentioned a fax. Financing concerns . . ."

Manchester dismissed the concern. "It never went out. It didn't feel right."

Stanbridge looked around the courtroom. "Go ahead and hold a press conference. Tell them we're going to work together." He paused. "But I'll have my own press conference later in the day. If I don't like what you've said, you're going to hear about it." He walked down the aisle and the Secret Service agents opened the large doors for him.

🏴

"Molly!" Dillon yelled so loudly that it scared him. "Molly!" he hollered as he reached the bottom of the massive marble steps in front of the Supreme Court building. She kept walking, picking up her pace. He ran down the sidewalk. His coat opened to the wind and flapped against his arms as he ran faster and caught up with her.

He grabbed her arm. "Molly!" he said breathless.

She stopped and turned, examined his face. "I guess that's the ruling you wanted," she said.

He fought to catch his breath. "Yeah, I think it was the right result."

"Now it's going back to the District Court. They may still find it unconstitutional."

Dillon tried to suppress a smile. "Yeah, I guess that could happen."

Molly turned toward the station. "Molly, please, I want to talk to you."

"What about?" she asked.

"I'm going to make this really easy for you. If you don't ever want to see me again because of everything that's happened, if my working for the Speaker of the House somehow makes me a bad person, then say so now. This is your chance. If you want me to get lost, say so."

She looked down at the sidewalk then into his eyes, "This whole . . . thing, the way Congress went out and ordered the Navy to go attack those people. It just seems so vindictive. So cold-blooded." She took her hands out of her pockets. "And the contortions you had to go through to claim authority to do it—I don't know; it just seems dishonest."

"It wasn't," Dillon said. "Anybody who says anything different from what you or the President believes is evil or wrong or dishonest?"

She looked at him coolly. "A lot of people died, Jim."

"Manchester *owed* it to the country to do something about it and he didn't. The fact that Congress did instead doesn't make it wrong."

"It isn't that simple," she said.

Dillon glanced over her shoulder at the Capitol building and the dome against the clear blue sky. Then he saw it. The same flag that was flying over the USS *Constitution* was flying over the Capitol. "Don't Tread on Me." He tried not to stare.

"Do you think Congress can do this anytime they feel like it?" Molly went on.

"Actually, I think they ought to do it a lot more often. I think the way we've done our little private wars through the CIA or the Contras or Surrogates, or anybody else that you can name, *that's* what's dishonest, Molly," he said, jamming his hands into his coat pockets. "For this country to be out there fighting and killing people and pretending like we aren't, for Congress *not* to be involved and to be able to wash their hands of it by saying, 'Well, it's all the President's doing,' *that's* dishonest. The power of going to war is given to Congress. *Not* the President. The idea of the President sending a bunch of troops overseas without Congress's approval and then arguing about the silly War Powers Act, *that's* dishonest. . . ."

Molly stood quietly. "But that attack, it felt wrong."

"That's because a Letter of Reprisal has never been done like this before. How do you think Congress felt when Truman sent troops under the UN to Korea? How do you think Congress felt when Kennedy, then Johnson, sent troops to Vietnam without a declaration of war? *Thousands* of Americans died. Where was Congress then? Why doesn't that feel wrong?"

Molly relaxed slightly. She searched Dillon's face. "I don't want to argue about it anymore. But I've got to know something."

"What?"

"You were there on the carrier," she said, noticing his involuntary wince. "We may disagree on whether it was right or now, whether it was legal, but did it feel good? Are you *glad?*"

Dillon closed his eyes momentarily to slow the watering from the cold. "It's funny, Admiral Billings asked me the same thing. Sort of. That's what surprised me. This wasn't really much of a war, and it got to me. I saw it personally, Molly. I went ashore with the Marines. I saw people get killed. I saw the head terrorist and he shot me twice." He could see the surprise on her face. "Hit my helmet and flak jacket. I only got bruises and a small cut," he said touching a half-inch scab by his ear. "And after

I got back to the carrier, I thought it would be like winning a football game, where everyone comes to their feet and cheers and claps. It's not like that at all. It's not a sport. So, no, I guess I'm not *glad*. It doesn't make me happy. It's made me, I don't know, different. I think I'd take it more seriously now than I ever would have before." He looked around at the President's motorcade pulling up. "But it was still the right thing to do."

Molly stepped closer to Dillon until they were nearly touching, her forehead just inches from his eyes. He could feel her warmth.

He studied her creamy complexion with the hint of freckles. "I still want a chance to be with you, Molly."

Molly pulled the windblown hair out of her mouth and looked up into his blue eyes, eyes set with determination but softened by integrity. "We'd have to work at it."

"I'm willing," Dillon replied.

Molly smiled. The warmest smile he had seen in a long time. "You're always willing."

"True enough. So what do you say?"

She hesitated. "I need to let this all settle in." She began to turn, then looked up at him. "When it does, I'll call you."

Dillon watched her walk away. He turned and walked toward the steps of the Supreme Court.

The Speaker stood at the bottom of the steps leading to the Supreme Court and watched President Manchester gather the press corps around him for his impromptu press conference.

Dillon walked over and stood next to Stanbridge, who glanced at him. The Speaker blew on his bare hands to warm them, then spoke to Dillon while they both watched Manchester.

"He's telling them all's well with the American government. We're all going to work together."

Dillon watched Manchester. "Are we?" he replied.

"Of course." Stanbridge smiled. "Just like always."

Acknowledgments

MANY PEOPLE HAVE HELPED IMMENSELY IN THE PREP-
aration of this book. I want to take this opportunity to
thank them for their help, support, and encouragement. I
want to thank my small cadre of loyal readers who have
read my writing for years with a critical eye and a supporting arm: Don Chartrand, Natalie Venezia, Mark
Hamer, and Dan Wien. I also want to thank Robin Ellis,
who helped me type the original manuscript.

I received technical assistance from several people
whose knowledge was invaluable: Chief Warrant Officer
G. Mike Johnson, U.S. Navy SEAL; former Clerk to the
Chief Justice of the United States and former Associate
White House Counsel, W. Neil Eggleston; Krister Holla-
day, Legislative Director for Congressman Newt Gin-
grich, Speaker of the House; and Commander Steven
Litwiller, USN.

I am especially grateful to my agent and friend, David
Gernert, who was willing to take a chance with an un-
known author. I am also grateful to his assistants, Matt
Williams and Amy Williams.

I want to thank my editor, Paul Bresnick, who has
shown enthusiasm and patience and taught me much in
the process of getting this book to print. I am also greatly
indebted to Paul Fedorko, the publisher of William Mor-

row, whose enthusiasm and support is far beyond what I could have ever hoped for from a publisher.

It is impossible to express with words my gratitude and appreciation to my wife, Dianna, who encouraged me and helped me through the long nights. I am also grateful to my children for their support and willingness to give up some of their time with me to allow me to complete this book.

I want to also express my infinite debt to my father, James A. Huston, author, mentor, and inspiration.

Above all, I thank God Almighty, the ultimate creator of everything.

—JAMES W. HUSTON

*Please turn the page
for an early look at*

THE PRICE OF POWER
by James W. Huston

*Available in hardcover from
William Morrow and Company*

THE BLACK CIGARETTE BOATS WERE BARELY DISCERN-
ible in the darkness. The low rumble of each boat's idling
engine merged with the other three as they drifted closer
together. The sea was unusually calm for a hot South Pacific night. The moon was just breaking over the horizon
and threw vague shadows on the water as the boats glided
toward the northwestern shore of Irian Jaya. A small Indonesian man in black clothing guided the lead boat under
a large tree and threw the engine into reverse to slow the
boat's momentum. As the boat nudged the shore another
man lowered himself over the side into waist-deep water
and strode up the bank with a line attached to the bow.
He wrapped the line around one of the massive trees ten
feet up from the shore. The other boats followed suit. The
engines fell silent and the boats bobbed along separated
only by black rubber bumpers. Without a sound, men
moved carefully but quickly to the bow of each boat and
let themselves down into the water. Each carried an assault rifle and a backpack. Each wore the same black
clothing. Their darkened faces were invisible.

When they had all gone ashore, the thirty men stood
around their leader in a clearing. He reviewed their instructions quietly. They nodded their understanding. They
checked their rifles and backpacks. When the leader was
satisfied, they squatted on their heels under the jungle canopy and waited. The leader looked at his watch several

times. Finally, after fifteen minutes, a half-naked figure emerged from the darkest part of the jungle. He had been watching them the entire time.

The leader was annoyed at having been made to wait; he was on a schedule. He went to the man and spoke to him in Indonesian. The half-naked man nodded and pointed. The leader motioned for him to go and for the rest to follow. They turned inland on a small trail in single file. The leader and guide set a quick but careful pace toward the largest gold mine in the world.

Dan Heidel stared out of the small window in his bedroom. He leaned forward, resting the weight of his shoulders on his hands, which grasped the window frame above his head. He drank in the smells and listened to the sounds of the jungle. He looked over his shoulder at his wife. "Smells like rain."

She slipped her white silk nightgown on and pulled her hair back. "It's a *rain* forest."

"It's so beautiful and peaceful. I love it," he said as he adjusted his striped pajama bottoms. He wasn't wearing a shirt. "Only nine more months. I'm going to miss it."

"I will too, but it'll be nice to go back. We're so *far* from everything."

"It's been good for my career."

Connie smiled as she brushed her hair. "Harvard MBA to sit in a jungle?"

He scratched his flat stomach. "No, to be the President of the biggest gold mine in the *world*." He sat in the wicker chair in the corner of the room. "Mind if I leave the windows open tonight instead of using the air conditioner? I'd like some fresh air."

"Fine with me." She sat on the edge of the sumptuous bed covered with pressed linens.

He opened the other window and walked to the door. She watched him prop the heavy wooden door open.

"We're not supposed to leave the door—"

"What could happen? We're in the middle of a compound. There are *guards* on our front porch."

"I know. It's just the rule—"

"Live dangerously for once," he said, looking for the book he had been reading. "Did you check on the kids?"

"They're fine. Both asleep." She turned around and faced him. "Have you thought about it?"

"What?"

"Sending the kids to live with your brother. Richard would be starting high school in the fall."

"They're doing fine."

"Don't you want them to be able to go to a football game?"

"Let's talk about it tomorrow." Heidel found his book and picked it up.

"You going to read?"

"Just for a few minutes."

She pulled the covers back. "I'm really tired."

"Okay. Night."

"Good night." She lay on her side facing the wall away from him. He turned off the overhead light and turned on a small brass lamp on his nightstand. He started to read as something screeched in a tree nearby.

It was so dark under the jungle canopy that when the men couldn't see each other they kept track by touching the man in front of them. They followed a small, almost imperceptible trail behind their guide, who strode confidently. Each of the men pointed his assault rifle out toward the jungle as they walked.

They walked for three hours. The moon would occasionally break through the cover of the trees to illuminate their black clothing. In spite of their rubber sandals, the birds and animals could hear them and grew quiet as they passed, afraid of the unknown predators.

The guide stopped in front of them and pointed. The

leader stood beside him and could see the high fence rising out of the jungle floor. They stood fifty feet back from
the fence and watched. They turned to their right to parallel the fence and kept moving. They walked for another
mile, back from the fence, out of sight. The guide slowed
and began nodding vigorously. The leader motioned for
them to kneel down. The gate of the gold mine was directly in front of them. Several of the men looked at each
other. Their eyes danced with excitement and fear.

The intruders watched two guards walk aimlessly by
from the gate toward their left. The guards had their rifles
slung over their shoulders as they casually smoked cigarettes and chatted in low voices. They didn't even glance
outside the fence. They didn't need to. They stood this
watch every night and nothing ever happened.

The guide, the tribesman, stood and walked toward the
gate. The other men began to fan out behind him in the
jungle making, a large semicircle. In front of the gate to
their right was a wide street in the darkened town of
maybe two hundred people. The town was developed by
the company primarily to provide clothing and food for
the employees.

The tribesman kneeled down just outside the fence. He
made an unusual calling noise with his mouth, like some
rare tropical bird that no Westerner had ever heard or
could possibly imitate. Twice. Three times. Finally, he
stood and walked boldly toward the front gate. He waited,
looked around, then yelled loudly in his native tongue.
The two guards ran toward the gate yelling at him to be
quiet. One was an American, and one, much smaller, appeared to be a native. The American guard turned a flashlight on him through the gate and spoke angrily, in
English, "Shut the hell up! What do you want?"

The guide spoke enthusiastically in his native language
and waved his arms frantically. He began jumping up and
down.

"What are you talking—"

The small guard pulled an automatic pistol with a silencer on it from inside his shirt and placed it against the American guard's chest. The American stared at him, confused, for two seconds. The small guard pulled the trigger and the American's body jerked back and fell to the ground. He twitched for a moment and then lay still in the night as a dark pool formed under his left arm. The small guard looked around, took out his keys, and unlocked the enormous wrought-iron gate. The two tribesmen, one in bare feet and the other in a guard's uniform, pushed the gate open and ran away.

The thirty intruders stayed in the shadows of the jungle and waited momentarily. They watched the gate, the fence, the shadows. Finally, on a signal, they sprang up as one and dashed through the gate. They headed up the slight hill to the left to the house of the president of the company a quarter mile from the gate. The house was dark. Two guards sat on the porch with automatic rifles on their laps. As the intruders approached, the two guards stood up and challenged them. Several sharp clicks from the attackers' silenced assault rifles answered. The guards were thrown against the wall of the house and slumped to the deck. Five of the intruders walked up the stairs and waited outside the screen door to the bedroom of the president of the South Sea Mining Company and listened.

Dan Heidel heard the noise and sat up quickly in bed trying to see through the darkness. "Connie, wake up. Wake up!" he whispered. Then more loudly toward the door, "Who's there?"

Connie sat up looking around, confused. "What? What is it?"

The intruders did not respond. Suddenly the screen door burst open as it was ripped from its hinges. Two men ran to each side of the bed. Heidel jumped at the first intruder. He didn't have a plan, he just knew he had to try to stop them. The first attacker timed his movement and struck him flat on his cheekbone with the butt of his rifle, knocking Heidel back onto the bed. The attacker climbed on his back and pushed his head down against the pillow with his rifle.

The two on the other side of the bed grabbed Connie as she watched in horror in the darkness. She began to scream. ''Dan! The childr—''

Heidel turned his head toward her, tearing his cheek on the rifle, ''Shut up!'' he cried.

One of the two men at her side forced her down onto the bed and climbed on top of her. She started to scream. He grabbed her jaw and forced it closed with his rough, callused hand. He grabbed a piece of tape that had been hanging from his shirt for just this moment and taped her mouth shut. He grabbed a nylon bag out of his pocket and pulled it over her head, her long blond hair splayed out on her neck.

The head intruder grabbed Heidel's hands and tied them behind his back. He turned him over and roughly pulled the piece of tape off his black shirt and taped Heidel's mouth shut, then whipped a nylon bag over his head.

The attackers pulled them out of the bed and taped their hands together more firmly behind their backs. They dragged them down the stairs, not caring that they were barefoot or what they were wearing. They stopped on the porch next to the two dead guards and looked around for the rest of the men. The compound was starkly quiet. The remaining guards had not been awakened and no one else was up. The intruders gathered quickly and headed out of the compound. Those in the back walked backward, their guns trained on the gold mine administrative buildings and guards' dormitory to stop anyone who came after them. They left quickly through the gate, leaving it open behind them, and joined with the two natives at the edge of the jungle.

Two of the men took off their backpacks and quickly assembled two sets of two long poles with netting in between, framing two rough hammocks. The American president and his wife were pushed to the ground and forced to lie on the netting with their hands still tied and their heads still covered. Two men then picked up each of the long poles, put them on their shoulders, and headed off into the jungle behind the tribesmen.

As the main group of intruders disappeared into the jungle, the leader called out and ten men returned with him to the compound as planned.

Each wore a backpack filled with Semtex, the Czech plastic explosive. They followed their leader in a trot. They headed toward the mouth of the actual gold mine. Four guards stood by the entrance and watched them come. They were confused by the orderly trot of the eleven men in black garb and rifles. They hesitated just too long as the ten began firing, killing the four guards instantly. Their bodies lay sprawled in front of the entrance to the mine.

The eleven men jumped over the guards and entered the mine. It was quiet. They walked into the shaft deep enough to satisfy their leader, who barked a command. They stopped, set their weapons on the ground, and took off their backpacks. They lined up in a prearranged order as their leader connected the cables protruding from the backpacks. The ten backpacks fit together in a sequence connected by the cables. The leader took out his own backpack and set a heavy metal device on the ground and hooked it by the cable to the first backpack. He turned a dial and pressed a large button, which caused an audible click. There were no other indicators on the box at all. The leader looked at his watch, nodded to the rest of his men, picked up his weapon and headed toward the entrance. They were surprised to encounter no other guards on their way out as they trotted down the streets and out the main gate to catch up with the others who had preceded them, carrying Heidel and his wife.

They moved quickly and precisely back along the path that had brought them to the gold mine. It was a long way and they had to make it to the coast before dawn. After fifteen minutes the two groups were back together. As the leader spoke with the others they heard a thunderous explosion behind them, much louder and bigger than even they had expected.

They increased their pace through the jungle night switching the load of the two Americans every fifteen minutes. The two tribesmen steered them around the creeks and rivers that would have slowed them. The sky began to lighten as they finally reached the small inlet where their four black Cigarette boats waited menacingly. The men who had been left to watch the boats started the engines. The deep rumble reassured the intruders as they gathered on the bank.

They waded into the ocean and passed the two Americans into the boats. Heidel and his wife were turned on their backs and lashed to the decks of two of the boats, two lumpy unhappy shapes with nylon bags over their heads with the hammock netting pinning them to the fiberglass boat deck. They were exposed to the elements.

The men scurried aboard as an Indonesian navy frigate appeared over the horizon. The leader yelled at them to hurry. They cut the lines to the shore. The black boats pivoted as one and turned their knifelike bows toward the open ocean. As they did, the frigate picked them up on its radar and turned toward the shore. The sky was light enough to see the smoke pouring from the stack of the frigate as it went to flank speed. Without warning the frigate began firing its one-hundred-millimeter gun. The first shot hit the shoreline with a *whumpf* that drove the intruders into furious action. The black boats accelerated instantly. The noise of their enormous engines assaulted the morning air. The boats quickly were up on step—most of their hulls out of the water—as they passed through twenty knots, then thirty and forty. They banged across the small waves at fifty knots, their speed still increasing. The best the frigate could make was thirty-three knots, but it hoped to reach the boats with its long-range gun. The black boats paralleled the coastline of Irian Jaya as closely as they could to camouflage their radar signature. The boats pulled farther away from the frigate every second.

The frigate's gun fired rapidly and recklessly at full speed, but against such a quick-moving target, a hit was unlikely. The shells began to fall behind the Cigarette boats as they sped away at nearly sixty knots. The frigate lagged, the shots fell short, and the speedboats, jumping across the waves, disappeared over the horizon into the Java Sea.